Robert Barr (16 September 1849 – 21 October 1912) was a Scottish-Canadian short story writer and novelist. Robert Barr was born in Barony, Lanark, Scotland to Robert Barr and Jane Watson. In 1854, he emigrated with his parents to Upper Canada at the age of four years old. His family settled on a farm near the village of Muirkirk. Barr assisted his father with his job as a carpenter, and developed a sound work ethic. Robert Barr then worked as a steel smelter for a number of years before he was educated at Toronto Normal School in 1873 to train as a teacher. After graduating Toronto Normal School, Barr became a teacher, and eventually headmaster/principal of the Central School of Windsor, Ontario in 1874. While Barr worked as head master of the Central School of Windsor, Ontario, he began to contribute short stories—often based on personal experiences, and recorded his work. On August 1876, when he was 27, Robert Barr married Ontario-born Eva Bennett, who was 21. (Source: Wikipedia)

Literary works:
"The Face And The Mask" (1894)
In the Midst of Alarms (1894, 1900, 1912)
From Whose Bourne (1896)
One Day's Courtship (1896)
Revenge!
The Strong Arm
A Woman Intervenes (1896)
Tekla: A Romance of Love and War (1898)
Jennie Baxter, Journalist (1899)
The Unchanging East (1900)
The Victors (1901)
A Prince of Good Fellows (1902)
Over The Border: A Romance (1903)
The O'Ruddy, A Romance, with Stephen Crane (1903)

ONE DAY'S COURTSHIP
&
IN THE MIDST OF ALARMS

ROBERT BARR

PRINCE CLASSICS

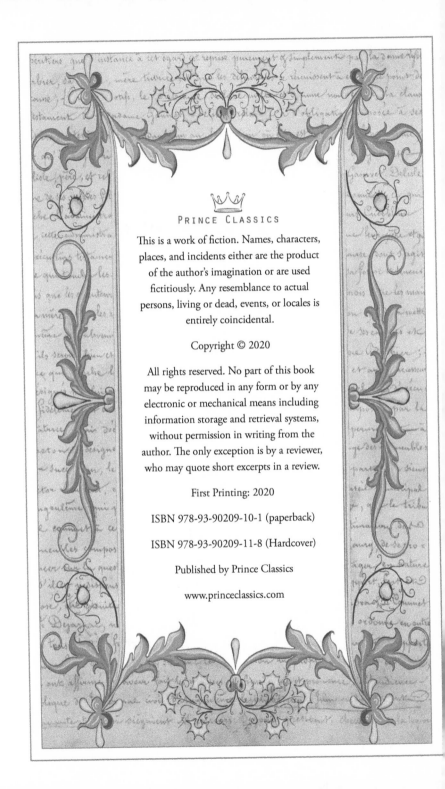

First Printing: 2020

ISBN 978-93-90209-10-1 (paperback)

ISBN 978-93-90209-11-8 (Hardcover)

Published by Prince Classics

www.princeclassics.com

Contents

ONE DAY'S COURTSHIP
&
IN THE MIDST OF ALARMS

ONE DAY'S COURTSHIP

One Day's Courtship

Chapter I

John Trenton, artist, put the finishing touches to the letter he was writing, and then read it over to himself. It ran as follows:—

"My Dear Ed.,

"I sail for England on the 27th. But before I leave I want to have another look at the Shawenegan Falls. Their roar has been in my ears ever since I left there. That tremendous hillside of foam is before my eyes night and day. The sketches I took are not at all satisfactory, so this time I will bring my camera with me, and try to get some snapshots at the falls.

"Now, what I ask is this. I want you to hold that canoe for me against all comers for Tuesday. Also, those two expert half-breeds. Tell them I am coming, and that there is money in it if they take me up and back as safely as they did before. I don't suppose there will be much demand for the canoe on that day; in fact, it astonishes me that Americans, who appreciate the good things of our country better than we do ourselves, practically know nothing of this superb cataract right at their own doors. I suppose your new canoe is not finished yet, and as the others are up in the woods I write so that you will keep this particular craft for me. I do not wish to take any risks, as I leave so soon. Please drop me a note to this hotel at Quebec, and I will meet you in Le Gres on Tuesday morning at daybreak.

"Your friend,

"John Trenton."

Mason was a millionaire and a lumber king, but every one called him Ed. He owned baronial estates in the pine woods, and saw-mills without number. Trenton had brought a letter of introduction to him from a mutual friend in Quebec, who had urged the artist to visit the Shawenegan Falls. He heard the Englishman inquire about the cataract, and told him that he knew the man who would give him every facility for reaching the falls. Trenton's acquaintance with Mason was about a fortnight old, but already they were the firmest of friends. Any one who appreciated the Shawenegan Falls found a ready path to the heart of the big lumberman. It was almost impossible to reach the falls without the assistance of Mr. Mason. However, he was no monopolist. Any person wishing to visit the cataract got a canoe from the lumber king free of all cost, except a tip to the two boatmen who acted as guides and watermen. The artist had not long to wait for his answer. It was—

"My **Dear John,**

"The canoe is yours; the boatmen are yours: and the Shawenegan is yours for Tuesday. Also,

"I am yours,

"E. Mason."

On Monday evening John Trenton stepped off the C. P. R. train at Three Rivers. With a roughing-it suit on, and his camera slung over his shoulders, no one would have taken him for the successful landscape artist who on Piccadilly was somewhat particular about his attire.

John Trenton was not yet R. A., nor even A. R. A., but all his friends would tell you that, if the Royal Academy was not governed by a clique, he would have been admitted long ago, and that anyhow it was only a question of time. In fact, John admitted this to himself, but to no one else.

He entered the ramshackle 'bus, and was driven a long distance through very sandy streets to the hotel on the St. Lawrence, and, securing a room, made arrangements to be called before daybreak. He engaged the same driver who had taken him out to "The Greys," as it was locally called, on the occasion of his former visit.

The morning was cold and dark. Trenton found the buckboard at the oor, and he put his camera under the one seat—a kind of a box for the olding of bits of harness and other odds and ends. As he buttoned up his vercoat he noticed that a great white steamer had come in the night, and was ied up in front of the hotel.

"The Montreal boat," explained the driver.

As they drove along the silent streets of Three Rivers, Trenton called to nind how, on the former occasion, he thought the Lower Canada buckboard ›y all odds, the most uncomfortable vehicle he had ever ridden in, and he elt that his present experience was going to corroborate this first impression. [he seat was set in the centre, between the front and back wheels, on springy ›oards, and every time the conveyance jolted over a log—a not unfrequent ›ccurrence—the seat went down and the back bent forward, as if to throw aim over on the heels of the patient horse.

The road at first was long and straight and sandy, but during the latter ›art of the ride there were plenty of hills, up many of which a plank roadway an; so that loads which it would be impossible to take through the deep sand, might be hauled up the steep incline.

At first the houses they passed had a dark and deserted look; then a light winkled here and there. The early habitant was making his fire. As daylight ›egan gradually to bring out the landscape, the sharp sound of the distant ıxe was heard. The early habitant was laying in his day's supply of firewood.

"Do you notice how the dawn slowly materialises the landscape?" said he artist to the boy beside him.

The boy saw nothing wonderful about that. Daylight always did it.

"Then it is not unusual in these parts? You see, I am very seldom up at this hour."

The boy wished that was his case.

"Does it not remind you of a photographer in a dark room carefully developing a landscape plate? Not one of those rapid plates, you know, but a slow, deliberate plate."

No, it didn't remind him of anything of the kind. He had never seen either a slow or a rapid plate developed.

"Then you have no prejudices as to which is the best developer, pyrogalli acid or ferrous oxalate, not to mention such recent decoctions as eikonogen quinol, and others?"

No, the boy had none.

"Well, that's what I like. I like a young man whose mind is open to conviction."

The boy was not a conversational success. He evidently did not enter into the spirit of the artist's remarks. He said most people got off at that point and walked to warm up, and asked Trenton if he would not like to follow their example.

"No, my boy," said the Englishman, "I don't think I shall. You see, I have paid for this ride, and I want to get all I can out of it. I shall shiver here and try to get the worth of my money. But with you it is different. If you want to get down, do so. I will drive."

The boy willingly handed over the reins, and sprang out on the road. Trenton, who was a boy himself that morning, at once whipped up the horse and dashed down the hill to get away from the driver. When a good half-mile had been worried out of the astonished animal, Trenton looked back to see the driver come panting after. The young man was calmly sitting on the back part of the buckboard, and when the horse began to walk again, the boy slid off, and, without a smile on his face, trotted along at the side.

"That fellow has evidently a quiet sense of humour, although he is so careful not to show it," said Trenton to himself.

On reaching the hilltop, they caught a glimpse of the rim of the sun rising gloriously over the treetops on the other side of the St. Maurice River. Trenton stopped the horse, and the boy looked up to see what was wrong. He could not imagine any one stopping merely to look at the sun.

"Isn't that splendid?" cried Trenton, with a deep breath, as he watched the great globe slowly ascend into the sky. The distant branches of the trees were delicately etched against its glowing surface, and seemed to cling to it like tendrils, slipping further and further down as the sun leisurely disentangled itself, and at last stood in its incomparable grandeur full above the forest.

The woods all around had on their marvellous autumn tints, and now the sun added a living lustre to them that made the landscape more brilliant than anything the artist had ever seen before.

"Ye gods!" he cried enthusiastically, "that scene is worth coming from England to have one glimpse of."

"See here," said the driver, "if you want to catch Ed. Mason before he's gone to the woods you'll have to hurry up. It's getting late."

"True, O driver. You have brought me from the sun to the earth. Have you ever heard of the person who fell from the sun to the earth?"

No, he hadn't.

"Well, that was before your time. You will never take such a tumble. I—I suppose they don't worship the sun in these parts?"

No, they didn't.

"When you come to think of it, that is very strange. Have you ever reflected that it is always in warm countries they worship the sun? Now, I should think it ought to be just the other way about. Do you know that when I got on with you this morning I was eighty years old, every day of it. What do you think my age is now?"

"Eighty years, sir."

"Not a bit of it. I'm eighteen. The sun did it. And yet they claim there is no fountain of youth. What fools people are, my boy!"

The young man looked at his fare slyly, and cordially agreed with him.

"You certainly have a concealed sense of humour," said the artist.

They wound down a deep cut in the hill, and got a view of the lumber village—their destination. The roar of the waters tumbling over the granite rocks—the rocks from which the village takes its name—came up the ravine. The broad river swept in a great semicircle to their right, and its dark waters were flecked with the foam of the small falls near the village, and the great cataract miles up the river. It promised to be a perfect autumn day. The sky, which had seemed to Trenton overcast when they started, was now one deep dome of blue without even the suggestion of a cloud.

The buckboard drew up at the gate of the house in which Mr. Mason lived when he was in the lumber village, although his home was at Three Rivers. The old Frenchwoman, Mason's housekeeper, opened the door for Trenton, and he remembered as he went in how the exquisite cleanliness of everything had impressed him during his former visit. She smiled as she recognised the genial Englishman. She had not forgotten his compliments in her own language on her housekeeping some months before, and perhaps she also remembered his liberality. Mr. Mason, she said, had gone to the river to see after the canoe, leaving word that he would return in a few minutes. Trenton, who knew the house, opened the door at his right, to enter the sitting-room and leave there his morning wraps, which the increasing warmth rendered no longer necessary. As he burst into the room in his impetuous way, he was taken aback to see standing at the window, looking out towards the river, a tall young woman. Without changing her position, she looked slowly around at the intruder. Trenton's first thought was a hasty wish that he were better dressed. His roughing-it costume, which up to that time had seemed so comfortable, now appeared uncouth and out of place. He felt as if he had suddenly found himself in a London drawing-room with a shooting-jacket on. But this sensation was quickly effaced by the look which the beauty gave him over her shoulder. Trenton, in all his experience, had never encountered such a glance of indignant scorn. It was a look of resentment and contempt, with just a dash of feminine reproach in it.

"What have I done?" thought the unhappy man; then he stammered aloud, "I—I—really—I beg your pardon. I thought the—ah—room was empty."

The imperious young woman made no reply. She turned to the window again, and Trenton backed out of the room as best he could.

"Well!" he said to himself, as he breathed with relief the outside air again, "that was the rudest thing I ever knew a lady to do. She is a lady, there is no doubt of that. There is nothing of the backwoods about her. But she might at least have answered me. What have I done, I wonder? It must be something terrible and utterly unforgivable, whatever it is. Great heavens!" he murmured, aghast at the thought, "I hope that girl isn't going up to the Shawenegan Falls."

Trenton was no ladies' man. The presence of women always disconcerted him, and made him feel awkward and boorish. He had been too much of a student in higher art to acquire the smaller art of the drawing-room. He felt ill at ease in society, and seemed to have a fatal predilection for saying the wrong thing, and suffered the torture afterwards of remembering what the right thing would have been.

Trenton stood at the gate for a moment, hoping Mason would come. Suddenly he remembered with confusion that he was directly in range of those disdainful eyes in the parlour, and he beat a hasty retreat toward the old mill that stood by the falls. The roar of the turbulent water over the granite rocks had a soothing effect on the soul of the man who knew he was a criminal, yet could not for the life of him tell what his crime had been. Then he wandered up the river-bank toward where he saw the two half-breeds placing the canoe in the still water at the further end of the village. Half-way there he was relieved to meet the genial Ed. Mason, who greeted him, as Trenton thought, with a somewhat overwrought effusion. There evidently was something on the genial Ed.'s mind.

"Hello, old man," he cried, shaking Trenton warmly by the hand. "Been here long? Well, I declare, I'm glad to see you. Going to have a splendid day for it, aren't you? Yes, sir, I am glad to see you."

"When a man says that twice in one breath, a fellow begins to doubt him. Now, you good-natured humbug, what's the matter? What have I done? How did you find me out? Who turned Queen's evidence? Look here, Edward Mason, why are you not glad to see me?"

"Nonsense; you know I am. No one could be more welcome. By the way, my wife's here. You never met her, I think?"

"I saw a young lady remarkably—"

"No, no; that is Miss —. By the way, Trenton, I want you to do me a favour, now that I think of it. Of course the canoe is yours for to-day, but that young woman wants to go up to the Shawenegan. You wouldn't mind her going up with you, would you? You see, I have no other canoe to-day, and she can't stay till to-morrow."

"I shall be delighted, I'm sure," answered Trenton. But he didn't look it.

Chapter II

Eva Sommerton, of Boston, knew that she lived in the right portion of that justly celebrated city, and this knowledge was evident in the poise of her queenly head, and in every movement of her graceful form. Blundering foreigners—foreigners as far as Boston is concerned, although they may be citizens of the United States—considered Boston to be a large city, with commerce and railroads and busy streets and enterprising newspapers, but the true Bostonian knows that this view is very incorrect. The real Boston is penetrated by no railroads. Even the jingle of the street-car bell does not disturb the silence of the streets of this select city. It is to the ordinary Boston what the empty, out-of-season London is to the rest of the busy metropolis. The stranger, jostled by the throng, may not notice that London is empty, but his lordship, if he happens during the deserted period to pass through, knows there is not a soul in town.

Miss Sommerton had many delusions, but fortunately for her peace of mind she had never yet met a candid friend with courage enough to tell her so. It would have required more bravery than the ordinary society person possesses to tell Miss Sommerton about any of her faults. The young gentlemen of her acquaintance claimed that she had no faults, and if her lady friends thought otherwise, they reserved the expression of such opinions for social gatherings not graced by the presence of Miss Sommerton.

Eva Sommerton thought she was not proud, or if there was any tinge of pride in her character, it was pride of the necessary and proper sort.

She also possessed the vain belief that true merit was the one essential, but if true merit had had the misfortune to be presented to Miss Sommerton without an introduction of a strictly unimpeachable nature, there is every reason to fear true merit would not have had the exquisite privilege of basking in the smiles of that young Bostonian. But perhaps her chief delusion was the belief that she was an artist. She had learned all that Boston could teach of drawing, and this thin veneer had received a beautiful foreign polish abroad. Her friends pronounced her sketches really wonderful. Perhaps Miss Sommerton's entire capital had been something less than her half-yearly income, she might have made a name for herself; but the rich man gets a foretaste of the scriptural difficulty awaiting him at the gates of heaven, when he endeavours to achieve an earthly success, the price of which is hard labour and not hard cash.

We are told that pride must have a fall, and there came an episode in Miss Sommerton's career as an artist which was a rude shock to her self-complacency. Having purchased a landscape by a celebrated artist whose work she had long admired, she at last ventured to write to him and enclose some of her own sketches, with a request for a candid judgment of them— that is, she said she wanted a candid judgment of them.

The reply seemed to her so ungentlemanly, and so harsh, that, in her vexation and anger, she tore the letter to shreds and stamped her pretty foot with a vehemence which would have shocked those who knew her only as the dignified and self-possessed Miss Eva Sommerton.

Then she looked at her libelled sketches, and somehow they did not appear to be quite so faultless as she had supposed them to be.

This inspection was followed by a thoughtful and tearful period of meditation; and finally, with contriteness, the young woman picked up from her studio floor the shreds of the letter and pasted them carefully together on a white sheet of paper, in which form she still preserved the first honest opinion she had ever received.

In the seclusion of her aesthetic studio Miss Sommerton made a heroic resolve to work hard. Her life was to be consecrated to art. She would win reluctant recognition from the masters. Under all this wave of heroic resolution was an under-current of determination to get even with the artist who had treated her work so contemptuously.

Few of us quite live up to our best intentions, and Miss Sommerton was no exception to the rule. She did not work as devotedly as she had hoped to do, nor did she become a recluse from society. A year after she sent to the artist some sketches which she had taken in Quebec—some unknown waterfalls, some wild river scenery—and received from him a warmer letter of commendation than she had hoped for. He remembered her former sketches, and now saw a great improvement. If the waterfall sketches were not exaggerations, he would like to see the originals. Where were they? The lady was proud of her discoveries in the almost unknown land of Northern Quebec, and she wrote a long letter telling all about them, and a polite note of thanks for the information ended the correspondence.

Miss Sommerton's favourite discovery was that tremendous downward plunge of the St. Maurice, the Falls of Shawenegan. She had sketched it from a dozen different standpoints, and raved about it to her friends, if such a dignified young person as Miss Sommerton could be said to rave over anything. Some Boston people, on her recommendation, had visited the falls, but their account of the journey made so much of the difficulties and discomforts, and so little of the magnificence of the cataract, that our amateur artist resolved to keep the falls, as it were, to herself. She made yearly pilgrimages to the St. Maurice, and came to have a kind of idea of possession which always amused Mr. Mason. She seemed to resent the fact that others went to look at the falls, and, worse than all, took picnic baskets there, actually lunching on its sacred shores, leaving empty champagne bottles and boxes of sardines that had evidently broken some one's favourite knife in the opening. This particular summer she had driven out to "The Greys," but finding that a party was going up in canoes every day that week, she promptly ordered her driver to take her back to Three Rivers, saying to Mr. Mason she would return when she could have the falls to herself.

"You remind me of Miss Porter," said the lumber king.

"Miss Porter! Who is she?"

"When Miss Porter visited England and saw Mr. Gladstone, he asked her if she had ever seen the Niagara Falls. 'Seen them?' she answered. 'Why, I own them!'"

"What did she mean by that? I confess I don't see the point, or perhaps it isn't a joke."

"Oh yes, it is. You mustn't slight my good stories in that way. She meant just what she said. I believe the Porter family own, or did own, Goat Island, and, I suppose, the other bank, and, therefore, the American Fall. The joke—I do dislike to have to explain jokes, especially to you cool, unsympathising Bostonians—is the ridiculousness of any mere human person claiming to own such a thing as the Niagara Falls. I believe, though, that you are quite equal to it—I do indeed."

"Thank you, Mr. Mason."

"I knew you would be grateful when I made myself clearly understood. Now, what I was going to propose is this. You should apply to the Canadian Government for possession of the Shawenegan. I think they would let it go at a reasonable figure. They look on it merely as an annoying impediment to the navigation of the river, and an obstruction which has caused them to spend some thousands of dollars in building a slide by the side of it, so that the logs may come down safely."

"If I owned it, the slide is the first thing I would destroy."

"What? And ruin the lumber industry of the Upper St. Maurice? Oh, you wouldn't do such a thing! If that is your idea, I give you fair warning that I will oppose your claims with all the arts of the lobbyist. If you want to become the private owner of the falls, you should tell the Government that you have some thoughts of encouraging the industries of the province by building a mill—"

"A mill?"

"Yes; why not? Indeed, I have half a notion to put a saw-mill there myself. It always grieves me to see so much magnificent power going to waste."

"Oh, seriously, Mr. Mason, you would never think of committing such an act of sacrilege?"

"Sacrilege, indeed! I like that. Why, the man who makes one saw-mill hum where no mill ever hummed before is a benefactor to his species. Don't they teach political economy at Boston? I thought you liked saw-mills. You drew a very pretty picture of the one down the stream."

"I admire a ruined saw-mill, as that one was; but not one in a state of activity, or of eruption, as a person might say."

"Well, won't you go up to the falls to-day, Miss Sommerton? I assure you we have a most unexceptionable party. Why, one of them is a Government official. Think of that!"

"I refuse to think of it; or, if I do think of it, I refuse to be dazzled by his magnificence. I want to see the Shawenegan, not a picnic party drinking.

"You wrong them, really you do, Miss Sommerton, believe me. You have got your dates mixed. It is the champagne party that goes to-day. The beer crowd is not due until to-morrow."

"The principle is the same."

"The price of the refreshment is not. I speak as a man of bitter experience. Let's see. If recollection holds her throne, I think there was a young lady from New England—I forget the name of the town at the moment—who took a lunch with her the last time she went to the Shawenegan. I merely give this as my impression, you know. I am open to contradiction."

"Certainly, I took a lunch. I always do. I would to-day if I were going up there, and Mrs. Mason would give me some sandwiches. You would give me a lunch, wouldn't you, dear?"

"I'll tell them to get it ready now, if you will only stay," replied that lady, on being appealed to.

"No, it isn't the lunch I object to. I object to people going there merely for the lunch. I go for the scenery; the lunch is incidental."

"When you get the deed of the falls, I'll tell you what we'll do," put in Mason. "We will have a band of trained Indians stationed at the landing, and they will allow no one to disembark who does not express himself in sufficiently ecstatic terms about the great cataract. You will draw up a set of adjectives, which I will give to the Indians, instructing them to allow no one to land who does not use at least three out of five of them in referring to the falls. People whose eloquent appreciation does not reach the required altitude will have to stay there till it does, that's all. We will treat them as we do our juries—starve them into a verdict, and the right verdict at that."

"Don't mind him, Eva. He is just trying to exasperate you. Think of what I have to put up with. He goes on like that all the time," said Mrs. Mason.

"Really, my dear, your flattery confuses me. You can't persuade any one that I keep up this brilliancy in the privacy of my own house. It is only turned on for company."

"Why, Mr. Mason, I didn't think you looked on me as company. I thought I enjoyed the friendship of the Mason family."

"Oh, you do, you do indeed! The company I referred to was the official party which has just gone to the falls. This is some of the brilliancy left over. But, really, you had better stay after coming all this distance."

"Yes, do, Eva. Let me go back with you to the Three Rivers, and then you stay with me till next week, when you can visit the falls all alone. It is very pleasant at Three Rivers just now. And besides, we can go for a day's shopping at Montreal."

"I wish I could."

"Why, of course you can," said Mason. "Imagine the delight of smuggling your purchases back to Boston. Confess that this is a pleasure you hadn't thought of."

"I admit the fascination of it all, but you see I am with a party that has gone on to Quebec, and I just got away for a day. I am to meet them there to-night or to-morrow morning. But I will return in the autumn, Mrs. Mason, when it is too late for the picnics. Then, Mr. Mason, take warning. I mean to have a canoe to myself, or—well, you know the way we Bostonians treated you Britishers once upon a time."

"Distinctly. But we will return good for evil, and give you warm tea ıstead of the cold mixture you so foolishly brewed in the harbour."

As the buckboard disappeared around the corner, and Mr. and Mrs. Mason walked back to the house, the lady said—

"What a strange girl Eva is."

"Very. Don't she strike you as being a trifle selfish?"

"Selfish? Eva Sommerton? Why, what could make you think such a thing? What an absurd idea! You cannot imagine how kind she was to me when I visited Boston."

"Who could help it, my dear? I would have been so myself if I had happened to meet you there."

"Now, Ed., don't be absurd."

"There is something absurd in being kind to a person's wife, isn't there? Well, it struck me her objection to any one else being at the falls, when her ladyship was there, might seem—not to me, of course, but to an outsider—a trifle selfish."

"Oh, you don't understand her at all. She has an artistic temperament, and she is quite right in wishing to be alone. Now, Ed., when she does come again I want you to keep anyone else from going up there. Don't forget it, as you do most of the things I tell you. Say to anybody who wants to go up that the canoes are out of repair."

"Oh, I can't say that, you know. Anything this side of a crime I am willing to commit; but to perjure myself, no, not for Venice. Can you think of any other method that will combine duplicity with a clear conscience? I'll tell you what I'll do. I will have the canoe drawn up, and gently, but firmly, slit it with my knife. One of the men can mend it in ten minutes. Then I can look even the official from Quebec in the face, and tell him truly that the canoe will not hold water. I suppose as long as my story will hold water you and Miss Sommerton will not mind?"

"If the canoe is ready for her when she comes, I shall be satisfied. Please to remember I am going to spend a week or two in Boston next winter."

"Oh ho, that's it, is it? Then it was not pure philanthropy—"

"Pure nonsense, Ed. I want the canoe to be ready, that's all."

When Mrs. Mason received the letter from Miss Sommerton, stating the time the young woman intended to pay her visit to the Shawenegan, she gave the letter to her husband, and reminded him of the necessity of keeping the canoe for that particular date. As the particular date was some weeks off, and as Ed. Mason was a man who never crossed a stream until he came to it, he said, "All right," put the letter in his inside pocket, and the next time he thought of it was on the fine autumn afternoon—Monday afternoon—when he saw Mrs. Mason drive up to the door of his lumber-woods residence with Miss Eva Sommerton in the buggy beside her. The young lady wondered, as Mr. Mason helped her out, if that genial gentleman, whom she regarded as the most fortunate of men, had in reality some secret, gnawing sorrow the world knew not of.

"Why, Ed., you look ill," exclaimed Mrs. Mason; "is there anything the matter?"

"Oh, it is nothing—at least, not of much consequence. A little business worry, that's all."

"Has there been any trouble?"

"Oh no—at the least, not yet."

"Trouble about the men, is it?"

"No, not about the men," said the unfortunate gentleman, with a somewhat unnecessary emphasis on the last word.

"Oh, Mr. Mason, I am afraid I have come at a wrong time. If so, don't hesitate to tell me. If I can do anything to help you, I hope I may be allowed."

"You have come just at the right time," said the lumberman, "and you are very welcome, I assure you. If I find I need help, as perhaps I may, you will be reminded of your promise."

To put off as long as possible the evil time of meeting his wife, Mason went with the man to see the horse put away, and he lingered an unnecessarily long time in ascertaining that everything was right in the stable. The man was astonished to find his master so particular that afternoon. A crisis may be postponed, but it can rarely be avoided altogether, and knowing he had to face the inevitable sooner or later, the unhappy man, with a sigh, betook himself to the house, where he found his wife impatiently waiting for him. She closed the door and confronted him.

"Now, Ed., what's the matter?"

"Where's Miss Sommerton?" was the somewhat irrelevant reply.

"She has gone to her room. Ed., don't keep me in suspense. What is wrong?"

"You remember John Trenton, who was here in the summer?"

"I remember hearing you speak of him. I didn't meet him, you know."

"Oh, that's so. Neither you did. You see, he's an awful good fellow, Trenton is—that is, for an Englishman."

"Well, what has Trenton to do with the trouble?"

"Everything, my dear—everything."

"I see how it is. Trenton visited the Shawenegan?"

"He did."

"And he wants to go there again?"

"He does."

"And you have gone and promised him the canoe for to-morrow?"

"The intuition of woman, my dear, is the most wonderful thing on earth."

"It is not half so wonderful as the negligence of man—I won't say the stupidity."

"Thank you, Jennie, for not saying it, but I really think I would feel better if you did."

"Now, what are you going to do about it?"

"Well, my dear, strange as it may appear, that very question has been racking my brain for the last ten minutes. Now, what would you do in my position?"

"Oh, I couldn't be in your position."

"No, that's so, Jennie. Excuse me for suggesting the possibility. I really think this trouble has affected my mind a little. But if you had a husband—if a sensible woman like you could have a husband who got himself into such a position—what would you advise him to do?"

"Now, Ed., don't joke. It's too serious."

"My dear, no one on earth can have such a realisation of its seriousness as I have at this moment. I feel as Mark Twain did with that novel he never finished. I have brought things to a point where I can't go any further. The game seems blocked. I wonder if Miss Sommerton would accept ten thousand feet of lumber f.o.b. and call it square."

"Really, Ed., if you can't talk sensibly, I have nothing further to say."

"Well, as I said, the strain is getting too much for me. Now, don't go away, Jennie. Here is what I am thinking of doing. I'll speak to Trenton. He won't mind Miss Sommerton's going in the canoe with him. In fact, I should think he would rather like it."

"Dear me, Ed., is that all the progress you've made? I am not troubling myself about Mr. Trenton. The difficulty will be with Eva. Do you think for a moment she will go if she imagined herself under obligations to a stranger for the canoe? Can't you get Mr. Trenton to put off his visit until the day after tomorrow? It isn't long to wait."

"No, that is impossible. You see, he has just time to catch his steamer as it is. No, he has the promise in writing, while Miss Sommerton has no legal evidence if this thing ever gets into the courts. Trenton has my written promise. You see, I did not remember the two dates were the same. When I wrote to Trenton—"

"Ed., don't try to excuse yourself. You had her letter in your pocket, you know you had. This is a matter for which there is no excuse, and it cannot be explained away."

"That's so, Jennie. I am down in the depths once more. I shall not try to crawl out again—at least, not while my wife is looking."

"No, your plan will not work. I don't know that any will. There is only one thing to try, and it is this—Miss Sommerton must think that the canoe is hers. You must appeal to her generosity to let Mr. Trenton go with her."

"Won't you make the appeal, Jen?"

"No, I will not. In the first place she'll be sorry for you, because you will make such a bungle of it. Trial is your only hope."

"Oh, if success lies in bungling, I will succeed."

"Don't be too sure. I suppose that man will be here by daybreak to-morrow?"

"Not so bad as that, Jennie. You always try to put the worst face on things. He won't be here till sunrise at the earliest."

"I will ask Eva to come down."

"You needn't hurry just because of me. Besides, I would like a few moments to prepare myself for my fate. Even a murderer is given a little time."

"Not a moment, Ed. We had better get this thing settled as soon as possible."

"Perhaps you are right," he murmured, with a deep sigh. "Well, if we Britishers, as Miss S. calls us, ever faced the Americans with as faint a heart as I do now, I don't wonder we got licked."

"Don't say 'licked,' Ed."

"I believe it's historical. Oh, I see. You object to the word, not to the allegation. Well, I won't cavil about that. All my sympathy just now is concentrated on one unfortunate Britisher. My dear, let the sacrifice begin."

Mrs. Mason went to the stairway and called—

"Eva, dear, can you come down for a moment? We want you to help us out of a difficulty."

Miss Sommerton appeared smilingly, smoothing down the front of the dress that had taken the place of the one she travelled in. She advanced towards Mason with sweet compassion in her eyes, and that ill-fated man thought he had never seen any one look so altogether charming—excepting, of course, his own wife in her youthful days. She seemed to have smoothed away all the Boston stiffness as she smoothed her dress.

"Oh, Mr. Mason," she said, sympathetically, as she approached, "I am so sorry anything has happened to trouble you, and I do hope I am not intruding."

"Indeed, you are not, Miss Eva. In fact, your sympathy has taken away half the trouble already, and I want to beg of you to help me off with the other half."

A glance at his wife's face showed him that he had not made a bad beginning.

"Miss Sommerton, you said you would like to kelp me. Now I am going to appeal to you. I throw myself on your mercy."

There was a slight frown on Mrs. Mason's face, and her husband felt that he was perhaps appealing too much.

"In fact, the truth is, my wife gave me—"

Here a cough interrupted him, and he paused and ran his hand through his hair. "Pray don't mind me, Mr. Mason," said Miss Sommerton, "if you would rather not tell—"

"Oh, but I must; that is, I want you to know."

He glanced at his wife, but there was no help there, so he plunged in eadlong.

"To tell the truth, there is a friend of mine who wants to go to the falls omorrow. He sails for Europe immediately, and has no other day."

The Boston rigidity perceptibly returned.

"Oh, if that is all, you needn't have had a moment's trouble. I can just s well put off my visit."

"Oh, can you?" cried Mason, joyously.

His wife sat down in the rocking-chair with a sigh of despair. Her nfatuated husband thought he was getting along famously.

"Then your friends are not waiting for you at Quebec this time, and you an stay a day or two with us."

"Eva's friends are at Montreal, Edward, and she cannot stay."

"Oh, then—why, then, to-morrow's your only day, too?"

"It doesn't matter in the least, Mr. Mason. I shall be most glad to put off ny visit to oblige your friend—no, I didn't mean that," she cried, seeing the ook of anguish on Mason's face, "it is to oblige you. Now, am I not good?"

"No, you are cruel," replied Mason. "You are going up to the falls. I nsist on that. Let's take that as settled. The canoe is yours." He caught an ncouraging look from his wife. "If you want to torture me you will say you vill not go. If you want to do me the greatest of favours, you will let my riend go in the canoe with you to the landing."

"What! go alone with a stranger?" cried Miss Sommerton, freezingly.

"No, the Indians will be there, you know."

"Oh, I didn't expect to paddle the canoe myself."

"I don't know about that. You strike me as a girl who would paddle her >wn canoe pretty well."

"Now, Edward," said his wife. "He wants to take some photographs o the falls, and—"

"Photographs? Why, Ed., I thought you said he was an artist."

"Isn't a photographer an artist?"

"You know he isn't."

"Well, my dear, you know they put on their signs, 'artist—photographe pictures taken in cloudy weather.' But he's an amateur photographer; a amateur is not so bad as a professional, is he, Miss Sommerton?"

"I think he's worse, if there is any choice. A professional at least take good pictures, such as they are."

"He is an elderly gentleman, and I am sure—"

"Oh, is he?" cried Miss Sommerton; "then the matter is settled. He sha go. I thought it was some young fop of an amateur photographer."

"Oh, quite elderly. His hair is grey, or badly tinged at least."

The frown on Miss Sommerton's brow cleared away, and she smilec in a manner that was cheering to the heart of her suppliant. He thought i reminded him of the sun breaking through the clouds over the hills beyon the St. Maurice.

"Why, Mr. Mason, how selfishly I've been acting, haven't I? You reall must forgive me. It is so funny, too, making you beg for a seat in your ow canoe."

"Oh no, it's your canoe—that is, after twelve o'clock to-night. That when your contract begins."

"The arrangement does not seem to me quite regular; but, then, this i the Canadian woods, and not Boston. But, I want to make my little proviso I do not wish to be introduced to this man; he must have no excuse fo beginning a conversation with me. I don't want to talk to-morrow."

"Heroic resolution," murmured Mason.

"So, I do not wish to see the gentleman until I go into the canoe. You can be conveniently absent. Mrs. Perrault will take me down there; she speaks no English, and it is not likely he can speak French."

"We can arrange that."

"Then it is settled, and all I hope for is a good day to-morrow."

Mrs. Mason sprang up and kissed the fair Bostonian, and Mason felt a sensation of joyous freedom that recalled his youthful days when a half-holiday was announced.

"Oh, it is too good of you," said the elder lady.

"Not a bit of it," whispered Miss Sommerton; "I hate the man before I have seen him."

Chapter III

When John Trenton came in to breakfast, he found his friend Mason waiting for him. That genial gentleman was evidently ill at ease, but he said in an offhand way—

"The ladies have already breakfasted. They are busily engaged in the preparations for the trip, and so you and I can have a snack together, and then we will go and see to the canoe."

After breakfast they went together to the river, and found the canoe and the two half-breeds waiting for them. A couple of rugs were spread on the bottom of the canoe rising over the two slanting boards which served as backs to the lowly seats.

"Now," said Mason with a blush, for he always told a necessary lie with some compunction, "I shall have to go and see to one of my men who was injured in the mill this morning. You had better take your place in the canoe, and wait for your passenger, who, as is usual with ladies, will probably be a little late. I think you should sit in the back seat, as you are the heavier of the two. I presume you remember what I told you about sitting in a canoe? Get in with caution while these two men hold the side of it; sit down carefully, and keep steady, no matter what happens. Perhaps you may as well put your camera here at the back, or in the prow."

"No," said Trenton, "I shall keep it slung over my shoulder. It isn't heavy, and I am always afraid of forgetting it if I leave it anywhere."

Trenton got cautiously into the canoe, while Mason bustled off with a very guilty feeling at his heart. He never thought of blaming Miss Sommerton for the course she had taken, and the dilemma into which she placed him, for he felt that the fault was entirely his own.

John Trenton pulled out his pipe, and, absent-mindedly, stuffed it full of tobacco. Just as he was about to light it, he remembered there was to be a lady in the party, and so with a grimace of disappointment he put the loaded pipe into his pocket again.

It was the most lovely time of the year. The sun was still warm, but the dreaded black fly and other insect pests of the region had disappeared before the sharp frosts that occurred every night. The hilly banks of the St. Maurice were covered with unbroken forest, and "the woods of autumn all around, the vale had put their glory on." Presently Trenton saw Miss Sommerton, accompanied by old Mrs. Perrault, coming over the brow of the hill. He attempted to rise, in order to assist the lady to a seat in the canoe, when the half-breed-said in French—:

"Better sit still. It is safer. We will help the lady."

Miss Sommerton was talking rapidly in French—with rather overdone eagerness—to Mrs. Perrault. She took no notice of her fellow-voyager as she lightly stepped exactly in the centre of the canoe, and sank down on the rug in front of him, with the ease of one thoroughly accustomed to that somewhat treacherous craft. The two stalwart boatmen—one at the prow, the other at the stern of the canoe—with swift and dexterous strokes, shot it out into the stream. Trenton could not but admire the knowledge of these two men and their dexterous use of it. Here they were on a swiftly flowing river, with a small fall behind them and a tremendous cataract several miles in front, yet these two men, by their knowledge of the currents, managed to work their way up stream with the least possible amount of physical exertion. The St. Maurice at this point is about half a mile wide, with an island here and there, and now and then a touch of rapids. Sometimes the men would dash right across the river to the opposite bank, and there fall in with a miniature Gulf Stream that would carry them onward without exertion. Sometimes they were near the densely wooded shore, sometimes in the center of the river. The half-breed who stood behind Trenton, leant over to him, and whispered—

"You can now smoke if you like, the wind is down stream."

Naturally, Mr. Trenton wished to smoke. The requesting of permission to do so, it struck him, might open the way to conversation. He was not an ardent conversationalist, but it seemed to him rather ridiculous that two persons should thus travel together in a canoe without saying a word to each other.

"I beg your pardon, madam," he began; "but would you have any objection to my smoking? I am ashamed to confess that I am a slave to the pernicious habit."

There was a moment or two of silence, broken only by the regular dip of the paddle, then Miss Sommerton said, "If you wish to desecrate this lovely spot by smoking, I presume anything I can say will not prevent you."

Trenton was amazed at the rudeness of this reply, and his face flushed with anger. Finally he said, "You must have a very poor opinion of me!"

Miss Sommerton answered tartly, "I have no opinion whatever of you." Then, with womanly inconsistency, she proceeded to deliver her opinion, saying, "A man who would smoke here would smoke in a cathedral."

"I think you are wrong there," said Mr. Trenton, calmly. "I would smoke here, but I would not think of smoking in a cathedral. Neither would I smoke in the humblest log-cabin chapel."

"Sir," said Miss Sommerton, turning partly round, "I came to the St. Maurice for the purpose of viewing its scenery. I hoped to see it alone. I have been disappointed in that, but I must insist on seeing it in silence. I do not wish to carry on a conversation, nor do I wish to enter into a discussion on any subject whatever. I am sorry to have to say this, but it seems to be necessary."

Her remarks so astonished Trenton that he found it impossible to get angrier than he had been when she first spoke. In fact, he found his anger receding rather than augmenting. It was something so entirely new to meet a lady who had such an utter disregard for the rules of politeness that obtain in any civilized society that Mr. Trenton felt he was having a unique and valuable experience.

"Will you pardon me," he said, with apparent submissiveness—"will you pardon me if I disregard your request sufficiently to humbly beg forgiveness for having spoken to you in the first place?"

To this Miss Sommerton made no reply, and the canoe glided along.

After going up the river for a few miles the boatmen came to a difficult ₊art of the voyage. Here the river was divided by an island. The dark waters ₊oved with great swiftness, and with the smoothness of oil, over the concealed ₊cks, breaking into foam at the foot of the rapids. Now for the first time the ₊dians had hard work. For quite half an hour they paddled as if in despair, ₊nd the canoe moved upward inch by inch. It was not only hard work, but it ₊as work that did not allow of a moment's rest until it was finished. Should ₊e paddles pause but an instant, the canoe would be swept to the bottom of ₊e rapids. When at last the craft floated into the still water above the rapids, ₊e boatmen rested and mopped the perspiration from their brows. Then, ₊ithout a word, they resumed their steady, easy swing of the paddle. In a ₊hort time the canoe drew up at a landing, from which a path ascended the ₊teep hill among the trees. The silence was broken only by the deep, distant, ₊w roar of the Shawenegan Falls. Mr. Trenton sat in his place, while the half-₊reeds held the canoe steady. Miss Sommerton rose and stepped with firm, ₊elf-reliant tread on the landing. Without looking backward she proceeded ₊p the steep hill, and disappeared among the dense foliage. Then Trenton ₊eisurely got out of the canoe.

"You had a hard time of it up that rapid," said the artist in French to the ₊oatmen. "Here is a five-dollar bill to divide when you get down; and, if you ₊ring us safely back, I shall have another ready for you."

The men were profusely grateful, as indeed they had a right to be, for the ₊nost they expected was a dollar each as a fee.

"Ah," said the elder, "if we had gentlemen like you to take up every day," ₊nd he gave an expressive shrug.

"You shouldn't take such a sordid view of the matter," said the artist. "I ₊hould think you would find great pleasure in taking up parties of handsome ₊adies such as I understand now and then visit the falls."

"Ah," said the boatman, "it is very nice, of course; but, except from Miss ₊ommerton, we don't get much."

"Really," said the artist; "and who is Miss Sommerton, pray?"

The half-breed nodded up the path.

"Oh, indeed, that is her name. I did not know."

"Yes," said the man, "she is very generous, and she always brings u tobacco in her pocket—good tobacco."

"Tobacco!" cried the artist. "The arrant hypocrite. She gives you tobacc does she? Did you understand what we were talking about coming up here?

The younger half-breed was about to say "Yes," and a gleam of intelligenc came into his face; but a frown on the other's brow checked him, and th elder gravely shook his head.

"We do not understand English," he said.

As Trenton walked slowly up the steep hillside, he said to himself, "Tha young woman does not seem to have the slightest spark of gratitude in he composition. Here I have been good-natured enough to share my canoe witl her, yet she treats me as if I were some low ruffian instead of a gentleman."

As Miss Sommerton was approaching the Shawenegan Falls, she saic to herself, "What an insufferable cad that man is? Mr. Mason doubtless tolc him that he was indebted to me for being allowed to come in the canoe, anc yet, although he must see I do not wish to talk with him, he tried to forc conversation on me."

Miss Sommerton walked rapidly along the very imperfect woodlanc path, which was completely shaded by the overhanging trees. After a walk o nearly a mile, the path suddenly ended at the top of a tremendous precipic of granite, and opposite this point the great hillside of tumbling whit foam plunged for ever downward. At the foot of the falls the waters flun, themselves against the massive granite barrier, and then, turning at a righ angle, plunged downward in a series of wild rapids that completely eclipsec in picturesqueness and grandeur and force even the famous rapids at Niagara Contemplating this incomparable scene, Miss Sommerton forgot all abou her objectionable travelling companion. She sat down on a fallen log, placing her sketch-book on her lap, but it lay there idly as, unconscious of the passing time, she gazed dreamily at the great falls and listened to their vibrating deafening roar. Suddenly the consciousness of some one near startled her from her reverie. She sprang to her feet, and had so completely forgotten her companion that she stared at him for a moment in dumb amazement. He stood back some distance from her, and beside him on its slender tripod was placed a natty little camera. Connected with the instantaneous shutter was a long black rubber tube almost as thin as a string. The bulb of this instantaneous attachment Mr. Trenton held in his hand, and the instant Miss Sommerton turned around, the little shutter, as if in defiance of her, gave a snap, and she knew her picture had been taken, and also that she was the principal object in the foreground.

"You have photographed me, sir!" cried the young woman, with her eyes blazing.

"I have photographed the falls, or, at least, I hope I have," replied Trenton.

"But my picture is in the foreground. You must destroy that plate."

"You will excuse me, Miss Sommerton, if I tell you I shall do nothing of the kind. It is very unusual with me to deny the request of a lady, but in this case I must do so. This is the last plate I have, and it may be the one successful picture of the lot. I shall, therefore, not destroy the plate."

"Then, sir, you are not a gentleman!" cried the impetuous young lady, her face aflame with anger.

"I never claimed to be one," answered Trenton, calmly.

"I shall appeal to Mr. Mason; perhaps he has some means of making you understand that you are not allowed to take a lady's photograph without her permission, and in defiance of her wishes."

"Will you allow me to explain why it is unnecessary to destroy the plate? If you understand anything about photography, you must be aware of the fact—"

41

"I am happy to say I know nothing of photography, and I desire to know nothing of it. I will not hear any explanation from you, sir. You have refused to destroy the plate. That is enough for me. Your conduct to-day has been entirely contemptible. In the first place you have forced yourself, through Mr. Mason, into my company. The canoe was mine for to-day, and you knew it. I granted you permission to come, but I made it a proviso that there should be no conversation. Now, I shall return in the canoe alone, and I shall pay the boatmen to come back for you this evening." With this she swept indignantly past Mr. Trenton, leaving the unfortunate man for the second or third time that day too much dumbfounded to reply. She marched down the path toward the landing. Arriving at the canoe, she told the boatmen they would have to return for Mr. Trenton; that she was going back alone, and she would pay them handsomely for their extra trip. Even the additional pay offered did not seem to quite satisfy the two half-breeds.

"It will be nearly dark before we can get back," grumbled the elder boatman.

"That does not matter," replied Miss Sommerton, shortly.

"But it is dangerous going down the river at night."

"That does not matter," was again the reply.

"But he has nothing—"

"The longer you stand talking here the longer it will be before you get back. If you are afraid for the safety of the gentleman, pray stay here with him and give me the paddle—I will take the boat down alone."

The boatman said nothing more, but shot the canoe out from the landing and proceeded rapidly down the stream.

Miss Sommerton meditated bitterly on the disappointments and annoyances of the day. Once fairly away, conscience began to trouble her, and she remembered that the gentleman so unceremoniously left in the woods without any possibility of getting away was a man whom Mr. Mason, her friend, evidently desired very much to please. Little had been said by the

42

boatmen, merely a brief word of command now and then from the elder who stood in the stern, until they passed down the rapids. Then Miss Sommerton caught a grumbling word in French which made her heart stand still.

"What is that you said?" she cried to the elder boatman.

He did not answer, but solemnly paddled onward.

"Answer me," demanded Miss Sommerton. "What is that you said about the gentleman who went up with us this morning?"

"I said," replied the half-breed, with a grim severity that even the remembrance of gifts of tobacco could not mitigate, "that the canoe belonged to him today."

"How dare you say such a thing! The canoe was mine. Mr. Mason gave it to me. It was mine for to-day."

"I know nothing about that," returned the boatman doggedly; "but I do know that three days ago Mr. Mason came to me with this gentleman's letter in his hand and said, 'Pierre, Mr. Trenton is to have the canoe for Tuesday. See it is in good order, and no one else is to have it for that day.' That is what Mr. Mason said, and when they were down at the canoe this morning, Mr. Mason asked Mr. Trenton if he would let you go up to the falls in his canoe, and he said 'Yes.'"

Miss Sommerton sat there too horrified to speak. A wild resentment against the duplicity of Ed. Mason arose for a moment in her heart, but it speedily sank as she viewed her own conduct in the light of this astounding revelation. She had abused an unknown gentleman like a pickpocket, and had finally gone off with his canoe, leaving him marooned, as it were, to whose courtesy she was indebted for being there at all. Overcome by the thoughts that crowded so quickly upon her, she buried her face in her hands and wept. But this was only for an instant. Raising her head again, with the imperious air characteristic of her, she said to the boatman—

"Turn back at once, please."

"We are almost there now," he answered, amazed at the feminine inconsistency of the command.

"Turn back at once, I say. You are not too tired to paddle up the river again, are you?"

"No, madame," he answered, "but it is so useless; we are almost there. We shall land you, and then the canoe will go up lighter."

"I wish to go with you. Do what I tell you, and I will pay you."

The stolid boatman gave the command; the man at the bow paddled one way, while the man at the stern paddled another, and the canoe swung round upstream again.

Chapter IV

The sun had gone down when Miss Sommerton put her foot once more in the landing.

"We will go and search for him," said the boatman.

"Stay where you are," she commanded, and disappeared swiftly up the path. Expecting to find him still at the falls, she faced the prospect of a good mile of rough walking in the gathering darkness without flinching. But at the brow of the hill, within hearing distance of the landing, she found the man of whom she was in search. In her agony of mind Miss Sommerton had expected to come upon him pacing moodily up and down before the falls, meditating on the ingratitude of womankind. She discovered him in a much less romantic attitude. He was lying at full length below a white birch-tree, with his camera-box under his head for a pillow. It was evident he had seen enough of the Shawenegan Falls for one day, and doubtless, because of the morning's early rising, and the day's long journey, had fallen soundly asleep. His soft felt hat lay on the ground beside him. Miss Sommerton looked at him for a moment, and thought bitterly of Mason's additional perjury in swearing that he was an elderly man. True, his hair was tinged with grey at the temples, but there was nothing elderly about his appearance. Miss Sommerton saw that he was a handsome man, and wondered this had escaped her notice before, forgetting that she had scarcely deigned to look at him. She thought he had spoken to her with inexcusable bluntness at the falls, in refusing to destroy his plate; but she now remembered with compunction that he had made no allusion to his ownership of the boat for that day, while she had boasted that it was hers. She determined to return and send one of the boatmen up to awaken him, but at that moment Trenton suddenly opened his eyes, as a person often does when some one looks at him in his sleep. He sprang quickly to his feet, and put up his hand in bewilderment to remove his hat, but found it wasn't there. Then he laughed uncomfortably, stooping to pick it up again.

"I—I—I wasn't expecting visitors," he stammered—

"Why did you not tell me," she said, "that Mr. Mason had promised yo the boat for the day?"

"Good gracious!" cried Trenton, "has Ed. Mason told you that?"

"I have not seen Mr. Mason," she replied; "I found it out by catchin an accidental remark made by one of the boatmen. I desire very humbly t apologise to you for my conduct."

"Oh, that doesn't matter at all, I assure you."

"What! My conduct doesn't?"

"No, I didn't mean quite that; but I—Of course, you did treat m rather abruptly; but then, you know, I saw how it was. You looked on me a an interloper, as it were, and I think you were quite justified, you know, i speaking as you did. I am a very poor hand at conversing with ladies, even a my best, and I am not at my best to-day. I had to get up too early, so ther is no doubt what I said was said very awkwardly indeed. But it really doesn matter, you know—that is, it doesn't matter about anything you said."

"I think it matters very much—at least, it matters very much to me. shall always regret having treated you as I did, and I hope you will forgive m for having done so."

"Oh, that's all right," said Mr. Trenton, swinging his camera over hi shoulder. "It is getting dark, Miss Sommerton; I think we should hurry dow to the canoe."

As they walked down the hill together, he continued—

"I wish you would let me give you a little lesson in photography, if yo don't mind."

"I have very little interest in photography, especially amateu photography," replied Miss Sommerton, with a partial return of her ol reserve.

"Oh, I don't wish to make an amateur photographer of you. You sketcl very nicely, and—"

46

"How do you know that?" asked Miss Sommerton, turning quickly towards him: "you have never seen any of my sketches."

"Ah, well," stammered Trenton, "no—that is—you know—are not those water-colours in Mason's house yours?"

"Mr. Mason has some of my sketches. I didn't know you had seen them."

"Well, as I was saying," continued Trenton, "I have no desire to convert you to the beauties of amateur photography. I admit the results in many cases are very bad. I am afraid if you saw the pictures I take myself you would not be much in love with the art. But what I wish to say is in mitigation of my refusal to destroy the plate when you asked me to."

"Oh, I beg you will not mention that, or refer to anything at all I have said to you. I assure you it pains me very much, and you know I have apologised once or twice already."

"Oh, it isn't that. The apology should come from me; but I thought I would like to explain why it is that I did not take your picture, as you thought I did."

"Not take my picture? Why I saw you take it. You admitted yourself you took it."

"Well, you see, that is what I want to explain. I took your picture, and then again I didn't take it. This is how it is with amateur photography. Your picture on the plate will be a mere shadow, a dim outline, nothing more. No one can tell who it is. You see, it is utterly impossible to take a dark object and one in pure white at the instantaneous snap. If the picture of the falls is at all correct, as I expect it will be, then your picture will be nothing but a shadow unrecognisable by any one."

"But they do take pictures with the cataract as a background, do they not? I am sure I have seen photos of groups taken at Niagara Falls; in fact, I have seen groups being posed in public for that purpose, and very silly they looked, I must say. I presume that is one of the things that has prejudiced me so much against the camera."

"Those pictures, Miss Sommerton, are not genuine; they are not at all what they pretend to be. The prints that you have seen are the results of the manipulation of two separate plates, one of the plates containing the group or the person photographed, and the other an instantaneous picture of the falls. If you look closely at one of those pictures you will see a little halo of light or dark around the person photographed. That, to an experienced photographer, shows the double printing. In fact, it is double dealing all round. The deluded victim of the camera imagines that the pictures he gets of the falls, with himself in the foreground, is really a picture of the falls taken at the time he is being photographed. Whereas, in the picture actually taken of him, the falls themselves are hopelessly over-exposed, and do not appear at all on the plate. So with the instantaneous picture I took; there will really be nothing of you on that plate that you would recognise as yourself. That was why I refused to destroy it."

"I am afraid," said Miss Sommerton, sadly, "you are trying to make my punishment harder and harder. I believe in reality you are very cruel. You know how badly I feel about the whole matter, and now even the one little point that apparently gave me any excuse is taken away by your scientific explanation."

"Candidly, Miss Sommerton, I am more of a culprit than you imagine, and I suppose it is the tortures of a guilty conscience that caused me to make this explanation. I shall now confess without reserve. As you sat there with your head in your hand looking at the falls, I deliberately and with malice aforethought took a timed picture, which, if developed, will reveal you exactly as you sat, and which will not show the falls at all."

Miss Sommerton walked in silence beside him, and he could not tell just how angry she might be. Finally he said, "I shall destroy that plate, if you order me to."

Miss Sommerton made no reply, until they were nearly at the canoe. Then she looked up at him with a smile, and said, "I think it a pity to destroy any pictures you have had such trouble to obtain."

"Thank you, Miss Sommerton," said the artist. He helped her into the canoe in the gathering dusk, and then sat down himself. But neither of them saw the look of anxiety on the face of the elder boatman. He knew the River St. Maurice.

Chapter V

From the words the elder boatman rapidly addressed to the younger, it was evident to Mr. Trenton that the half-breed was anxious to pass the rapids before it became very much darker.

The landing is at the edge of comparatively still water. At the bottom of the falls the river turns an acute angle and flows to the west. At the landing it turns with equal abruptness, and flows south.

The short westward section of the river from the falls to the point where they landed is a wild, turbulent rapid, in which no boat can live for a moment. From the Point downwards, although the water is covered with foam, only one dangerous place has to be passed. Toward that spot the stalwart half-breeds bent all their energy in forcing the canoe down with the current. The canoe shot over the darkening rapid with the speed of an arrow. If but one or two persons had been in it, the chances are the passage would have been made in safety. As it was one wrong turn of the paddle by the younger half-breed did the mischief. The bottom barely touched a sharp-pointed hidden rock, and in an instant the canoe was slit open as with a knife.

As he sat there Trenton felt the cold water rise around him with a quickness that prevented his doing anything, even if he had known what to do.

"Sit still!" cried the elder boatman; and then to the younger he shouted sharply, "The shore!"

They were almost under the hanging trees when the four found themselves in the water. Trenton grasped an overhanging branch with one hand, and with the other caught Miss Sommerton by the arm. For a moment it was doubtful whether the branch would hold. The current was very swift, and it threw each of them against the rock bank, and bent the branch down into the water.

"Catch hold of me!" cried Trenton. "Catch hold of my coat; I need both ands."

Miss Sommerton, who had acted with commendable bravery throughout, did as she was directed. Trenton, with his released hand, worked himself slowly up the branch, hand over hand, and finally catching a sapling that grew close to the water's edge, with a firm hold, reached down and helped Miss Sommerton on the bank. Then he slowly drew himself up to a safe position and looked around for any signs of the boatmen. He shouted loudly, but there was no answer.

"Are they drowned, do you think?" asked Miss Sommerton, anxiously.

"No, I don't suppose they are; I don't think you could drown a half-breed. They have done their best to drown us, and as we have escaped I see no reason why they should drown."

"Oh, it's all my fault! all my fault!" wailed Miss Sommerton.

"It is, indeed," answered Trenton, briefly.

She tried to straighten herself up, but, too wet and chilled and limp to be heroic, she sank on a rock and began to cry.

"Please don't do that," said the artist, softly. "Of course I shouldn't have agreed with you. I beg pardon for having done so, but now that we are here, you are not to shirk your share of the duties. I want you to search around and get materials for a fire."

"Search around?" cried Miss Sommerton dolefully.

"Yes, search around. Hunt, as you Americans say. You have got us into this scrape, so I don't propose you shall sit calmly by and not take any of the consequences."

"Do you mean to insult me, Mr. Trenton, now that I am helpless?"

"If it is an insult to ask you to get up and gather some wood and bring it here, then I do mean to insult you most emphatically. I shall gather some, too, for we shall need a quantity of it."

Miss Sommerton rose indignantly, and was on the point of threatening to leave the place, when a moment's reflection showed her that she didn't know where to go, and remembering she was not as brave in the darkness and in the woods as in Boston, she meekly set about the search for dry twigs and sticks. Flinging down the bundle near the heap Trenton had already collected the young woman burst into a laugh.

"Do you see anything particularly funny in the situation?" asked Trenton, with chattering teeth. "I confess I do not."

"The funniness of the situation is that we should gather wood, when, if there is a match in your pocket, it must be so wet as to be useless."

"Oh, not at all. You must remember I come from a very damp climate and we take care of our matches there. I have been in the water before now on a tramp, and my matches are in a silver case warranted to keep out the wet." As he said this Trenton struck a light, and applied it to the small twigs and dry autumn leaves. The flames flashed up through the larger sticks, and in a very few moments a cheering fire was blazing, over which Trenton threw armful after armful of the wood he had collected.

"Now," said the artist, "if you will take off what outer wraps you have on, we can spread them here, and dry them. Then if you sit, first facing the fire and next with your back to it, and maintain a sort of rotatory motion, it will not be long before you are reasonably dry and warm."

Miss Sommerton laughed, but there was not much merriment in her laughter.

"Was there ever anything so supremely ridiculous?" she said. "A gentleman from England gathering sticks, and a lady from Boston gyrating before the fire. I am glad you are not a newspaper man, for you might be tempted to write about the situation for some sensational paper."

"How do you know I am not a journalist?"

"Well, I hope you are not. I thought you were a photographer."

"Oh, not a professional photographer, you know."

"I am sorry; I prefer the professional to the amateur."

"I like to hear you say that."

"Why? It is not very complimentary, I am sure."

"The very reason I like to hear you say it. If you were complimentary I would be afraid you were going to take a chill and be ill after this disaster; but now that you are yourself again, I have no such fear."

"Myself again!" blazed the young woman. "What do you know about me? How do you know whether I am myself or somebody else? I am sure our acquaintance has been very short."

"Counted by time, yes. But an incident like this, in the wilderness, does more to form a friendship, or the reverse, than years of ordinary acquaintance in Boston or London. You ask how I know that you are yourself. Shall I tell you?"

"If you please."

"Well, I imagine you are a young lady who has been spoilt. I think probably you are rich, and have had a good deal of your own way in this world. In fact, I take it for granted that you have never met any one who frankly told you your faults. Even if such good fortune had been yours, I doubt if you would have profited by it. A snub would have been the reward of the courageous person who told Miss Sommerton her failings."

"I presume you have courage enough to tell me my faults without the fear of a snub before your eyes."

"I have the courage, yes. You see I have already received the snub three or four times, and it has lost its terrors for me."

"In that case, will you be kind enough to tell me what you consider my faults?"

"If you wish me to."

"I do wish it."

"Well, then, one of them is inordinate pride."

"Do you think pride a fault?"

"It is not usually reckoned one of the virtues."

"In this country, Mr. Trenton, we consider that every person should have a certain amount of pride."

"A certain amount may be all right. It depends entirely on how much the certain amount is."

"Well, now for fault No. 2."

"Fault No. 2 is a disregard on your part for the feelings of others. This arises, I imagine, partly from fault No. 1. You are in the habit of classing the great mass of the public very much beneath you in intellect and other qualities, and you forget that persons whom you may perhaps dislike, have feelings which you have no right to ignore."

"I presume you refer to this morning," said Miss Sommerton, seriously. "I apologised for that two or three times, I think. I have always understood that a gentleman regards an apology from another gentleman as blotting out the original offence. Why should he not regard it in the same light when it comes from a woman?"

"Oh, now you are making a personal matter of it. I am talking in an entirely impersonal sense. I am merely giving you, with brutal rudeness, opinions formed on a very short acquaintance. Remember, I have done so at your own request."

"I am very much obliged to you, I am sure. I think you are more than half right. I hope the list is not much longer."

"No, the list ends there. I suppose you imagine that I am one of the rudest men you ever met?"

"No, we generally expect rudeness from Englishmen."

"Oh, do you really? Then I am only keeping up the reputation my countrymen have already acquired in America. Have you had the pleasure of meeting a rude Englishman before?"

"No, I can't say that I have. Most Englishmen I have met have been what we call very gentlemanly indeed. But the rudest letter I ever received was from an Englishman; not only rude, but ungrateful, for I had bought at a very high price one of his landscapes. He was John Trenton, the artist, of London. Do you know him?"

"Yes," hesitated Trenton, "I know him. I may say I know him very well. In fact, he is a namesake of mine."

"Why, how curious it is I had never thought of that. Is your first name J—, the same as his?"

"Yes."

"Not a relative, is he?"

"Well, no. I don't think I can call him a relative. I don't know that I can even go so far as to call him my friend, but he is an acquaintance."

"Oh, tell me about him," cried Miss Sommerton, enthusiastically. "He is one of the Englishmen I have longed very much to meet."

"Then you forgave him his rude letter?"

"Oh, I forgave that long ago. I don't know that it was rude, after all. It was truthful. I presume the truth offended me."

"Well," said Trenton, "truth has to be handled very delicately, or it is apt to give offence. You bought a landscape of his, did you? Which one, do you remember?"

"It was a picture of the Thames valley."

"Ah, I don't recall it at the moment. A rather hackneyed subject, too. Probably he sent it to America because he couldn't sell it in England."

"Oh, I suppose you think we buy anything here that the English refuse, I beg to inform you this picture had a place in the Royal Academy, and was very highly spoken of by the critics. I bought it in England."

"Oh yes, I remember it now, 'The Thames at Sonning.' Still, it was a hackneyed subject, although reasonably well treated."

"Reasonably well! I think it one of the finest landscape pictures of the century."

"Well, in that at least Trenton would agree with you."

"He is very conceited, you mean?"

"Even his enemies admit that."

"I don't believe it. I don't believe a man of such talent could be so conceited."

"Then, Miss Sommerton, allow me to say you have very little knowledge of human nature. It is only reasonable that a great man should know he is a great man. Most of our great men are conceited. I would like to see Trenton's letter to you. I could then have a good deal of amusement at his expense when I get back."

"Well, in that case I can assure you that you will never see the letter."

"Ah, you destroyed it, did you?"

"Not for that reason."

"Then you did destroy it?"

"I tore it up, but on second thoughts I pasted it together again, and have it still."

"In that case, why should you object to showing me the letter?"

"Well, because I think it rather unusual for a lady to be asked by a gentleman show him a letter that has been written to her by another gentleman."

"In matters of the heart that is true; but in matters of art it is not."

"Is that intended for a pun?"

"It is as near to one as I ever allow myself to come, I should like very

56

uch to see Mr. Trenton's letter. It was probably brutally rude. I know the an, you see."

"It was nothing of the sort," replied Miss Sommerton, hotly. "It was a ruthful, well-meant letter."

"And yet you tore it up?"

"But that was the first impulse. The pasting it together was the apology."

"And you will not show it to me?"

"No, I will not."

"Did you answer it?"

"I will tell you nothing more about it. I am sorry I spoke of the letter at ll. You don't appreciate Mr. Trenton's work."

"Oh, I beg your pardon, I do. He has no greater admirer in England han I am—except himself, of course."

"I suppose it makes no difference to you to know that I don't like a emark like that."

"Oh, I thought it would please you. You see, with the exception of myself, Mr. Trenton is about the rudest man in England. In fact, I begin to uspect it was Mr. Trenton's letter that led you to a wholesale condemning of he English race, for you admit the Englishmen you have met were not rude."

"You forget I have met you since then."

"Well bowled, as we say in cricket."

"Has Mr. Trenton many friends in London?"

"Not a great number. He is a man who sticks rather closely to his work, nd, as I said before, he prides himself on telling the truth. That doesn't do in London any more than it does in Boston."

"Well, I honour him for it."

"Oh, certainly; everybody does in the abstract. But it is not a quality that tends to the making or the keeping of friends, you know."

"If you see Mr. Trenton when you return, I wish you would tell him there is a lady in America who is a friend of his; and if he has any pictures th people over there do not appreciate, ask him to send them to Boston, and hi friend will buy them."

"Then you must be rich, for his pictures bring very good prices, even i England."

"Yes," said Miss Sommerton, "I am rich."

"Well, I suppose it's very jolly to be rich," replied the artist, with a sigh

"You are not rich, then, I imagine?"

"No, I am not. That is, not compared with your American fortunes. have enough of money to let me roam around the world if I wish to, and ge half drowned in the St. Maurice River."

"Oh, is it not strange that we have heard nothing from those boatmen You surely don't imagine they could have been drowned?"

"I hardly think so. Still, it is quite possible."

"Oh, don't say that; it makes me feel like a murderer."

"Well, I think it was a good deal your fault, don't you know." Miss Sommerton looked at him.

"Have I not been punished enough already?" she said.

"For the death of two men—if they are dead? Bless me! no. Do you imagine for a moment there is any relation between the punishment and the fault?"

Miss Sommerton buried her face in her hands.

"Oh, I take that back," said Trenton. "I didn't mean to say such a thing."

"It is the truth—it is the truth!" wailed the young woman. "Do you honestly think they did not reach the shore?"

58

"Of course they did. If you want to know what has happened, I'll tell you exactly, and back my opinion by a bet if you like. An Englishman is always ready to back his opinion, you know. Those two men swam with the current until they came to some landing-place. They evidently think we are drowned. Nevertheless, they are now making their way through the woods to the settlement. Then comes the hubbub. Mason will stir up the neighbourhood, and the men who are back from the woods with the other canoes will be roused and pressed into service, and some time to-night we will be rescued."

"Oh, I hope that is the case," cried Miss Sommerton, looking brightly at him.

"It is the case. Will you bet about it?"

"I never bet," said Miss Sommerton.

"Ah, well, you miss a good deal of fun then. You see I am a bit of a mind reader. I can tell just about where the men are now."

"I don't believe much in mind reading."

"Don't you? Shall I give you a specimen of it? Take that letter we have spoken so much about. If you think it over in your mind I will read you the letter—not word for word, perhaps, but I shall give you gist of it, at least."

"Oh, impossible!"

"Do you remember it?"

"I have it with me."

"Oh, have you? Then, if you wish to preserve it, you should spread it out upon the ground to dry before the fire."

"There is no need of my producing the letter," replied Miss Sommerton; "I remember every word it."

"Very well, just think it over in your mind, and see if I cannot repeat it. Are you thinking about it?"

"Yes, I am thinking about it."

"Here goes, then. 'Miss Edith Sommerton—'"

"Wrong," said that young lady.

"The Sommerton is right, is it not?"

"Yes, but the first name is not."

"What is it, then?"

"I shall not tell you."

"Oh, very well. Miss Sommerton,—'I have some hesitation in answering your letter.' Oh, by the way, I forgot the address. That is the first sentence of the letter, but the address is some number which I cannot quite see, 'Beacon Street, Boston.' Is there any such street in that city?"

"There is," said Miss Sommerton. "What a question to ask."

"Ah, then Beacon Street is one of the principal streets, is it?"

"One of them? It is the street. It is Boston."

"Very good. I will now proceed with the letter. 'I have some hesitation in answering your letter, because the sketches you send are so bad, that it seems to me no one could seriously forward them to an artist for criticism. However, if you really desire criticism, and if the pictures are sent in good faith, I may say I see in them no merit whatever, not even good drawing; while the colours are put on in a way that would seem to indicate you have not yet learned the fundamental principle of mixing the paints. If you are thinking of earning a livelihood with your pencil, I strongly advise you to abandon the idea. But if you are a lady of leisure and wealth, I suppose there is no harm in your continuing as long as you see fit.—Yours truly, JOHN TRENTON.'"

Miss Sommerton, whose eyes had opened wider and wider as this reading went on, said sharply—

"He has shown you the letter. You have seen it before it was sent."

"I admit that," said the artist.

"Well—I will believe all you like to say about Mr. John Trenton."

"Now, stop a moment; do not be too sweeping in your denunciation of him. I know that Mr. Trenton showed the letter to no one."

"Why, I thought you said a moment ago that he showed it to you."

"He did. Yet no one but himself saw the letter."

The young lady sprang to her feet.

"Are you, then, John Trenton, the artist?"

"Miss Sommerton, I have to plead guilty."

Chapter VI

Miss Eva Sommerton and Mr. John Trenton stood on opposite sides of the blazing fire and looked at each other. A faint smile hovered around the lips of the artist, but Miss Sommerton's face was very serious. She was the first to speak.

"It seems to me," she said, "that there is something about all this that smacks of false pretences."

"On my part, Miss Sommerton?"

"Certainly on your part. You must have known all along that I was the person who had written the letter to you. I think, when you found that out, you should have spoken of it."

"Then you do not give me credit for the honesty of speaking now. You ought to know that I need not have spoken at all, unless I wished to be very honest about the matter."

"Yes, there is that to be said in your favour, of course."

"Well, Miss Sommerton, I hope you will consider anything that happens to be in my favour. You see, we are really old friends, after all."

"Old enemies, you mean."

"Oh, I don't know about that. I would rather look on myself as your friend than your enemy."

"The letter you wrote me was not a very friendly one."

"I am not so sure. We differ on that point, you know."

"I am afraid we differ on almost every point."

"No, I differ with you there again. Still, I must admit I would prefer being your enemy—"

"To being my friend?" said Miss Sommerton, quickly.

"No, to being entirely indifferent to you."

"Really, Mr. Trenton, we are getting along very rapidly, are we not?" said he young lady, without looking up at him.

"Now, I am pleased to be able to agree with you there, Miss Sommerton. As I said before, an incident like this does more to ripen acquaintance or friendship, or—" The young man hesitated, and did not complete his sentence.

"Well," said the artist, after a pause, "which is it to be, friends or enemies?"

"It shall be exactly as you say," she replied.

"If you leave the choice to me, I shall say friends. Let us shake hands on that."

She held out her hand frankly to him as he crossed over to her side, and as he took it in his own, a strange thrill passed through him, and acting on the impulse of the moment, he drew her toward him and kissed her.

"How dare you!" she cried, drawing herself indignantly from him. "Do you think I am some backwoods girl who is flattered by your preference after a day's acquaintance?"

"Not a day's acquaintance, Miss Sommerton—a year, two years, ten years. In fact, I feel as though I had known you all my life."

"You certainly act as if you had. I did think for some time past that you were a gentleman. But you take advantage now of my unprotected position."

"Miss Sommerton, let me humbly apologise!"

"I shall not accept your apology. It cannot be apologised for. I must ask you not to speak to me again until Mr. Mason comes. You may consider yourself very fortunate when I tell you I shall say nothing of what has passed to Mr. Mason when he arrives."

John Trenton made no reply, but gathered another armful of wood and flung it on the fire.

Miss Sommerton sat very dejectedly looking at the embers.

For half an hour neither of them said anything.

Suddenly Trenton jumped up and listened intently.

"What is it?" cried Miss Sommerton, startled by his action.

"Now," said Trenton, "that is unfair. If I am not to be allowed to speak to you, you must not ask me any questions."

"I beg your pardon," said Miss Sommerton, curtly.

"But really I wanted to say something, and I wanted you to be the first to break the contract imposed. May I say what I wish to? I have just thought about something."

"If you have thought of anything that will help us out of our difficulty, I shall be very glad to hear it indeed."

"I don't know that it will help us out of our difficulties, but I think it will help us now that we're in them. You know, I presume, that my camera, like John Brown's knapsack, was strapped on my back, and that it is one of the few things rescued from the late disaster?"

He paused for a reply, but she said nothing. She evidently was not interested in his camera.

"Now, that camera-box is water-tight. It is really a very natty arrangement, although you regard it so scornfully."

He paused a second time, but there was no reply.

"Very well; packed in that box is, first the camera, then the dry plates, but most important of all, there are at least two or three very nice Three Rivers sandwiches. What do you say to our having supper?"

Miss Sommerton smiled in spite of herself, and Trenton busily unstrapped the camera-box, pulled out the little instrument, and fished up from the bottom a neatly-folded white table-napkin, in which were wrapped several sandwiches.

"Now," he continued, "I have a folding drinking-cup and a flask of sherry. It shows how absent-minded I am, for I ought to have thought of the wine long ago. You should have had a glass of sherry the moment we landed here. By the way, I wanted to say, and I say it now in case I shall forget it, that when I ordered you so unceremoniously to go around picking up sticks for the fire, it was not because I needed assistance, but to keep you, if possible, from getting a chill."

"Very kind of you," remarked Miss Sommerton.

But the Englishman could not tell whether she meant just what she said or not.

"I wish you would admit that you are hungry. Have you had anything to eat to-day?"

"I had, I am ashamed to confess," she answered. "I took lunch with me and I ate it coming down in the canoe. That was what troubled me about you. I was afraid you had eaten nothing all day, and I wished to offer you some lunch when we were in the canoe, but scarcely liked to. I thought we would soon reach the settlement. I am very glad you have sandwiches with you."

"How little you Americans really know of the great British nation, after all. Now, if there is one thing more than another that an Englishman looks after, it is the commissariat."

After a moment's silence he said—

"Don't you think, Miss Sommerton, that notwithstanding any accident or disaster, or misadventure that may have happened, we might get back at least on the old enemy footing again? I would like to apologise"—he paused for a moment, and added, "for the letter I wrote you ever so many years ago."

"There seem to be too many apologies between us," she replied. "I shall neither give nor take any more."

"Well," he answered, "I think after all that is the best way. You ought to treat me rather kindly though, because you are the cause of my being here."

"That is one of the many things I have apologised for. You surely do not wish to taunt me with it again?"

"Oh, I don't mean the recent accident. I mean being here in America. Your sketches of the Shawenegan Falls, and your description of the Quebec district, brought me out to America; and, added to that—I expected to meet you."

"To meet me?"

"Certainly. Perhaps you don't know that I called at Beacon Street, and found you were from home—with friends in Canada, they said—and I want to say, in self-defence, that I came very well introduced. I brought letters to people in Boston of the most undoubted respectability, and to people in New York, who are as near the social equals of the Boston people as it is possible for mere New York persons to be. Among other letters of introduction I had two to you. I saw the house in Beacon Street. So, you see, I have no delusions about your being a backwoods girl, as you charged me with having a short time since."

"I would rather not refer to that again, if you please."

"Very well. Now, I have one question to ask you—one request to make. Have I your permission to make it?"

"It depends entirely on what your request is."

"Of course, in that case you cannot tell until I make it. So I shall now make my request, and I want you to remember, before you refuse it, that you are indebted to me for supper. Miss Sommerton, give me a plug of tobacco."

Miss Sommerton stood up in dumb amazement.

"You see," continued the artist, paying no heed to her evident resentment, "I have lost my tobacco in the marine disaster, but luckily I have my pipe. I admit the scenery is beautiful here, if we could only see it; but darkness is all around, although the moon is rising. It can therefore be no desecration for me to smoke a pipeful of tobacco, and I am sure the tobacco you keep will be the very best that can be bought. Won't you grant my request, Miss Sommerton?"

At first Miss Sommerton seemed to resent the audacity of this request. Then a conscious light came into her face, and instinctively her hand pressed the side of her dress where her pocket was supposed to be.

"Now," said the artist, "don't deny that you have the tobacco. I told you I was a bit of a mind reader, and besides, I have been informed that young ladies in America are rarely without the weed, and that they only keep the best."

The situation was too ridiculous for Miss Sommerton to remain very long indignant about it. So she put her hand in her pocket and drew out a plug of tobacco, and with a bow handed it to the artist.

"Thanks," he replied; "I shall borrow a pipeful and give you back the remainder. Have you ever tried the English birdseye? I assure you it is a very nice smoking tobacco."

"I presume," said Miss Sommerton, "the boatmen told you I always gave them some tobacco when I came up to see the falls?"

"Ah, you will doubt my mind-reading gift. Well, honestly, they did tell me, and I thought perhaps you might by good luck have it with you now. Besides, you know, wasn't there the least bit of humbug about your objection to smoking as we came up the river? If you really object to smoking, of course I shall not smoke now."

"Oh, I haven't the least objection to it. I am sorry I have not a good cigar to offer you."

"Thank you. But this is quite as acceptable. We rarely use plug tobacco in England, but I find some of it in this country is very good indeed."

"I must confess," said Miss Sommerton, "that I have very little interest in the subject of tobacco. But I cannot see why we should not have good tobacco in this country. We grow it here."

"That's so, when you come to think of it," answered the artist.

Trenton sat with his back against the tree, smoking in a meditative manner, and watching the flicker of the firelight on the face of his companion, whose thoughts seemed to be concentrated on the embers.

"Miss Sommerton," he said at last, "I would like permission to ask you a second question.

"You have it," replied that lady, without looking up. "But to prevent disappointment, I may say this is all the tobacco I have. The rest I left in the canoe when I went up to the falls."

"I shall try to bear the disappointment as well as I may. But in this case the question is of a very different nature. I don't know just exactly how to put it. You may have noticed that I am rather awkward when it comes to saying the right thing at the right time. I have not been much accustomed to society, and I am rather a blunt man."

"Many persons," said Miss Sommerton with some severity, "pride themselves on their bluntness. They seem to think it an excuse for saying rude things. There is a sort of superstition that bluntness and honesty go together."

"Well, that is not very encouraging, However, I do not pride myself on my bluntness, but rather regret it. I was merely stating a condition of things, not making a boast. In this instance I imagine I can show that honesty is the accompaniment. The question I wished to ask was something like this: Suppose I had had the chance to present to you my letters of introduction, and suppose that we had known each other for some time, and suppose that everything had been very conventional, instead of somewhat unconventional; supposing all this, would you have deemed a recent action of mine so unpardonable as you did a while ago?"

"You said you were not referring to smoking."

"Neither am I. I am referring to my having kissed you. There's bluntness for you."

"My dear sir," replied Miss Sommerton, shading her face with her hand, you know nothing whatever of me."

"That is rather evading the question."

"Well, then, I know nothing whatever of you."

"That is the second evasion. I am taking it for granted that we each now something of the other."

"I should think it would depend entirely on how the knowledge nfluenced each party in the case. It is such a purely supposititious state of hings that I cannot see how I can answer your question. I suppose you have ieard the adage about not crossing a bridge until you come to it."

"I thought it was a stream."

"Well, a stream then. The principle is the same.'"

"I was afraid I would not be able to put the question in a way to make 'ou understand it. I shall now fall back on my bluntness again, and with this juestion, are you betrothed?"

"We generally call it engaged in this country."

"Then I shall translate my question into the language of the country, ind ask if—"

"Oh, don't ask it, please. I shall answer before you do ask it by saying, No. I do not know why I should countenance your bluntness, as you call it, >y giving you an answer to such a question; but I do so on condition that the juestion is the last."

"But the second question cannot be the last. There is always the third eading of a bill. The auctioneer usually cries, 'Third and last time,' not Second and last time,' and the banns of approaching marriage are called out hree times. So, you see, I have the right to ask you one more question."

"Very well. A person may sometimes have the right to do a thing, and 'et be very foolish in exercising that right."

"I accept your warning," said the artist, "and reserve my right."

"What time is it, do you think?" she asked him.

"I haven't the least idea," he replied; "my watch has stopped. That case was warranted to resist water, but I doubt if it has done so."

"Don't you think that if the men managed to save themselves they would have been here by this time?"

"I am sure I don't know. I have no idea of the distance. Perhaps they may have taken it for granted we are drowned, and so there is one chance in a thousand that they may not come back at all."

"Oh, I do not think such a thing is possible. The moment Mr. Mason heard of the disaster he would come without delay, no matter what he might believe the result of the accident to be."

"Yes, I think you are right. I shall try to get out on this point and see if I can discover anything of them. The moon now lights up the river, and if they are within a reasonable distance I think I can see them from this point of rock."

The artist climbed up on the point, which projected over the river. The footing was not of the safest, and Miss Sommerton watched him with some anxiety as he slipped and stumbled and kept his place by holding on to the branches of the overhanging trees.

"Pray be careful, Mr. Trenton," she said; "remember you are over the water there, and it is very swift."

"The rocks seem rather slippery with the dew," answered the artist; "but I am reasonably surefooted."

"Well, please don't take any chances; for, disagreeable as you are, I don't wish to be left here alone."

"Thank you, Miss Sommerton."

The artist stood on the point of rock, and, holding by a branch of a tree, peered out over the river.

"Oh, Mr. Trenton, don't do that!" cried the young lady, with alarm.

"Please come back."

"Say 'John,' then," replied the gentleman.

"Oh, Mr. Trenton, don't!" she cried as he leaned still further over the water, straining the branch to its utmost.

"Say 'John.'"

"Mr. Trenton."

"'John.'"

The branch cracked ominously as Trenton leaned yet a little further.

"John!" cried the young lady, sharply, "cease your fooling and come down from that rock."

The artist instantly recovered his position, and, coming back, sprang down to the ground again.

Miss Sommerton drew back in alarm; but Trenton merely put his hands in his pockets, and said—

"Well, Eva, I came back because you called me."

"It was a case of coercion," she said. "You English are too fond of coercion. We Americans are against it."

"Oh, I am a Home Ruler, if you are," replied the artist. "Miss Eva, I am going to risk my third and last question, and I shall await the answer with more anxiety than I ever felt before in my life. The question is this: Will—"

"Hello! there you are. Thank Heaven! I was never so glad to see anybody in my life," cried the cheery voice of Ed. Mason, as he broke through the bushes towards them.

Trenton looked around with anything but a welcome on his brow. If Mason had never been so glad in his life to see anybody, it was quite evident his feeling was not entirely reciprocated by the artist.

"How the deuce did you get here?" asked Trenton. "I was just looking for you down the river."

"Well, you see, we kept pretty close to the shore. I doubt if you could have seen us. Didn't you hear us shout?"

"No, we didn't hear anything. We didn't hear them shout, did we, Miss Sommerton?"

"No," replied that young woman, looking at the dying fire, whose glowing embers seemed to redden her face.

"Why, do you know," said Mason, "it looks as if you had been quarrelling. I guess I came just in the nick of time."

"You are always just in time, Mr. Mason," said Miss Sommerton. "For we were quarrelling, as you say. The subject of the quarrel is which of us was rightful owner of that canoe."

Mason laughed heartily, while Miss Sommerton frowned at him with marked disapprobation.

"Then you found me out, did you? Well, I expected you would before the day was over. You see, it isn't often that I have to deal with two such particular people in the same day. Still, I guess the ownership of the canoe doesn't amount to much now. I'll give it to the one who finds it."

"Oh, Mr. Mason," cried Miss Sommerton, "did the two men escape all right?"

"Why, certainly, I have just been giving them 'Hail Columbia,' because they didn't come back to you; but you see, a little distance down, the bank gets very steep—so much so that it is impossible to climb it, and then the woods here are thick and hard to work a person's way through. So they thought it best to come down and tell me, and we have brought two canoes up with us."

"Does Mrs. Mason know of the accident?"

"No, she doesn't; but she is just as anxious as if she did. She can't think what in the world keeps you."

"She doesn't realise," said the artist, "what strong attractions the

Shawenegan Falls have for people alive to the beauties of nature."

"Well," said Mason, "we mustn't stand here talking. You must be about frozen to death." Here he shouted to one of the men to come up and put out the fire.

"Oh, don't bother," said the artist; "it will soon burn out."

"Oh yes," put in Ed. Mason; "and if a wind should happen to rise in the night, where would my pine forest be? I don't propose to have a whole section of the country burnt up to commemorate the quarrel between you two."

The half-breed flung the biggest brand into the river, and speedily trampled out the rest, carrying up some water in his hat to pour on the centre of the fire. This done, they stepped into the canoe and were soon on their way down the river. Reaching the landing, the artist gave his hand to Miss Sommerton and aided her out on the bank.

"Miss Sommerton," he whispered to her, "I intended to sail to-morrow. I shall leave it for you to say whether I shall go or not."

"You will not sail," said Miss Sommerton promptly.

"Oh, thank you," cried the artist; "you do not know how happy that makes me."

"Why should it?"

"Well, you know what I infer from your answer."

"My dear sir, I said that you would not sail, and you will not, for this reason: To sail you require to catch to-night's train for Montreal, and take the train from there to New York to get your boat. You cannot catch to-night's train, and, therefore, cannot get to your steamer. I never before saw a man so glad to miss his train or his boat. Good-night, Mr. Trenton. Good-night, Mr. Mason," she cried aloud to that gentleman, as she disappeared toward the house.

"You two appear to be quite friendly," said Mr. Mason to the artist.

"Do we? Appearances are deceitful. I really cannot tell at this moment whether we are friends or enemies."

"Well, not enemies, I am sure. Miss Eva is a very nice girl when you understand her."

"Do you understand her?" asked the artist.

"I can't say that I do. Come to think of it, I don't think anybody does."

"In that case, then, for all practical purposes, she might just as well not be a nice girl."

"Ah, well, you may change your opinion some day—when you get better acquainted with her," said Mason, shaking hands with his friend. "And now that you have missed your train, anyhow, I don't suppose you care for a very early start to-morrow. Good-night."

Chapter VII

After Trenton awoke next morning he thought the situation over very calmly, and resolved to have question number three answered that day if possible.

When called to breakfast he found Ed. Mason at the head of the table.

"Shan't we wait for the ladies?" asked the artist.

"I don't think we'd better. You see we might have to wait quite a long time. I don't know when Miss Sommerton will be here again, and it will be a week at least before Mrs. Mason comes back. They are more than half-way to Three Rivers by this time."

"Good gracious!" cried Trenton, abashed; "why didn't you call me? I should have liked very much to have accompanied them."

"Oh, they wouldn't hear of your being disturbed; and besides, Mr. Trenton, our American ladies are quite in the habit of looking after themselves. I found that out long ago."

"I suppose there is nothing for it but get out my buckboard and get back to Three Rivers."

"Oh, I dismissed your driver long ago," said the lumberman. "I'll take you there in my buggy. I am going out to Three Rivers to-day anyhow."

"No chance of overtaking the ladies?" asked Trenton.

"I don't think so. We may overtake Mrs. Mason but I imagine Miss Sommerton will be either at Quebec or Montreal before we reach Three Rivers. I don't know in which direction she is going. You seem to be somewhat interested in that young lady. Purely artistic admiration, I presume. She is rather a striking girl. Well, you certainly have made the most of your opportunities. Let's see, you have known her now for quite a long while. Must be nearly twenty-four hours."

"Oh, don't underestimate it, Mason; quite thirty-six hours at least."

"So long as that? Ah, well, I don't wish to discourage you; but I wouldn't be too sure of her if I were you."

"Sure of her! Why, I am not sure of anything."

"Well, that is the proper spirit. You Englishmen are rather apt to take things for granted. I think you would make a mistake in this case if you were too sure. You are not the only man who has tried to awaken the interest of Miss Sommerton of Boston."

"I didn't suppose that I was. Nevertheless, I am going to Boston."

"Well, it's a nice town," said Mason, with a noncommittal air. "It hasn't the advantages of Three Rivers, of course; but still it is a very attractive place in some respects."

"In some respects, yes," said the artist.

* * * * *

Two days later Mr. John Trenton called at the house on Beacon Street.

"Miss Sommerton is not at home," said the servant. "She is in Canada somewhere."

And so Mr. Trenton went back to his hotel.

The artist resolved to live quietly in Boston until Miss Sommerton returned. Then the fateful number three could be answered. He determined not to present any of his letters of introduction. When he came to Boston first, he thought he would like to see something of society, of the art world in that city, if there was an art world, and of the people; but he had come and gone without being invited anywhere, and now he anticipated no trouble in living a quiet life, and thinking occasionally over the situation. But during his absence it appeared Boston had awakened to the fact that in its midst had resided a real live artist of prominence from the other side, and nothing had been done to overcome his prejudices, and show him that, after all, the real intellectual centre of the world was not London, but the capital of

Massachusetts.

The first day he spent in his hotel he was called upon by a young gentleman whose card proclaimed him a reporter on one of the large daily papers.

"You are Mr. Trenton, the celebrated English artist, are you not?"

"My name is Trenton, and by profession I am an artist. But I do not claim the adjective, 'celebrated.'"

"All right. You are the man I am after. Now, I should like to know what you think of the art movement in America?"

"Well, really, I have been in America but a very short time, and during that time I have had no opportunity of seeing the work of your artists or of visiting any collections, so you see I cannot give an opinion."

"Met any of our American artists?"

"I have in Europe, yes. Quite a number of them, and very talented gentlemen some of them are, too."

"I suppose Europe lays over this country in the matter of art, don't it?"

"I beg your pardon."

"Knocks the spots out of us in pictures?"

"I don't know that I quite follow you. Do you mean that we produce pictures more rapidly than you do here?"

"No, I just mean the whole tout ensemble of the thing. They are 'way ahead of us, are they not, in art?"

"Well, you see, as I said before—really, I am not in a position to make any comparison, because I am entirely ignorant of American painting. It seems to me that certain branches of art ought to flourish here. There is no country in the world with grander scenery than America."

"Been out to the Rockies?"

"Where is that?"

"To the Rocky Mountains?"

"Oh no, no. You see I have been only a few weeks in this country. I have confined my attention to Canada mainly, the Quebec region and around there, although I have been among the White Mountains, and the Catskills, and the Adirondacks."

"What school of art do you belong to?"

"School? Well, I don't know that I belong to any. May I ask if you are a connoisseur in art matters. Are you the art critic of your journal?"

"Me? No—oh no. I don't know the first darn thing about it. That's why they sent me."

"Well, I should have thought, if he wished to get anything worth publishing, your editor would have sent somebody who was at least familiar with the subject he has to write about."

"I dare say; but, that ain't the way to get snappy articles written. You take an art man, now, for instance; he's prejudiced. He thinks one school is all right, and another school isn't; and he is apt to work in his own fads. Now, if our man liked the French school, and despised the English school, or the German school, if there is one, or the Italian school, whatever it happened to be, and you went against that; why, don't you see, he would think you didn't know anything, and write you up that way. Now, I am perfectly unprejudiced. I want to write a good readable article, and I don't care a hang which school is the best or the worst, or anything else about it."

"Ah! I see. Well, in that case, you certainly approach your work without bias."

"You bet I do. Now, who do you think is the best painter in England?"

"In what line?"

"Well, in any line. Who stands ahead? Who's the leader? Who tops them all? Who's the Raphael?"

"I don't know that we have any Raphael? We have good painters each in his own branch."

"Isn't there one, in your opinion, that is 'way ahead of all the rest?"

"Well, you see, to make an intelligent comparison, you have to take into consideration the specialty of the painter. You could hardly compare Alma Tadema, for instance, with Sir John Millais, or Sir Frederic Leighton with Hubert Herkomer, or any of them with some of your own painters. Each has his specialty, and each stands at the head of it."

"Then there is no one man in England like Old Man Rubens, or Van Dyke, or those other fellows, I forget their names, who are head and shoulders above everybody else? Sort of Jay Gould in art, you know."

"No, I wouldn't like to say there is. In fact, all of your questions require some consideration. Now, if you will write them down for me, and give me time to think them over, I will write out such answers as occur to me. It would be impossible for me to do justice to myself, or to art, or to your paper, by attempting to answer questions off-hand in this way."

"Oh, that's too slow for our time here. You know this thing comes out to-morrow morning, and I have got to do a column and a half of it. Sometimes, you know, it is very difficult; but you are different from most Englishmen I have talked with. You speak right out, and you talk to a fellow. I can make a column and a half out of what you have said now."

"Dear me! Can you really? Well, now, I should be careful, if I were you. I am afraid that, if you don't understand anything about art, you may give the public some very erroneous impressions."

"Oh, the public don't care a hang. All they want is to read something snappy and bright. That's what the public want. No, sir, we have catered too long for the public not to know what its size is. You might print the most learned article you could get hold of, it might be written by What's-his-name De Vinci, and be full of art slang, and all that sort of thing, but it wouldn't touch the general public at all."

"I don't suppose it would."

"What do you think of our Sunday papers here? You don't have any Sunday papers over in London."

"Oh yes, we do. But none of the big dailies have Sunday editions."

"They are not as big, or as enterprising as ours, are they? One Sunday paper, you know, prints about as much as two or three thirty-five cent magazines."

"What, the Sunday paper does?"

"Yes, the Sunday paper prints it, but doesn't sell for that. We give 'em more for the money than any magazine you ever saw."

"You certainly print some very large papers."

With this the reporter took his leave, and next morning Mr. Trenton saw the most astonishing account of his ideas on art matters imaginable. What struck him most forcibly was, that an article written by a person who admittedly knew nothing at all about art should be in general so free from error. The interview had a great number of head lines, and it was evident the paper desired to treat the artist with the utmost respect, and that it felt he showed his sense in preferring Boston to New York as a place of temporary residence; but what appalled him was the free and easy criticisms he was credited with having made on his own contemporaries in England. The principal points of each were summed up with a great deal of terseness and force, and in many cases were laughably true to life. It was evident that whoever touched up that interview possessed a very clear opinion and very accurate knowledge of the art movement in England.

Mr. Trenton thought he would sit down and write to the editor of the paper, correcting some of the more glaring inaccuracies; but a friend said—

"Oh, it is no use. Never mind. Nobody pays any attention to that. It's all right anyhow."

"Yes, but suppose the article should be copied in England, or suppose some of the papers should get over there?"

"Oh, that'll be all right," said his friend, with easy optimism. "Don't bother about it. They all know what a newspaper interview is; if they don't, why, you can tell them when you get back."

It was not long before Mr. Trenton found himself put down at all the principal clubs, both artistic and literary; and he also became, with a suddenness that bewildered him, quite the social lion for the time being. He was astonished to find that the receptions to which he was invited, and where he was, in a way, on exhibition, were really very grand occasions, and compared favourably with the finest gatherings he had had experience of in London.

His hostess at one of these receptions said to him, "Mr. Trenton, I want to introduce you to some of our art lovers in this city, whom I am sure you will be pleased to meet. I know that as a general thing the real artists are apt to despise the amateurs; but in this instance I hope you will be kind enough not to despise them, for my sake. We think they are really very clever indeed, and we like to be flattered by foreign preference."

"Am I the foreign preference in this instance?"

"You are, Mr. Trenton."

"Now, I think it is too bad of you to say that, just when I have begun to feel as much at home in Boston as I do in London. I assure you I do not feel in the least foreign here. Neither do I maintain, like Mrs. Brown, that you are the foreigners."

"How very nice of you to say so, Mr. Trenton. Now I hope you will say something like that to the young lady I want you to meet. She is really very charming, and I am sure you will like her; and I may say, in parenthesis, that she, like the rest of us, is perfectly infatuated with your pictures."

As the lady said this, she brought Mr. Trenton in her wake, as it were, and said, "Miss Sommerton, allow me to present to you Mr. Trenton."

Miss Sommerton rose with graceful indolence, and held out her hand frankly to the artist. "Mr. Trenton," she said, "I am very pleased indeed to meet you. Have you been long in Boston?"

"Only a few days," replied Trenton. "I came up to Boston from Canada a short time since."

"Up? You mean down. We don't say up from Canada."

"Oh, don't you? Well, in England, you know, we say up to London, no matter from what part of the country we approach it. I think you are wrong in saying down, I think it really ought to be up to Boston from wherever you come."

His hostess appeared to be delighted with this bit of conversation, and she said, "I shall leave you two together for a few moments to get acquainted. Mr. Trenton, you know you are in demand this evening."

"Do you think that is true?" said Trenton to Miss Sommerton.

"What?"

"Well, that I am in demand."

"I suppose it is true, if Mrs. Lennox says it is. You surely don't intend to cast any doubt on the word of your hostess, do you?"

"Oh, not at all. I didn't mean in a general way, you know, I meant in particular."

"I don't think I understand you, Mr. Trenton. By the way, you said you had been in Canada. Do you not think it is a very charming country?"

"Charming, Miss Sommerton, isn't the word for it. It is the most delightful country in the world."

"Ah, you say that because it belongs to England. I admit it is very delightful; but then there are other places on the Continent quite as beautiful as any part of Canada. You seem to have a prejudice in favour of monarchical institutions."

"Oh, is Canada monarchical? I didn't know that. I thought Canada was quite republican in its form of government."

"Well, it is a dependency; that's what I despise about Canada. Think o a glorious country like that, with hundreds of thousands of square miles, in fact, millions, I think, being dependent on a little island, away there among the fogs and rains, between the North Sea and the Atlantic Ocean. To be a dependency of some splendid tyrannical power like Russia wouldn't be so bad; but to be dependent on that little island—I lose all my respect for Canada when I think of it."

"Well, you know, the United States were colonies once."

"Ah, that is a very unfortunate comparison, Mr. Trenton. The moment the colonies, as you call them, came to years of discretion, they soon shook off their dependency. You must remember you are at Boston, and that the harbour is only a short distance from here."

"Does that mean that I should take advantage of its proximity and leave?"

"Oh, not at all. I could not say anything so rude, Mr. Trenton. Perhaps you are not familiar with the history of our trouble with England? Don't you remember it commenced in Boston Harbour practically?"

"Oh yes, I recollect now. I had forgotten it. Something about tea, was it not?"

"Yes, something about tea."

"Well, talking of tea, Miss Sommerton, may I take you to the conservatory and bring you a cup of it?"

"May I have an ice instead of the tea, if I prefer it, Mr. Trenton?"

"Why, certainly. You see how I am already dropping into the American phraseology."

"Oh, I think you are improving wonderfully, Mr. Trenton."

When they reached the conservatory, Miss Sommerton said—

"This is really a very great breach of good manners on both your part and mine. I have taken away the lion of the evening, and the lion has forgotten his duty to his hostess and to the other guests."

"Well, you see, I wanted to learn more of your ideas in the matter of dependencies. I don't at all agree with you on that. Now, I think if a country is conquered, it ought to be a dependency of the conquering people. It is the right of conquest. I—I am a thorough believer in the right of conquest."

"You seem to have very settled opinions on the matter, Mr. Trenton."

"I have indeed, Miss Sommerton. It is said that an Englishman never knows when he is conquered. Now I think that is a great mistake. There is no one so quick as an Englishman to admit that he has met his match."

"Why, have you met your match already, Mr. Trenton? Let me congratulate you."

"Well, don't congratulate me just yet. I am not at all certain whether I shall need any congratulations or not."

"I am sure I hope you will be very successful."

"Do you mean that?"

Miss Sommerton looked at him quietly for a moment.

"Do you think," she said, "I am in the habit of saying things I do not mean?"

"I think you are."

"Well, you are not a bit more complimentary than—than—you used to be."

"You were going to say than I was on the banks of the St. Maurice?"

"Oh, you visited the St. Maurice, did you? How far away from Boston that seems, doesn't it?"

"It is indeed a great distance, Miss Sommerton. But apparently not half as long as the round-about way we are traveling just now. Miss Sommerton, I waited and waited in Boston for you to return. I want to be a dependence. I

84

admit the conquest. I wish to swear fealty to Miss Eva Sommerton of Boston, and now I ask my third question, will you accept the allegiance?"

Miss Sommerton was a little slow in replying, and before she had spoken Mrs. Lennox bustled in, and said—

"Oh, Mr. Trenton, I have been looking everywhere for you. There are a hundred people here who wish to be introduced, and all at once. May I have him, Miss Sommerton?"

"Well, Mrs. Lennox, you know, if I said 'Yes,' that would imply a certain ownership in him."

"I brought Miss Sommerton here to get her to accept an ice from me, which as yet I have not had the privilege of bringing. Will you accept—the ice, Miss Sommerton?"

The young lady blushed, as she looked at the artist.

"Yes," she said with a sigh; the tone was almost inaudible.

The artist hurried away to bring the refreshment.

"Why, Eva Sommerton," cried Mrs. Lennox, "you accept a plate of ice cream as tragically as if you were giving the answer to a proposal."

Mrs. Lennox said afterward that she thought there was something very peculiar about Miss Sommerton's smile in reply to her remark.

IN THE MIDST OF ALARMS

CHAPTER I.

In the marble-floored vestibule of the Metropolitan Grand Hotel in Buffalo, Professor Stillson Renmark stood and looked about him with the anxious manner of a person unused to the gaudy splendor of the modern American house of entertainment. The professor had paused halfway between the door and the marble counter, because he began to fear that he had arrived at an inopportune time, that something unusual was going on. The hurry and bustle bewildered him.

An omnibus, partly filled with passengers, was standing at the door, its steps backed over the curbstone, and beside it was a broad, flat van, on which stalwart porters were heaving great square, iron-bound trunks belonging to commercial travelers, and the more fragile, but not less bulky, saratogas, doubtless the property of the ladies who sat patiently in the omnibus. Another vehicle which had just arrived was backing up to the curb, and the irate driver used language suitable to the occasion; for the two restive horses were not behaving exactly in the way he liked.

A man with a stentorian, but monotonous and mournful, voice was filling the air with the information that a train was about to depart for Albany, Saratoga, Troy, Boston, New York, and the East. When he came to the words "the East," his voice dropped to a sad minor key, as if the man despaired of the fate of those who took their departure in that direction. Every now and then a brazen gong sounded sharply; and one of the negroes who sat in a row on a bench along the marble-paneled wall sprang forward to the counter, took somebody's handbag, and disappeared in the direction of the elevator with the newly arrived guest following him. Groups of men stood here and there conversing, heedless of the rush of arrival and departure around them.

Before the broad and lofty plate-glass windows sat a row of men, some talking, some reading, and some gazing outside, but all with their feet on the brass rail which had been apparently put there for that purpose. Nearly everybody was smoking a cigar. A lady of dignified mien came down the hall to the front of the counter, and spoke quietly to the clerk, who bent his well-groomed head deferentially on one side as he listened to what she had to say. The men instantly made way for her. She passed along among them as composedly as if she were in her own drawing room, inclining her head slightly to one or other of her acquaintances, which salutation was gravely acknowledged by the raising of the hat and the temporary removal of the cigar from the lips.

All this was very strange to the professor, and he felt himself in a new world, with whose customs he was not familiar. Nobody paid the slightest attention to him as he stood there among it all with his satchel in his hand. As he timidly edged up to the counter, and tried to accumulate courage enough to address the clerk, a young man came forward, flung his handbag on the polished top of the counter, metaphorically brushed the professor aside, pulled the bulky register toward him, and inscribed his name on the page with a rapidity equaled only by the illegibility of the result.

"Hello, Sam!" he said to the clerk. "How's things? Get my telegram?"

"Yes," answered the clerk; "but I can't give you 27. It's been taken for a week. I reserved 85 for you, and had to hold on with my teeth to do that."

The reply of the young man was merely a brief mention of the place of torment.

"It is hot," said the clerk blandly. "In from Cleveland?"

"Yes. Any letters for me?"

"Couple of telegrams. You'll find them up in 85."

"Oh, you were cocksure I'd take that room?"

"I was cocksure you'd have to. It is that or the fifth floor. We're full. Couldn't give a better room to the President if he came."

"Oh, well, what's good enough for the President I can put up with for a couple of days."

The hand of the clerk descended on the bell. The negro sprang forward

90

and took the "grip."

"Eighty-five," said the clerk; and the drummer and the Negro disappeared.

"Is there any place where I could leave my bag for a while?" the professor at last said timidly to the clerk.

"Your bag?"

The professor held it up in view.

"Oh, your grip. Certainly. Have a room, sir?" And the clerk's hand hovered over the bell.

"No. At least, not just yet. You see, I'm———"

"All right. The baggage man there to the left will check it for you."

"Any letters for Bond?" said a man, pushing himself in front of the professor. The clerk pulled out a fat bunch of letters from the compartment marked "B," and handed the whole lot to the inquirer, who went rapidly over them, selected two that appeared to be addressed to him, and gave the letters a push toward the clerk, who placed them where they were before.

The professor paused a moment, then, realizing that the clerk had forgotten him, sought the baggage man, whom he found in a room filled with trunks and valises. The room communicated with the great hall by means of a square opening whose lower ledge was breast high. The professor stood before it, and handed the valise to the man behind this opening, who rapidly attached one brass check to the handle with a leather thong, and flung the other piece of brass to the professor. The latter was not sure but there was something to pay, still he quite correctly assumed that if there had been the somewhat brusque man would have had no hesitation in mentioning the fact; in which surmise his natural common sense proved a sure guide among strange surroundings. There was no false delicacy about the baggage man.

Although the professor was to a certain extent bewildered by the condition of things, there was still in his nature a certain dogged persistence that had before now stood him in good stead, and which had enabled him to distance, in the long run, much more brilliant men. He was not at all satisfied with his brief interview with the clerk. He resolved to approach that busy individual again, if he could arrest his attention. It was some time before he caught the speaker's eye, as it were, but when he did so, he said:

"I was about to say to you that I am waiting for a friend from New York who may not yet have arrived. His name is Mr. Richard Yates of the——"

"Oh, Dick Yates! Certainly. He's here." Turning to the negro, he said: "Go down to the billiard room and see if Mr. Yates is there. If he is not, look for him at the bar."

The clerk evidently knew Mr. Dick Yates. Apparently not noticing the look of amazement that had stolen over the professor's face, the clerk said:

"If you wait in the reading room, I'll send Yates to you when he comes. The boy will find him if he's in the house; but he may be uptown."

The professor, disliking to trouble the obliging clerk further, did not ask him where the reading room was. He inquired, instead, of a hurrying porter, and received the curt but comprehensive answer:

"Dining room next floor. Reading, smoking, and writing rooms up the hall. Billiard room, bar, and lavatory downstairs."

The professor, after getting into the barber shop and the cigar store, finally found his way into the reading room. Numerous daily papers were scattered around on the table, each attached to a long, clumsy cleft holder made of wood; while other journals, similarly encumbered, hung from racks against the wall. The professor sat down in one of the easy leather-covered chairs, but, instead of taking up a paper, drew a thin book from his pocket, in which he was soon so absorbed that he became entirely unconscious of his strange surroundings. A light touch on the shoulder brought him up from his book into the world again, and he saw, looking down on him, the stern face of a heavily mustached stranger.

"I beg your pardon, sir, but may I ask if you are a guest of this house?"

A shade of apprehension crossed the professor's face as he slipped the ook into his pocket. He had vaguely felt that he was trespassing when he first ntered the hotel, and now his doubts were confirmed.

"I—I am not exactly a guest," he stammered.

"What do you mean by not exactly a guest?" continued the other, egarding the professor with a cold and scrutinizing gaze. "A man is either a uest or he is not, I take it. Which is it in your case?"

"I presume, technically speaking, I am not."

"Technically speaking! More evasions. Let me ask you, sir, as an ostensibly onest man, if you imagine that all this luxury—this—this elegance—is naintained for nothing? Do you think, sir, that it is provided for any man ho has cheek enough to step out of the street and enjoy it? Is it kept up, I sk, for people who are, technically speaking, not guests?"

The expression of conscious guilt deepened on the face of the unfortunate rofessor. He had nothing to say. He realized that his conduct was too flagrant o admit of defense, so he attempted none. Suddenly the countenance of his uestioner lit up with a smile, and he smote the professor on the shoulder.

"Well, old stick-in-the-mud, you haven't changed a particle in fifteen ears! You don't mean to pretend you don't know me?"

"You can't—you can't be Richard Yates?"

"I not only can, but I can't be anybody else. I know, because I have often ried. Well, well, well, well! Stilly we used to call you; don't you remember? 'll never forget that time we sang 'Oft in the stilly night' in front of your vindow when you were studying for the exams. You always were a quiet ellow, Stilly. I've been waiting for you nearly a whole day. I was up just 10w with a party of friends when the boy brought me your card—a little hilanthropic gathering—sort of mutual benefit arrangement, you know: ach of us contributed what we could spare to a general fund, which was iven to some deserving person in the crowd."

"Yes," said the professor dryly. "I heard the clerk telling the boy where he would be most likely to find you."

"Oh, you did, eh?" cried Yates, with a laugh. "Yes, Sam generally know where to send for me; but he needn't have been so darned public about it Being a newspaper man, I know what ought to go in print and what shoul have the blue pencil run through it. Sam is very discreet, as a general thing but then he knew, of course, the moment he set eyes on you, that you wer an old pal of mine."

Again Yates laughed, a very bright and cheery laugh for so evidentl wicked a man.

"Come along," he said, taking the professor by the arm. "We must ge you located."

They passed out into the hall, and drew up at the clerk's counter.

"I say, Sam," cried Yates, "can't you do something better for us than th fifth floor? I didn't come to Buffalo to engage in ballooning. No sky parlor for me, if I can help it."

"I'm sorry, Dick," said the clerk; "but I expect the fifth floor will be gon when the Chicago express gets in."

"Well, what can you do for us, anyhow?"

"I can let you have 518. That's the next room to yours. Really, they'r the most comfortable rooms in the house this weather. Fine lookout over th lake. I wouldn't mind having a sight of the lake myself, if I could leave th desk."

"All right. But I didn't come to look at the lake, nor yet at the railroa tracks this side, nor at Buffalo Creek either, beautiful and romantic as i is, nor to listen to the clanging of the ten thousand locomotives that pas within hearing distance for the delight of your guests. The fact is that, alway excepting Chicago, Buffalo is more like—for the professor's sake I'll sa Hades, than any other place in America."

"Oh, Buffalo's all right," said the clerk, with that feeling of local loyalt which all Americans possess. "Say, are you here on this Fenian snap?"

"What Fenian snap?" asked the newspaper man.

"Oh! don't you know about it? I thought, the moment I saw you, that you were here for this affair. Well, don't say I told you, but I can put you on to one of the big guns if you want the particulars. They say they're going to take Canada. I told 'em that I wouldn't take Canada as a gift, let alone fight for it. I've been there."

Yates' newspaper instinct thrilled him as he thought of the possible sensation. Then the light slowly died out of his eyes when he looked at the professor, who had flushed somewhat and compressed his lips as he listened to the slighting remarks on his country.

"Well, Sam," said the newspaper man at last, "it isn't more than once in a lifetime that you'll find me give the go-by to a piece of news, but the fact is I'm on my vacation just now. About the first I've had for fifteen years; so, you see, I must take care of it. No, let the Argus get scooped, if it wants to. They'll value my services all the more when I get back. No. 518, I think you said?"

The clerk handed over the key, and the professor gave the boy the check for his valise at Yates' suggestion.

"Now, get a move on you," said Yates to the elevator boy. "We're going right through with you."

And so the two friends were shot up together to the fifth floor.

CHAPTER II.

The sky parlor, as Yates had termed it, certainly commanded a very extensive view. Immediately underneath was a wilderness of roofs. Farther along were the railway tracks that Yates objected to; and a line of masts and propeller funnels marked the windings of Buffalo Creek, along whose banks arose numerous huge elevators, each marked by some tremendous letter of the alphabet, done in white paint against the somber brown of the big building. Still farther to the west was a more grateful and comforting sight for a hot day. The blue lake, dotted with white sails and an occasional trail of smoke, lay shimmering under the broiling sun. Over the water, through the distant summer haze, there could be seen the dim line of the Canadian shore.

"Sit you down," cried Yates, putting both hands on the other's shoulders, and pushing him into a chair near the window. Then, placing his finger on the electric button, he added: "What will you drink?"

"I'll take a glass of water, if it can be had without trouble," said Renmark.

Yates' hand dropped from the electric button hopelessly to his side, and he looked reproachfully at the professor.

"Great Heavens!" he cried, "have something mild. Don't go rashly in for Buffalo water before you realize what it is made of. Work up to it gradually. Try a sherry cobbler or a milk shake as a starter."

"Thank you, no. A glass of water will do very well for me. Order what you like for yourself."

"Thanks, I can be depended on for doing that." He pushed the button, and, when the boy appeared, said: "Bring up an iced cobbler, and charge it to Professor Renmark, No. 518. Bring also a pitcher of ice water for Yates, No. 520. There," he continued gleefully, "I'm going to have all the drinks, except the ice water, charged to you. I'll pay the bill, but I'll keep the account to hold over your head in the future. Professor Stillson Renmark, debtor to Metropolitan Grand—one sherry cobbler, one gin sling, one whisky cocktail, and so on. Now, then, Stilly, let's talk business. You're not married, I take it, or you wouldn't have responded to my invitation so promptly." The professor shook his head. "Neither am I. You never had the courage to propose to a girl; and I never had the time."

"Lack of self-conceit was not your failing in the old days, Richard," said Renmark quietly.

Yates laughed. "Well, it didn't hold me back any, to my knowledge. Now I'll tell you how I've got along since we attended old Scragmore's academy together, fifteen years ago. How time does fly! When I left, I tried teaching for one short month. I had some theories on the education of our youth which did not seem to chime in with the prejudices the school trustees had already formed on the subject."

The professor was at once all attention. Touch a man on his business, and he generally responds by being interested.

"And what were your theories?" he asked.

"Well, I thought a teacher should look after the physical as well as the mental welfare of his pupils. It did not seem to me that his duty to those under his charge ended with mere book learning."

"I quite agree with you," said the professor cordially.

"Thanks. Well, the trustees didn't. I joined the boys at their games, hoping my example would have an influence on their conduct on the playground as well as in the schoolroom. We got up a rattling good cricket club. You may not remember that I stood rather better in cricket at the academy than I did in mathematics or grammar. By handicapping me with several poor players, and having the best players among the boys in opposition, we made a pretty evenly matched team at school section No. 12. One day, at noon, we began a game. The grounds were in excellent condition, and the opposition boys were at their best. My side was getting the worst of it. I was very much interested; and, when one o'clock came, I thought it a pity to call school and spoil so good and interesting a contest. The boys were unanimously of the same opinion. The girls were happy, picnicking under the trees. So we played cricket all the afternoon."

"I think that was carrying your theory a little too far," said the professor dubiously.

"Just what the trustees thought when they came to hear of it. So they dismissed me; and I think my leaving was the only case on record where the pupils genuinely mourned a teacher's departure. I shook the dust of Canada from my feet, and have never regretted it. I tramped to Buffalo, continuing to shake the dust off at every step. (Hello! here's your drinks at last, Stilly. I had forgotten about them—an unusual thing with me. That's all right, boy; charge it to room 518. Ah! that hits the spot on a hot day.) Well, where was I? Oh, yes, at Buffalo. I got a place on a paper here, at just enough to keep life in me; but I liked the work. Then I drifted to Rochester at a bigger salary, afterward to Albany at a still bigger salary, and of course Albany is only a few hours from New York, and that is where all newspaper men ultimately land, if they are worth their salt. I saw a small section of the war as special correspondent, got hurt, and rounded up in the hospital. Since then, although only a reporter, I am about the top of the tree in that line, and make enough money to pay my poker debts and purchase iced drinks to soothe the asperities of the game. When there is anything big going on anywhere in the country, I am there, with other fellows to do the drudgery; I writing the picturesque descriptions and interviewing the big men. My stuff goes red-hot over the telegraph wire, and the humble postage stamp knows my envelopes no more. I am acquainted with every hotel clerk that amounts to anything from New York to San Francisco. If I could save money, I should be rich, for I make plenty; but the hole at the top of my trousers pocket has lost me a lot of cash, and I don't seem to be able to get it mended. Now, you've listened with your customary patience in order to give my self-esteem, as you called it, full sway. I am grateful. I will reciprocate. How about yourself?"

The professor spoke slowly. "I have had no such adventurous career," he began. "I have not shaken Canadian dust from my feet, and have not made any great success. I have simply plodded; and am in no danger of becoming rich, although I suppose I spend as little as any man. After you were expel—after you left the aca——"

"Don't mutilate the good old English language, Stilly. You were right in the first place. I am not thin-skinned. You were saying after I was expelled. Go on."

"I thought perhaps it might be a sore subject. You remember, you were very indignant at the time, and———"

"Of course I was—and am still, for that matter. It was an outrage!"

"I thought it was proved that you helped to put the pony in the principal's room."

"Oh, certainly. That. Of course. But what I detested was the way the principal worked the thing. He allowed that villain Spink to turn evidence against us, and Spink stated I originated the affair, whereas I could claim no such honor. It was Spink's own project, which I fell in with, as I did with every disreputable thing proposed. Of course the principal believed at once that I was the chief criminal. Do you happen to know if Spink has been hanged yet?"

"I believe he is a very reputable business man in Montreal, and much respected."

"I might have suspected that. Well, you keep your eye on the respected Spink. If he doesn't fail some day, and make a lot of money, I'm a Dutchman. But go on. This is digression. By the way, just push that electric button. You're nearest, and it is too hot to move. Thanks. After I was expelled———"

"After your departure I took a diploma, and for a year or two taught a class in the academy. Then, as I studied during my spare time, I got a chance as master of a grammar school near Toronto, chiefly, as I think, though the recommendation of Principal Scragmore. I had my degree by this time. Then———"

There was a gentle tap at the door.

"Come in!" shouted Yates. "Oh, it's you. Just bring up another cooling cobbler, will you? and charge it, as before, to Professor Renmark, room 518. Yes; and then———"

"And then there came the opening in University College, Toronto. I had the good fortune to be appointed. There I am still, and there I suppose I shall stay. I know very few people, and am better acquainted with books than with men. Those whom I have the privilege of knowing are mostly studious persons, who have made, or will make, their mark in the world of learning. I have not had your advantage, of meeting statesmen who guide the destinies of a great empire.

"No; you always were lucky, Stilly. My experience is that the chaps who do the guiding are more anxious about their own pockets, or their own political advancement, than they are of the destinies. Still, the empire seems to take its course westward just the same. So old Scragmore's been your friend, has he?"

"He has, indeed."

"Well, he insulted me only the other day."

"You astonish me. I cannot imagine so gentlemanly and scholarly a man as Principal Scragmore insulting anybody."

"Oh, you don't know him as I do. It was like this: I wanted to find out where you were, for reasons that I shall state hereafter. I cudgeled my brains, and then thought of old Scrag. I wrote him, and enclosed a stamped and addressed envelope, as all unsought contributors should do. He answered— But I have his reply somewhere. You shall read it for yourself."

Yates pulled from his inside pocket a bundle of letters, which he hurriedly fingered over, commenting in a low voice as he did so: "I thought I answered that. Still, no matter. Jingo! haven't I paid that bill yet? This pass is run out. Must get another." Then he smiled and sighed as he looked at a letter in dainty handwriting; but apparently he could not find the document he sought.

"Oh, well, it doesn't matter. I have it somewhere. He returned me the prepaid envelope, and reminded me that United States stamps were of no use in Canada, which of course I should have remembered. But he didn't pay the postage on his own letter, so that I had to fork out double. Still, I don't mind

100

that, only as an indication of his meanness. He went on to say that, of all the members of our class, you—you!—were the only one who had reflected credit on it. That was the insult. The idea of his making such a statement, when I had told him I was on the New York Argus! Credit to the class, indeed! I wonder if he ever heard of Brown after he was expelled. You know, of course. No? Well, Brown, by his own exertions, became president of the Alum Bank in New York, wrecked it, and got off to Canada with a clear half million. Yes, sir. I saw him in Quebec not six months ago. Keeps the finest span and carriage in the city, and lives in a palace. Could buy out old Scragmore a thousand times, and never feel it. Most liberal contributor to the cause of education that there is in Canada. He says education made him, and he's not a man to go back on education. And yet Scragmore has the cheek to say that you were the only man in the class who reflects credit on it!"

The professor smiled quietly as the excited journalist took a cooling sip of the cobbler.

"You see, Yates, people's opinions differ. A man like Brown may not be Principal Scragmore's ideal. The principal may be local in his ideals of a successful man, or of one who reflects credit on his teaching."

"Local? You bet he's local. Too darned local for me. It would do that man good to live in New York for a year. But I'm going to get even with him. I'm going to write him up. I'll give him a column and a half; see if I don't. I'll get his photograph, and publish a newspaper portrait of him. If that doesn't make him quake, he's a cast-iron man. Say, you haven't a photograph of old Scrag that you can lend me, have you?"

"I have; but I won't lend it for such a purpose. However, never mind the principal. Tell me your plans. I am at your disposal for a couple of weeks, or longer if necessary."

"Good boy! Well, I'll tell you how it is. I want rest and quiet, and the woods, for a week or two. This is how it happened: I have been steadily at the grindstone, except for a while in the hospital; and that, you will admit, is not much of a vacation. The work interests me, and I am always in the thick of it. Now, it's like this in the newspaper business: Your chief is never the person to suggest that you take a vacation. He is usually short of men and long on things to do, so if you don't worry him into letting you off, he won't lose any sleep over it. He's content to let well enough alone every time. Then there is always somebody who wants to get away on pressing business,—grandmother's funeral, and that sort of thing,—so if a fellow is content to work right along, his chief is quite content to let him. That's the way affairs have gone for years with me. The other week I went over to Washington to interview a senator on the political prospects. I tell you what it is, Stilly, without bragging, there are some big men in the States whom no one but me can interview. And yet old Scrag says I'm no credit to his class! Why, last year my political predictions were telegraphed all over this country, and have since appeared in the European press. No credit! By Jove, I would like to have old Scrag in a twenty-four-foot ring, with thin gloves on, for about ten minutes!"

"I doubt if he would shine under those circumstances. But never mind him. He spoke, for once, without due reflection, and with perhaps an exaggerated remembrance of your school-day offenses. What happened when you went to Washington?"

"A strange thing happened. When I was admitted to the senator's library, I saw another fellow, whom I thought I knew, sitting there. I said to the senator: 'I will come when you are alone.' The senator looked up in surprise, and said: 'I am alone.' I didn't say anything, but went on with my interview; and the other fellow took notes all the time. I didn't like this, but said nothing, for the senator is not a man to offend, and it is by not offending these fellows that I can get the information I do. Well, the other fellow came out with me, and as I looked at him I saw that he was myself. This did not strike me as strange at the time, but I argued with him all the way to New York, and tried to show him that he wasn't treating me fairly. I wrote up the interview, with the other fellow interfering all the while, so I compromised, and half the time put in what he suggested, and half the time what I wanted in myself. When the political editor went over the stuff, he looked alarmed. I told him frankly just how I had been interfered with, and he looked none the less alarmed when I had finished. He sent at once for a doctor. The doctor metaphorically took me to pieces, and then said to my chief: 'This man is simply worked to death.

102

He must have a vacation, and a real one, with absolutely nothing to think of, or he is going to collapse, and that with a suddenness which will surprise everybody.' The chief, to my astonishment, consented without a murmur, and even upbraided me for not going away sooner. Then the doctor said to me: 'You get some companion—some man with no brains, if possible, who will not discuss politics, who has no opinion on anything that any sane man would care to talk about, and who couldn't say a bright thing if he tried for a year. Get such a man to go off to the woods somewhere. Up in Maine or in Canada. As far away from post offices and telegraph offices as possible. And, by the way, don't leave your address at the Argus office.' Thus it happened, Stilly, when he described this man so graphically, I at once thought of you."

"I am deeply gratified, I am sure," said the professor, with the ghost of a smile, "to be so promptly remembered in such a connection, and if I can be of service to you, I shall be very glad. I take it, then, that you have no intention of stopping in Buffalo?"

"You bet I haven't. I'm in for the forest primeval, the murmuring pines and the hemlock, bearded with moss and green in the something or other—I forget the rest. I want to quit lying on paper, and lie on my back instead, on the sward or in a hammock. I'm going to avoid all boarding houses or delightful summer resorts, and go in for the quiet of the forest."

"There ought to be some nice places along the lake shore."

"No, sir. No lake shore for me. It would remind me of the Lake Shore Railroad when it was calm, and of Long Branch when it was rough. No, sir. The woods, the woods, and the woods. I have hired a tent and a lot of cooking things. I'm going to take that tent over to Canada to-morrow; and then I propose we engage a man with a team to cart it somewhere into the woods, fifteen or twenty miles away. We shall have to be near a farmhouse, so that we can get fresh butter, milk, and eggs. This, of course, is a disadvantage; but I shall try to get near someone who has never even heard of New York."

"You may find that somewhat difficult."

"Oh, I don't know. I have great hopes of the lack of intelligence in the

Canadians."

"Often the narrowest," said the professor slowly, "are those who think themselves the most cosmopolitan."

"Right you are," cried Yates, skimming lightly over the remark, and seeing nothing applicable to his case in it. "Well, I've laid in about half a ton, more or less, of tobacco, and have bought an empty jug."

"An empty one?"

"Yes. Among the few things worth having that the Canadians possess, is good whisky. Besides, the empty jar will save trouble at the customhouse. I don't suppose Canadian rye is as good as the Kentucky article, but you and I will have to scrub along on it for a while. And, talking of whisky, just press the button once again."

The professor did so, saying:

"The doctor made no remark, I suppose, about drinking less or smoking less, did he?"

"In my case? Well, come to think of it, there was some conversation in that direction. Don't remember at the moment just what it amounted to; but all physicians have their little fads, you know. It doesn't do to humor them too much. Ah, boy, there you are again. Well, the professor wants another drink. Make it a gin fizz this time, and put plenty of ice in it; but don't neglect the gin on that account. Certainly; charge it to room 518."

CHAPTER III.

"What's all this tackle?" asked the burly and somewhat red-faced customs officer at Fort Erie.

"This," said Yates, "is a tent, with the poles and pegs appertaining thereto. These are a number of packages of tobacco, on which I shall doubtless have to pay something into the exchequer of her Majesty. This is a jug used for the holding of liquids. I beg to call your attention to the fact that it is at present empty, which unfortunately prevents me making a libation to the rites of good-fellowship. What my friend has in that valise I don't know, but I suspect a gambling outfit, and would advise you to search him."

"My valise contains books principally, with some articles of wearing apparel," said the professor, opening his grip.

The customs officer looked with suspicion on the whole outfit, and evidently did not like the tone of the American. He seemed to be treating the customs department in a light and airy manner, and the officer was too much impressed by the dignity of his position not to resent flippancy. Besides, there were rumors of Fenian invasion in the air, and the officer resolved that no Fenian should get into the country without paying duty.

"Where are you going with this tent?"

"I'm sure I don't know. Perhaps you can tell us. I don't know the country about here. Say, Stilly, I'm off uptown to attend to the emptiness in this stone utensil. I've been empty too often myself not to sympathize with its condition. You wrestle this matter out about the tent. You know the ways of the country, whereas I don't."

It was perhaps as well that Yates left negotiations in the hands of his friend. He was quick enough to see that he made no headway with the officer, but rather the opposite. He slung the jar ostentatiously over his shoulder, to the evident discomfort of the professor, and marched up the hill to the nearest tavern, whistling one of the lately popular war tunes.

"Now," he said to the barkeeper, placing the jar tenderly on the bar, "fi that up to the nozzle with the best rye you have. Fill it with the old familia juice, as the late poet Omar saith."

The bartender did as he was requested.

"Can you disguise a little of that fluid in any way, so that it may be take internally without a man suspecting what he is swallowing?"

The barkeeper smiled. "How would a cocktail fill the vacancy?"

"I can suggest nothing better," replied Yates. "If you are sure you know how to make it."

The man did not resent this imputation of ignorance. He merely said with the air of one who gives an incontrovertible answer:

"I am a Kentucky man myself."

"Shake!" cried Yates briefly, as he reached his hand across the bar. "How is it you happened to be here?"

"Well, I got in to a little trouble in Louisville, and here I am, where I ca at least look at God's country."

"Hold on," protested Yates. "You're making only one cocktail."

"Didn't you say one?" asked the man, pausing in the compounding.

"Bless you, I never saw one cocktail made in my life. You are with m on this."

"Just as you say," replied the other, as he prepared enough for two.

"Now I'll tell you my fix," said Yates confidentially. "I've got a tent an some camp things down below at the customhouse shanty, and I want to ge them taken into the woods, where I can camp out with a friend. I want place where we can have absolute rest and quiet. Do you know the countr round here? Perhaps you could recommend a spot."

"Well, for all the time I've been here, I know precious little about th

106

back country. I've been down the road to Niagara Falls, but never back in the woods. I suppose you want some place by the lake or the river?"

"No, I don't. I want to get clear back into the forest—if there is a forest."

"Well, there's a man in to-day from somewhere near Ridgeway, I think. He's got a hay rack with him, and that would be just the thing to take your tent and poles. Wouldn't be very comfortable traveling for you, but it would be all right for the tent, if it's a big one."

"That will suit us exactly. We don't care a cent about the comfort. Roughing it is what we came for. Where will I find him?"

"Oh, he'll be along here soon. That's his team tied there on the side street. If he happens to be in good humor, he'll take your things, and as like as not give you a place to camp in his woods. Hiram Bartlett's his name. And, talking of the old Nick himself, here he is. I say, Mr. Bartlett, this gentleman was wondering if you couldn't tote out some of his belongings. He's going out your way."

Bartlett was a somewhat uncouth and wiry specimen of the Canadian farmer who evidently paid little attention to the subject of dress. He said nothing, but looked in a lowering way at Yates, with something of contempt and suspicion in his glance.

Yates had one receipt for making the acquaintance of all mankind. "Come in, Mr. Bartlett," he said cheerily, "and try one of my friend's excellent cocktails."

"I take mine straight," growled Bartlett gruffly, although he stepped inside the open door. "I don't want no Yankee mixtures in mine. Plain whisky's good enough for any man, if he is a man. I don't take no water, neither. I've got trouble enough."

The bartender winked at Yates as he shoved the decanter over to the newcomer.

"Right you are," assented Yates cordially.

The farmer did not thaw out in the least because of this prompt

107

agreement with him, but sipped his whisky gloomily, as if it were a most disagreeable medicine.

"What did you want me to take out?" he said at last.

"A friend and a tent, a jug of whisky and a lot of jolly good tobacco."

"How much are you willing to pay?"

"Oh, I don't know. I'm always willing to do what's right. How would five dollars strike you?"

The farmer scowled and shook his head.

"Too much," he said, as Yates was about to offer more. "'Taint worth it. Two and a half would be about the right figure. Don'no but that's too much. I'll think on it going home, and charge you what it's worth. I'll be ready to leave in about an hour, if that suits you. That's my team on the other side of the road. If it's gone when you come back, I'm gone, an' you'll have to get somebody else."

With this Bartlett drew his coat sleeve across his mouth and departed.

"That's him exactly," said the barkeeper. "He's the most cantankerous crank in the township. And say, let me give you a pointer. If the subject of 1812 comes up,—the war, you know,—you'd better admit that we got thrashed out of our boots; that is, if you want to get along with Hiram. He hates Yankees like poison."

"And did we get thrashed in 1812?" asked Yates, who was more familiar with current topics than with the history of the past.

"Blessed if I know. Hiram says we did. I told him once that we got what we wanted from old England, and he nearly hauled me over the bar. So I give you the warning, if you want to get along with him."

"Thank you. I'll remember it. So long."

This friendly hint from the man in the tavern offers a key to the solution of the problem of Yates' success on the New York press. He could get news when no other man could. Flippant and shallow as he undoubtedly was, he somehow got into the inner confidences of all sorts of men in a way that made them give him an inkling of anything that was going on for the mere love of him; and thus Yates often received valuable assistance from his acquaintances which other reporters could not get for money.

The New Yorker found the professor sitting on a bench by the customhouse, chatting with the officer, and gazing at the rapidly flowing broad blue river in front of them.

"I have got a man," said Yates, "who will take us out into the wilderness in about an hour's time. Suppose we explore the town. I expect nobody will run away with the tent till we come back."

"I'll look after that," said the officer; and, thanking him, the two friends strolled up the street. They were a trifle late in getting back, and when they reached the tavern, they found Bartlett just on the point of driving home. He gruffly consented to take them, if they did not keep him more than five minutes loading up. The tent and its belongings were speedily placed on the hay rack, and then Bartlett drove up to the tavern and waited, saying nothing, although he had been in such a hurry a few moments before. Yates did not like to ask the cause of the delay; so the three sat there silently. After a while Yates said as mildly as he could:

"Are you waiting for anyone, Mr. Bartlett?"

"Yes," answered the driver in a surly tone. "I'm waiting for you to go in fur that jug. I don't suppose you filled it to leave it on the counter."

"By Jove!" cried Yates, springing off, "I had forgotten all about it, which shows the extraordinary effect this country has on me already." The professor frowned, but Yates came out merrily, with the jar in his hand, and Bartlett started his team. They drove out of the village and up a slight hill, going for a mile or two along a straight and somewhat sandy road. Then they turned into the Ridge Road, as Bartlett called it, in answer to a question by the professor, and there was no need to ask why it was so termed. It was a good highway, but rather stony, the road being, in places, on the bare rock. It paid not the slightest attention to Euclid's definition of a straight line, and in this respect was rather a welcome change from the average American road. Sometimes they passed along avenues of overbranching trees, which were evidently relics of the forest that once covered all the district. The road followed the ridge, and on each side were frequently to be seen wide vistas of lower lying country. All along the road were comfortable farmhouses; and it was evident that a prosperous community flourished along the ridge.

Bartlett spoke only once, and then to the professor, who sat next to him.

"You a Canadian?"

"Yes."

"Where's he from?"

"My friend is from New York," answered the innocent professor.

"Humph!" grunted Bartlett, scowling deeper than ever, after which he became silent again. The team was not going very fast, although neither the load nor the road was heavy. Bartlett was muttering a good deal to himself, and now and then brought down his whip savagely on one or the other of the horses; but the moment the unfortunate animals quickened their pace he hauled them in roughly. Nevertheless, they were going quickly enough to be overtaking a young woman who was walking on alone. Although she must have heard them coming over the rocky road she did not turn her head, but walked along with the free and springy step of one who is not only accustomed to walking, but who likes it. Bartlett paid no attention to the girl; the professor was endeavoring to read his thin book as well as a man might who is being jolted frequently; but Yates, as soon as he recognized that the pedestrian was young, pulled up his collar, adjusted his necktie with care, and placed his hat in a somewhat more jaunty and fetching position.

"Are you going to offer that girl a ride?" he said to Bartlett.

"No, I'm not."

"I think that is rather uncivil," he added, forgetting the warning he had had.

110

"You do, eh? Well, you offer her a ride. You hired the team."

"By Jove! I will," said Yates, placing his hand on the outside of the rack, nd springing lightly to the ground.

"Likely thing," growled Bartlett to the professor, "that she's going to ride vith the like of him."

The professor looked for a moment at Yates, politely taking off his hat to he apparently astonished young woman, but he said nothing.

"Fur two cents," continued Bartlett, gathering up the reins, "I'd whip up he horses, and let him walk the rest of the way."

"From what I know of my friend," answered the professor slowly, "I hink he would not object in the slightest."

Bartlett muttered something to himself, and seemed to change his mind bout galloping his horses.

Meanwhile, Yates, as has been said, took off his hat with great politeness o the fair pedestrian, and as he did so he noticed, with a thrill of admiration, hat she was very handsome. Yates always had an eye for the beautiful.

"Our conveyance," he began, "is not as comfortable as it might be, yet I hall be very happy if you will accept its hospitalities."

The young woman flashed a brief glance at him from her dark eyes, and or a moment Yates feared that his language had been rather too choice for er rural understanding, but before he could amend his phrase she answered riefly:

"Thank you. I prefer to walk."

"Well, I don't know that I blame you. May I ask if you have come all the vay from the village?"

"Yes."

"That is a long distance, and you must be very tired." There was no eply; so Yates continued. "At least, I thought it a long distance; but perhaps that was because I was riding on Bartlett's hay rack. There is no 'downy be of ease' about his vehicle."

As he spoke of the wagon he looked at it, and, striding forward to it side, said in a husky whisper to the professor:

"Say, Stilly, cover up that jug with a flap of the tent."

"Cover it up yourself," briefly replied the other; "it isn't mine."

Yates reached across and, in a sort of accidental way, threw the flap o the tent over the too conspicuous jar. As an excuse for his action he took u his walking cane and turned toward his new acquaintance. He was flattered to see that she was loitering some distance behind the wagon, and he speedil rejoined her. The girl, looking straight ahead, now quickened her pace, an rapidly shortened the distance between herself and the vehicle. Yates, with the quickness characteristic of him, made up his mind that this was a cas of country diffidence, which was best to be met by the bringing down of hi conversation to the level of his hearer's intelligence.

"Have you been marketing?" he asked.

"Yes."

"Butter and eggs, and that sort of thing?"

"We are farmers," she answered, "and we sell butter and eggs"— pause—"and that sort of thing."

Yates laughed in his light and cheery way. As he twirled his cane h looked at his pretty companion. She was gazing anxiously ahead toward turn in the road. Her comely face was slightly flushed, doubtless with th exercise of walking.

"Now, in my country," continued the New Yorker, "we idolize ou women. Pretty girls don't tramp miles to market with butter and eggs."

"Aren't the girls pretty—in your country?"

Yates made a mental note that there was not as much rurality about thi

112

girl as he had thought at first. There was a piquancy about the conversation which he liked. That she shared his enjoyment was doubtful, for a slight line of resentment was noticeable on her smooth brow.

"You bet they're pretty! I think all American girls are pretty. It seems their birthright. When I say American, I mean the whole continent, of course. I'm from the States myself—from New York." He gave an extra twirl to his cane as he said this, and bore himself with that air of conscious superiority which naturally pertains to a citizen of the metropolis. "But over in the States we think the men should do all the work, and that the women should—well, spend the money. I must do our ladies the justice to say that they attend strictly to their share of the arrangement."

"It should be a delightful country to live in—for the women."

"They all say so. We used to have an adage to the effect that America was paradise for women, purgatory for men, and—well, an entirely different sort of place for oxen."

There was no doubt that Yates had a way of getting along with people. As he looked at his companion he was gratified to note just the faintest suspicion of a smile hovering about her lips. Before she could answer, if she had intended to do so, there was a quick clatter of hoofs on the hard road ahead, and next instant an elegant buggy, whose slender jet-black polished spokes flashed and twinkled in the sunlight, came dashing past the wagon. On seeing the two walking together the driver hauled up his team with a suddenness that was evidently not relished by the spirited dappled span he drove.

"Hello, Margaret!" he cried; "am I late? Have you walked in all the way?"

"You are just in good time," answered the girl, without looking toward Yates, who stood aimlessly twirling his cane. The young woman put her foot on the buggy step, and sprang lightly in beside the driver. It needed no second glance to see that he was her brother, not only on account of the family resemblance between them, but also because he allowed her to get into the buggy without offering the slightest assistance, which, indeed, was

113

not needed, and graciously permitted her to place the duster that covered his knees over her own lap as well. The restive team trotted rapidly down the road for a few rods, until they came to a wide place in the highway, and then whirled around, seemingly within an ace of upsetting the buggy; but the young man evidently knew his business, and held them in with a firm hand. The wagon was jogging along where the road was very narrow, and Bartlett kept his team stolidly in the center of the way.

"Hello, there, Bartlett!" shouted the young man in the buggy; "half the road, you know—half the road."

"Take it," cried Bartlett over his shoulder.

"Come, come, Bartlett, get out of the way, or I'll run you down."

"You just try it."

Bartlett either had no sense of humor or his resentment against his young neighbor smothered it, since otherwise he would have recognized that a heavy wagon was in no danger of being run into by a light and expensive buggy. The young man kept his temper admirably, but he knew just where to touch the elder on the raw. His sister's hand was placed appealingly on his arm. He smiled, and took no notice of her.

"Come, now, you move out, or I'll have the law on you."

"The law!" roared Bartlett; "you just try it on."

"Should think you'd had enough of it by this time."

"Oh, don't, don't, Henry!" protested the girl in distress.

"There aint no law," yelled Bartlett, "that kin make a man with a load move out fur anything."

"You haven't any load, unless it's in that jug."

Yates saw with consternation that the jar had been jolted out from under its covering, but the happy consolation came to him that the two in the buggy would believe it belonged to Bartlett. He thought, however, that this dog-in-the-manger policy had gone far enough. He stepped briskly forward, and said to Bartlett:

"Better drive aside a little, and let them pass."

"You 'tend to your own business," cried the thoroughly enraged farmer.

"I will," said Yates shortly, striding to the horses' heads. He took them by the bits and, in spite of Bartlett's maledictions and pulling at the lines, he drew them to one side, so that the buggy got by.

"Thank you!" cried the young man. The light and glittering carriage rapidly disappeared up the Ridge Road.

Bartlett sat there for one moment the picture of baffled rage. Then he threw the reins down on the backs of his patient horses, and descended.

"You take my horses by the head, do you, you good-fur-nuthin' Yank? You do, eh? I like your cheek. Touch my horses an' me a-holdin' the lines! Now you hear me? Your traps comes right off here on the road. You hear me?"

"Oh, anybody within a mile can hear you."

"Kin they? Well, off comes your pesky tent."

"No, it doesn't."

"Don't it, eh? Well, then, you'll lick me fust; and that's something no Yank ever did nor kin do."

"I'll do it with pleasure."

"Come, come," cried the professor, getting down on the road, "this has gone far enough. Keep quiet, Yates. Now, Mr. Bartlett, don't mind it; he means no disrespect."

"Don't you interfere. You're all right, an' I aint got nothin' ag'in you. But I'm goin' to thrash this Yank within an inch of his life; see if I don't. We met 'em in 1812, an' we fit 'em an' we licked 'em, an' we can do it ag'in. I'll learn ye to take my horses by the head."

"Teach," suggested Yates tantalizingly.

Before he could properly defend himself, Bartlett sprang at him and grasped him round the waist. Yates was something of a wrestler himself, but his skill was of no avail on this occasion. Bartlett's right leg became twisted around his with a steel-like grip that speedily convinced the younger man he would have to give way or a bone would break. He gave way accordingly, and the next thing he knew he came down on his back with a thud that seemed to shake the universe.

"There, darn ye!" cried the triumphant farmer; "that's 1812 and Queenstown Heights for ye. How do you like 'em?"

Yates rose to his feet with some deliberation, and slowly took off his coat.

"Now, now, Yates," said the professor soothingly, "let it go at this. You're not hurt, are you?" he asked anxiously, as he noticed how white the young man was around the lips.

"Look here, Renmark; you're a sensible man. There is a time to interfere and a time not to. This is the time not to. A certain international element seems to have crept into this dispute. Now, you stand aside, like a good fellow, for I don't want to have to thrash both of you."

The professor stood aside, for he realized that, when Yates called him by his last name, matters were serious.

"Now, old chucklehead, perhaps you would like to try that again."

"I kin do it a dozen times, if ye aint satisfied. There aint no Yank ever raised on pumpkin pie that can stand ag'in that grapevine twist."

"Try the grapevine once more."

Bartlett proceeded more cautiously this time, for there was a look in the young man's face he did not quite like. He took a catch-as-catch-can attitude, and moved stealthily in a semi-circle around Yates, who shifted his position constantly so as to keep facing his foe. At last Bartlett sprang forward, and the next instant found himself sitting on a piece of the rock of the country, with a thousand humming birds buzzing in his head, while stars and the landscape ound joined in a dance together. The blow was sudden, well placed, and om the shoulder.

"That," said Yates, standing over him, "is 1776—the Revolution— hen, to use your own phrase, we met ye, fit ye, and licked ye. How do you ke it? Now, if my advice is of any use to you, take a broader view of history an you have done. Don't confine yourself too much to one period. Study p the War of the Revolution a bit."

Bartlett made no reply. After sitting there for a while, until the urrounding landscape assumed its normal condition, he arose leisurely, ithout saying a word. He picked the reins from the backs of the horses and atted the nearest animal gently. Then he mounted to his place and drove off. he professor had taken his seat beside the driver, but Yates, putting on his oat and picking up his cane, strode along in front, switching off the heads of Canada thistles with his walking stick as he proceeded.

CHAPTER IV.

Bartlett was silent for a long time, but there was evidently somethin
on his mind, for he communed with himself, his mutterings growing loude
and louder, until they broke the stillness; then he struck the horses, pulle
them in, and began his soliloquy over again. At last he said abruptly to th
professor:

"What's this Revolution he talked about?"

"It was the War of Independence, beginning in 1776."

"Never heard of it. Did the Yanks fight us?"

"The colonies fought with England."

"What colonies?"

"The country now called the United States."

"They fit with England, eh? Which licked?"

"The colonies won their independence."

"That means they licked us. I don't believe a word of it. 'Pears to me I'
'a' heard of it; fur I've lived in these parts a long time."

"It was a little before your day."

"So was 1812; but my father fit in it, an' I never heard him tell o
this Revolution. He'd 'a' known, I sh'd think. There's a nigger in the fenc
somewheres."

"Well, England was rather busy at the time with the French."

"Ah, that was it, was it? I'll bet England never knew the Revolution wa
a-goin' on till it was over. Old Napoleon couldn't thrash 'em, and it don'
stand to reason that the Yanks could. I thought there was some skullduggery
Why, it took the Yanks four years to lick themselves. I got a book at home al

about Napoleon. He was a tough cuss."

The professor did not feel called upon to defend the character of Napoleon, and so silence once more descended upon them. Bartlett seemed a good deal disturbed by the news he had just heard of the Revolution, and he growled to himself, while the horses suffered more than usual from the whip and the hauling back that invariably followed the stroke. Yates was some distance ahead, and swinging along at a great rate, when the horses, apparently of their own accord, turned in at an open gateway and proceeded, in their usual leisurely fashion, toward a large barn, past a comfortable frame house with a wide veranda in front.

"This is my place," said Bartlett shortly.

"I wish you had told me a few minutes ago," replied the professor, springing off, "so that I might have called to my friend."

"I'm not frettin' about him," said Bartlett, throwing the reins to a young man who came out of the house.

Renmark ran to the road and shouted loudly to the distant Yates. Yates apparently did not hear him, but something about the next house attracted the pedestrian's attention, and after standing for a moment and gazing toward the west he looked around and saw the professor beckoning to him. When the two men met, Yates said:

"So we have arrived, have we? I say, Stilly, she lives in the next house. I saw the buggy in the yard."

"She? Who?"

"Why, that good-looking girl we passed on the road. I'm going to buy our supplies at that house, Stilly, if you have no objections. By the way, how is my old friend 1812?"

"He doesn't seem to harbor any harsh feelings. In fact, he was more troubled about the Revolution than about the blow you gave him."

"News to him, eh? Well, I'm glad I knocked something into his head."

119

"You certainly did it most unscientifically."

"How do you mean—unscientifically?"

"In the delivery of the blow. I never saw a more awkwardly delivered undercut."

Yates looked at his friend in astonishment. How should this calm, learned man know anything about undercuts or science in blows?

"Well, you must admit I got there just the same."

"Yes, by brute force. A sledge hammer would have done as well. But you had such an opportunity to do it neatly and deftly, without any display of surplus energy, that I regretted to see such an opening thrown away."

"Heavens and earth, Stilly, this is the professor in a new light! What do you teach in Toronto University, anyhow? The noble art of self-defense?"

"Not exactly; but if you intend to go through Canada in this belligerent manner, I think it would be worth your while to take a few hints from me."

"With striking examples, I suppose. By Jove! I will, Stilly."

As the two came to the house they found Bartlett sitting in a wooden rocking chair on the veranda, looking grimly down the road.

"What an old tyrant that man must be in his home!" said Yates. There was no time for the professor to reply before they came within earshot.

"The old woman's setting out supper," said the farmer gruffly, that piece of information being apparently as near as he could get toward inviting them to share his hospitality. Yates didn't know whether it was meant for an invitation or not, but he answered shortly:

"Thanks, we won't stay."

"Speak fur yourself, please," snarled Bartlett.

"Of course I go with my friend," said Renmark; "but we are obliged for the invitation."

120

"Please yourselves."

"What's that?" cried a cheery voice from the inside of the house, as a stout, rosy, and very good-natured-looking woman appeared at the front door. "Won't stay? Who won't stay? I'd like to see anybody leave my house hungry when there's a meal on the table! And, young men, if you can get a better meal anywhere on the Ridge than what I'll give you, why, you're welcome to go there next time, but this meal you'll have here, inside of ten minutes. Hiram, that's your fault. You always invite a person to dinner as if you wanted to wrastle with him!"

Hiram gave a guilty start, and looked with something of mute appeal at the two men, but said nothing.

"Never mind him," continued Mrs. Bartlett. "You're at my house; and, whatever my neighbors may say ag'in me, I never heard anybody complain of the lack of good victuals while I was able to do the cooking. Come right in and wash yourselves, for the road between here and the fort is dusty enough, even if Hiram never was taken up for fast driving. Besides, a wash is refreshing after a hot day."

There was no denying the cordiality of this invitation, and Yates, whose natural gallantry was at once aroused, responded with the readiness of a courtier. Mrs. Bartlett led the way into the house; but as Yates passed the farmer the latter cleared his throat with an effort, and, throwing his thumb over his shoulder in the direction his wife had taken, said in a husky whisper:

"No call to—to mention the Revolution, you know."

"Certainly not," answered Yates, with a wink that took in the situation. "Shall we sample the jug before or after supper?"

"After, if it's all the same to you;" adding, "out in the barn."

Yates nodded, and followed his friend into the house.

The young men were shown into a bedroom of more than ordinary size, on the upper floor. Everything about the house was of the most dainty and scrupulous cleanliness, and an air of cheerful comfort pervaded the place.

Mrs. Bartlett was evidently a housekeeper to be proud of. Two large pitchers of cool, soft water awaited them, and the wash, as had been predicted, was most refreshing.

"I say," cried Yates, "it's rather cheeky to accept a man's hospitality after knocking him down."

"It would be for most people, but I think you underestimate your cheek, as you call it."

"Bravo, Stilly! You're blossoming out. That's repartee, that is. With the accent on the rap, too. Never you mind; I think old 1812 and I will get on all right after this. It doesn't seem to bother him any, so I don't see why it should worry me. Nice motherly old lady, isn't she?"

"Who? 1812?"

"No; Mrs. 1812. I'm sorry I complimented you on your repartee. You'll get conceited. Remember that what in the newspaper man is clever, in a grave professor is rank flippancy. Let's go down."

The table was covered with a cloth as white and spotless as good linen can well be. The bread was genuine homemade, a term so often misused in the cities. It was brown as to crust, and flaky and light as to interior. The butter, cool from the rock cellar, was of a refreshing yellow hue. The sight of the well-loaded table was most welcome to the eyes of hungry travelers. There was, as Yates afterward remarked, "abundance, and plenty of it."

"Come, father!" cried Mrs. Bartlett, as the young men appeared; they heard the rocking chair creak on the veranda in prompt answer to the summons.

"This is my son, gentlemen," said Mrs. Bartlett, indicating the young man who stood in a noncommittal attitude near a corner of the room. The professor recognized him as the person who had taken charge of the horses when his father came home. There was evidently something of his father's demeanor about the young man, who awkwardly and silently responded to the recognition of the strangers.

122

"And this is my daughter," continued the good woman. "Now, what might your names be?"

"My name is Yates, and this is my friend Professor Renmark of T'ronto," pronouncing the name of the fair city in two syllables, as is, alas! too often done. The professor bowed, and Yates cordially extended his hand to the young woman. "How do you do, Miss Bartlett?" he said, "I am happy to meet you."

The girl smiled very prettily, and said she hoped they had a pleasant trip out from Fort Erie.

"Oh, we had," said Yates, looking for a moment at his host, whose eyes were fixed on the tablecloth, and who appeared to be quite content to let his wife run the show. "The road's a little rocky in places, but it's very pleasant."

"Now, you sit down here, and you here," said Mrs. Bartlett; "and I do hope you have brought good appetites with you."

The strangers took their places, and Yates had a chance to look at the younger member of the family, which opportunity he did not let slip. It was hard to believe that she was the daughter of so crusty a man as Hiram Bartlett. Her cheeks were rosy, with dimples in them that constantly came and went in her incessant efforts to keep from laughing. Her hair, which hung about her plump shoulders, was a lovely golden brown. Although her dress was of the cheapest material, it was neatly cut and fitted; and her dainty white apron added that touch of wholesome cleanliness which was so noticeable everywhere in the house. A bit of blue ribbon at her white throat, and a pretty spring flower just below it, completed a charming picture, which a more critical and less susceptible man than Yates might have contemplated with pleasure.

Miss Bartlett sat smilingly at one end of the table, and her father grimly at the other. The mother sat at the side, apparently looking on that position as one of vantage for commanding the whole field, and keeping her husband and her daughter both under her eye. The teapot and cups were set before the young woman. She did not pour out the tea at once, but seemed to be waiting instructions from her mother. That good lady was gazing with some sternnes at her husband, he vainly endeavoring to look at the ceiling or anywhere bu at her. He drew his open hand nervously down his face, which was of unusua gravity even for him. Finally he cast an appealing glance at his wife, wh sat with her hands folded on her lap, but her eyes were unrelenting. Afte a moment's hopeless irresolution Bartlett bent his head over his plate an murmured:

"For what we are about to receive, oh, make us truly thankful. Amen."

Mrs. Bartlett echoed the last word, having also bowed her head whe she saw surrender in the troubled eyes of her husband.

Now, it happened that Yates, who had seen nothing of this silent strugg of the eyes, being exceedingly hungry, was making every preparation for th energetic beginning of the meal. He had spent most of his life in hotels an New York boarding houses, so that if he ever knew the adage, "Grace befor meat," he had forgotten it. In the midst of his preparations came the devou words, and they came upon him as a stupefying surprise. Although naturall a resourceful man, he was not quick enough this time to cover his confusior Miss Bartlett's golden head was bowed, but out of the corner of her eye sh saw Yates' look of amazed bewilderment and his sudden halt of surprise When all heads were raised, the young girl's still remained where it was, whil her plump shoulders quivered. Then she covered her face with her apron, an the silvery ripple of a laugh came like a smothered musical chime tricklin through her fingers.

"Why, Kitty!" cried her mother in astonishment, "whatever is the matte with you?"

The girl could no longer restrain her mirth. "You'll have to pour out th tea, mother!" She exclaimed, as she fled from the room.

"For the land's sake!" cried the astonished mother, rising to take he frivolous daughter's place, "what ails the child? I don't see what there is t laugh at."

Hiram scowled down the table, and was evidently also of the opinio that there was no occasion for mirth. The professor was equally in the dark.

"I am afraid, Mrs. Bartlett," said Yates, "that I am the innocent cause of Miss Kitty's mirth. You see, madam—it's a pathetic thing to say, but really I have had no home life. Although I attend church regularly, of course," he added with jaunty mendacity, "I must confess that I haven't heard grace at meals for years and years, and—well, I wasn't just prepared for it. I have no doubt I made an exhibition of myself, which your daughter was quick to see."

"It wasn't very polite," said Mrs. Bartlett with some asperity.

"I know that," pleaded Yates with contrition, "but I assure you it was unintentional on my part."

"Bless the man!" cried his hostess. "I don't mean you. I mean Kitty. But that girl never could keep her face straight. She always favored me more than her father."

This statement was not difficult to believe, for Hiram at that moment looked as if he had never smiled in his life. He sat silent throughout the meal, but Mrs. Bartlett talked quite enough for two.

"Well, for my part," she said, "I don't know what farming's coming to! Henry Howard and Margaret drove past here this afternoon as proud as Punch in their new covered buggy. Things is very different from what they was when I was a girl. Then a farmer's daughter had to work. Now Margaret's took her diploma at the ladies' college, and Arthur he's begun at the university, and Henry's sporting round in a new buggy. They have a piano there, with the organ moved out into the back room."

"The whole Howard lot's a stuck-up set," muttered the farmer.

But Mrs. Bartlett wouldn't have that. Any detraction that was necessary she felt competent to supply, without help from the nominal head of the house.

"No, I don't go so far as to say that. Neither would you, Hiram, if you hadn't lost your lawsuit about the line fence; and served you right, too, for it wouldn't have been begun if I had been at home at the time. Not but what

125

Margaret's a good housekeeper, for she wouldn't be her mother's daughter if she wasn't that; but it does seem to me a queer way to raise farmers' children, and I only hope they can keep it up. There were no pianos nor French and German in my young days."

"You ought to hear her play! My lands!" cried young Bartlett, who spoke for the first time. His admiration for her accomplishment evidently went beyond his powers of expression.

Bartlett himself did not relish the turn the conversation had taken, and he looked somewhat uneasily at the two strangers. The professor's countenance was open and frank, and he was listening with respectful interest to Mrs. Bartlett's talk. Yates bent over his plate with flushed face, and confined himself strictly to the business in hand.

"I am glad," said the professor innocently to Yates, "that you made the young lady's acquaintance. I must ask you for an introduction."

For once in his life Yates had nothing to say, but he looked at his friend with an expression that was not kindly. The latter, in answer to Mrs. Bartlett's inquiries, told how they had passed Miss Howard on the road, and how Yates, with his usual kindness of heart, had offered the young woman the hospitalities of the hay rack. Two persons at the table were much relieved when the talk turned to the tent. It was young Hiram who brought about this boon. He was interested in the tent, and he wanted to know. Two things seemed to bother the boy: First, he was anxious to learn what diabolical cause had been at work to induce two apparently sane men to give up the comforts of home and live in this exposed manner, if they were not compelled to do so. Second, he desired to find out why people who had the privilege of living in large cities came of their own accord into the uninteresting country, anyhow. Even when explanations were offered, the problem seemed still beyond him.

After the meal they all adjourned to the veranda, where the air was cool and the view extensive. Mrs. Bartlett would not hear of the young men pitching the tent that night. "Goodness knows, you will have enough of it, with the rain and the mosquitoes. We have plenty of room here, and you will have one comfortable night on the Ridge, at any rate. Then in the morning

126

you can find a place in the woods to suit you, and my boy will take an ax and cut stakes for you, and help to put up your precious tent. Only remember that when it rains you are to come to the house, or you will catch your deaths with cold and rheumatism. It will be very nice till the novelty wears off; then you are quite welcome to the front rooms upstairs, and Hiram can take the tent back to Erie the first time he goes to town."

Mrs. Bartlett had a way of taking things for granted. It never seemed to occur to her that any of her rulings might be questioned. Hiram sat gazing silently at the road, as if all this was no affair of his.

Yates had refused a chair, and sat on the edge of the veranda, with his back against one of the pillars, in such a position that he might, without turning his head, look through the open doorway into the room. where Miss Bartlett was busily but silently clearing away the tea things. The young man caught fleeting glimpses of her as she moved airily about her work. He drew a cigar from his case, cut off the end with his knife, and lit a match on the sole of his boot, doing this with an easy automatic familiarity that required no attention on his part; all of which aroused the respectful envy of young Hiram, who sat on a wooden chair, leaning forward, eagerly watching the man from New York.

"Have a cigar?" said Yates, offering the case to young Hiram.

"No, no; thank you," gasped the boy, aghast at the reckless audacity of the proposal.

"What's that?" cried Mrs. Bartlett. Although she was talking volubly to the professor, her maternal vigilance never even nodded, much less slept. "A cigar? Not likely! I'll say this for my husband and my boy: that, whatever else they may have done, they have never smoked nor touched a drop of liquor since I've known them, and, please God, they never will."

"Oh, I guess it wouldn't hurt them," said Yates, with a lack of tact that was not habitual. He fell several degrees in the estimation of his hostess.

"Hurt 'em?" cried Mrs. Bartlett indignantly. "I guess it won't get a chance to." She turned to the professor, who was a good listener—respectful and deferential, with little to say for himself. She rocked gently to and fro as she talked.

Her husband sat unbendingly silent, in a sphinxlike attitude that gave no outward indication of his mental uneasiness. He was thinking gloomily that it would be just his luck to meet Mrs. Bartlett unexpectedly in the streets of Fort Erie on one of those rare occasions when he was enjoying the pleasures of sin for a season. He had the most pessimistic forebodings of what the future might have in store for him. Sometimes, when neighbors or customers "treated" him in the village, and he felt he had taken all the whisky that cloves would conceal, he took a five-cent cigar instead of a drink. He did not particularly like the smoking of it, but there was a certain devil-may-care recklessness in going down the street with a lighted cigar in his teeth, which had all the more fascination for him because of its manifest danger. He felt at these times that he was going the pace, and that it is well our women do not know of all the wickedness there is in this world. He did not fear that any neighbor might tell his wife, for there were depths to which no person could convince Mrs. Bartlett he would descend. But he thought with horror of some combination of circumstances that might bring his wife to town unknown to him on a day when he indulged. He pictured, with a shudder, meeting her unexpectedly on the uncertain plank sidewalk of Fort Erie, he smoking a cigar. When this nightmare presented itself to him, he resolved never to touch a cigar again; but he well knew that the best resolutions fade away if a man is excited with two or three glasses of liquor.

When Mrs. Bartlett resumed conversation with the professor, Yates looked up at young Hiram and winked. The boy flushed with pleasure under the comprehensiveness of that wink. It included him in the attractive halo of crime that enveloped the fascinating personality of the man from New York. It seemed to say:

"That's all right, but we are men of the world. We know."

Young Hiram's devotion to the Goddess Nicotine had never reached the altitude of a cigar. He had surreptitiously smoked a pipe in a secluded corner behind the barn in days when his father was away. He feared both his father

nd his mother, and so was in an even more embarrassing situation than old
Hiram himself. He had worked gradually up to tobacco by smoking cigarettes
f cane made from abandoned hoop-skirts. Crinoline was fashionable, even
n the country, in those days, and ribs of cane were used before the metallic
istenders of dresses came in. One hoop-skirt, whose usefulness as an article
f adornment was gone, would furnish delight and smoking material for a
ompany of boys for a month. The cane smoke made the tongue rather raw,
ut the wickedness was undeniable. Yates' wink seemed to recognize young
Hiram as a comrade worthy to offer incense at the shrine, and the boy was a
irm friend of Yates from the moment the eyelid of the latter drooped.

The tea things having been cleared away, Yates got no more glimpses
f the girl through the open door. He rose from his lowly seat and strolled
oward the gate, with his hands in his pockets. He remembered that he had
orgotten something, and cudgeled his brains to make out what it was. He
azed down the road at the house of the Howards, which naturally brought to
is recollection his meeting with the young girl on the road. There was a pang
f discomfiture in this thought when he remembered the accomplishments
ttributed to her by Mrs. Bartlett. He recalled his condescending tone to
er, and recollected his anxiety about the jar. The jar! That was what he had
orgotten. He flashed a glance at old Hiram, and noted that the farmer was
ooking at him with something like reproach in his eyes. Yates moved his head
lmost imperceptibly toward the barn, and the farmer's eyes dropped to the
loor of the veranda. The young man nonchalantly strolled past the end of
he house.

"I guess I'll go to look after the horses," said the farmer, rising.

"The horses are all right, father. I saw to them," put in his son, but the
ld man frowned him down, and slouched around the corner of the house.
Mrs. Bartlett was too busy talking to the professor to notice. So good a listener
lid not fall to her lot every day.

"Here's looking at you," said Yates, strolling into the barn, taking a
elescopic metal cup from his pocket, and clinking it into receptive shape by
 jerk of the hand. He offered the now elongated cup to Hiram, who declined

129

any such modern improvement.

"Help yourself in that thing. The jug's good enough for me."

"Three fingers" of the liquid gurgled out into the patented vessel, and the farmer took the jar, after a furtive look over his shoulder.

"Well, here's luck." The newspaper man tossed off the potion with the facility of long experience, shutting up the dish with his thumb and finger, as if it were a metallic opera hat.

The farmer drank silently from the jar itself. Then he smote in the cork with his open palm.

"Better bury it in the wheat bin," he said morosely. "The boy might find it if you put it among the oats—feedin' the horses, ye know."

"Mighty good place," assented Yates, as the golden grain flowed in a wave over the submerged jar. "I say, old man, you know the spot; you've been here before."

Bartlett's lowering countenance indicated resentment at the imputation, but he neither affirmed nor denied. Yates strolled out of the barn, while the farmer went through a small doorway that led to the stable. A moment later he heard Hiram calling loudly to his son to bring the pails and water the horses.

"Evidently preparing an alibi," said Yates, smiling to himself, as he sauntered toward the gate.

CHAPTER V.

"What's up? what's up?" cried Yates drowsily next morning, as a prolonged hammering at his door awakened him.

"Well, you're not, anyhow." He recognized the voice of young Hiram. "I say, breakfast's ready. The professor has been up an hour."

"All right; I'll be down shortly," said Yates, yawning, adding to himself: "Hang the professor!" The sun was streaming in through the east window, but Yates never before remembered seeing it such a short distance above the horizon in the morning. He pulled his watch from the pocket of his vest, hanging on the bedpost. It was not yet seven o'clock. He placed it to his ear, thinking it had stopped, but found himself mistaken.

"What an unearthly hour," he said, unable to check the yawns. Yates' years on a morning newspaper had made seven o'clock something like midnight to him. He had been unable to sleep until after two o'clock, his usual time of turning in, and now this rude wakening seemed thoughtless cruelty. However, he dressed, and yawned himself downstairs.

They were all seated at breakfast when Yates entered the apartment, which was at once dining room and parlor.

"Waiting for you," said young Hiram humorously, that being one of a set of jokes which suited various occasions. Yates took his place near Miss Kitty, who looked as fresh and radiant as a spirit of the morning.

"I hope I haven't kept you waiting long," he said.

"No fear," cried Mrs. Bartlett. "If breakfast's a minute later than seven o'clock, we soon hear of it from the men-folks. They get precious hungry by that time."

"By that time?" echoed Yates. "Then do they get up before seven?"

"Laws! what a farmer you would make, Mr. Yates!" exclaimed Mrs.

Bartlett, laughing.

"Why, everything's done about the house and barn; horses fed, cows milked—everything. There never was a better motto made than the one you learned when you were a boy, and like as not have forgotten all about:

"Early to bed and early to rise

Makes a man healthy, wealthy, and wise.'

I'm sorry you don't believe in it, Mr. Yates."

"Oh, that's all right," said Yates with some loftiness; "but I'd like to see a man get out a morning paper on such a basis. I'm healthy enough, quite as wealthy as the professor here, and everyone will admit that I'm wiser than he is; yet I never go to bed until after two o'clock, and rarely wake before noon."

Kitty laughed at this, and young Hiram looked admiringly at the New Yorker, wishing he was as clever.

"For the land's sake!" cried Mrs. Bartlett, with true feminine profanity, "What do you do up so late as that?"

"Writing, writing," said Yates airily; "articles that make dynasties tremble next morning, and which call forth apologies or libel suits afterward, as the case may be."

Young Hiram had no patience with one's profession as a topic of conversation. The tent and its future position was the burning question with him. He mumbled something about Yates having slept late in order to avoid the hearing of the words of thankfulness at the beginning of the meal. What his parents caught of this remark should have shown them how evil communications corrupt good manners; for, big as he was, the boy had never before ventured even to hint at ridicule on such a subject. He was darkly frowned upon by his silent father, and sharply reprimanded by his voluble mother. Kitty apparently thought it rather funny, and would like to have laughed. As it was, she contented herself with a sly glance at Yates, who, incredible as it may seem, actually blushed at young Hiram's allusion to the confusing incident of the day before.

132

The professor, who was a kind-hearted man, drew a herring across the scent.

"Mr. Bartlett has been good enough," said he, changing the subject, "to say we may camp in the woods at the back of the farm. I have been out there this morning, and it certainly is a lovely spot."

"We're awfully obliged, Mr. Bartlett," said Yates. "Of course Renmark went out there merely to show the difference between the ant and the butterfly. You'll find out what a humbug he is by and by, Mrs. Bartlett. He looks honest; but you wait."

"I know just the spot for the tent," cried young Hiram—"down in the hollow by the creek. Then you won't need to haul water."

"Yes, and catch their deaths of fever and ague," said Mrs. Bartlett. Malaria had not then been invented. "Take my advice, and put your tent—if you will put it up at all—on the highest ground you can find. Hauling water won't hurt you."

"I agree with you, Mrs. Bartlett. It shall be so. My friend uses no water— you ought to have seen his bill at the Buffalo hotel. I have it somewhere, and am going to pin it up on the outside of the tent as a warning to the youth of this neighborhood—and what water I need I can easily carry up from the creek."

The professor did not defend himself, and Mrs. Bartlett evidently took a large discount from all that Yates said. She was a shrewd woman.

After breakfast the men went out to the barn. The horses were hitched to the wagon, which still contained the tent and fittings. Young Hiram threw an ax and a spade among the canvas folds, mounted to his place, and drove up the lane leading to the forest, followed by Yates and Renmark on foot, leaving the farmer in his barnyard with a cheery good-by, which he did not see fit to return.

First, a field of wheat; next, an expanse of waving hay that soon would be ready for the scythe; then, a pasture field, in which some young horses galloped to the fence, gazing for a moment at the harnessed horses, whinnying sympathetically, off the next with flying heels wildly flung in the air, rejoicing in their own contrast of liberty, standing at the farther corner and snorting defiance to all the world; last, the cool shade of the woods into which the lane ran, losing its identity as a wagon road in diverging cow paths. Young Hiram knew the locality well, and drove direct to an ideal place for camping. Yates was enchanted. He included all that section of the country in a sweeping wave of his hand, and burst forth:

> "'This is the spot, the center of the grove:
>
> There stands the oak, the monarch of the wood.
>
> In such a place as this, at such an hour,
>
> We'll raise a tent to ward off sun and shower.'

Shakespeare improved."

"I think you are mistaken," said Renmark.

"Not a bit it. Couldn't be a better camping ground."

"Yes; I know that. I picked it out two hours ago. But you were wrong in your quotation. It is not by Shakespeare and yourself, as you seem to think."

"Isn't it? Some other fellow, eh? Well, if Shake is satisfied, I am. Do you know, Renny, I calculate that, line for line, I've written about ten times as much as Shakespeare. Do the literati recognize that fact? Not a bit of it. This is an ungrateful world, Stilly."

"It is, Dick. Now, what are you going to do toward putting up the tent?"

"Everything, my boy, everything. I know more about putting up tents than you do about science, or whatever you teach. Now, Hiram, my boy, you cut me some stakes about two feet long—stout ones. Here, professor, throw off that coat and négligé manner, and grasp this spade. I want some trenches dug."

Yates certainly made good his words. He understood the putting up of tents, his experience in the army being not yet remote. Young Hiram gazed with growing admiration at Yates' deftness and evident knowledge of what he was about, while his contempt for the professor's futile struggle with a spade entangled in tree roots was hardly repressed.

"Better give me that spade," he said at length; but there was an element of stubbornness in Renmark's character. He struggled on.

At last the work was completed, stakes driven, ropes tightened, trenches dug.

Yates danced, and gave the war whoop of the country.

"Thus the canvas tent has risen,

All the slanting stakes are driven,

Stakes of oak and stakes of beechwood:

Mops his brow, the tired professor;

Grins with satisfaction, Hiram;

Dances wildly, the reporter—

Calls aloud for gin and water.

Longfellow, old man, Longfellow. Bet you a dollar on it!" And the frivolous Yates poked the professor in the ribs.

"Richard," said the latter, "I can stand only a certain amount of this sort of thing. I don't wish to call any man a fool, but you act remarkably like one."

"Don't be mealy-mouthed, Renny; call a spade a spade. By George! young Hiram has gone off and forgotten his—And the ax, too! Perhaps they're left for us. He's a good fellow, is young Hiram. A fool? Of course I'm a fool. That's what I came for, and that's what I'm going to be for the next two weeks. 'A fool—a fool, I met a fool i' the forest'—just the spot for him. Who could be wise here after years of brick and mortar?

"Where are your eyes, Renny," he cried, "that you don't grow wild when you look around you? See the dappled sunlight filtering through the leaves; listen to the murmur of the wind in the branches; hear the trickle of the brook down there; notice the smooth bark of the beech and the rugged covering of the oak; smell the wholesome woodland scents. Renmark, you have no soul, or you could not be so unmoved. It is like paradise. It is—Say, Renny, by Jove, I've forgotten that jug at the barn!"

"It will be left there."

"Will it? Oh, well, if you say so."

"I do say so. I looked around for it this morning to smash it, but couldn't find it."

"Why didn't you ask old Bartlett?"

"I did; but he didn't know where it was."

Yates threw himself down on the moss and laughed, flinging his arms and legs about with the joy of living.

"Say, Culture, have you got any old disreputable clothes with you? Well, then, go into the tent and put them on; then come out and lie on your back and look up at the leaves. You're a good fellow, Renny, but decent clothes spoil you. You won't know yourself when you get ancient duds on your back. Old clothes mean freedom, liberty, all that our ancestors fought for. When you come out, we'll settle who's to cook and who to wash dishes. I've settled it already in my own mind, but I am not so selfish as to refuse to discuss the matter with you."

When the professor came out of the tent, Yates roared. Renmark himself smiled; he knew the effect would appeal to Yates.

"By Jove! old man, I ought to have included a mirror in the outfit. The look of learned respectability, set off with the garments of a disreputable tramp, makes a combination that is simply killing. Well, you can't spoil that suit, anyhow. Now sprawl."

"I'm very comfortable standing up, thank you."

"Get down on your back. You hear me?"

"Put me there."

"You mean it?" asked Yates, sitting up.

"Certainly."

"Say, Renny, beware. I don't want to hurt you."

"I'll forgive you for once."

"On your head be it."

"On my back, you mean."

"That's not bad, Renny," cried Yates, springing to his feet. "Now, it will hurt. You have fair warning. I have spoken."

The young men took sparring attitudes. Yates tried to do it gently at first, but, finding he could not touch his opponent, struck out more earnestly, again giving a friendly warning. This went on ineffectually for some time, when the professor, with a quick movement, swung around his foot with the airy grace of a dancing master, and caught Yates just behind the knee, at the same time giving him a slight tap on the breast. Yates was instantly on his back.

"Oh, I say, Renny, that wasn't fair. That was a kick."

"No, it wasn't. It is merely a little French touch. I learned it in Paris. They do kick there, you know; and it is good to know how to use your feet as well as your fists if you are set on by three, as I was one night in the Latin Quarter."

Yates sat up.

"Look here, Renmark; when were you in Paris?"

"Several times."

Yates gazed at him for a few moments, then said:

"Renny, you improve on acquaintance. I never saw a Bool-var in my life.

You must teach me that little kick."

"With pleasure," said Renmark, sitting down, while the other sprawled at full length. "Teaching is my business, and I shall be glad to exercise any talents I may have in that line. In endeavoring to instruct a New York man the first step is to convince him that he doesn't know everything. That is the difficult point. Afterward everything is easy."

"Mr. Stillson Renmark, you are pleased to be severe. Know that you are forgiven. This delicious sylvan retreat does not lend itself to acrimonious dispute, or, in plain English, quarreling. Let dogs delight, if they want to; I refuse to be goaded by your querulous nature into giving anything but the soft answer. Now to business. Nothing is so conducive to friendship, when two people are camping out, as a definition of the duties of each at the beginning. Do you follow me?"

"Perfectly. What do you propose?"

"I propose that you do the cooking and I wash the dishes. We will forage for food alternate days."

"Very well. I agree to that."

Richard Yates sat suddenly upright, looking at his friend with reproach in his eyes. "See here, Renmark; are you resolved to force on an international complication the very first day? That's no fair show to give a man."

"What isn't?"

"Why, agreeing with him. There are depths of meanness in your character, Renny, that I never suspected. You know that people who camp out always object to the part assigned them by their fellow-campers. I counted on that. I'll do anything but wash dishes."

"Then why didn't you say so?"

"Because any sane man would have said 'no' when I suggested cooking, merely because I suggested it. There is no diplomacy about you, Renmark. A man doesn't know where to find you when you act like that. When you

138

refused to do the cooking, I would have said: 'Very well, then, I'll do it,' and everything would have been lovely; but now——"

Yates lay down again in disgust. There are moments in life when language fails a man.

"Then it's settled that you do the cooking and I wash the dishes?" said the professor.

"Settled? Oh yes, if you say so; but all the pleasure of getting one's own way by the use of one's brains is gone. I hate to be agreed with in that objectionably civil manner."

"Well, that point being arranged, who begins the foraging—you or I?"

"Both, Herr Professor, both. I propose to go to the house of the Howards, and I need an excuse for the first visit; therefore I shall forage to a limited extent. I go ostensibly for bread. As I may not get any, you perhaps should bring some from whatever farmhouse you choose as the scene of your operations. Bread is always handy in the camp, fresh or stale. When in doubt, buy more bread. You can never go wrong, and the bread won't."

"What else should I get? Milk, I suppose?"

"Certainly; eggs, butter—anything. Mrs. Bartlett will give you hints on what to get that will be more valuable than mine."

"Have you all the cooking utensils you need?"

"I think so. The villain from whom I hired the outfit said it was complete. Doubtless he lied; but we'll manage, I think."

"Very well. If you wait until I change my clothes, I'll go with you as far as the road."

"My dear fellow, be advised, and don't change. You'll get everything twenty per cent. cheaper in that rig-out. Besides, you are so much more picturesque. Your costume may save us from starvation if we run short of cash. You can get enough for both of us as a professional tramp. Oh, well, if you insist, I'll wait. Good advice is thrown away on a man like you."

CHAPTER VI.

Margaret Howard stood at the kitchen table kneading dough. The room was called the kitchen, which it was not, except in winter. The stove was moved out in spring to a lean-to, easily reached through the open door leading to the kitchen veranda.

When the stove went out or came in, it marked the approach or the departure of summer. It was the heavy pendulum whose swing this way or that indicated the two great changes of the year. No job about the farm was so much disliked by the farmer and his boys as the semiannual removal of the stove. Soot came down, stovepipes gratingly grudged to go together again; the stove was heavy and cumbersome, and many a pain in a rural back dated from the journey of the stove from outhouse to kitchen.

The kitchen itself was a one-story building, which projected back from the two-story farmhouse, giving the whole a T-shape. There was a veranda on each side of the kitchen, as well as one along the front of the house itself.

Margaret's sleeves were turned back nearly to her elbows, showing a pair of white and shapely arms. Now and then she deftly dusted the kneading board with flour to prevent the dough sticking, and as she pressed her open palms into the smooth, white, spongy mass, the table groaned protestingly. She cut the roll with a knife into lumps that were patted into shape, and placed side by side, like hillocks of snow, in the sheet-iron pan.

At this moment there was a rap at the open kitchen door, and Margaret turned round, startled, for visitors were rare at that hour of the day; besides, neighbors seldom made such a concession to formality as to knock. The young girl flushed as she recognized the man who had spoken to her the day before. He stood smiling in the doorway, with his hat in his hand. She uttered no word of greeting or welcome, but stood looking at him, with her hand on the floury table.

"Good-morning, Miss Howard," said Yates blithely; "may I come in? I have been knocking for some time fruitlessly at the front door, so I took the liberty of coming around."

"I did not hear you knock," answered Margaret. She neglected to invite him in, but he took the permission for granted and entered, seating himself as one who had come to stay. "You must excuse me for going on with my work," she added; "bread at this stage will not wait."

"Certainly, certainly. Please do not let me interrupt you. I have made my own bread for years, but not in that way. I am glad that you are making bread, for I have come to see if I can buy some."

"Really? Perhaps I can sell you some butter and eggs as well."

Yates laughed in that joyous, free-hearted manner of his which had much to do with his getting on in the world. It was difficult to remain long angry with so buoyant a nature.

"Ah, Miss Howard, I see you haven't forgiven me for that remark. You surely could not have thought I meant it. I really intended it for a joke, but I am willing to admit, now that I look back on it, that the joke was rather poor; but, then, most of my jokes are rather shopworn."

"I am afraid I lack a sense of humor."

"All women do," said Yates with easy confidence. "At least, all I've ever met."

Yates was sitting in a wooden chair, which he now placed at the end of the table, tilting it back until his shoulders rested against the wall. His feet were upon the rung, and he waved his hat back and forth, fanning himself, for it was warm. In this position he could look up at the face of the pretty girl before him, whose smooth brow was touched with just the slightest indication of a faint frown. She did not even glance at the self-confident young man, but kept her eyes fixed resolutely on her work. In the silence the table creaked as Margaret kneaded the dough. Yates felt an unaccustomed sensation of embarrassment creeping over him, and realized that he would have to re-erect the conversation on a new basis. It was manifestly absurd that a resourceful New Yorker, who had conversed unabashed with presidents, senators, generals, and other great people of a great nation, should be put out of countenance by the unaccountable coldness of a country girl in the wilds of Canada.

"I have not had an opportunity of properly introducing myself," he said at last, when the creaking of the table, slight as it was, became insupportable. "My name is Richard Yates, and I come from New York. I am camping out in this neighborhood to relieve, as it were, a mental strain—the result of years of literary work."

Yates knew from long experience that the quickest and surest road to a woman's confidence was through her sympathy. "Mental strain" struck him as a good phrase, indicating midnight oil and the hollow eye of the devoted student.

"Is your work mental, then?" asked Margaret incredulously, flashing, for the first time, a dark-eyed look at him.

"Yes," Yates laughed uneasily. He had manifestly missed fire. "I notice by your tone that you evidently think my equipment meager. You should not judge by appearances, Miss Howard. Most of us are better than we seem, pessimists to the contrary notwithstanding. Well, as I was saying, the camping company consists of two partners. We are so different in every respect that we are the best of friends. My partner is Mr. Stillson Renmark, professor of something or other in University College, Toronto."

For the first time Margaret exhibited some interest in the conversation.

"Professor Renmark? I have heard of him."

"Dear me! I had no idea the fame of the professor had penetrated beyond the precincts of the university—if a university has precincts. He told me it had all the modern improvements, but I suspected at the time that was merely Renny's brag."

The frown on the girl's brow deepened, and Yates was quick to see that he had lost ground again, if, indeed, he had ever gained any, which he began o doubt. She evidently did not relish his glib talk about the university. He was just about to say something deferentially about that institution, for he was not a man who would speak disrespectfully of the equator if he thought he might curry favor with his auditor by doing otherwise, when it occurred to him that Miss Howard's interest was centered in the man, and not in the university.

"In this world, Miss Howard," he continued, "true merit rarely finds its reward; at least, the reward shows some reluctance in making itself visible in time for man to enjoy it. Professor Renmark is a man so worthy that I was rather astonished to learn that you knew of him. I am glad for his sake that it is so, for no man more thoroughly deserves fame than he."

"I know nothing of him," said Margaret, "except what my brother has written. My brother is a student at the university."

"Is he really? And what is he going in for?"

"A good education."

Yates laughed.

"Well, that is an all-round handy thing for a person to have about him. I often wish I had had a university training. Still, it is not valued in an American newspaper office as much as might be. Yet," he added in a tone that showed he did not desire to be unfair to a man of education, "I have known some university men who became passably good reporters in time."

The girl made no answer, but attended strictly to the work in hand. She had the rare gift of silence, and these intervals of quiet abashed Yates, whose most frequent boast was that he could outtalk any man on earth. Opposition, or even abuse, merely served as a spur to his volubility, but taciturnity disconcerted him.

"Well," he cried at length, with something like desperation, "let us abandon this animated discussion on the subject of education, and take up the more practical topic of bread. Would you believe, Miss Howard, that I am an expert in bread making?"

"I think you said already that you made your bread."

"Ah, yes, but I meant then that I made it by the sweat of my good lead pencil. Still, I have made bread in my time, and I believe that some of those who subsisted upon it are alive to-day. The endurance of the human frame is something marvelous, when you come to think of it. I did the baking in a lumber camp one winter. Used to dump the contents of a sack of flour into a trough made out of a log, pour in a pail or two of melted snow, and mix with a hoe after the manner of a bricklayer's assistant making mortar. There was nothing small or mean about my bread making. I was in the wholesale trade."

"I pity the unfortunate lumbermen."

"Your sympathy is entirely misplaced, Miss Howard. You ought to pity me for having to pander to such appetites as those men brought in from the woods with them. They never complained of the quality of the bread, although there was occasionally some grumbling about the quantity. I have fed sheaves to a threshing machine and logs to a sawmill, but their voracity was nothing to that of a big lumberman just in from felling trees. Enough, and plenty of it, is what he wants. No 'tabbledote' for him. He wants it all at once, and he wants it right away. If there is any washing necessary, he is content to do it after the meal. I know nothing, except a morning paper, that has such an appetite for miscellaneous stuff as the man of the woods."

The girl made no remark, but Yates could see that she was interested in his talk in spite of herself. The bread was now in the pans, and she had drawn out the table to the middle of the floor; the baking board had disappeared, and the surface of the table was cleaned. With a light, deft motion of her two hands she had whisked over its surface the spotlessly white cloth, which flowed in waves over the table and finally settled calmly in its place like the placid face of a pond in the moonlight. Yates realized that the way to success lay in keeping the conversation in his own hands and not depending on any response. In this way a man may best display the store of knowledge he possesses, to the admiration and bewilderment of his audience, even though his store consists merely of samples like the outfit of a commercial traveler; yet a commercial traveler who knows his business can so arrange his samples

144

on the table of his room in a hotel that they give the onlooker an idea of the vastness and wealth of the warehouses from which they are drawn.

"Bread," said Yates with the serious air of a very learned man, "is a most interesting subject. It is a historical subject—it is a biblical subject. As an article of food it is mentioned oftener in the Bible than any other. It is used in parable and to point a moral. 'Ye must not live on bread alone.'"

From the suspicion of a twinkle in the eye of his listener he feared he had not quoted correctly. He knew he was not now among that portion of his samples with which he was most familiar, so he hastened back to the historical aspect of his subject. Few people could skate over thinner ice than Richard Yates, but his natural shrewdness always caused him to return to more solid footing.

"Now, in this country bread has gone through three distinct stages, and although I am a strong believer in progress, yet, in the case of our most important article of food, I hold that the bread of to-day is inferior to the bread our mothers used to make, or perhaps, I should say, our grandmothers. This is, unfortunately, rapidly becoming the age of machinery—and machinery, while it may be quicker, is certainly not so thorough as old-fashioned hand work. There is a new writer in England named Ruskin who is very bitter against machinery. He would like to see it abolished—at least, so he says. I will send for one of his books, and show it to you, if you will let me."

"You, in New York, surely do not call the author of 'Modern Painters' and 'The Seven Lamps of Architecture' a new man. My father has one of his books which must be nearly twenty years old."

This was the longest speech Margaret had made to him, and, as he said afterward to the professor in describing its effects, it took him right off his feet. He admitted to the professor, but not to the girl, that he had never read a word of Ruskin in his life. The allusion he had made to him he had heard someone else use, and he had worked it into an article before now with telling effect. "As Mr. Ruskin says" looked well in a newspaper column, giving an air of erudition and research to it. Mr. Yates, however, was not at the present moment prepared to enter into a discussion on either the age or the merits of the English writer.

"Ah, well," he said, "technically speaking, of course, Ruskin is not a new man. What I meant was that he is looked on—ah—in New York as—that is—you know—as comparatively new—comparatively new. But, as I was saying about bread, the old log-house era of bread, as I might call it, produced the most delicious loaf ever made in this country. It was the salt-rising kind, and was baked in a round, flat-bottomed iron kettle. Did you ever see the baking kettle of other days?"

"I think Mrs. Bartlett has one, although she never uses it now. It was placed on the hot embers, was it not?"

"Exactly," said Yates, noting with pleasure that the girl was thawing, as he expressed it to himself. "The hot coals were drawn out and the kettle placed upon them. When the lid was in position, hot coals were put on he top of it. The bread was firm and white and sweet inside, with the most delicious golden brown crust all around. Ah, that was bread! but perhaps I appreciated it because I was always hungry in those days. Then came the alleged improvement of the tin Dutch oven. That was the second stage in the evolution of bread in this country. It also belonged to the log-house and open-fireplace era. Bread baked by direct heat from the fire and reflected heat from the polished tin. I think our present cast-iron stove arrangement is preferable to that, although not up to the old-time kettle."

If Margaret had been a reader of the New York Argus, she would have noticed that the facts set forth by her visitor had already appeared in that paper, much elaborated, in an article entitled "Our Daily Bread." In the pause that ensued after Yates had finished his dissertation on the staff of life the stillness was broken by a long wailing cry. It began with one continued, sustained note, and ended with a wail half a tone below the first. The girl paid no attention to it, but Yates started to his feet.

"In the name of—What's that?"

Margaret smiled, but before she could answer the stillness was again broken by what appeared to be the more distant notes of a bugle.

146

"The first," she said, "was Kitty Bartlett's voice calling the men home from the field for dinner. Mrs. Bartlett is a very good housekeeper and is usually a few minutes ahead of the neighbors with the meals. The second was the sound of a horn farther up the road. It is what you would deplore as the age of tin applied to the dinner call, just as your tin oven supplanted the better bread maker. I like Kitty's call much better than the tin horn. It seems to me more musical, although it appeared to startle you."

"Oh, you can talk!" cried Yates with audacious admiration, at which the girl colored slightly and seemed to retire within herself again. "And you can make fun of people's historical lore, too. Which do you use—the tin horn or the natural voice?"

"Neither. If you will look outside, you will see a flag at the top of a pole. That is our signal."

It flashed across the mind of Yates that this was intended as an intimation that he might see many things outside to interest him. He felt that his visit had not been at all the brilliant success he had anticipated. Of course the quest for bread had been merely an excuse. He had expected to be able to efface the unfavorable impression he knew he had made by his jaunty conversation on the Ridge Road the day before, and he realized that his position was still the same. A good deal of Yates' success in life came from the fact that he never knew when he was beaten. He did not admit defeat now, but he saw he had, for some reason, not gained any advantage in a preliminary skirmish. He concluded it would be well to retire in good order, and renew the contest at some future time. He was so unused to anything like a rebuff that all his fighting qualities were up in arms, and he resolved to show this unimpressionable girl that he was not a man to be lightly valued.

As he rose the door from the main portion of the house opened, and there entered a woman hardly yet past middle age, who had once been undoubtedly handsome, but on whose worn and faded face was the look of patient weariness which so often is the result of a youth spent in helping a husband to overcome the stumpy stubbornness of an American bush farm. When the farm is conquered, the victor is usually vanquished. It needed no second glance to see that she was the mother from whom the daughter had inherited her good looks. Mrs. Howard did not appear surprised to see a stranger standing there; in fact, the faculty of being surprised at anything seemed to have left her. Margaret introduced them quietly, and went about her preparation for the meal. Yates greeted Mrs. Howard with effusion. He had come, he said, on a bread mission. He thought he knew something about bread, but he now learned he came too early in the day. He hoped he might have the privilege of repeating his visit.

"But you are not going now?" said Mrs. Howard with hospitable anxiety.

"I fear I have already stayed too long," answered Yates lingeringly. "My partner, Professor Renmark, is also on a foraging expedition at your neighbors', the Bartletts. He is doubtless back in camp long ago, and will be expecting me."

"No fear of that. Mrs. Bartlett would never let anyone go when there is a meal on the way."

"I am afraid I shall be giving extra trouble by staying. I imagine there is quite enough to do in every farmhouse without entertaining any chance tramp who happens along. Don't you agree with me for once, Miss Howard?"

Yates was reluctant to go, and yet he did not wish to stay unless Margaret added her invitation to her mother's. He felt vaguely that his reluctance did him credit, and that he was improving. He could not remember a time when he had not taken without question whatever the gods sent, and this unaccustomed qualm of modesty caused him to suspect that there were depths in his nature hitherto unexplored. It always flatters a man to realize that he is deeper than he thought.

Mrs. Howard laughed in a subdued manner because Yates likened himself to a tramp, and Margaret said coldly:

"Mother's motto is that one more or less never makes any difference."

"And what is your motto, Miss Howard?"

"I don't think Margaret has any," said Mrs. Howard, answering for he

148

daughter. "She is like her father. She reads a great deal and doesn't talk much. He would read all the time, if he did not have to work. I see Margaret has already invited you, for she has put an extra plate on the table."

"Ah, then," said Yates, "I shall have much pleasure in accepting both the verbal and the crockery invitation. I am sorry for the professor at his lonely meal by the tent; for he is a martyr to duty, and I feel sure Mrs. Bartlett will not be able to keep him."

Before Mrs. Howard could reply there floated in to them, from the outside, where Margaret was, a cheery voice which Yates had no difficulty in recognizing as belonging to Miss Kitty Bartlett.

"Hello, Margaret!" she said. "Is he here?"

The reply was inaudible.

"Oh, you know whom I mean. That conceited city fellow."

There was evidently an admonition and a warning.

"Well, I don't care if he does. I'll tell him so to his face. It might do him good."

Next moment there appeared a pretty vision in the doorway. On the fair curls, which were flying about her shoulders, had been carelessly placed her brother's straw hat, with a broad and torn brim. Her face was flushed with running; and of the fact that she was a very lovely girl there was not the slightest doubt.

"How de do?" she said to Mrs. Howard, and, nodding to Yates, cried: "I knew you were here, but I came over to make sure. There's going to be war in our house. Mother's made a prisoner of the professor already, but he doesn't know it. He thinks he's going back to the tent, and she's packing up the things he wanted, and doing it awfully slow, till I get back. He said you would be sure to be waiting for him out in the woods. We both told him there was no fear of that. You wouldn't leave a place where there was good cooking for all the professors in the world."

"You are a wonderful judge of character, Miss Bartlett," said Yates,

149

somewhat piqued by her frankness.

"Of course I am. The professor knows ever so much more than you, but he doesn't know when he's well off, just the same. You do. He's a quiet, stubborn man."

"And which do you admire the most, Miss Bartlett—a quiet, stubborn man, or one who is conceited?"

Miss Kitty laughed heartily, without the slightest trace of embarrassment. "Detest, you mean. I'm sure I don't know. Margaret, which is the most objectionable?"

Margaret looked reproachfully at her neighbor on being thus suddenly questioned, but said nothing.

Kitty, laughing again, sprang toward her friend, dabbed a little kiss, like the peck of a bird, on each cheek, cried: "Well, I must be off, or mother will have to tie up the professor to keep him," and was off accordingly with the speed and lightness of a young fawn.

"Extraordinary girl," remarked Yates, as the flutter of curls and calico dress disappeared.

"She is a good girl," cried Margaret emphatically.

"Bless me, I said nothing to the contrary. But don't you think she is somewhat free with her opinions about other people?" asked Yates.

"She did not know that you were within hearing when she first spoke, and after that she brazened it out. That's her way. But she's a kind girl and good-hearted, otherwise she would not have taken the trouble to come over here merely because your friend happened to be surly."

"Oh, Renny is anything but surly," said Yates, as quick to defend his friend as she was to stand up for hers. "As I was saying a moment ago, he is a martyr to duty, and if he thought I was at the camp, nothing would keep him. Now he will have a good dinner in peace when he knows I am not waiting for him, and a good dinner is more than he will get when I take to the cooking."

By this time the silent signal on the flagpole had done its work, and Margaret's father and brother arrived from the field. They put their broad straw hats on the roof of the kitchen veranda, and, taking water in a tin basin from the rain barrel, placed it on a bench outside and proceeded to wash vigorously.

Mr. Howard was much more interested in his guest than his daughter had apparently been. Yates talked glibly, as he could always do if he had a sympathetic audience, and he showed an easy familiarity with the great people of this earth that was fascinating to a man who had read much of them, but who was, in a measure, locked out of the bustling world. Yates knew many of the generals in the late war, and all of the politicians. Of the latter there was not an honest man among them, according to the reporter; of the former there were few who had not made the most ghastly mistakes. He looked on the world as a vast hoard of commonplace people, wherein the men of real genius were buried out of sight, if there were any men of genius, which he seemed to doubt, and those on the top were there either through their own intrigues or because they had been forced up by circumstances. His opinions sometimes caused a look of pain to cross the face of the older man, who was enthusiastic in his quiet way, and had his heroes. He would have been a strong Republican if he had lived in the States; and he had watched the four-years' struggle, through the papers, with keen and absorbed interest. The North had been fighting, in his opinion, for the great and undying principle of human liberty, and had deservedly won. Yates had no such delusion. It was a politicians' war, he said. Principle wasn't in it. The North would have been quite willing to let slavery stand if the situation had not been forced by the firing on Fort Sumter. Then the conduct of the war did not at all meet the approval of Mr. Yates.

"Oh, yes," he said, "I suppose Grant will go down into history as a great general. The truth is that he simply knew how to subtract. That is all there is in it. He had the additional boon of an utter lack of imagination. We had many generals who were greater than Grant, but they were troubled with imaginations. Imagination will ruin the best general in the world. Now, take yourself, for example. If you were to kill a man unintentionally, your conscience would trouble you all the rest of your life. Think how you would feel, then, if you were to cause the death of ten thousand men all in a lump. It would break you down. The mistake an ordinary man makes may result in the loss of a few dollars, which can be replaced; but if a general makes a mistake, the loss can never be made up, for his mistakes are estimated by the lives of men. He says 'Go' when he should have said 'Come.' He says 'Attack' when he should have said 'Retreat.' What is the result? Five, ten, or fifteen thousand men, many of them better men than he is, left dead on the field. Grant had nothing of this feeling. He simply knew how to subtract, as I said before. It is like this: You have fifty thousand men and I have twenty-five thousand. When I kill twenty-five thousand of your men and you kill twenty-five thousand of my men, you have twenty-five thousand left and I have none. You are the victor, and the thoughtless crowd howls about you, but that does not make you out the greatest general by a long shot. If Lee had had Grant's number, and Grant had Lee's, the result would have been reversed. Grant set himself to do this little sum in subtraction, and he did it—did it probably as quickly as any other man would have done it, and he knew that when it was done the war would have to stop. That's all there was to it."

The older man shook his head. "I doubt," he said, "if history will take your view either of the motives of those in power or of the way the war was carried on. It was a great and noble struggle, heroically fought by those deluded people who were in the wrong, and stubbornly contested at immense self-sacrifice by those who were in the right."

"What a pity it was," said young Howard to the newspaper man, with a rudeness that drew a frown from his father, "that you didn't get to show 'em how to carry on the war."

"Well," said Yates, with a humorous twinkle in his eye, "I flatter myself that I would have given them some valuable pointers. Still, it is too late to bemoan their neglect now."

"Oh, you may have a chance yet," continued the unabashed young man. "They say the Fenians are coming over here this time sure. You ought to volunteer either on our side or on theirs, and show how a war ought to be rried on."

"Oh, there's nothing in the Fenian scare! They won't venture over. They ght with their mouths. It's the safest way."

"I believe you," said the youth significantly.

Perhaps it was because the boy had been so inconsiderate as to make ese remarks that Yates received a cordial invitation from both Mr. and Mrs. oward to visit the farm as often as he cared to do so. Of this privilege Yates solved to avail himself, but he would have prized it more if Miss Margaret ad added her word—which she did not, perhaps because she was so busy ooking after the bread. Yates knew, however, that with a woman apparent rogress is rarely synonymous with real progress. This knowledge soothed his isappointment.

As he walked back to the camp he reviewed his own feelings with omething like astonishment. The march of events was rapid even for him, ho was not slow in anything he undertook.

"It is the result of leisure," he said to himself. "It is the first breathing me I have had for fifteen years. Not two days of my vacation gone, and here am hopelessly in love!"

CHAPTER VII.

Yates had intended to call at the Bartletts' and escort Renmark back to the woods; but when he got outside he forgot the existence of the professor and wandered somewhat aimlessly up the side road, switching at the weeds that always grow in great profusion along the ditches of a Canadian country thoroughfare. The day was sunny and warm, and as Yates wandered on in the direction of the forest he thought of many things. He had feared that he would find life deadly dull so far from New York, without even the consolation of a morning-paper, the feverish reading of which had become a sort of vice with him, like smoking. He had imagined that he could not exist without his morning paper, but he now realized that it was not nearly so important a factor in life as he had supposed; yet he sighed when he thought of it, and wished he had one with him of current date. He could now, for the first time in many years, read a paper without that vague fear which always possessed him when he took up an opposition sheet, still damp from the press. Before he could enjoy it his habit was to scan it over rapidly to see if it contained any item of news which he himself had missed the previous day. The impending "scoop" hangs over the head of the newspaper man like the sword so often quoted. Great as the joy of beating the opposition press is, it never takes the poignancy of the sting away from a beating received. If a terrible disaster took place, and another paper gave fuller particulars than the Argus did, Yates found himself almost wishing the accident had not occurred, although he recognized such a wish as decidedly unprofessional.

Richard's idea of the correct spirit in a reporter was exemplified by an old broken-down, out-of-work morning newspaper man, who had not long before committed suicide at an hour in the day too late for the evening paper to get the sensational item. He had sent in to the paper for which he formerly worked a full account of the fatality, accurately headed and sub-headed; and in his note to the city editor, he told why he had chosen the hour of 7 P.M. as the time for his departure from an unappreciative world.

"Ah, well," said Yates under his breath, and suddenly pulling himself together, "I mustn't think of New York if I intend to stay here for a couple of weeks. I'll be city-sick the first thing I know, and then I'll make a break for the metropolis. This will never do. The air here is enchanting, it fills a man with new life. This is the spot for me, and I'll stick to it till I'm right again. Hang New York! But I mustn't think of Broadway or I'm done for."

He came to the spot in the road where he could see the white side of the tent under the dark trees, and climbed up on the rail fence, sitting there for a few moments. The occasional call of a quail from a neighboring field was the only sound that broke the intense stillness. The warm smell of spring was in the air. The buds had but recently broken, and the woods, intensely green, had a look of newness and freshness that was comforting to the eye and grateful to the other senses. The world seemed to be but lately made. The young man breathed deeply of the vivifying air, and said: "No, there's nothing the matter with this place, Dick. New York's a fool to it." Then, with a sigh, he added: "If I can stand it for two weeks. I wonder how the boys are getting on without me."

In spite of himself his thoughts kept drifting back to the great city, although he told himself that it wouldn't do. He gazed at the peaceful, spreading landscape, but his eyes were vacant and he saw nothing. The roar of the streets was in his ears. Suddenly his reverie was broken by a voice from the forest.

"I say, Yates, where's the bread?"

Yates looked quickly around, somewhat startled, and saw the professor coming toward him.

"The bread? I forgot all about it. No; I didn't either. They were baking—that was it. I am to go for it later in the day. What loot did you rake in, professor?"

"Vegetables mostly."

"That's all right. Have a good dinner?"

"Excellent."

"So did I. Renny, when you interrupted me, I was just counting the farmhouses in sight. What do you say to boarding round among them? You are a schoolmaster, and ought to know all about it. Isn't education in this country encouraged by paying the teacher as little as possible, and letting him take it out in eating his way from one house to another? Ever board around, Renny?"

"Never. If the custom once existed in Canada, it is out of date now."

"That's a pity. I hate to face my own cooking, Renmark. We become less brave as we grow older. By the way, how is old man Bartlett? As well as could be expected?"

"He seemed much as usual. Mrs. Bartlett has sent out two chairs to the tent; she fears we will get rheumatism if we sit on the ground."

"She is a kind woman, Renny, and a thoughtful. And that reminds me: I have a hammock somewhere among my belongings. I will swing it up. Chairs are comfortable, but a hammock is luxury."

Yates slid down from the fence top, and together the two men walked to the tent. The hammock was unfurled and slung between two trees. Yates tested it cautiously, and finally trusted himself to its restful folds of network. He was swaying indolently several feet from the ground when he said to Renmark:

"I call this paradise—paradise regained; but it will be paradise lost next month. Now, professor, I am ready to do the cooking, but I have a fancy for doing it by proxy. The general directs, and the useful prosaic man executes. Where are your vegetables, Renny? Potatoes and carrots, eh? Very good. Now, you may wash them, Renny; but first you must bring some water from the spring."

The professor was a patient man, and he obeyed. Yates continued to swing in the hammock alternating directions with rhapsodies on the beauties of the day and the stillness of the woods. Renmark said but little, and attended strictly to the business in hand. The vegetables finished, he took a book from his valise, tilted a chair back against a tree, and began to read.

156

"I'm depending upon you for the bread," he said to the drowsy man in the hammock.

"Right you are, Renny. Your confidence is not misplaced. I shall presently journey down into the realms of civilization, and fill the long-felt want. I shall go to the Howards by way of the Bartlett homestead, but I warn you that if there is a meal on, at either place, you will not have me here to test your first efforts at cooking. So you may have to wait until breakfast for my opinion."

Yates extricated himself slowly and reluctantly from the hammock, and looked regretfully at it when he stood once more on the ground.

"This mad struggle for bread, professor, is the curse of life here below. It is what we are all after. If it were not for the necessity of bread and clothing, what a good time a fellow might have. Well, my blessing, Renny. Good-by."

Yates strolled slowly through the woods, until he came to the beginning of a lane which led to the Bartlett homestead. He saw the farmer and his son at work in the back fields. From between the distant house and barn there arose, straight up into the still air, a blue column of smoke, which, reaching a certain height, spread out like a thin, hazy cloud above the dwelling. At first Yates thought that some of the outhouses were on fire, and he quickened his pace to a run; but a moment's reflection showed him that the column was plainly visible to the workers in the fields, and that if anything were wrong they would not continue placidly at their labor. When he had walked the long length of the lane, and had safely rounded the corner of the barn, he saw, in the open space between that building and the house, a huge camp fire blazing. From a pole, upheld by two crotched supports, hung a big iron kettle over the flames. The caldron was full nearly to the brim, and the steam was already beginning to rise from its surface, although the fire had evidently been but recently kindled. The smoke was not now so voluminous, but Kitty Bartlett stood there with a big-brimmed straw hat in her hands, fanning it away from her face, while the hat at the same time protected her rosy countenance from the fire. She plainly was not prepared to receive visitors, and she started when the young man addressed her, flushing still more deeply, apparently annoyed at his unwelcome appearance.

"Good-afternoon," he said cordially. "Preparing for washing? I thought Monday was washing day."

"It is."

"Then I have not been misinformed. And you are not preparing for washing?"

"We are."

Yates laughed so heartily that Kitty, in spite of herself, had to permit a smile to brighten her own features. She always found it difficult remain solemn for any length of time.

"This is obviously a conundrum," said Yates, ticking off the items on his four fingers. "First, Monday is washing day. Second, this is not Monday. Third, neither is to-morrow. Fourth, we are preparing for washing. I give it up, Miss Bartlett. Please tell me the answer."

"The answer is that I am making soap; soft soap, if you know what that is."

"Practically, I don't know what it is; but I have heard the term used in a political connection. In the States we say that if a man is very diplomatic he uses soft soap, so I suppose it has lubricating qualities. Sam Slick used the term 'soft sawder' in the same way; but what sawder is, soft or hard, I haven't the slightest idea."

"I thought you knew everything, Mr. Yates."

"Me? Bless you, no. I'm a humble gleaner in the field of knowledge. That's why I brought a Toronto professor with me. I want to learn something. Won't you teach me how to make soap?"

"I'm very busy just now. When I said that we were preparing for washing, I should perhaps have told you there was something else we are not prepared for to-day."

"What is that?"

"A visitor."

"Oh, I say, Miss Bartlett, you are a little hard on me. I'm not a visitor. I'm a friend of the family. I want to help. You will find me a most diligent student. Won't you give me a chance?"

"All the hard work's done. But perhaps you knew that before you came."

Yates looked at her reproachfully, and sighed deeply.

"That's what it is to be a misunderstood man. So you think, among other bad qualities, I have the habit of shirking work? Let me tell you, Miss Bartlett, that the reason I am here is because I have worked too hard. Now, confess that you are sorry for what you said—trampling on an already downtrodden man."

Kitty laughed merrily at this, and Yates laughed also, for his sense of comradeship was strong.

"You don't look as if you had ever worked in your life; I don't believe you know what work is."

"But there are different kinds of labor. Don't you call writing work?"

"No."

"That's just where you're mistaken. It is, and hard work, too. I'll tell you about the newspaper business if you'll tell me about soap making. Fair exchange. I wish you would take me as a pupil, Miss Bartlett; you would find me quick at picking up things."

"Well, then, pick up that pail and draw a pailful of water."

"I'll do it," cried Yates sternly; "I'll do it, though it blast me."

Yates picked up the wooden pail, painted blue on the outside, with a red stripe near the top for ornament, and cream-colored inside. It was called a "patent pail" in those days, as it was a comparatively recent innovation, being cheaper, lighter, and stronger than the tin pail which it was rapidly replacing. At the well was a stout pole, pinned through the center to the upright support on which it swung, like the walking-beam of an engine. The thick end, which rested on the ground, was loaded with heavy stones; while

159

from the thin end, high in the air, there dangled over the mouth of the well a slim pole with a hook. This hook was ingeniously furnished with a spring of hickory, which snapped when the handle of the pail was placed on the hook, and prevented the "patent" utensil from slipping off when it was lowered to the surface of the water. Yates speedily recognized the usefulness of this contrivance, for he found that the filling of a wooden pail in a deep well was not the simple affair it looked. The bucket bobbed about on the surface of the water. Once he forgot the necessity of keeping a stout grip on the pole, and the next instant the pail came up to the sunlight with a suddenness that was terrifying. Only an equally sudden backward jump on Yates' part saved his head. Miss Bartlett was pleased to look upon this incident as funny. Yates was so startled by the unexpected revolt of the pail that his native courtesy did not get a chance to prevent Kitty from drawing up the water herself. She lowered the vessel, pulling down the pole in a hand-over-hand manner that the young man thought decidedly fetching, and then she gave an almost imperceptible twist to the arrangement that resulted in instant success. The next thing Yates knew the full pail was resting on the well curb, and the hickory spring had given the click that released the handle.

"There," said Kitty, suppressing her merriment, "that's how it's done."

"I see the result, Miss Bartlett; but I'm not sure I can do the trick. These things are not so simple as they seem. What is the next step?"

"Pour the water into the leach."

"Into the what?"

"Into the leach, I said. Where else?"

"Oh, I'm up a tree again. I see I don't even know the A B C of this business. In the old days the leech was a physician. You don't mean I'm to drown a doctor?"

"This is the leach," said Kitty, pointing to a large, yellowish, upright wooden cylinder, which rested on some slanting boards, down the surface of which ran a brownish liquid that dripped into a trough.

As Yates stood on a bench with the pail in his hand he saw that the cylinder was filled nearly to the top with sodden wood ashes. He poured in the water, and it sank quickly out of sight.

"So this is part of the soap-making equipment?" he said, stepping down; "I thought the iron kettle over the fire was the whole factory. Tell me about the leach."

"That is where the hard work of soap making comes in," said Kitty, stirring the contents of the iron kettle with a long stick. "Keeping the leach supplied with water at first is no fun, for then the ashes are dry. If you put in five more pails of water, I will tell you about it."

"Right!" cried Yates, pleased to see that the girl's evident objection to his presence at first was fast disappearing. "Now you'll understand how energetic I am. I'm a handy man about a place."

When he had completed his task, she was still stirring the thickening liquid in the caldron, guarding her face from the fire with her big straw hat. Her clustering, tangled fair hair was down about her shoulders; and Yates, as he put the pail in its place, when it had been emptied the fifth time, thought she formed a very pretty picture standing there by the fire, even if she were making soft soap.

"The wicked genii has finished the task set him by the fairy princess. Now for the reward. I want all the particulars about the leach. In the first place, where do you get this huge wooden cylinder that I have, without apparent effect, been pouring water into? Is it manufactured or natural?"

"Both. It is a section of the buttonwood tree."

"Buttonwood? I don't think I ever heard of that. I know the beech and the maple, and some kinds of oak, but there my wood lore ends. Why the buttonwood?"

"The buttonwood happens to be exactly suited to the purpose. It is a tree that is very fine to look at. It seems all right, but it generally isn't. It is hollow or rotten within, and, even when sound, the timber made from it is of little value, as it doesn't last. Yet you can't tell until you begin to chop whether it is of any use or not." Kitty shot a quick glance at the young man, who was sitting on a log watching her.

"Go on, Miss Bartlett; I see what you mean. There are men like the buttonwood tree. The woods are full of them. I've met lots of that kind, fair to look upon, but hollow. Of course you don't mean anything personal; for you must have seen my worth by the way I stuck to the water hauling. But go on."

"Dear me, I never thought of such a thing; but a guilty conscience, they say——" said Kitty, with a giggle.

"Of course they say; but it's wrong, like most other things they say. It's the man with the guilty conscience who looks you straight in the eye. Now that the buttonwood is chopped down, what's the next thing to be done?"

"It is sawn off at the proper length, square at one end and slanting at the other."

"Why slanting?"

"Don't you see, the foundation of plank on which it rests is inclined, so the end of the leach that is down must be slantingly cut, otherwise it would not stand perpendicularly. It would topple over in the first windstorm."

"I see, I see. Then they haul it in and set it up?"

"Oh, dear no; not yet. They build a fire in it when it gets dry enough."

"Really? I think I understand the comprehensive scheme, but I slip up on the details, as when I tried to submerge that wooden pail. What's the fire for?"

"To burn out what remains of the soft inside wood, so as to leave only the hard outside shell. Then the charring of the inner surface is supposed to make the leach better—more water-tight, perhaps."

"Quite so. Then it is hauled in and set up?"

"Yes; and gradually filled with ashes. When it is full, we pour the water in it, and catch the lye as it drips out. This is put in the caldron with grease,

162

pigskins, and that sort of thing, and when it boils long enough, the result is soft soap."

"And if you boil it too long, what is the result?"

"Hard soap, I suppose. I never boil it too long."

The conversation was here interrupted by a hissing in the fire, caused by the tumultuous boiling over of the soap. Kitty hurriedly threw in a basin of cold lye, and stirred the mixture vigorously.

"You see," she said reproachfully, "the result of keeping me talking nonsense to you. Now you will have to make up for it by bringing in some wood and putting more water into the leach."

"With the utmost pleasure," cried Yates, springing to his feet. "It is a delight to atone for a fault by obeying your commands."

The girl laughed. "Buttonwood," she said. Before Yates could think of anything to say in reply Mrs. Bartlett appeared at the back door.

"How is the soap getting on, Kitty?" she asked. "Why, Mr. Yates, are you here?"

"Am I here? I should say I was. Very much here. I'm the hired man. I'm the hewer of wood and the hauler of water, or, to speak more correctly, I'm the hauler of both. And, besides, I've been learning how to make soap, Mrs. Bartlett."

"Well, it won't hurt you to know how."

"You bet it won't. When I get back to New York, the first thing I shall do will be to chop down a buttonwood tree in the park, if I can find one, and set up a leach for myself. Lye comes useful in running a paper."

Mrs. Bartlett's eyes twinkled, for, although she did not quite understand his nonsense, she knew it was nonsense, and she had a liking for frivolous persons, her own husband being so somber-minded.

"Tea is ready," she said. "Of course you will stay, Mr. Yates."

"Really, Mrs. Bartlett, I cannot conscientiously do so. I haven't earned a meal since the last one. No; my conscience won't let me accept, but thank you all the same."

"Nonsense; my conscience won't let you go away hungry. If nobody were to eat but those who earn their victuals, there would be more starving people in the world than there are. Of course you'll stay."

"Now, that's what I like, Mrs. Bartlett. I like to have a chance of refusing an invitation I yearn for, and then be forced to accept. That's true hospitality." Then in a whisper he added to Kitty; "If you dare to say 'buttonwood,' Miss Bartlett, you and I will quarrel."

But Kitty said nothing, now that her mother had appeared on the scene, but industriously stirred the contents of the iron kettle.

"Kitty," said the mother, "you call the men to supper."

"I can't leave this," said Kitty, flushing; "it will boil over. You call, mother."

So Mrs. Bartlett held her open palms on each side of her mouth, and gave the long wailing cry, which was faintly answered from the fields, and Yates, who knew a thing or two, noted with secret satisfaction that Kitty had refused doubtless because he was there.

CHAPTER VIII.

"I tell you what it is, Renny," said Yates, a few days after the soap episode, as he swung in his hammock at the camp, "I'm learning something new every day."

"Not really?" asked the professor in surprise.

"Yes, really. I knew it would astonish you. My chief pleasure in life, professor, is the surprising of you. I sometimes wonder why it delights me; it is so easily done."

"Never mind about that. What have you been learning?"

"Wisdom, my boy; wisdom in solid chunks. In the first place, I am learning to admire the resourcefulness of these people around us. Practically, they make everything they need. They are the most self-helping people that I was ever thrown among. I look upon theirs as the ideal life."

"I think you said something like that when we first came here."

"I said that, you ass, about camping out. I am talking now about farm life. Farmers eliminate the middleman pretty effectually, and that in itself is going a long way toward complete happiness. Take the making of soap, that I told you about; there you have it, cheap and good. When you've made it, you know what is in it, and I'll be hanged if you do when you pay a big price for it in New York. Here they make pretty nearly everything they need, except the wagon and the crockery; and I'm not sure but they made them a few years back. Now, when a man with a good sharp ax and a jack-knife can do anything from building his house to whittling out a chair, he's the most independent man on earth. Nobody lives better than these people do. Everything is fresh, sweet, and good. Perhaps the country air helps; but it seems to me I never tasted such meals as Mrs. Bartlett, for instance, gets up. They buy nothing at the stores except the tea, and I confess I prefer milk myself. My tastes were always simple."

"And what is the deduction?"

"Why, that this is the proper way to live. Old Hiram has an anvil and an amateur forge. He can tinker up almost anything, and that eliminates the blacksmith. Howard has a bench, saws, hammers, and other tools, and that eliminates the carpenter. The women eliminate the baker, the soap boiler, and a lot of other parasites. Now, when you have eliminated all the middlemen, then comes independence, and consequently complete happiness. You can't keep happiness away with a shotgun then."

"But what is to become of the blacksmith, the carpenter, and all the rest?"

"Let them take up land and be happy too; there's plenty of land. The land is waiting for them. Then look how the master is eliminated. That's the most beautiful riddance of all. Even the carpenter and blacksmith usually have to work under a boss; and if not, they have to depend on the men who employ them. The farmer has to please nobody but himself. That adds to his independence. That's why old Hiram is ready to fight the first comer on the slightest provocation. He doesn't care whom he offends, so long as it isn't his wife. These people know how to make what they want, and what they can't make they do without. That's the way to form a great nation. You raise, in this way, a self-sustaining, resolute, unconquerable people. The reason the North conquered the South was because we drew our armies mostly from the self-reliant farming class, while we had to fight a people accustomed for generations to having things done for them."

"Why don't you buy a farm, Yates?"

"Several reasons. I am spoiled for the life here. I am like the drunkard who admires a temperate life, yet can't pass a ginshop. The city virus is in my blood. And then, perhaps, after all, I am not quite satisfied with the tendency of farm life; it is unfortunately in a transition state. It is at the frame-house stage, and will soon blossom into the red-brick stage. The log-house era is what I yearn for. Then everything a person needed was made on the farm. When the brick-house era sets in, the middleman will be rampant. I saw the other day at the Howards' a set of ancient stones that interested me a much as an Assyrian marble would interest you. They were old, home-made millstones, and they have not been used since the frame house was built. The grist mill at the village put them out of date. And just here, notice the subtlety of the crafty middleman. The farmer takes his grist to the mill, and the miller does not charge him cash for grinding it. He takes toll out of the bags, and the farmer has a vague idea that he gets his grinding for almost nothing. The old way was the best, Renny, my boy. The farmer's son won't be as happy in the brick house which the mason will build for him as his grandfather was in the log house he built for himself. And fools call this change the advance of civilization."

"There is something to be said for the old order of things," admitted Renmark. "If a person could unite the advantages of what we call civilization with the advantages of a pastoral life, he would inaugurate a condition of things that would be truly idyllic."

"That's so, Renmark, that's so!" cried Yates enthusiastically. "A brownstone mansion on Fifth Avenue, and a log hut on the shores of Lake Superior! That would suit me down to the ground. Spend half the year in each place."

"Yes," said the professor meditatively; "a log hut on the rocks and under the trees, with the lake in front, would be very nice if the hut had a good library attached."

"And a daily paper. Don't forget the press."

"No. I draw the line there. The daily paper would mean the daily steamer or the daily train. The one would frighten away the fish, and the other would disturb the stillness with its whistle."

Yates sighed. "I forgot about the drawbacks," he said. "That's the trouble with civilization. You can't have the things you want without bringing in their trail so many things you don't want. I shall have to give up the daily paper."

"Then there is another objection, worse than either steamer or train."

"What's that?"

"The daily paper itself."

167

Yates sat up indignantly.

"Renmark!" he cried, "that's blasphemy. For Heaven's sake, man, hold something sacred. If you don't respect the press, what do you respect? Not my most cherished feelings, at any rate, or you wouldn't talk in that flippant manner. If you speak kindly of my daily paper, I'll tolerate your library."

"And that reminds me: Have you brought any books with you, Yates? I have gone through most of mine already, although many of them will bear going over again; still, I have so much time on my hands that I think I may indulge in a little general reading. When you wrote asking me to meet you in Buffalo, I thought you perhaps intended to tramp through the country, so I did not bring as many books with me as I should have done if I had known you were going to camp out."

Yates sprang from the hammock.

"Books? Well, I should say so! Perhaps you think I don't read anything but the daily papers. I'd have you know that I am something of a reader myself. You mustn't imagine you monopolize all the culture in the township, professor."

The young man went into the tent, and shortly returned with an armful of yellow-covered, paper-bound small volumes, which he flung in profusion at the feet of the man from Toronto. They were mostly Beadle's Dime Novels, which had a great sale at the time.

"There," he said, "you have quantity, quality, and variety, as I have before remarked. 'The Murderous Sioux of Kalamazoo;' that's a good one. A hair-raising Indian story in every sense of the word. The one you are looking at is a pirate story, judging by the burning ship on the cover. But for first-class highwaymen yarns, this other edition is the best. That's the 'Sixteen String Jack set.' They're immense, if they do cost a quarter each. You must begin at the right volume, or you'll be sorry. You see, they never really end, although every volume is supposed to be complete in itself. They leave off at the most exciting point, and are continued in the next volume. I call that a pretty good idea, but it's rather exasperating if you begin at the last book. You'll enjoy this lot. I'm glad I brought them along."

"It is a blessing," said Renmark, with the ghost of a smile about his lips. "I can truthfully say that they are entirely new to me."

"That's all right, my boy," cried Yates loftily, with a wave of his hand. "Use them as if they were your own."

Renmark arose leisurely and picked up a quantity of the books.

"These will do excellently for lighting our morning camp fire," he said. "And if you will allow me to treat them as if they were my own, that is the use to which I will put them. You surely do not mean to say that you read such trash as this, Yates?"

"Trash?" exclaimed Yates indignantly. "It serves me right. That's what a man gets for being decent to you, Renny. Well, you're not compelled to read them; but if you put one of them in the fire, your stupid treatises will follow, if they are not too solid to burn. You don't know good literature when you see it."

The professor, buoyed up, perhaps, by the conceit which comes to a man through the possession of a real sheepskin diploma, granted by a university of good standing, did not think it necessary to defend his literary taste. He busied himself in pruning a stick he had cut in the forest, and finally he got it into the semblance of a walking cane. He was an athletic man, and the indolence of camp life did not suit him as it did Yates. He tested the stick in various ways when he had trimmed it to his satisfaction.

"Are you ready for a ten-mile walk?" he asked of the man in the hammock.

"Good gracious, no. Man wants but little walking here below, and he doesn't want it ten miles in length either. I'm easily satisfied. You're off, are you? Well, so long. And I say, Renny, bring back some bread when you return to camp. It's the one safe thing to do."

CHAPTER IX.

Renmark walked through the woods and then across the fields, until he came to the road. He avoided the habitations of man as much as he could, for he was neither so sociably inclined nor so frequently hungry as was his companion. He strode along the road, not caring much where it led him. Everyone he met gave him "Good-day," after the friendly custom of the country. Those with wagons or lighter vehicles going in his direction usually offered him a ride, and went on, wondering that a man should choose to walk when it was not compulsory. The professor, like most silent men, found himself good company, and did not feel the need of companionship in his walks. He had felt relieved rather than disappointed when Yates refused to accompany him. And Yates, swinging drowsily in his hammock, was no less gratified. Even where men are firm and intimate friends, the first few days of camping out together is a severe strain on their regard for each other. If Damon and Pythias had occupied a tent together for a week, the worst enemy of either, or both, might at the end of that time have ventured into the camp in safety, and would have been welcome.

Renmark thought of these things as he walked along. His few days' intimacy with Yates had shown him how far apart they had managed to get by following paths that diverged more and more widely the farther they were trodden. The friendship of their youth had turned out to be merely ephemeral. Neither would now choose the other as an intimate associate. Another illusion had gone.

"I have surely enough self-control," said Renmark to himself, as he walked on, "to stand his shallow flippancy for another week, and not let him see what I think of him."

Yates at the same time was thoroughly enjoying the peaceful silence of the camp. "That man is an exaggerated schoolmaster, with all the faults of the species abnormally developed. If I once open out on him, he will learn more truth about himself in ten minutes than he ever heard in his life before. What an unbearable prig he has grown to be." Thus ran Yates' thoughts as he swung in his hammock, looking up at the ceiling of green leaves.

Nevertheless, the case was not so bad as either of them thought. If it had been, then were marriage not only a failure, but a practical impossibility. If two men can get over the first few days in camp without a quarrel, life becomes easier, and the tension relaxes.

Renmark, as he polished off his ten miles, paid little heed to those he met; but one driver drew up his horse and accosted him.

"Good-day," he said. "How are you getting on in the tent?"

The professor was surprised at the question. Had their tenting-out eccentricity gone all over the country? He was not a quick man at recognizing people, belonging, as he did, to the "I-remember-your-face-but-can't-recall-your-name" fraternity. It had been said of him that he never, at any one time, knew the names of more than half a dozen students in his class; but this was an undergraduate libel on him. The young man who had accosted him was driving a single horse, attached to what he termed a "democrat"—a four-wheeled light wagon, not so slim and elegant as a buggy, nor so heavy and clumsy as a wagon. Renmark looked up at the driver with confused unrecognition, troubled because he vaguely felt that he had met him somewhere before. But his surprise at being addressed speedily changed into amazement as he looked from the driver to the load. The "democrat" was heaped with books. The larger volumes were stuck along the sides with some regularity, and in this way kept the miscellaneous pile from being shaken out on the road. His eye glittered with a new interest as it rested on the many-colored bindings; and he recognized in the pile the peculiar brown covers of the "Bohn" edition of classic translations, that were scattered like so many turnips over the top of this ridge of literature. He rubbed his eyes to make sure he was not dreaming. How came a farmer's boy to be driving a wagon load of books in the wilds of the country as nonchalantly as if they were so many bushels of potatoes?

The young driver, who had stopped his horse, for the load was heavy and the sand was deep, saw that the stranger not only did not recognize him, but that from the moment he saw the books he had forgotten everything else. It was evidently necessary to speak again.

"If you are coming back, will you have a ride?" he asked.

"I—I think I will," said the professor, descending to earth again and climbing up beside the boy.

"I see you don't remember me," said the latter, starting his horse again. "My name is Howard. I passed you in my buggy when you were coming in with your tent that day on the Ridge. Your partner—what's his name—Yates, isn't it?—had dinner at our house the other day."

"Ah, yes. I recollect you now. I thought I had seen you before; but it was only for a moment, you know. I have a very poor memory so far as people are concerned. It has always been a failing of mine. Are these your books? And how do you happen to have such a quantity?"

"Oh, this is the library," said young Howard.

"The library?"

"Yes, the township library, you know."

"Oh! The township has a library, then? I didn't know."

"Well, it's part of it. This is a fifth part. You know about township libraries, don't you? Your partner said you were a college man."

Renmark blushed at his own ignorance, but he was never reluctant to admit it.

"I ought to be ashamed to confess it, but I know nothing of township libraries. Please, tell me about them."

Young Howard was eager to give information to a college man, especially on the subject of books, which he regarded as belonging to the province of college-bred men. He was pleased also to discover that city people did not know everything. He had long had the idea that they did, and this belief had been annoyingly corroborated by the cocksureness of Yates. The professor evidently was a decent fellow, who did not pretend to universal knowledge

172

This was encouraging. He liked Renmark better than Yates, and was glad he had offered him a ride, although, of course, that was the custom; still, a person with one horse and a heavy load is exempt on a sandy road.

"Well, you see," he said in explanation, "it's like this: The township votes a sum of money, say a hundred dollars, or two hundred, as the case may be. They give notice to the Government of the amount voted, and the Government adds the same amount to the township money. It's like the old game: you think of a number, and they double it. The Government has a depository of books, in Toronto, I think, and they sell them cheaper than the bookstores do. At any rate, the four hundred dollars' worth are bought, or whatever the amount is, and the books are the property of the township. Five persons are picked out in the township as librarians, and they have to give security. My father is librarian for this section. The library is divided into five parts, and each librarian gets a share. Once a year I go to the next section and get all their books. They go to the next section, again, and get all the books at that place. A man comes to our house to-day and takes all we have. So we get a complete change every year, and in five years we get back the first batch, which by that time we have forgotten all about. To-day is changing day all around."

"And the books are lent to any person in each section who wishes to read them?" asked the professor.

"Yes. Margaret keeps a record, and a person can have a book out for two weeks; after that time there is a fine, but Margaret never fines anyone."

"And do people have to pay to take out the books?"

"Not likely!" said Howard with fine contempt. "You wouldn't expect people to pay for reading books; would you, now?"

"No, I suppose not. And who selected the volumes?"

"Well, the township can select the books if it likes, or it can send a committee to select them; but they didn't think it worth the trouble and expense. People grumbled enough at wasting money on books as it was, even if they did buy them at half price. Still, others said it was a pity not to get the

173

money out of the Government when they had the chance. I don't believe any of them cared very much about the books, except father and a few others. So the Government chose the books. They'll do that if you leave it to them. And a queer lot of trash they sent, if you take my word for it. I believe they shoved off on us all the things no one else would buy. Even when they did pick out novels, they were just as tough as the history books. 'Adam Bede' is one. They say that's a novel. I tried it, but I would rather read the history of Josephus any day. There's some fighting in that, if it is a history. Then there's any amount of biography books. They're no good. There's a 'History of Napoleon.' Old Bartlett's got that, and he won't give it up. He says he was taxed for the library against his will. He dares them to go to law about it, and it aint worth while for one book. The other sections are all asking for that book; not that they want it, but the whole country knows that old Bartlett's a-holding on to it, so they'd like to see some fun. Bartlett's read that book fourteen times, and it's all he knows. I tell Margaret she ought to fine him, and keep on fining, but she won't do it. I guess Bartlett thinks the book belongs to him by this time. Margaret likes Kitty and Mrs. Bartlett,—so does everybody,—but old Bartlett's a seed. There he sits now on his veranda, and it's a wonder he's not reading the 'History of Napoleon.'"

They were passing the Bartlett house, and young Howard raised his voice and called out:

"I say, Mr. Bartlett, we want that Napoleon book. This is changing day you know. Shall I come up for it, or will you bring it down? If you fetch it to the gate, I'll cart it home now."

The old man paid no heed to what was said to him; but Mrs. Bartlett, attracted by the outcry, came to the door.

"You go along with your books, you young rascal!" she cried, coming down to the gate when she saw the professor. "That's a nice way to carry bound books, as if they were a lot of bricks. I'll warrant you have lost a dozen between Mallory's and here. But easy come, easy go. It's plain to be seen they didn't cost you anything. I don't know what the world's a-coming to when the township spends its money in books, as if taxes weren't heavy enough already.

174

Won't you come in, Mr. Renmark? Tea's on the table."

"Mr. Renmark's coming with me this trip, Mrs. Bartlett," young Howard said before the professor had time to reply; "but I'll come over and take tea, if you'll invite me, as soon as I have put the horse up."

"You go along with your nonsense," she said; "I know you." Then in a lower voice she asked: "How is your mother, Henry—and Margaret?"

"They're pretty well, thanks."

"Tell them I'm going to run over to see them some day soon, but that need not keep them from coming to see me. The old man's going to town to-morrow," and with this hint, after again inviting the professor to a meal, she departed up the path to the house.

"I think I'll get down here," said Renmark, halfway between the two houses. "I am very much obliged to you for the ride, and also for what you told me about the books. It was very interesting."

"Nonsense!" cried young Howard; "I'm not going to let you do anything of the sort. You're coming home with me. You want to see the books, don't you? Very well, then, come along, Margaret is always impatient on changing day, she's so anxious to see the books, and father generally comes in early from the fields for the same reason."

As they approached the Howard homestead they noticed Margaret waiting for them at the gate; but when the girl saw that a stranger was in the wagon, she turned and walked into the house. Renmark, seeing this retreat, regretted he had not accepted Mrs. Bartlett's invitation. He was a sensitive man, and did not realize that others were sometimes as shy as himself. He felt he was intruding, and that at a sacred moment—the moment of the arrival of the library. He was such a lover of books, and valued so highly the privilege of being alone with them, that he fancied he saw in the abrupt departure of Margaret the same feeling of resentment he would himself have experienced if a visitor had encroached upon him in his favorite nook in the fine room that held the library of the university.

When the wagon stopped in the lane, Renmark said hesitatingly:

"I think I'll not stay, if you don't mind. My friend is waiting for me at the camp, and will be wondering what has become of me."

"Who? Yates? Let him wonder. I guess he never bothers about anybody else as long as he is comfortable himself. That's how I sized him up, at any rate. Besides, you're never going back on carrying in the books, are you? I counted on your help. I don't want to do it, and it don't seem the square thing to let Margaret do it all alone; does it, now?"

"Oh, if I can be of any assistance, I shall——"

"Of course you can. Besides, I know my father wants to see you, anyhow. Don't you, father?"

The old man was coming round from the back of the house to meet them.

"Don't I what?" he asked.

"You said you wanted to see Professor Renmark when Margaret told you what Yates had said to her about him."

Renmark reddened slightly at finding so many people had made him the subject of conversation, rather suspecting at the same time that the boy was making fun of him. Mr. Howard cordially held out his hand.

"So this is Professor Renmark, is it? I am very pleased to see you. Yes, as Henry was saying, I have been wanting to see you ever since my daughter spoke of you. I suppose Henry told you that his brother is a pupil of yours?"

"Oh! is Arthur Howard your son?" cried Renmark, warming up at once. "I did not know it. There are many young men at the college, and I have but the vaguest idea from what parts of the country they all come. A teacher should have no favorites, but I must confess to a strong liking for your son. He is a good boy, which cannot be said about every member of my class."

"Arthur was always studious, so we thought we would give him a chance. I am glad to hear he behaves himself in the city. Farming is hard work, and I hope my boys will have an easier time than I had. But come in, come in. The

missus and Margaret will be glad to see you, and hear how the boy is coming
n with his studies."

So they went in together.

CHAPTER X.

"Hello! Hello, there! Wake up! Breakfa-a-a-st! I thought that would fetch you. Gosh! I wish I had your job at a dollar a day!"

Yates rubbed his eyes, and sat up in the hammock. At first he thought the forest was tumbling down about his ears, but as he collected his wits he saw that it was only young Bartlett who had come crashing through the woods on the back of one horse, while he led another by a strap attached to a halter. The echo of his hearty yell still resounded in the depths of the woods, and rang in Yates' ears as he pulled himself together.

"Did you—ah—make any remarks?" asked Yates quietly.

The boy admired his gift of never showing surprise.

"I say, don't you know that it's not healthy to go to sleep in the middle of the day?"

"Is it the middle of the day? I thought it was later. I guess I can stand it, if the middle of the day can. I've a strong constitution. Now, what do you mean by dashing up on two horses into a man's bedroom in that reckless fashion?"

The boy laughed.

"I thought perhaps you would like a ride. I knew you were alone, for I saw the professor go mooning up the road a little while ago."

"Oh! Where was he going?"

"Hanged if I know, and he didn't look as if he knew himself. He's a queer fish, aint he?"

"He is. Everybody can't be as sensible and handsome as we are, you know. Where are you going with those horses, young man?"

"To get them shod. Won't you come along? You can ride the horse I'm on. It's got a bridle. I'll ride the one with the halter."

"How far away is the blacksmith's shop?"

"Oh, a couple of miles or so; down at the Cross Roads."

"Well," said Yates, "there's merit in the idea. I take it your generous offer is made in good faith, and not necessarily for publication."

"I don't understand. What do you mean?"

"There is no concealed joke, is there? No getting me on the back of one of those brutes to make a public exhibition of me? Do they bite or kick or buck, or playfully roll over a person?"

"No," cried, young Bartlett indignantly. "This is no circus. Why, a baby could ride this horse."

"Well, that's about the style of horse I prefer. You see, I'm a trifle out of practice. I never rode anything more spirited than a street car, and I haven't been on one of them for a week."

"Oh, you can ride all right. I guess you could do most things you set your mind to."

Yates was flattered by this evidently sincere tribute to his capacity, so he got out of the hammock. The boy, who had been sitting on the horse with both feet on one side, now straightened his back and slipped to the ground.

"Wait till I throw down the fence," he said.

Yates mounted with some difficulty, and the two went trotting down the road. He managed to hold his place with some little uncertainty, but the joggling up and down worried him. He never seemed to alight in quite the same place on the horse's back, and this gave an element of chance to his position which embarrassed him. He expected to come down some time and find the horse wasn't there. The boy laughed at his riding, but Yates was too much engaged in keeping his position to mind that very much.

"D-d-dirt is s-s-said to b-b-be matter out of place, and that's what's the m-m-mat-matter w-w-with me." His conversation seemed to be shaken out of him by the trotting of the horse. "I say, Bartlett, I can't stand this any longer. I'd rather walk."

"You're all right," said the boy; "we'll make him canter."

He struck the horse over the flank with the loose end of the halter rein.

"Here!" shouted Yates, letting go the bridle and grasping the mane. "Don't make him go faster, you young fiend. I'll murder you when I get off—and that will be soon."

"You're all right," repeated young Bartlett, and, much to his astonishment, Yates found it to be so. When the horse broke into a canter, Yates thought the motion as easy as swinging in a hammock, and as soothing as a rocking chair.

"This is an improvement. But we've got to keep it up, for if this brute suddenly changes to a trot, I'm done for."

"We'll keep it up until we come in sight of the Corners, then we'll slow down to a walk. There's sure to be a lot of fellows at the blacksmith's shop, so we'll come in on them easy like."

"You're a good fellow, Bartlett," said Yates. "I suspected you of tricks at first. I'm afraid, if I had got another chap in such a fix, I wouldn't have let him off as easily as you have me. The temptation would have been too great."

When they reached the blacksmith's shop at the Corners, they found four horses in the building ahead of them. Bartlett tied his team outside, and then, with his comrade, entered the wide doorway of the smithy. The shop was built of rough boards, and the inside was blackened with soot. It was not well lighted, the two windows being obscured with much smoke, so that they were useless as far as their original purpose was concerned; but the doorway, as wide as that of a barn, allowed all the light to come in that the smith needed for his work. At the far end and darkest corner of the place stood the forge, with the large bellows behind it, concealed, for the most part, by the chimney. The forge was perhaps six feet square and three or four feet high, built of plank and filled in with earth. The top was covered with cinders and coal, while in the center glowed the red core of the fire, with blue flames hovering over it. The man who worked the bellows chewed tobacco, and now and then projected the juice with deadly accuracy right into the center of the fire, where it made a momentary hiss and dark spot. All the frequenters of the smithy admired Sandy's skill in expectoration, and many tried in vain to emulate it. The envious said it was due to the peculiar formation of his front teeth, the upper row being prominent, and the two middle teeth set far apart, as if one were missing. But this was jealousy; Sandy's perfection in the art was due to no favoritism of nature, but to constant and long-continued practice. Occasionally with his callous right hand, never removing his left from the lever, Sandy pulled an iron bar out of the fire and examined it critically. The incandescent end of the bar radiated a blinding white light when it was gently withdrawn, and illuminated the man's head, making his beardless face look, against its dark background, like the smudged countenance of some cynical demon glowing with a fire from within. The end of the bar which he held must have been very hot to an ordinary mortal, as everyone in the shop knew, all of them, at their initiation to the country club, having been handed a black piece of iron from Sandy's hand, which he held unflinchingly, but which the innocent receiver usually dropped with a yell. This was Sandy's favorite joke, and made life worth living for him. It was perhaps not so good as the blacksmith's own bit of humor, but public opinion was divided on that point. Every great man has his own particular set of admirers; and there were some who said,—under their breaths, of course,—that Sandy could turn a horseshoe as well as Macdonald himself. Experts, however, while admitting Sandy's general genius, did not go so far as this.

About half a dozen members of the club were present, and most of them stood leaning against something with hands deep in their trousers pockets; one was sitting on the blacksmith's bench, with his legs dangling down. On the bench tools were scattered around so thickly that he had had to clear a place before he could sit down; the taking of this liberty proved the man to be an old and privileged member. He sat there whittling a stick, aimlessly bringing it to a fine point, examining it frequently with a critical air, as if he were engaged in some delicate operation which required great discrimination.

The blacksmith himself stooped with his back to one of the horses, the hind hoof of the animal, between his knees, resting on his leathern apron. The horse was restive, looking over its shoulder at him, not liking what was going on. Macdonald swore at it fluently, and requested it to stand still, holding the foot as firmly as if it were in his own iron vise, which was fixed to the table near the whittler. With his right hand he held a hot horseshoe, attached to an iron punch that had been driven into one of the nail holes, and this he pressed against the upraised hoof, as though sealing a document with a gigantic seal. Smoke and flame rose from the contact of the hot iron with the hoof, and the air was filled with the not unpleasant odor of burning horn. The smith's tool box, with hammer, pinchers, and nails, lay on the earthern floor within easy reach. The sweat poured from his grimy brow; for it was a hot job, and Macdonald was in the habit of making the most of his work. He was called the hardest working man in that part of the country, and he was proud of the designation. He was a standing reproach to the loafers who frequented his shop, and that fact gave him pleasure in their company. Besides, a man must have an audience when he is an expert in swearing. Macdonald's profanity was largely automatic,—a natural gift, as it were,—and he meant nothing wrong by it. In fact, when you got him fighting angry, he always forgot to swear; but in his calm moments oaths rolled easily and picturesquely from his lips, and gave fluency to his conversation. Macdonald enjoyed the reputation round about of being a wicked man, which he was not; his language was against him, that was all. This reputation had a misty halo thrown around it by Macdonald's unknown doings "down East," from which mystical region he had come. No one knew just what Macdonald had done, but it was admitted on all sides that he must have had some terrible experiences, although he was still a young man and unmarried. He used to say: "When you have come through what I have, you won't be so ready to pick a quarrel with a man."

This must have meant something significant, but the blacksmith never took anyone into his confidence; and "down East" is a vague place, a sort of indefinite, unlocalized no-man's-land, situated anywhere between Toronto and Quebec. Almost anything might have happened in such a space of country. Macdonald's favorite way of crushing an opponent was to say: "When you've had some of my experiences, young man, you'll know better'n to talk like that." All this gave a certain fascination to friendship with the blacksmith; and the farmers' boys felt that they were playing with fire when in his company, getting, as it were, a glimpse of the dangerous side of life. As for work, the blacksmith reveled in it, and made it practically his only vice. He did everything with full steam on, and was, as has been said, a constant reproach to loafers all over the country. When there was no work to do, he made work. When there was work to do, he did it with a rush, sweeping the sweat from his grimy brow with his hooked fore finger, and flecking it to the floor with a flirt of the right hand, loose on the wrist, in a way that made his thumb and fore finger snap together like the crack of a whip. This action was always accompanied with a long-drawn breath, almost a sigh, that seemed to say: "I wish I had the easy times you fellows have." In fact, since he came to the neighborhood the current phrase, "He works like a steer" had given way to, "He works like Macdonald," except with the older people, who find it hard to change phrases. Yet everyone liked the blacksmith, and took no special offense at his untiring industry, looking at it rather as an example to others.

He did not look up as the two newcomers entered, but industriously pared down the hoof with a curiously formed knife turned like a hook at the point, burned in the shoe to its place, nailed it on, and rasped the hoof into shape with a long, broad file. Not till he let the foot drop on the earthen floor, and slapped the impatient horse on the flank, did he deign to answer young Bartlett's inquiry.

"No," he said, wringing the perspiration from his forehead, "all these horses aint ahead of you, and you won't need to come next week. That's the last hoof of the last horse. No man needs to come to my shop and go away again, while the breath of life is left in me. And I don't do it, either, by sitting on a bench and whittling a stick."

"That's so. That's so," said Sandy, chuckling, in the admiring tone of one who intimated that, when the boss spoke, wisdom was uttered. "That's one on you, Sam."

"I guess I can stand it, if he can," said the whittler from the bench; which was considered fair repartee.

"Sit it, you mean," said young Bartlett, laughing with the others at his own joke.

"But," said the blacksmith severely, "we're out of shoes, and you'll have to wait till we turn some, that is, if you don't want the old ones reset. Are they good enough?"

"I guess so, if you can find 'em; but they're out in the fields. Didn't think I'd bring the horses in while they held on, did you?" Then, suddenly remembering his duties, he said by, way of general introduction: "Gentlemen, this is my friend Mr. Yates from New York."

The name seemed to fall like a wet blanket on the high spirits of the crowd. They had imagined from the cut of his clothes that he was a storekeeper from some village around, or an auctioneer from a distance, these two occupations being the highest social position to which a man might attain. They were prepared to hear that he was from Welland, or perhaps St. Catherines; but New York! that was a crusher. Macdonald, however, was not a man to be put down in his own shop and before his own admirers. He was not going to let his prestige slip from him merely because a man from New York had happened along. He could not claim to know the city, for the stranger would quickly detect the imposture and probably expose him; but the slightly superior air which Yates wore irritated him, while it abashed the others. Even Sandy was silent.

"I've met some people from New York down East," he said in an offhand manner, as if, after all, a man might meet a New Yorker and still not sink into the ground.

"Really?" said Yates. "I hope you liked them."

"Oh, so-so," replied the blacksmith airily. "There's good and bad among them, like the rest of us."

"Ah, you noticed that," said Yates. "Well, I've often thought the same myself. It's a safe remark to make; there is generally no disputing it."

The condescending air of the New Yorker was maddening, and

184

Macdonald realized that he was losing ground. The quiet insolence of Yates' tone was so exasperating to the blacksmith that he felt any language at his disposal inadequate to cope with it. The time for the practical joke had arrived. The conceit of this man must be taken down. He would try Sandy's method, and, if that failed, it would at least draw attention from himself to his helper.

"Being as you're from New York, maybe you can decide a little bet Sandy here wants to have with somebody."

Sandy, quick to take the hint, picked up the bar that always lay near enough the fire to be uncomfortably warm.

"How much do you reckon that weighs?" he said, with critical nicety estimating its ounces in his swaying hand. Sandy had never done it better. There was a look of perfect innocence on his bland, unsophisticated countenance, and the crowd looked on in breathless suspense.

Bartlett was about to step forward and save his friend, but a wicked glare from Macdonald restrained him; besides, he felt, somehow, that his sympathies were with his neighbors, and not with the stranger he had brought among them. He thought resentfully that Yates might have been less high and mighty. In fact, when he asked him to come he had imagined his brilliancy would be instantly popular, and would reflect glory on himself. Now he fancied he was included in the general scorn Yates took such little pains to conceal.

Yates glanced at the piece of iron and, without taking his hands from his pockets, said carelessly:

"Oh, I should imagine it weighed a couple of pounds."

"Heft it," said Sandy beseechingly, holding it out to him.

"No, thank you," replied Yates, with a smile. "Do you think I have never picked up a hot horseshoe before? If you are anxious to know its weight, why don't you take it over to the grocery store and have it weighed?"

"'Taint hot," said Sandy, as he feebly smiled and flung the iron back on the forge. "If it was, I couldn't have held it s'long."

"Oh, no," returned Yates, with a grin, "of course not. I don't know what a blacksmith's hands are, do I? Try something fresh."

Macdonald saw there was no triumph over him among his crowd, for they all evidently felt as much involved in the failure of Sandy's trick as he did himself; but he was sure that in future some man, hard pushed in argument, would fling the New Yorker at him. In the crisis he showed the instinct of a Napoleon.

"Well, boys," he cried, "fun's fun, but I've got to work. I have to earn my living, anyhow."

Yates enjoyed his victory; they wouldn't try "getting at" him again, he said to himself.

Macdonald strode to the forge and took out the bar of white-hot iron. He gave a scarcely perceptible nod to Sandy, who, ever ready with tobacco juice, spat with great directness on the top of the anvil. Macdonald placed the hot iron on the spot, and quickly smote it a stalwart blow with the heavy hammer. The result was appalling. An instantaneous spreading fan of apparently molten iron lit up the place as if it were a flash of lightning. There was a crash like the bursting of a cannon. The shop was filled for a moment with a shower of brilliant sparks, that flew like meteors to every corner of the place. Everyone was prepared for the explosion except Yates. He sprang back with a cry, tripped, and, without having time to get the use of his hands to ease his fall, tumbled and rolled to the horses' heels. The animals, frightened by the report, stamped around; and Yates had to hustle on his hands and knees to safer quarters, exhibiting more celerity than dignity. The blacksmith never smiled, but everyone else roared. The reputation of the country was safe. Sandy doubled himself up in his boisterous mirth.

"There's no one like the old man!" he shouted. "Oh, lordy! lordy! He's all wool, and a yard wide."

Yates picked himself up and dusted himself off, laughing with the rest of them.

"If I ever knew that trick before, I had forgotten it. That's one on me, as this youth in spasms said a moment ago. Blacksmith, shake! I'll treat the crowd, if there's a place handy."

CHAPTER XI.

People who have but a superficial knowledge of the life and times here set down may possibly claim that the grocery store, and not the blacksmith's shop, used to be the real country club—the place where the politics of the country were discussed; where the doings of great men were commended or condemned, and the government criticised. It is true that the grocery store was the club of the village, when a place like the Corners grew to be a village; but the blacksmith's shop was usually the first building erected on the spot where a village was ultimately to stand. It was the nucleus. As a place grew, and enervating luxury set in, the grocery store slowly supplanted the blacksmith's shop, because people found a nail keg, or a box of crackers, more comfortable to sit on than the limited seats at their disposal in a smithy; moreover, in winter the store, with its red-hot box stove, was a place of warmth and joy, but the reveling in such an atmosphere of comfort meant that the members of the club had to live close at hand, for no man would brave the storms of a Canadian winter night, and journey a mile or two through the snow, to enjoy even the pleasures of the store. So the grocery was essentially a village club, and not a rural club.

Of course, as civilization advanced, the blacksmith found it impossible to compete with the grocer. He could not offer the same inducements. The grocery approached more nearly than the smithy the grateful epicurism of the Athenaeum, the Reform, or the Carlton. It catered to the appetite of man, besides supplying him with the intellectual stimulus of debate. A box of soda crackers was generally open, and, although such biscuits were always dry, they were good to munch, if consumed slowly. The barrel of hazel nuts never had a lid on. The raisins, in their square box, with blue-tinted paper, setting forth the word "Malaga" under the colored picture of joyous Spanish grape pickers, stood on the shelves behind the counter, at an angle suited to display the contents to all comers, requiring an exceptionally long reach, and more than an ordinary amount of cheek, before they were got at; but the barrel of Muscavado brown sugar was where everyone could dip his hand in; while the man on the keg of tenpenny nails might extend his arm over into the display window, where the highly colored candies exhibited themselves, although the person who meddled often with them was frowned upon, for it was etiquette in the club not to purloin things which were expensive. The grocer himself drew the line at the candies, and a second helping usually brought forth the mild reproof:

"Shall I charge that, Sam; or would you rather pay for it now?"

All these delicacies were taken in a somewhat surreptitious way, and the takers generally wore an absent-minded look, as if the purloining was not quite intentional on their part. But they were all good customers of the grocer, and the abstractions were doubtless looked on by him as being in the way of trade; just as the giving of a present with a pound of tea, or a watch with a suit of clothes, became in later days. Be that as it may, he never said anything unless his generosity was taken advantage of, which was rarely the case.

Very often on winter nights there was a hilarious feast, that helped to lighten the shelves and burden the till. This ordinarily took the form of a splurge in cove oysters. Cove oysters came from Baltimore, of course, in round tins; they were introduced into Canada long before the square tin boxes that now come in winter from the same bivalvular city. Cove oysters were partly cooked before being tinned, so that they would, as the advertisements say, keep in any climate. They did not require ice around them, as do the square tins which now contain the raw oysters. Someone present would say:

"What's the matter with having a feed of cove oysters?"

He then collected a subscription of ten cents or so from each member, and the whole was expended in several cans of oysters and a few pounds of crackers. The cooking was done in a tin basin on the top of the hot stove. The contents of the cans were emptied into this handy dish, milk was added, and broken crackers, to give thickness and consistency to the result. There were always plenty of plates, for the store supplied the crockery of the neighborhood. There were also plenty of spoons, for everything was to be had at the grocery. What more could the most exacting man need? On a particularly reckless night the feast ended with several tins of peaches, which needed no cooking, but only a sprinkling of sugar. The grocer was always an expert at cooking cove oysters and at opening tins of peaches.

There was a general feeling among the members that, by indulging in these banquets, they were going the pace rather; and some of the older heads feebly protested against the indulgence of the times, but it was noticed that they never refrained from doing their share when it came to spoon work.

"A man has but one life to live," the younger and more reckless would say, as if that excused the extravagance; for a member rarely got away without being fifteen cents out of pocket, especially when they had peaches as well as oysters.

The grocery at the Corners had been but recently established and as yet the blacksmith's shop had not looked upon it as a rival. Macdonald was monarch of all he surveyed, and his shop was the favorite gathering place for miles around. The smithy was also the patriotic center of the district, as a blacksmith's shop must be as long as anvils can take the place of cannon for saluting purposes. On the 24th of May, the queen's birthday, celebrated locally as the only day in the year, except Sundays, when Macdonald's face was clean and when he did no work, the firing of the anvils aroused the echoes of the locality. On that great day the grocer supplied the powder, which was worth three York shillings a pound—a York shilling being sixpence halfpenny. It took two men to carry an anvil, with a good deal of grunting; but Macdonald, if the crowd were big enough, made nothing of picking it up, hoisting it on his shoulder, and flinging it down on the green in front of his shop. In the iron mass there is a square hole, and when the anvil was placed upside down, the hole was uppermost. It was filled with powder, and a wooden plug, with a notch cut in it, was pounded in with a sledge hammer. Powder was sprinkled from the notch over the surface of the anvil, and then the crowd stood back and held its breath. It was a most exciting moment. Macdonald would come running out of the shop bareheaded, holding a long iron bar, the wavering, red-hot end of which descended on the anvil, while the blacksmith shouted in a terrifying voice: "Look out, there!" The loose powder hissed and spat for a moment, then bang went the cannon, and a

190

great cloud of smoke rolled upward, while the rousing cheers came echoing back from the surrounding forests. The helper, with the powder-horn, would spring to the anvil and pour the black explosive into the hole, while another stood ready with plug and hammer. The delicious scent of burned gunpowder filled the air, and was inhaled by all the youngsters with satisfaction, for now they realized what real war was. Thus the salutes were fired, and thus the royal birthday was fittingly celebrated.

Where two anvils were to be had, the cannonade was much brisker, as then a plug was not needed. The hole in the lower anvil was filled with powder, and the other anvil was placed over it. This was much quicker than pounding in a plug, and had quite as striking and detonating an effect. The upper anvil gave a heave, like Mark Twain's shot-laden frog, and fell over on its side. The smoke rolled up as usual, and the report was equally gratifying.

Yates learned all these things as he sat in the blacksmith's shop, for they were still in the month of May, and the smoke of the echoing anvils had hardly yet cleared away. All present were eager to tell him of the glory of the day. One or two were good enough to express regret that he had not been there to see. After the disaster which had overturned Yates things had gone on very smoothly, and he had become one of the crowd, as it were. The fact that he was originally a Canadian told in his favor, although he had been contaminated by long residence in the States.

Macdonald worked hard at the turning of horseshoes from long rods of iron. Usually an extended line of unfinished shoes bestrode a blackened scantling, like bodiless horsemen, the scantling crossing the shop overhead, just under the roof. These were the work of Macdonald's comparatively leisure days, and they were ready to be fitted to the hoofs of any horse that came to be shod, but on this occasion there had been such a run on his stock that it was exhausted, a depletion the smith seemed to regard as a reproach on himself, for he told Yates several times that he often had as many as three dozen shoes up aloft for a rainy day.

When the sledge hammer work was to be done, one of those present stepped forward and swung the heavy sledge, keeping stroke for stroke with

191

Macdonald's one-handed hammer, all of which required a nice ear for time. This assistance was supposed to be rendered by Sandy; but, as he remarked, he was no hog, and anyone who wished to show his skill was at liberty to do so. Sandy seemed to spend most of his time at the bellows, and when he was not echoing the sentiments of the boss, as he called him, he was commending the expertness of the pro tem. amateur, the wielder of the sledge. It was fun to the amateur, and it was an old thing with Sandy, so he never protested against this interference with his duty, believing in giving everyone a chance, especially when it came to swinging a heavy hammer. The whole scene brought back to Yates the days of his youth, especially when Macdonald, putting the finishing strokes to his shoe, let his hammer periodically tinkle with musical clangor on the anvil, ringing forth a tintinnabulation that chimed melodiously on the ear—a sort of anvil-chorus accompaniment to his mechanical skill. He was a real sleight-of-hand man, and the anvil was his orchestra.

Yates soon began to enjoy his visit to the rural club. As the members thawed out he found them all first-rate fellows, and, what was more, they were appreciative listeners. His stories were all evidently new to them, and nothing puts a man into a genial frame of mind so quickly as an attentive, sympathetic audience. Few men could tell a story better than Yates, but he needed the responsive touch of interested hearers. He hated to have to explain the points of his anecdotes, as, indeed, what story-teller does not? A cold and critical man like the professor froze the spring of narration at its source. Besides, Renmark had an objectionable habit of tracing the recital to its origin; it annoyed Yates to tell a modern yarn, and then discover that Aristophanes, or some other prehistoric poacher on the good things men were to say, had forestalled him by a thousand years or so. When a man is quick to see the point of your stories, and laughs heartily at them, you are apt to form a high opinion of his good sense, and to value his companionship.

When the horses were shod, and young Bartlett, who was delighted at the impression Yates had made, was preparing to go, the whole company protested against the New Yorker's departure. This was real flattery.

"What's your hurry, Bartlett?" asked the whittler. "You can't do anything this afternoon, if you do go home. It's a poor time this to mend a bad day's work. If you stay, he'll stay; won't you, Mr. Yates? Macdonald is going to set tires, and he needs us all to look on and see that he does it right; don't you, Mac?"

"Yes; I get a lot of help from you while there's a stick to whittle," replied the smith.

"Then there's the protracted meeting to-night at the schoolhouse," put in another, anxious that all the attractions of the place should be brought forward.

"That's so," said the whittler; "I had forgotten about that. It's the first night, so we must all be there to encourage old Benderson. You'll be on hand to-night, won't you, Macdonald?"

The blacksmith made no answer, but turned to Sandy and asked him savagely what in —— and —-nation he was standing gawking there for. Why didn't he go outside and get things ready for the tire setting? What in thunder was he paying him for, anyhow? Wasn't there enough loafers round, without him joining the ranks?

Sandy took this rating with equanimity, and, when the smith's back was turned, he shrugged his shoulders, took a fresh bite of tobacco from the plug which he drew from his hip pocket, winking at the others as he did so. He leisurely followed Macdonald out of the shop, saying in a whisper as he passed the whittler:

"I wouldn't rile the old man, if I were you."

The club then adjourned to the outside, all except those who sat on the bench. Yates asked:

"What's the matter with Macdonald? Doesn't he like protracted meetings? And, by the way, what are protracted meetings?"

"They're revival meetings—religious meetings, you know, for converting sinners."

"Really?" said Yates. "But why protracted? Are they kept on for a week or two?"

"Yes; I suppose that's why, although, to tell the truth, I never knew the reason for the name. Protracted meetings always stood for just the same thing ever since I was a boy, and we took it as meaning that one thing, without thinking why."

"And doesn't Macdonald like them?"

"Well, you see, it's like this: He never wants to go to a protracted meeting, yet he can't keep away. He's like a drunkard and the corner tavern. He can't pass it, and he knows if he goes in he will fall. Macdonald's always the first one to go up to the penitent bench. They rake him in every time. He has religion real bad for a couple of weeks, and then he backslides. He doesn't seem able to stand either the converting or the backsliding. I suppose some time they will gather him in finally, and he will stick and become a class leader, but he hasn't stuck up to date."

"Then he doesn't like to hear the subject spoken of?"

"You bet he don't. It isn't safe to twit him about it either. To tell the truth, I was pleased when I heard him swear at Sandy; then I knew it was all right, and Sandy can stand it. Macdonald is a bad man to tackle when he's mad. There's nobody in this district can handle him. I'd sooner get a blow from a sledge hammer than meet Mac's fist when his dander is up. But so long as he swears it's all right. Say, you'll stay down for the meeting, won't you?"

"I think I will. I'll see what young Bartlett intends to do. It isn't very far to walk, in any case."

"There will be lots of nice girls going your way to-night after the meeting. I don't know but I'll jog along in that direction myself when it's over. That's the principal use I have for the meetings, anyhow."

The whittler and Yates got down from the bench, and joined the crowd outside. Young Bartlett sat on one of the horses, loath to leave while the tire setting was going on.

"Are you coming, Yates?" he shouted, as his comrade appeared.

194

"I think I'll stay for the meeting," said Yates, approaching him and patting the horse. He had no desire for mounting and riding away in the presence of that critical assemblage.

"All right," said young Bartlett. "I guess I'll be down at the meeting, too; then I can show you the way home."

"Thanks," said Yates; "I'll be on the lookout for you."

Young Bartlett galloped away, and was soon lost to sight in a cloud of dust. The others had also departed with their shod horses; but there were several new arrivals, and the company was augmented rather than diminished. They sat around on the fence, or on the logs dumped down by the wayside.

Few smoked, but many chewed tobacco. It was a convenient way of using the weed, and required no matches, besides being safer for men who had to frequent inflammable barns.

A circular fire burned in front of the shop, oak bark being the main fuel used. Iron wagon tires lay hidden in this burning circle. Macdonald and Sandy bustled about making preparations, their faces, more hideous in the bright sunlight than in the comparative obscurity of the shop, giving them the appearance of two evil spirits about to attend some incantation scene of which the circular fire was the visible indication. Crosstrees, of four pieces of squared timber, lay near the fire, with a tireless wheel placed flat upon them, the hub in the square hole at the center. Shiftless farmers always resisted having tires set until they would no longer stay on the wheel. The inevitable day was postponed, time and again, by a soaking of the wheels overnight in some convenient puddle of water; but as the warmer and dryer weather approached this device, supplemented by wooden wedges, no longer sufficed, and the tires had to be set for summer work. Frequently the tire rolled off on the sandy highway, and the farmer was reluctantly compelled to borrow a rail from the nearest fence, and place it so as to support the axle; he then put the denuded wheel and its tire on the wagon, and drove slowly to the nearest blacksmith's shop, his vehicle "trailing like a wounded duck," the rail leaving a snake's track behind it on the dusty road.

The blacksmith had previously cut and welded the tire, reducing its circumference, and when it was hot enough, he and Sandy, each with a pair of tongs, lifted it from the red-hot circle of fire. It was pressed and hammered down on the blazing rim of the wheel, and instantly Sandy and Macdonald, with two pails of water that stood handy, poured the cold liquid around the red-hot zone, enveloping themselves in clouds of steam, the quick contraction clamping the iron on the wood until the joints cracked together. There could be no loitering; quick work was necessary, or a spoiled wheel was the result. Macdonald, alternately spluttering through fire and steam, was in his element. Even Sandy had to be on the keen jump, without a moment to call his plug of tobacco his own. Macdonald fussed and fussed, but got through an immense amount of work in an incredibly short space of time, cursing Sandy pretty much all the while; yet that useful man never replied in kind, contenting himself with a wink at the crowd when he got the chance, and saying under his breath:

"The old man's in great fettle to-day."

Thus everybody enjoyed himself: Macdonald, because he was the center figure in a saturnalia of work; Sandy, because no matter how hard a man has to work he can chew tobacco all the time; the crowd, because the spectacle of fire, water, and steam was fine, and they didn't have to do anything but sit around and look on. The sun got lower and lower as, one by one, the spectators departed to do their chores, and prepare for the evening meeting. Yates at the invitation of the whittler went home with him, and thoroughly relished his evening meal.

CHAPTER XII.

Margaret had never met any man but her father who was so fond of books as Professor Renmark. The young fellows of her acquaintance read scarcely anything but the weekly papers; they went with some care through the yellow almanac that was given away free, with the grocer's name printed on the back. The marvelous cures the almanac recorded were of little interest, and were chiefly read by the older folk, but the young men reveled in the jokes to be found at the bottom of every page, their only drawback being that one could never tell the stories at a paring-bee or other social gathering, because everyone in the company had read them. A few of the young men came sheepishly round to get a book out of the library, but it was evident that their interest was not so much in the volume as in the librarian, and when that fact became apparent to the girl, she resented it. Margaret was thought to be cold and proud by the youth of the neighborhood, or "stuck-up," as they expressed it.

To such a girl a man like Renmark was a revelation. He could talk of other things than the weather, live stock, and the prospects for the crops. The conversation at first did not include Margaret, but she listened to every word of it with interest. Her father and mother were anxious to hear about their boy; and from that engrossing subject the talk soon drifted to university life, and the differences between city and country. At last the farmer, with a sigh, arose to go. There is little time for pleasant talk on a farm while daylight lasts. Margaret, remembering her duties as librarian, began to take in the books from the wagon to the front room. Renmark, slow in most things, was quick enough to offer his assistance on this occasion; but he reddened somewhat as he did so, for he was unused to being a squire of dames.

"I wish you would let me do the porterage," he said. "I would like to earn the right to look at these books sometimes, even though I may not have the privilege of borrowing, not being a taxable resident of the township."

"The librarian," answered Margaret, with a smile, "seems to be at liberty to use her own discretion in the matter of lending. No one has authority to look over her accounts, or to censure her if she lends recklessly. So, if you wish to borrow books, all you have to do is to ask for them."

"You may be sure I shall avail myself of the permission. But my conscience will be easier if I am allowed to carry them in."

"You will be permitted to help. I like carrying them. There is no more delicious armful than books."

As Renmark looked at the lovely girl, her face radiant with enthusiasm, the disconcerting thought came suddenly that perhaps her statement might not be accurate. No such thought had ever suggested itself to him before, and it now filled him with guilty confusion. He met the clear, honest gaze of her eyes for a moment, then he stammered lamely:

"I—I too am very fond of books."

Together they carried in the several hundred volumes, and then began to arrange them.

"Have you no catalogue?" he asked.

"No. We never seem to need one. People come and look over the library, and take out whatever book they fancy."

"Yes, but still every library ought to be catalogued. Cataloguing is an art in itself. I have paid a good deal of attention to it, and will show you how it is done, if you care to know."

"Oh, I wish you would."

"How do you keep a record of the volumes that are out?"

"I just write the name of the person, the title, and the date in this blank book. When the volume is returned, I score out the record."

"I see," said Renmark dubiously.

"That isn't right, is it? Is there a better way?"

"Well, for a small library, that ought to do; but if you were handling many books, I think confusion might result."

"Do tell me the right way. I should like to know, even if it is a small library."

"There are several methods, but I am by no means sure your way is not the simplest, and therefore the best in this instance."

"I'm not going to be put off like that," said Margaret, laughing. "A collection of books is a collection of books, whether large or small, and deserves respect and the best of treatment. Now, what method is used in large libraries?"

"Well, I should suggest a system of cards, though slips of paper would do. When any person wants to take out a book, let him make out a card, giving the date and the name or number of the book; he then must sign the card, and there you are. He cannot deny having had the book, for you have his own signature to prove it. The slips are arranged in a box according to dates, and when a book is returned, you tear up the recording paper."

"I think that is a very good way, and I will adopt it."

"Then let me send to Toronto and get you a few hundred cards. We'll have them here in a day or two."

"Oh, I don't want to put you to that trouble."

"It is no trouble at all. Now, that is settled, let us attack the catalogue. Have you a blank book anywhere about? We will first make an alphabetical list; then we will arrange them under the heads of history, biography, fiction, and so on."

Simple as it appeared, the making of a catalogue took a long time. Both were absorbed in their occupation. Cataloguing in itself is a straight and narrow path, but in this instance there were so many delightful side excursions that rapid progress could not be expected. To a reader the mere mention of a book brings up recollections. Margaret was reading out the names; Renmark, on slips of paper, each with a letter on it, was writing them down.

"Oh, have you that book?" he would say, looking up as a title was mentioned. "Have you ever read it?"

"No; for, you see, this part of the library is all new to me. Why, here is one of which the leaves are not even cut. No one has read it. Is it good?"

"One of the best," Renmark would say, taking the volume. "Yes, I know this edition. Let me read you one passage."

And Margaret would sit in the rocking while he cut the leaves and found the place. One extract was sure to suggest another, and time passed before the title of the book found its way to the proper slip of paper. These excursions into literature were most interesting to both excursionists, but they interfered with cataloguing. Renmark read and read, ever and anon stopping to explain some point, or quote what someone else had said on the same subject, marking the place in the book, as he paused, with inserted fore finger. Margaret swayed back and forth in the comfortable rocking chair, and listened intently, her large dark eyes fixed upon him so earnestly that now and then, when he met them, he seemed disconcerted for a moment. But the girl did not notice this. At the end of one of his dissertations she leaned her elbow on the arm of the chair, with her cheek resting against her hand, and said:

"How very clear you make everything, Mr. Renmark."

"Do you think so?" he said with a smile. "It's my business, you know."

"I think it's a shame that girls are not allowed to go to the university; don't you?"

"Really, I never gave any thought to the subject, and I am not quite prepared to say."

"Well, I think it most unfair. The university is supported by the Government, is it not? Then why should half of the population be shut out from its advantages?"

"I'm afraid it wouldn't do, you know."

"Why?"

"There are many reasons," he replied evasively.

200

"What are they? Do you think girls could not learn, or are not as capable of hard study as well as——"

"It isn't that," he interrupted; "there are plenty of girls' schools in the country, you know. Some very good ones in Toronto itself, for that matter."

"Yes; but why shouldn't I go to the university with my brother? There are plenty of boys' schools, too, but the university is the university. I suppose my father helps to support it. Why, then, should one child be allowed to attend and the other not? It isn't at all just."

"It wouldn't do," said the professor more firmly, the more he thought about it.

"Would you take that as a satisfying reason from one or your students?"

"What?"

"The phrase, 'It wouldn't do.'"

Renmark laughed.

"I'm afraid not," he said; "but, then, I'm very exacting in class. Now, if you want to know, why do you not ask your father?"

"Father and I have discussed the question, often, and he quite agrees with me in thinking it unfair."

"Oh, does he?" said Renmark, taken aback; although, when he reflected, he realized that the father doubtless knew as little about the dangers of the city as the daughter did.

"And what does your mother say?"

"Oh, mother thinks if a girl is a good housekeeper it is all that is required. So you will have to give me a good reason, if there is one, for nobody else in this house argues on your side of the question."

"Well," said Renmark in an embarrassed manner, "if you don't know by the time you are twenty-five, I'll promise to discuss the whole subject with you."

201

Margaret sighed as she leaned back in her chair.

"Twenty-five?" she cried, adding with the unconscious veracity of youth: "That will be seven years to wait. Thank you, but I think I'll find out before that time."

"I think you will," Renmark answered.

They were interrupted by the sudden and unannounced entrance of her brother.

"Hello, you two!" he shouted with the rude familiarity of a boy. "It seems the library takes a longer time to arrange than usual."

Margaret rose with dignity.

"We are cataloguing," she said severely.

"Oh, that's what you call it, is it? Can I be of any assistance, or is two company when they're cataloguing? Have you any idea what time it is?"

"I'm afraid I must be off," said the professor, rising. "My companion in camp won't know what has become of me."

"Oh, he's all right!" said Henry. "He's down at the Corners, and is going to stay there for the meeting to-night. Young Bartlett passed a while ago; he was getting the horses shod, and your friend went with him. I guess Yates can take care of himself, Mr. Renmark. Say, sis, will you go to the meeting? I'm going. Young Bartlett's going, and so is Kitty. Won't you come, too, Mr. Renmark? It's great fun."

"Don't talk like that about a religious gathering, Henry," said his sister, frowning.

"Well, that's what it is, anyhow."

"Is it a prayer meeting?" asked the professor, looking at the girl.

"You bet it is!" cried Henry enthusiastically, giving no one a chance to speak but himself. "It's a prayer meeting, and every other kind of meeting all rolled into one. It's a revival meeting; a protracted meeting, that's what it is.

You had better come with us, Mr. Renmark, and then you can see what it is like. You can walk home with Yates."

This attractive dénouement did not seem to appeal so strongly to the professor as the boy expected, for he made no answer.

"You will come, sis; won't you?" urged the boy.

"Are you sure Kitty is going?"

"Of course she is. You don't think she'd miss it, do you? They'll soon be here, too; better go and get ready."

"I'll see what mother says," replied Margaret as she left the room. She shortly returned, dressed ready for the meeting, and the professor concluded he would go also.

CHAPTER XIII.

Anyone passing the Corners that evening would have quickly seen that something important was on. Vehicles of all kinds lined the roadway, drawn in toward the fence, to the rails of which the horses were tied. Some had evidently come from afar, for the fame of the revivalist was widespread. The women, when they arrived, entered the schoolhouse, which was brilliantly lighted with oil lamps. The men stood around outside in groups, while many sat in rows on the fences, all conversing about every conceivable topic except religion. They apparently acted on the theory that there would be enough religion to satisfy the most exacting when they went inside. Yates sat on the top rail of the fence with the whittler, whose guest he had been. It was getting too dark for satisfactory whittling, so the man with the jack-knife improved the time by cutting notches in the rail on which he sat. Even when this failed, there was always a satisfaction in opening and shutting a knife that had a powerful spring at the back of it, added to which was the pleasurable danger of cutting his fingers. They were discussing the Fenian question, which at that time was occupying the minds of Canadians to some extent. Yates was telling them what he knew of the brotherhood in New York, and the strength of it, which his auditors seemed inclined to underestimate. Nobody believed that the Fenians would be so foolhardy as to attempt an invasion of Canada; but Yates held that if they did they would give the Canadians more trouble than was expected.

"Oh, we'll turn old Bartlett on them, if they come over here. They'll be glad enough to get back if he tackles them."

"With his tongue," added another.

"By the way," said the whittler, "did young Bartlett say he was coming to-night? I hope he'll bring his sister if he does. Didn't any of you fellows ask him to bring her? He'd never think of it if he wasn't told. He has no consideration for the rest of us."

"Why didn't you ask him? I hear you have taken to going in that direction yourself."

"Who? Me?" asked the whittler, quite unconcerned. "I have no chance in that quarter, especially when the old man's around."

There was a sound of singing from the schoolhouse. The double doors were wide open, and as the light streamed out the people began to stream in.

"Where's Macdonald?" asked Yates.

"Oh, I guess he's taken to the woods. He washes his face, and then he hides. He has the sense to wash his face first, for he knows he will have to come. You'll see him back before they start the second hymn."

"Well, boys!" said one, getting down from the fence and stretching his arms above his head with a yawn, "I guess, if we're going in, it's about time."

One after another they got down from the fence, the whittler shutting his knife with a reluctant snap, and putting it in his pocket with evident regret. The schoolhouse, large as it was, was filled to its utmost capacity— women on one side of the room, and men on the other; although near the door there was no such division, all the occupants of the back benches being men and boys. The congregation was standing, singing a hymn, when Yates and his comrades entered, so their quiet incoming was not noticed. The teacher's desk had been moved from the platform on which it usually stood, and now occupied a corner on the men's side of the house. It was used as a seat by two or three, who wished to be near the front, and at the same time keep an eye on the rest of the assemblage. The local preacher stood on the edge of the platform, beating time gently with his hymn book, but not singing, as he had neither voice nor ear for music, and happily recognized the fact. The singing was led by a man in the middle of the room.

At the back of the platform, near the wall, were two chairs, on one of which sat the Rev. Mr. Benderson, who was to conduct the revival. He was a stout, powerful-looking man, but Yates could not see his face, for it was buried in his hands, his head being bowed in silent prayer. It was generally understood that he had spent a youth of fearful wickedness, and he always referred to himself as a brand snatched from the burning. It was even hinted that at one time he had been a card player, but no one knew this for a fact. Many of the local preachers had not the power of exhortation, therefore a man like the Rev. Mr. Benderson, who had that gift abnormally developed, was too valuable to be localized; so he spent the year going from place to place, sweeping, driving, coaxing, or frightening into the fold those stray sheep that hovered on the outskirts; once they were within the religious ring-fence the local minister was supposed to keep them there. The latter, who had given out the hymn, was a man of very different caliber. He was tall, pale, and thin, and his long black coat hung on him as if it were on a post. When the hymn was finished; and everyone sat down, Yates, and those with him, found seats as best they could at the end near the door. This was the portion of the hall where the scoffers assembled, but it was also the portion which yielded most fruit, if the revival happened to be a successful one. Yates, seeing the place so full, and noticing two empty benches up at the front, asked the whittler why they were not occupied.

"They'll be occupied pretty soon."

"Who are they being kept for?"

"Perhaps you, perhaps me, perhaps both of us. You never can tell. That's the penitents' bench."

The local preacher knelt on the platform, and offered up a prayer. He asked the Lord to bless the efforts of the brother who was with them there that night, and to crown his labors with success; through his instrumentality to call many wandering sinners home. There were cries of "Amen" and "Bless the Lord" from different parts of the hall as the prayer was being made. On rising, another hymn was given out:

"Joy to the world, the Lord is come.

Let earth receive her King."

The leader of the singing started it too low. The tune began high, and ran down to the bottom of the scale by the time it reached the end of the first line. When the congregation had got two-thirds of the way down, they found they could go no farther, not even those who sang bass. The leader, in some confusion, had to pitch the tune higher, and his miscalculation was looked upon as exceedingly funny by the reckless spirits at the back of the hall. The door opened quietly; and they all turned expecting to see Macdonald, but it was only Sandy. He had washed his face with but indifferent success, and the bulge in his cheek, like a wen, showed that he had not abandoned tobacco on entering the schoolhouse. He tiptoed to a place beside his friends.

"The old man's outside," he whispered to the youth who sat nearest him, holding his hand to the side of his mouth so that the sound would not travel. Catching sight of Yates, he winked at him in a friendly sort of way.

The hymn gathered volume and spirit as it went on, gradually recovering from the misadventure at starting. When it was finished, the preacher sat down beside the revivalist. His part of the work was done, as there was no formal introduction of speaker to audience to be gone through. The other remained as he was with bowed head, for what appeared to be a long time.

A deep silence fell on all present. Even the whisperings among the scoffers ceased.

At last Mr. Benderson slowly raised his head, arose, and came to the front of the platform. He had a strong, masterful, clean-shaven face, with the heavy jaw of a stubborn man—a man not easily beaten. "Open the door," he said in a quiet voice.

In the last few meetings he had held he had found this an effective beginning. It was new to his present audience. Usually a knot of people stood outside, and if they were there, he made an appeal to them, through the open door, to enter. If no one was there, he had a lesson to impart, based on the silence and the darkness. In this instance it was hard to say which was the more surprised, the revivalist or the congregation. Sandy, being on his feet, stepped to the door, and threw it open. He was so astonished at what he saw that he slid behind the open door out of sight. Macdonald stood there, against the darkness beyond, in a crouching attitude, as if about to spring. He had evidently been trying to see what was going on through the keyhole; and, being taken unawares by the sudden opening of the door, had not had time to recover himself. No retreat was now possible. He stood up

207

with haggard face, like a man who has been on a spree, and, without a word, walked in. Those on the bench in front of Yates moved together a little closer, and the blacksmith sat down on the vacant space left at the outside. In his confusion he drew his hand across his brow, and snapped his fingers loudly in the silence. A few faces at the back wore a grin, and would have laughed had not Sandy, closing the door quietly, given them one menacing look which quelled their merriment. He was not going to have the "old man" made fun of in his extremity; and they all had respect enough for Sandy's fist not to run the risk of encountering it after the meeting was over. Macdonald himself was more to be dreaded in a fight; but the chances were that for the next two or three weeks, if the revival were a success, there would be no danger from that quarter. Sandy, however, was permanently among the unconverted, and therefore to be feared, as being always ready to stand up for his employer, either with voice or blow. The unexpected incident Mr. Benderson had witnessed suggested no remarks at the time, so, being a wise man, he said nothing. The congregation wondered how he had known Macdonald was at the door, and none more than Macdonald himself. It seemed to many that the revivalist had a gift of divination denied to themselves, and this belief left them in a frame of mind more than ever ready to profit by the discourse they were about to hear.

Mr. Benderson began in a low monotone, that nevertheless penetrated to every part of the room. He had a voice of peculiar quality, as sweet as the tones of a tenor, and as pleasant to hear as music; now and then there was a manly ring in it which thrilled his listeners. "A week ago to-night," he said, "at this very hour, I stood by the deathbed of one who is now among the blessed. It is four years since he found salvation, by the mercy of God, through the humble instrumentality of the least of his servants. It was my blessed privilege to see that young man—that boy almost—pledge his soul to Jesus. He was less than twenty when he gave himself to Christ, and his hopes of a long life were as strong as the hopes of the youngest here to-night. Yet he was struck down in the early flush of manhood—struck down almost without warning. When I heard of his brief illness, although knowing nothing of its seriousness, something urged me to go to him, and at once. When I reached the house, they told me that he had asked to see me, and that they had just

208

sent a messenger to the telegraph office with a dispatch for me. I said: 'God telegraphed to me.' They took me to the bedside of my young friend, whom I had last seen as hearty and strong as anyone here.'"

Mr. Benderson then, in a voice quivering with emotion, told the story of the deathbed scene. His language was simple and touching, and it was evident to the most callous auditor that he spoke from the heart, describing in pathetic words the scene he had witnessed. His unadorned eloquence went straight home to every listener, and many an eye dimmed as he put before them a graphic picture of the serenity attending the end of a well-spent life.

"As I came through among you to-night," he continued, "as you stood together in groups outside this building, I caught a chance expression that one of you uttered. A man was speaking of some neighbor who, at this busy season of the year, had been unable to get help. I think the one to whom this man was speaking had asked if the busy man were here, and the answer was: 'No; he has not a minute to call his own.' The phrase has haunted me since I heard it, less than an hour ago. 'Not a minute to call his own!' I thought of it as I sat before you. I thought of it as I rose to address you. I think of it now. Who has a minute to call his own?" The soft tones of the preacher's voice had given place to a ringing cry that echoed from the roof down on their heads. "Have you? Have I? Has any king, any prince, any president, any ruler over men, a minute or a moment he can call his own? Not one. Not one of all the teeming millions on this earth. The minutes that are past are yours. What use have you made of them? All your efforts, all your prayers, will not change the deeds done in any one of those minutes that are past, and those only are yours. The chiseled stone is not more fixed than are the deeds of the minutes that are past. Their record is for you or against you. But where now are those minutes of the future—those minutes that, from this time onward, you will be able to call your own when they are spent? They are in the hand of God—in his hand to give or to withhold. And who can count them in the hand of God? Not you, not I, not the wisest man upon the earth. Man may number the miles from here to the farthest visible star; but he cannot tell you,—you; I don't mean your neighbor, I mean you,—he cannot tell YOU whether your minutes are to be one or a thousand. They are doled out to you, and you are responsible for them. But there will come a moment,—it may be to-night, it may be a year hence,—when the hand of God will close, and you will have had your sum. Then time will end for you, and eternity begin. Are you prepared for that awful moment—that moment when the last is given you, and the next withheld? What if it came now? Are you prepared for it? Are you ready to welcome it, as did our brother who died at this hour one short week ago? His was not the only deathbed I have attended. Some scenes have been so seared into my brain that I can never forget them. A year ago I was called to the bedside of a dying man, old in years and old in sin. Often had he been called, but he put Christ away from him, saying: 'At a more convenient season.' He knew the path, but he walked not therein. And when at last God's patience ended, and this man was stricken down, he, foolish to the last, called for me, the servant, instead of to God, the Master. When I reached his side, the stamp of death was on his face. The biting finger of agony had drawn lines upon his haggard brow. A great fear was upon him, and he gripped my hand with the cold grasp of death itself. In that darkened room it seemed to me I saw the angel of peace standing by the bed, but it stood aloof, as one often offended. It seemed to me at the head of the bed the demon of eternal darkness bent over, whispering to him: 'It is too late! it is too late!' The dying man looked at me—oh, such a look! May you never be called upon to witness its like. He gasped: 'I have lived—I have lived a sinful life. Is it too late?' 'No,' I said, trembling. 'Say you believe.' His lips moved, but no sound came. He died as he had lived. The one necessary minute was withheld. Do you hear? It—was—withheld! He had not the minute to call his own. Not that minute in which to turn from everlasting damnation. He—went—down—into—hell, dying as he had lived."

The preacher's voice rose until it sounded like a trumpet blast. His eyes shone, and his face flushed with the fervor of his theme. Then followed, as rapidly as words could utter, a lurid, awful picture of hell and the day of judgment. Sobs and groans were heard in every part of the room. "Come—now—now!" he cried, "Now is the appointed time, now is the day of salvation. Come now; and as you rise pray God that in his mercy he may spare you strength and life to reach the penitent bench."

Suddenly the preacher ceased talking. Stretching out his hands, he broke

210

forth, with his splendid tenor voice, into the rousing hymn, with its spirited marching time:

[Musical score: Come ye sinners, poor and needy,

Weak and wounded, sick and sore;

Jesus ready stands to save you.

Full of pity, love, and power.]

The whole congregation joined him. Everyone knew the words and the tune. It seemed a relief to the pent-up feelings to sing at the top of the voice. The chorus rose like a triumphal march:

[Musical score: Turn to the Lord, and seek salvation,

Sound the praise of His dear name;

Glory, honour, and salvation,

Christ the Lord has come to reign.]

As the congregation sang the preacher in stentorian tones urged sinners to seek the Lord while he was yet to be found.

Yates felt the electric thrill in the air, and he tugged at his collar, as if he were choking. He could not understand the strange exaltation that had come over him. It seemed as if he must cry aloud. All those around him were much moved. There were now no scoffers at the back of the room. Most of them seemed frightened, and sat looking one at the other. It only needed a beginning, and the penitent bench would be crowded. Many eyes were turned on Macdonald. His face was livid, and great beads of perspiration stood on his brow. His strong hand clutched the back of the seat before him, and the muscles stood out on the portion of his arm that was bare. He stared like a hypnotized man at the preacher. His teeth were set, and he breathed hard, as would a man engaged in a struggle. At last the hand of the preacher seemed to be pointed directly at him. He rose tremblingly to his feet and staggered down the aisle, flinging himself on his knees, with his head on his arms, beside the penitent bench, groaning aloud.

"Bless the Lord!" cried the preacher.

It was the starting of the avalanche. Up the aisle, with pale faces, many with tears streaming from their eyes, walked the young men and the old. Mothers, with joy in their hearts and a prayer on their lips, saw their sons fall prostrate before the penitent bench. Soon the contrite had to kneel wherever they could. The ringing salvation march filled the air, mingled with cries of joy and devout ejaculations.

"God!" cried Yates, tearing off his collar, "what is the matter with me? I never felt like this before. I must get into the open air."

He made for the door, and escaped unnoticed in the excitement of the moment. He stood for a time by the fence outside, breathing deeply of the cool, sweet air. The sound of the hymn came faintly to him. He clutched the fence, fearing he was about to faint. Partially recovering himself at last, he ran with all his might up the road, while there rang in his ears the marching words:

> [Musical score: Turn to the Lord, and seek salvation,
>
> Sound the praise of His dear Name.
>
> Glory, honour and salvation,
>
> Christ the Lord has come to reign.]

CHAPTER XIV.

When people are thrown together, especially when they are young, the mutual relationship existing between them rarely remains stationary. It drifts toward like or dislike; and cases have been known where it progressed into love or hatred.

Stillson Renmark and Margaret Howard became at least very firm friends. Each of them would have been ready to admit this much. These two had a good foundation on which to build up an acquaintance in the fact that Margaret's brother was a student in the university of which the professor was a worthy member. They had also a subject of difference, which, if it leads not to heated argument, but is soberly discussed, lends itself even more to the building of friendship than subjects of agreement. Margaret held, as has been indicated in a previous chapter, that the university was wrong in closing its doors to women. Renmark, up to the time of their first conversation on the subject, had given the matter but little thought; yet he developed an opinion contrary to that of Margaret, and was too honest a man, or too little of a diplomatist, to conceal it. On one occasion Yates had been present, and he threw himself, with the energy that distinguished him, into the woman side of the question—cordially agreeing with Margaret, citing instances, and holding those who were against the admission of women up to ridicule, taunting them with fear of feminine competition. Margaret became silent as the champion of her cause waxed the more eloquent; but whether she liked Richard Yates the better for his championship who that is not versed in the ways of women can say? As the hope of winning her regard was the sole basis of Yates' uncompromising views on the subject, it is likely that he was successful, for his experiences with the sex were large and varied. Margaret was certainly attracted toward Renmark, whose deep scholarship even his excessive self-depreciation could not entirely conceal; and he, in turn, had naturally a schoolmaster's enthusiasm over a pupil who so earnestly desired advancement in knowledge. Had he described his feelings to Yates, who was an expert in many matters, he would perhaps have learned that he was in love;

but Renmark was a reticent man, not much given either to introspection or to being lavish with his confidences. As to Margaret, who can plummet the depth of a young girl's regard until she herself gives some indication? All that one is able to record is that she was kinder to Yates than she had been at the beginning.

Miss Kitty Bartlett probably would not have denied that she had a sincere liking for the conceited young man from New York. Renmark fell into the error of thinking Miss Kitty a frivolous young person, whereas she was merely a girl who had an inexhaustible fund of high spirits, and one who took a most deplorable pleasure in shocking a serious man. Even Yates made a slight mistake regarding her on one occasion, when they were having an evening walk together, with that freedom from chaperonage which is the birthright of every American girl, whether she belongs to a farmhouse or to the palace of a millionaire.

In describing the incident afterward to Renmark, (for Yates had nothing of his comrade's reserve in these matters) he said:

"She left a diagram of her four fingers on my cheek that felt like one of those raised maps of Switzerland. I have before now felt the tap of a lady's fan in admonition, but never in my life have I met a gentle reproof that felt so much like a censure from the paw of our friend Tom Sayers."

Renmark said with some severity that he hoped Yates would not forget that he was, in a measure, a guest of his neighbors.

"Oh, that's all right," said Yates. "If you have any spare sympathy to bestow, keep it for me. My neighbors are amply able, and more than willing, to take care of themselves."

And now as to Richard Yates himself. One would imagine that here, at least, a conscientious relater of events would have an easy task. Alas! such is far from being the fact. The case of Yates was by all odds the most complex and bewildering of the four. He was deeply and truly in love with both of the girls. Instances of this kind are not so rare as a young man newly engaged to an innocent girl tries to make her believe. Cases have been known where a chance meeting with one girl, and not with another, has settled who was to be a young man's companion during a long life. Yates felt that in multitude of counsel there is wisdom, and made no secret of his perplexity to his friend. He complained sometimes that he got little help toward the solution of the problem, but generally he was quite content to sit under the trees with Renmark and weigh the different advantages of each of the girls. He sometimes appealed to his friend, as a man with a mathematical turn of mind, possessing an education that extended far into conic sections and algebraic formulae, to balance up the lists, and give him a candid and statistical opinion as to which of the two he should favor with serious proposals. When these appeals for help were coldly received, he accused his friend of lack of sympathy with his dilemma, said that he was a soulless man, and that if he had a heart it had become incrusted with the useless debris of a higher education, and swore to confide in him no more. He would search for a friend, he said, who had something human about him. The search for the sympathetic friend, however, seemed to be unsuccessful; for Yates always returned to Renmark, to have, as he remarked, ice water dashed upon his duplex-burning passion.

It was a lovely afternoon in the latter part of May, 1866, and Yates was swinging idly in the hammock, with his hands clasped under his head, gazing dreamily up at the patches of blue sky seen through the green branches of the trees overhead, while his industrious friend was unromantically peeling potatoes near the door of the tent.

"The human heart, Renny," said the man in the hammock reflectively, "is a remarkable organ, when you come to think of it. I presume, from your lack of interest, that you haven't given the subject much study, except, perhaps, in a physiological way. At the present moment it is to me the only theme worthy of a man's entire attention. Perhaps that is the result of spring, as the poet says; but, anyhow, it presents new aspects to me each hour. Now, I have made this important discovery: that the girl I am with last seems to me the most desirable. That is contrary to the observation of philosophers of bygone days. Absence makes the heart grow fonder, they say. I don't find it so. Presence is what plays the very deuce with me. Now, how do you account for it, Stilly?"

The professor did not attempt to account for it, but silently attended to the business in hand. Yates withdrew his eyes from the sky, and fixed them on the professor, waiting for the answer that did not come.

"Mr. Renmark," he drawled at last, "I am convinced that your treatment of the potato is a mistake. I think potatoes should not be peeled the day before, and left to soak in cold water until to-morrow's dinner. Of course I admire the industry that gets work well over before its results are called for. Nothing is more annoying than work left untouched until the last moment, and then hurriedly done. Still, virtue may be carried to excess, and a man may be too previous."

"Well, I am quite willing to relinquish the work into your hands. You may perhaps remember that for two days I have been doing your share as well as my own."

"Oh, I am not complaining about that, at all," said the hammock magnanimously. "You are acquiring practical knowledge, Renny, that will be of more use to you than all the learning taught at the schools. My only desire is that your education should be as complete as possible, and to this end I am willing to subordinate my own yearning desire for scullery work. I should suggest that, instead of going to the trouble of entirely removing the covering of the potato in that laborious way, you should merely peel a belt around its greatest circumference. Then, rather than cook the potatoes in the slow and soggy manner that seems to delight you, you should boil them quickly, with some salt placed in the water. The remaining coat would then curl outward, and the resulting potato would be white and dry and mealy, instead of being in the condition of a wet sponge."

"The beauty of a precept, Yates, is the illustrating of it. If you are not satisfied with my way of boiling potatoes, give me a practical object lesson."

The man in the hammock sighed reproachfully.

"Of course an unimaginative person like you, Renmark, cannot realize the cruelty of suggesting that a man as deeply in love as I am should demean himself by attending to the prosaic details of household affairs. I am doubly in love, and much more, therefore, as that old bore Euclid used to say, is your suggestion unkind and uncalled for."

"All right, then; don't criticise."

"Yes, there is a certain sweet reasonableness in your curt suggestion. A man who is unable, or unwilling, to work in the vineyard should not find fault with the pickers. And now, Renny, for the hundredth time of asking, add to the many obligations already conferred, and tell me, like the good fellow you are, what you would do if you were in my place. To which of those two charming, but totally unlike, girls would you give the preference?"

"Damn!" said the professor quietly.

"Hello, Renny!" cried Yates, raising his head. "Have you cut your finger? I should have warned you about using too sharp a knife."

But the professor had not cut his finger. His use of the word given above is not to be defended; still, as it was spoken by him, it seemed to lose all relationship with swearing. He said it quietly, mildly, and, in a certain sense, innocently. He was astonished at himself for using it, but there had been moments during the past few days when the ordinary expletives used in the learned volumes of higher mathematics did not fit the occasion.

Before anything more could be said there was a shout from the roadway near them.

"Is Richard Yates there?" hailed the voice.

"Yes. Who wants him?" cried Yates, springing out of the hammock.

"I do," said a young fellow on horseback. He threw himself off a tired horse, tied the animal to a sapling,—which, judging by the horse's condition, was an entirely unnecessary operation,—jumped over the rail fence, and approached through the woods. The young men saw, coming toward them, a tall lad in the uniform of the telegraph service.

"I'm Yates. What is it?"

"Well," said the lad, "I've had a hunt and a half for you. Here's a telegram."

217

"How in the world did you find out where I was? Nobody has my address."

"That's just the trouble. It would have saved somebody in New York a pile of money if you had left it. No man ought to go to the woods without leaving his address at a telegraph office, anyhow." The young man looked at the world from a telegraph point of view. People were good or bad according to the trouble they gave a telegraph messenger. Yates took the yellow envelope, addressed in lead pencil, but, without opening it, repeated his question:

"But how on earth did you find me?"

"Well, it wasn't easy;" said the boy. "My horse is about done out. I'm from Buffalo. They telegraphed from New York that we were to spare no expense; and we haven't. There are seven other fellows scouring the country on horseback with duplicates of that dispatch, and some more have gone along the lake shore on the American side. Say, no other messenger has been here before me, has he?" asked the boy with a touch of anxiety in his voice.

"No; you are the first."

"I'm glad of that. I've been 'most all over Canada. I got on your trail about two hours ago, and the folks at the farmhouse down below said you were up here. Is there any answer?"

Yates tore open the envelope. The dispatch was long, and he read it with a deepening frown. It was to this effect:

"Fenians crossing into Canada at Buffalo. You are near the spot; get there as quick as possible. Five of our men leave for Buffalo to-night. General O'Neill is in command of Fenian army. He will give you every facility when you tell him who you are. When five arrive, they will report to you. Place one or two with Canadian troops. Get one to hold the telegraph wire, and send over all the stuff the wire will carry. Draw on us for cash you need; and don't spare expense."

When Yates finished the reading of this, he broke forth into a line of language that astonished Renmark, and drew forth the envious admiration of the Buffalo telegraph boy.

"Heavens and earth and the lower regions! I'm here on my vacation. I'm not going to jump into work for all the papers in New York. Why couldn't those fools of Fenians stay at home? The idiots don't know when they're well off. The Fenians be hanged!"

"Guess that's what they will be," said the telegraph boy. "Any answer, sir?"

"No. Tell 'em you couldn't find me."

"Don't expect the boy to tell a lie," said the professor, speaking for the first time.

"Oh, I don't mind a lie!" exclaimed the boy, "but not that one. No, sir. I've had too much trouble finding you. I'm not going to pretend I'm no good. I started out for to find you, and I have. But I'll tell any other lie you like, Mr. Yates, if it will oblige you."

Yates recognized in the boy the same emulous desire to outstrip his fellows that had influenced himself when he was a young reporter, and he at once admitted the injustice of attempting to deprive him of the fruits of his enterprise.

"No," he said, "that won't do. No; you have found me, and you're a young fellow who will be president of the telegraph company some day, or perhaps hold the less important office of the United States presidency. Who knows? Have you a telegraph blank?"

"Of course," said the boy, fishing out a bundle from the leathern wallet by his side. Yates took the paper, and flung himself down under the tree.

"Here's a pencil," said the messenger.

"A newspaper man is never without a pencil, thank you," replied Yates, taking one out of his inside pocket. "Now, Renmark, I'm not going to tell a lie on this occasion," he continued.

"I think the truth is better on all occasions."

"Right you are. So here goes for the solid truth."

Yates, as he lay on the ground, wrote rapidly on the telegraph blank. Suddenly he looked up and said to the professor: "Say, Renmark, are you a doctor?"

"Of laws," replied his friend.

"Oh, that will do just as well." And he finished his writing.

"How is this?" he cried, holding the paper at arm's length:

"L. F. SPENCER,

"Managing Editor 'Argus,' New York:

"I'm flat on my back. Haven't done a hand's turn for a week. Am under the constant care, night and day, of one of the most eminent doctors in Canada, who even prepares my food for me. Since leaving New York trouble of the heart has complicated matters, and at present baffles the doctor. Consultations daily. It is impossible for me to move from here until present complications have yielded to treatment.

"Simson would be a good man to take charge in my absence."

"YATES.

"There," said Yates, with a tone of satisfaction, when he had finished the reading. "What do you think of that?"

The professor frowned, but did not answer. The boy, who partly saw through it, but not quite, grinned, and said: "Is it true?"

"Of course it's true!" cried Yates, indignant at the unjust suspicion. "It is a great deal more true than you have any idea of. Ask the doctor, there, if it isn't true. Now, my boy, will you give this in when you get back to the office? Tell 'em to rush it through to New York. I would mark it 'rush' only that never does any good, and always makes the operator mad."

The boy took the paper, and put it in his wallet.

"It's to be paid for at the other end," continued Yates.

"Oh, that's all right," answered the messenger with a certain condescension, as if he were giving credit on behalf of the company. "Well, so long," he added. "I hope you'll soon be better, Mr. Yates."

Yates sprang to his feet with a laugh, and followed him to the fence.

"Now, youngster, you are up to snuff, I can see that. They'll perhaps question you when you get back. What will you say?"

"Oh, I'll tell 'em what a hard job I had to find you, and let 'em know nobody else could 'a' done it, and I'll say you're a pretty sick man. I won't tell 'em you gave me a dollar!"

"Right you are, sonny; you'll get along. Here's five dollars, all in one bill. If you meet any other of the messengers, take them back with you. There's no use of their wasting valuable time in this little neck of the woods."

The boy stuffed the bill into his vest pocket as carelessly as if it represented cents instead of dollars, mounted his tired horse, and waved his hand in farewell to the newspaper man. Yates turned and walked slowly back to the tent. He threw himself once more into the hammock. As he expected, the professor was more taciturn than ever, and, although he had been prepared for silence, the silence irritated him. He felt ill used at having so unsympathetic a companion.

"Look here, Renmark; why don't you say something?"

"There is nothing to say."

"Oh, yes, there is. You don't approve of me, do you?"

"I don't suppose it makes any difference whether I approve or not."

"Oh, yes, it does. A man likes to have the approval of even the humblest of his fellow-creatures. Say, what will you take in cash to approve of me? People talk of the tortures of conscience, but you are more uncomfortable than the most cast-iron conscience any man ever had. One's own conscience one can deal with, but a conscience in the person of another man is beyond one's control. Now, it is like this: I am here for quiet and rest. I have earned both, and I think I am justified in——"

"Now, Mr. Yates, please spare me any cheap philosophy on the question. I am tired of it."

"And of me, too, I suppose?"

"Well, yes, rather—if you want to know."

Yates sprang out of the hammock. For the first time since the encounter with Bartlett on the road Renmark saw that he was thoroughly angry. The reporter stood with clenched fists and flashing eyes, hesitating. The other, his heavy brows drawn, while not in an aggressive attitude, was plainly ready for an attack. Yates concluded to speak, and not to strike. This was not because he was afraid, for he was not a coward. The reporter realized that he had forced the conversation, and remembered he had invited Renmark to accompany him. Although this recollection stayed his hand, it had no effect on his tongue.

"I believe," he said slowly, "that it would do you good for once to hear a straight, square, unbiased opinion of yourself. You have associated so long with pupils, to whom your word is law, that it may interest you to know what a man of the world thinks of you. A few years of schoolmastering is enough to spoil an archangel. Now, I think, of all the——"

The sentence was interrupted by a cry from the fence:

"Say, do you gentlemen know where a fellow named Yates lives?"

The reporter's hand dropped to his side. A look of dismay came over his face, and his truculent manner changed with a suddenness that forced a smile even to the stern lips of Renmark.

Yates backed toward the hammock like a man who had received an unexpected blow.

"I say, Renny," he wailed, "it's another of those cursed telegraph messengers. Go, like a good fellow, and sign for the dispatch. Sign it 'Dr. Renmark, for R. Yates.' That will give it a sort of official, medical-bulletin look. I wish I had thought of that when the other boy was here. Tell him

222

I'm lying down." He flung himself into the hammock, and Renmark, after a moment's hesitation, walked toward the boy at the fence, who had repeated his question in a louder voice. In a short time he returned with the yellow envelope, which he tossed to the man in the hammock. Yates seized it savagely, tore it into a score of pieces, and scattered the fluttering bits around him on the ground. The professor stood there for a few moments in silence.

"Perhaps," he said at last, "you'll be good enough to go on with your remarks."

"I was merely going to say," answered Yates wearily, "that you are a mighty good fellow, Renny. People who camp out always have rows. That is our first; suppose we let it be the last. Camping out is something like married life, I guess, and requires some forbearance on both sides. That philosophy may be cheap, but I think it is accurate. I am really very much worried about this newspaper business. I ought, of course, to fling myself into the chasm like that Roman fellow; but, hang it! I've been flinging myself into chasms for fifteen years, and what good has it done? There's always a crisis in a daily newspaper office. I want them to understand in the Argus office that I am on my vacation."

"They will be more apt to understand from the telegram that you're on your deathbed."

Yates laughed. "That's so," he said; "but, you see, Renny, we New Yorkers live in such an atmosphere of exaggeration that if I did not put it strongly it wouldn't have any effect. You've got to give a big dose to a man who has been taking poison all his life. They will take off ninety per cent. from any statement I make, anyhow; so, you see, I have to pile it up pretty high before the remaining ten per cent. amounts to anything."

The conversation was interrupted by the crackling of the dry twigs behind them, and Yates, who had been keeping his eye nervously on the fence, turned round. Young Bartlett pushed his way through the underbrush. His face was red; he had evidently been running.

"Two telegrams for you, Mr. Yates," he panted. "The fellows that brought 'em said they were important; so I ran out with them myself, for fear they wouldn't find you. One of them's from Port Colborne, the other's from Buffalo."

Telegrams were rare on the farm, and young Bartlett looked on the receipt of one as an event in a man's life. He was astonished to see Yates receive the double event with a listlessness that he could not help thinking was merely assumed for effect. Yates held them in his hand, and did not tear them up at once out of consideration for the feelings of the young man, who had had a race to deliver them.

"Here's two books they wanted you to sign. They're tired out, and mother's giving them something to eat."

"Professor, you sign for me, won't you?" said Yates.

Bartlett lingered a moment, hoping that he would hear something of the contents of the important messages; but Yates did not even open the envelopes, although he thanked the young man heartily for bringing them.

"Stuck-up cuss!" muttered young Bartlett to himself, as he shoved the signed books into his pocket and pushed his way through the underbrush again. Yates slowly and methodically tore the envelopes and their contents into little pieces, and scattered them as before.

"Begins to look like autumn," he said, "with the yellow leaves strewing the ground."

224

CHAPTER XV.

Before night three more telegraph boys found Yates, and three more telegrams in sections helped to carpet the floor of the forest. The usually high spirits of the newspaper man went down and down under the repeated visitations. At last he did not even swear, which, in the case of Yates, always indicated extreme depression. As night drew on he feebly remarked to the professor that he was more tired than he had ever been in going through an election campaign. He went to his tent bunk early, in a state of such utter dejection that Renmark felt sorry for him, and tried ineffectually to cheer him up.

"If they would all come together," said Yates bitterly, "so that one comprehensive effort of malediction would include the lot and have it over, it wouldn't be so bad; but this constant dribbling in of messengers would wear out the patience of a saint."

As he sat in his shirt sleeves on the edge of his bunk Renmark said that things would look brighter in the morning—which was a safe remark to make, for the night was dark.

Yates sat silently, with his head in his hands, for some moments. At last he said slowly: "There is no one so obtuse as the thoroughly good man. It is not the messenger I am afraid of, after all. He is but the outward symptom of the inward trouble. What you are seeing is an example of the workings of conscience where you thought conscience was absent. The trouble with me is that I know the newspaper depends on me, and that it will be the first time I have failed. It is the newspaper man's instinct to be in the center of the fray. He yearns to scoop the opposition press. I will get a night's sleep if I can, and to-morrow, I know, I shall capitulate. I will hunt out General O'Neill, and interview him on the field of slaughter. I will telegraph pages. I will refurbish my military vocabulary, and speak of deploying and massing and throwing out advance guards, and that sort of thing. I will move detachments and advance brigades, and invent strategy. We will have desperate fighting in the columns of the Argus, whatever there is on the fields of Canada. But to a man who has seen real war this opéra-bouffe masquerade of fighting——I don't want to say anything harsh, but to me it is offensive."

He looked up with a wan smile at his partner, sitting on the bottom of an upturned pail, as he said this. Then he reached for his hip pocket and drew out a revolver, which he handed, butt-end forward, to the professor, who, not knowing his friend carried such an instrument, instinctively shrank from it.

"Here, Renny, take this weapon of devastation and soak it with the potatoes. If another messenger comes in on me to-night, I know I shall riddle him if I have this handy. My better judgment tells me he is innocent, and I don't want to shed the only blood that will be spilled during this awful campaign."

How long they had been asleep they did not know, as the ghost-stories have it, but both were suddenly awakened by a commotion outside. It was intensely dark inside the tent, but as the two sat up they noticed a faint moving blur of light, which made itself just visible through the canvas.

"It's another of those fiendish messengers," whispered Yates. "Gi' me that revolver."

"Hush!" said the other below his breath. "There's about a dozen men out there, judging by the footfalls. I heard them coming."

"Let's fire into the tent and be done with it," said a voice outside.

"No, no," cried another; "no man shoot. It makes too much noise, and there must be others about. Have ye all got yer bayonets fixed?"

There was a murmur, apparently in the affirmative.

"Very well, then. Murphy and O'Rourick, come round to this side. You three stay where you are. Tim, you go to that end; and, Doolin, come with me."

"The Fenian army, by all the gods!" whispered Yates, groping for his clothes. "Renny, give me that revolver, and I'll show you more fun than funeral."

"No, no. They're at least three to our one. We're in a trap here, and helpless."

"Oh, just let me jump out among 'em and begin the fireworks. Those I didn't shoot would die of fright. Imagine scouts scouring the woods with a lantern—with a lantern, Renny! Think of that! Oh, this is pie! Let me at 'em."

"Hush! Keep quiet! They'll hear you."

"Tim, bring the lantern round to this side." The blur of light moved along the canvas. "There's a man with his back against the wall of the tent. Just touch him up with your bayonet, Murphy, and let him know we're here."

"There may be twenty in the tent," said Murphy cautiously.

"Do what I tell you," answered the man in command.

Murphy progged his bayonet through the canvas, and sunk the deadly point of the instrument into the bag of potatoes.

"Faith, he sleeps sound," said Murphy with a tremor of fear in his voice, as there was no demonstration on the part of the bag.

The voice of Yates rang out from the interior of the tent:

"What the old Harry do you fellows think you're doing, anyhow? What's the matter with you? What do you want?"

There was a moment's silence, broken only by a nervous scuffling of feet and the clicking of gun-locks.

"How many are there of you in there?" said the stern voice of the chief.

"Two, if you want to know, both unarmed, and one ready to fight the lot of you if you are anxious for a scrimmage."

"Come out one by one," was the next command.

"We'll come out one by one," said Yates, emerging in his shirt sleeves, 'but you can't expect us to keep it up long, as there are only two of us."

The professor next appeared, with his coat on. The situation certainly did not look inviting. The lantern on the ground threw up a pallid glow on the severe face of the commander, as the footlights might illuminate the figure of a brigand in a wood on the stage. The face of the officer showed that he was greatly impressed with the importance and danger of his position. Yates glanced about him with a smile, all his recent dejection gone now that he was in the midst of a row.

"Which is Murphy," he said, "and which is Doolin? Hello, alderman!" he cried, as his eyes rested on one tall, strapping, red-haired man who held his bayonet ready to charge, with a fierce determination in his face that might have made an opponent quail. "When did you leave New York? and who's running the city now that you're gone?"

The men had evidently a sense of humor, in spite of their bloodthirsty business, for a smile flickered on their faces in the lantern light, and several bayonets were unconsciously lowered. But the hard face of the commander did not relax.

"You are doing yourself no good by your talk," he said solemnly. "What you say will be used against you."

"Yes, and what you do will be used against you; and don't forget that fact. It's you who are in danger—not I. You are, at this moment, making about the biggest ass of yourself there is in Canada."

"Pinion these men!" cried the captain gruffly.

"Pinion nothing!" shouted Yates, shaking off the grasp of a man who had sprung to his side. But both Yates and Renmark were speedily overpowered; and then an unseen difficulty presented itself. Murphy pathetically remarked that they had no rope. The captain was a man of resource.

"Cut enough rope from the tent to tie them."

"And when you're at it, Murphy," said Yates, "cut off enough more to hang yourself with. You'll need it before long. And remember that any damage you do to that tent you'll have to pay for. It's hired."

Yates gave them all the trouble he could while they tied his elbows and wrists together, offering sardonic suggestions and cursing their clumsiness. Renmark submitted quietly. When the operation was finished, the professor said with the calm confidence of one who has an empire behind him and knows it:

"I warn you, sir, that this outrage is committed on British soil; and that I, on whom it is committed, am a British subject."

"Heavens and earth, Renmark, if you find it impossible to keep your mouth shut, do not use the word 'subject' but 'citizen.'"

"I am satisfied with the word, and with the protection given to those who use it."

"Look here, Renmark; you had better let me do the talking. You will only put your foot in it. I know the kind of men I have to deal with; you evidently don't."

In tying the professor they came upon the pistol in his coat pocket. Murphy held it up to the light.

"I thought you said you were unarmed?" remarked the captain severely, taking the revolver in his hand.

"I was unarmed. The revolver is mine, but the professor would not let me use it. If he had, all of you would be running for dear life through the woods."

"You admit that you are a British subject?" said the captain to Renmark, ignoring Yates.

"He doesn't admit it, he brags of it," said the latter before Renmark could speak. "You can't scare him; so quit this fooling, and let us know how long we are to stand here trussed up like this."

"I propose, captain," said the red-headed man, "that we shoot these men where they stand, and report to the general. They are spies. They are armed, and they denied it. It's according to the rules of war, captain."

"Rules of war? What do you know of the rules of war, you red-headed Senegambian? Rules of Hoyle! Your line is digging sewers, I imagine. Come, captain, undo these ropes, and make up your mind quickly. Trot us along to General O'Neill just as fast as you can. The sooner you get us there the more time you will have for being sorry over what you have done."

The captain still hesitated, and looked from one to the other of his men, as if to make up his mind whether they would obey him if he went to extremities. Yates' quick eye noted that the two prisoners had nothing to hope for, even from the men who smiled. The shooting of two unarmed and bound men seemed to them about the correct way of beginning a great struggle for freedom.

"Well," said the captain at length, "we must do it in proper form, so I suppose we should have a court-martial. Are you agreed?"

They were unanimously agreed.

"Look here," cried Yates, and there was a certain impressiveness in his voice in spite of his former levity; "this farce has gone just as far as it is going. Go inside the tent, there, and in my coat pocket you will find a telegram, the first of a dozen or two received by me within the last twenty-four hours. Then you will see whom you propose to shoot."

The telegram was found, and the captain read it, while Tim held the lantern. He looked from under his knitted brows at the newspaper man.

"Then you are one of the Argus staff."

"I am chief of the Argus staff. As you see, five of my men will be with General O'Neill to-morrow. The first question they will ask him will be: 'Where is Yates?' The next thing that will happen will be that you will be hanged for your stupidity, not by Canada nor by the State of New York, but by your general, who will curse your memory ever after. You are fooling not with a subject this time, but with a citizen; and your general is not such an idiot as to monkey with the United States Government; and, what is a blamed sight worse, with the great American press. Come, captain, we've had enough of this. Cut these cords just as quickly as you can, and take us to the general. We were going to see him in the morning, anyhow."

230

"But this man says he is a Canadian."

"That's all right. My friend is me. If you touch him, you touch me. Now, hurry up, climb down from your perch. I shall have enough trouble now, getting the general to forgive all the blunders you have made to-night, without your adding insult to injury. Tell your men to untie us, and throw the ropes back into the tent. It will soon be daylight. Hustle, and let us be off."

"Untie them," said the captain, with a sigh.

Yates shook himself when his arms regained their freedom.

"Now, Tim," he said, "run into that tent and bring out my coat. It's chilly here."

Tim did instantly as requested, and helped Yates on with the coat.

"Good boy!" said, Yates. "You've evidently been porter in a hotel."

Tim grinned.

"I think," said Yates meditatively, "that if I you look under the right-hand bunk, Tim, you will find a jug. It belongs to the professor, although he has hidden it under my bed to divert suspicion from himself. Just fish it out and bring it here. It is not as full as it was, but there's enough to go round, if the professor does not take more than his share."

The gallant troop smacked their lips in anticipation, and Renmark looked astonished to see the jar brought forth. "You first, professor," said Yates; and Tim innocently offered him the vessel. The learned man shook his head. Yates laughed, and took it himself.

"Well, here's to you, boys," he said. "And may you all get back as safely to New York as I will." The jar passed down along the line, until Tim finished its contents.

"Now, then, for the camp of the Fenian army," cried Yates, taking Renmark's arm; and they began their march through the woods. "Great Caesar! Stilly," he continued to his friend, "this is rest and quiet with a vengeance, isn't it?"

CHAPTER XVI.

The Fenians, feeling that they had to put their best foot foremost in the presence of their prisoners, tried at first to maintain something like military order in marching through the woods. They soon found, however, that this was a difficult thing to do. Canadian forests are not as trimly kept as English parks. Tim walked on ahead with the lantern, but three times he tumbled over some obstruction, and disappeared suddenly from view, uttering maledictions. His final effort in this line was a triumph. He fell over the lantern and smashed it. When all attempts at reconstruction failed, the party tramped on in go-as-you-please fashion, and found they did better without the light than with it. In fact, although it was not yet four o'clock, daybreak was already filtering through the trees, and the woods were perceptibly lighter.

"We must be getting near the camp," said the captain.

"Will I shout, sir?" asked Murphy.

"No, no; we can't miss it. Keep on as you are doing."

They were nearer the camp than they suspected. As they blundered on among the crackling underbrush and dry twigs the sharp report of a rifle echoed through the forest, and a bullet whistled above their heads.

"Fat the divil are you foiring at, Mike Lynch?" cried the alderman, who recognized the shooter, now rapidly falling back.

"Oh, it's you, is it?" said the sentry, stopping in his flight. The captain strode angrily toward him.

"What do you mean by firing like that? Don't you know enough to ask for the counter-sign before shooting?"

"Sure, I forgot about it, captain, entirely. But, then, ye see, I never car hit anything; so it's little difference it makes."

The shot had roused the camp, and there was now wild commotion everybody thinking the Canadians were upon them.

A strange sight met the eye of Yates and Renmark. Both were astonished to see the number of men that O'Neill had under his command. They found a motley crowd. Some tattered United States uniforms were among them, but the greater number were dressed as ordinary individuals, although a few had trimmings of green braid on their clothes. Sleeping out for a couple of nights had given the gathering the unkempt appearance of a great company of tramps. The officers were indistinguishable from the men at first, but afterward Yates noticed that they, mostly in plain clothes and slouch hats, had sword belts buckled around them; and one or two had swords that had evidently seen service in the United States cavalry.

"It's all right, boys," cried the captain to the excited mob. "It was only that fool Lynch who fired at us. There's nobody hurt. Where's the general?"

"Here he comes," said half a dozen voices at once, and the crowd made way for him.

General O'Neill was dressed in ordinary citizen's costume, and did not wear even a sword belt. On his head of light hair was a black soft felt hat. His face was pale, and covered with freckles. He looked more like a clerk from a grocery store than the commander of an army. He was evidently somewhere between thirty-five and forty years of age.

"Oh, it's you, is it?" he said. "Why are you back? Any news?"

The captain saluted, military fashion, and replied:

"We took two prisoners, sir. They were encamped in a tent in the woods. One of them says he is an American citizen, and says he knows you, so I brought them in."

"I wish you had brought in the tent, too," said the general with a wan smile. "It would be an improvement on sleeping in the open air. Are these the prisoners? I don't know either of them."

"The captain makes a mistake in saying that I claimed a personal acquaintance with you, general. What I said was that you would recognize, somewhat quicker than he did, who I was, and the desirability of treating me with reasonable decency. Just show the general that telegram you took from my coat pocket, captain."

The paper was produced, and O'Neill read it over once or twice.

"You are on the New York Argus, then?"

"Very much so, general."

"I hope you have not been roughly used?"

"Oh, no; merely tied up in a hard knot, and threatened with shooting—that's all."

"Oh, I'm sorry to hear that. Still, you must make some allowance at a time like this. If you will come with me, I will write you a pass which will prevent any similar mistake happening in the future." The general led the way to a smoldering camp fire, where, out of a valise, he took writing materials and, using the valise as a desk, began to write. After he had written "Headquarters of the Grand Army of the Irish Republic" he looked up, and asked Yates his Christian name. Being answered, he inquired the name of his friend.

"I want nothing from you," interposed Renmark. "Don't put my name on the paper."

"Oh, that's all right," said Yates. "Never mind him, general. He's a learned man who doesn't know when to talk and when not to. As you march up to our tent, general, you will see an empty jug, which will explain everything. Renmark's drunk, not to put too fine a point upon it; and he imagines himself a British subject."

The Fenian general looked up at the professor.

"Are you a Canadian?" he asked.

"Certainly I am."

"Well, in that case, if I let you leave camp, you must give me your word that, should you fall in with the enemy, you will give no information to them of our position, numbers, or of anything else you may have seen while with us."

"I shall not give my word. On the contrary, if I should fall in with the Canadian troops, I will tell them where you are, that you are from eight hundred to one thousand strong, and the worst looking set of vagabonds I have ever seen out of jail."

General O'Neill frowned, and looked from one to the other.

"Do you realize that you confess to being a spy, and that it becomes my duty to have you taken out and shot?"

"In real war, yes. But this is mere idiotic fooling. All of you that don't escape will be either in jail or shot before twenty-four hours."

"Well, by the gods, it won't help you any. I'll have you shot inside of ten minutes, instead of twenty-four hours."

"Hold on, general, hold on!" cried Yates, as the angry man rose and confronted the two. "I admit that he richly deserves shooting, if you were the fool killer, which you are not. But it won't do, I will be responsible for him. Just finish that pass for me, and I will take care of the professor. Shoot me if you like, but don't touch him. He hasn't any sense, as you can see; but I am not to blame for that, nor are you. If you take to shooting everybody who is an ass, general, you won't have any ammunition left with which to conquer Canada."

The general smiled in spite of himself, and resumed the writing of the pass. "There," he said, handing the paper to Yates. "You see, we always like to oblige the press. I will risk your belligerent friend, and I hope you will exercise more control over him, if you meet the Canadians, than you were able to exert here. Don't you think, on the whole, you had better stay with us? We are going to march in a couple of hours, when the men have had a little rest." He added in a lower voice, so that the professor could not hear: "You didn't see anything of the Canadians, I suppose?"

"Not a sign. No, I don't think I'll stay. There will be five of our fellows here some time to-day, I expect, and that will be more than enough. I'm really here on a vacation. Been ordered rest and quiet. I'm beginning to think I have made a mistake in location."

Yates bade good-by to the commander, and walked with his friend out of the camp. They threaded their way among sleeping men and groups of stacked guns. On the top of one of the bayonets was hung a tall silk hat, which looked most incongruous in such a place.

"I think," said Yates, "that we will make for the Ridge Road, which must lie somewhere in this direction. It will be easier walking than through the woods; and, besides, I want to stop at one of the farmhouses and get some breakfast. I'm as hungry as a bear after tramping so long."

"Very well," answered the professor shortly.

The two stumbled along until they reached the edge of the wood; then, crossing some open fields, they came presently upon the road, near the spot where the fist fight had taken place between Yates and Bartlett. The comrades, now with greater comfort, walked silently along the road toward the west, with the reddening east behind them. The whole scene was strangely quiet and peaceful, and the recollection of the weird camp they had left in the woods seemed merely a bad dream. The morning air was sweet, and the birds were beginning to sing. Yates had intended to give the professor a piece of his mind regarding the lack of tact and common sense displayed by Renmark in the camp, but, somehow, the scarcely awakened day did not lend itself to controversy, and the serene stillness soothed his spirit. He began to whistle softly that popular war song, "Tramp, tramp, tramp, the boys are marching," and then broke in with the question:

"Say, Renny, did you notice that plug hat on the bayonet?"

"Yes," answered the professor; "and I saw five others scattered around the camp."

"Jingo! you were observant. I can imagine nothing quite so ridiculous as a man going to war in a tall silk hat."

The professor made no reply, and Yates changed his whistling to "Rally round the flag."

"I presume," he said at length, "there is little use in attempting to improve the morning hour by trying to show you, Renmark, what a fool you made of yourself in the camp? Your natural diplomacy seemed to be slightly off the center."

"I do not hold diplomatic relations with thieves and vagabonds."

"They may be vagabonds; but so am I, for that matter. They may also be well-meaning, mistaken men; but I do not think they are thieves."

"While you were talking with the so-called general, one party came in with several horses that had been stolen from the neighboring farmers, and another party started out to get some more."

"Oh, that isn't stealing, Renmark; that's requisitioning. You mustn't use such reckless language. I imagine the second party has been successful; for here are three of them all mounted."

The three horsemen referred to stopped their steeds at the sight of the two men coming round the bend of the road, and awaited their approach. Like so many of the others, they wore no uniform, but two of them held revolvers in their hands ready for action. The one who had no visible revolver moved his horse up the middle of the road toward the pedestrians, the other two taking positions on each side of the wagon way.

"Who are you? Where do you come from, and where are you going?" cried the foremost horseman, as the two walkers came within talking distance.

"It's all right, commodore," said Yates jauntily, "and the top of the morning to you. We are hungry pedestrians. We have just come from the camp, and we are going to get something to eat."

"I must have a more satisfactory answer than that."

"Well, here you have it, then," answered Yates, pulling out his folded pass, and handing it up to the horseman. The man read it carefully. "You find that all right, I expect?"

"Right enough to cause your immediate arrest."

"But the general said we were not to be molested further. That is in his own handwriting."

"I presume it is, and all the worse for you. His handwriting does not run quite as far as the queen's writ in this country yet. I arrest you in the name of the queen. Cover these men with your revolvers, and shoot them down if they make any resistance." So saying, the rider slipped from his horse, whipped out of his pocket a pair of handcuffs joined by a short, stout steel chain, and, leaving his horse standing, grasped Renmark's wrist.

"I'm a Canadian," said the professor, wrenching his wrist away. "You mustn't put handcuffs on me."

"You are in very bad company, then. I am a constable of this county; if you are what you say, you will not resist arrest."

"I will go with you, but you mustn't handcuff me."

"Oh, mustn't I?" And, with a quick movement indicative of long practice with resisting criminals, the constable deftly slipped on one of the clasps, which closed with a sharp click and stuck like a burr.

Renmark became deadly pale, and there was a dangerous glitter in his eyes. He drew back his clinched fist, in spite of the fact that the cocked revolver was edging closer and closer to him, and the constable held his struggling manacled hand with grim determination.

"Hold on!" cried Yates, preventing the professor from striking the representative of the law. "Don't shoot," he shouted to the man on horseback; "it is all a little mistake that will be quickly put right. You are three armed and mounted men, and we are only two, unarmed and on foot. There is no need of any revolver practice. Now, Renmark, you are more of a rebel at the present moment than O'Neill. He owes no allegiance, and you do. Have you no respect for the forms of law and order? You are an anarchist at heart, for all your professions. You would sing 'God save the Queen!' in the wrong place a while ago, so now be satisfied that you have got her, or, rather, that she has go

238

you. Now, constable, do you want to hitch the other end of that arrangement on my wrist? or have you another pair for my own special use?

"I'll take your wrist, if you please."

"All right; here you are." Yates drew back his coat sleeve, and presented his wrist. The dangling cuff was speedily clamped upon it. The constable mounted the patient horse that stood waiting for him, watching him all the while with intelligent eye. The two prisoners, handcuffed together, took the middle of the road, with a horseman on each side of them, the constable bringing up the rear; thus they marched on, the professor gloomy from the indignity put upon them, and the newspaper man as joyous as the now thoroughly awakened birds. The scouts concluded to go no farther toward the enemy, but to return to the Canadian forces with their prisoners. They marched down the road, all silent except Yates, who enlivened the morning air with the singing of "John Brown."

"Keep quiet," said the constable curtly.

"All right, I will. But look here; we shall pass shortly the house of a friend. We want to go and get something to eat."

"You will get nothing to eat until I deliver you up to the officers of the volunteers."

"And where, may I ask, are they?"

"You may ask, but I will not answer."

"Now, Renmark," said Yates to his companion, "the tough part of this episode is that we shall have to pass Bartlett's house, and feast merely on the remembrance of the good things which Mrs. Bartlett is always glad to bestow on the wayfarer. I call that refined cruelty."

As they neared the Bartlett homestead they caught sight of Miss Kitty on the veranda, shading her eyes from the rising sun, and gazing earnestly at the approaching squad. As soon as she recognized the group she disappeared, with a cry, into the house. Presently there came out Mrs. Bartlett, followed by her son, and more slowly by the old man himself.

They all came down to the gate and waited.

"Hello, Mrs. Bartlett!" cried Yates cheerily. "You see, the professor has got his desserts at last; and I, being in bad company, share his fate, like the good dog Tray."

"What's all this about?" cried Mrs. Bartlett.

The constable, who knew both the farmer and his wife, nodded familiarly to them. "They're Fenian prisoners," he said.

"Nonsense!" cried Mrs. Bartlett—the old man, as usual, keeping his mouth grimly shut when his wife was present to do the talking—"they're not Fenians. They've been camping on our farm for a week or more."

"That may be," said the constable firmly, "but I have the best of evidence against them; and, if I'm not very much mistaken, they'll hang for it."

Miss Kitty, who had been partly visible through the door, gave a cry of anguish at this remark, and disappeared again.

"We have just escaped being hanged by the Fenians themselves, Mrs. Bartlett, and I hope the same fate awaits us at the hands of the Canadians."

"What! hanging?"

"No, no; just escaping. Not that I object to being hanged,—I hope I am not so pernickety as all that,—but, Mrs. Bartlett, you will sympathize with me when I tell you that the torture I am suffering from at this moment is the remembrance of the good things to eat which I have had in your house. I am simply starved to death, Mrs. Bartlett, and this hard-hearted constable refuses to allow me to ask you for anything."

Mrs. Bartlett came out through the gate to the road in a visible state of indignation.

"Stoliker," she exclaimed, "I'm ashamed of you! You may hang a man if you like, but you have no right to starve him. Come straight in with me," she said to the prisoners.

"Madam," said Stoliker severely, "you must not interfere with the course of the law."

"The course of stuff and nonsense!" cried the angry woman. "Do you think I am afraid of you, Sam Stoliker? Haven't I chased you out of this very orchard when you were a boy trying to steal my apples? Yes, and boxed your ears, too, when I caught you, and then was fool enough to fill your pockets with the best apples on the place, after giving you what you deserved. Course of the law, indeed! I'll box your ears now if you say anything more. Get down off your horse, and have something to eat yourself. I dare say you need it."

"This is what I call a rescue," whispered Yates to his linked companion.

What is a stern upholder of the law to do when the interferer with justice is a determined and angry woman accustomed to having her own way? Stoliker looked helplessly at Hiram, as the supposed head of the house, but the old man merely shrugged his shoulders, as much as to say: "You see how it is yourself. I am helpless."

Mrs. Bartlett marched her prisoners through the gate and up to the house.

"All I ask of you now," said Yates, "is that you will give Renmark and me seats together at the table. We cannot bear to be separated, even for an instant."

Having delivered her prisoners to the custody of her daughter, at the same time admonishing her to get breakfast as quickly as possible, Mrs. Bartlett went to the gate again. The constable was still on his horse. Hiram had asked, by way of treating him to a noncontroversial subject, if this was the colt he had bought from old Brown, on the second concession, and Stoliker had replied that it was. Hiram was saying he thought he recognized the horse by his sire when Mrs. Bartlett broke in upon them.

"Come, Sam," she said, "no sulking, you know. Slip off the horse and come in. How's your mother?"

"She's pretty well, thank you," said Sam sheepishly, coming down on his feet again.

Kitty Bartlett, her gayety gone and her eyes red, waited on the prisoners, but absolutely refused to serve Sam Stoliker, on whom she looked with the utmost contempt, not taking into account the fact that the poor young man had been merely doing his duty, and doing it well.

"Take off these handcuffs, Sam," said Mrs. Bartlett, "until they have breakfast, at least."

Stoliker produced a key and unlocked the manacles, slipping them into his pocket.

"Ah, now!" said Yates, looking at his red wrist, "we can breathe easier; and I, for one, can eat more."

The professor said nothing. The iron had not only encircled his wrist, but had entered his soul as well. Although Yates tried to make the early meal as cheerful as possible, it was rather a gloomy festival. Stoliker began to feel, poor man, that the paths of duty were unpopular. Old Hiram could always be depended upon to add somberness and taciturnity to a wedding feast; the professor, never the liveliest of companions, sat silent, with clouded brow, and vexed even the cheerful Mrs. Bartlett by having evidently no appetite. When the hurried meal was over, Yates, noticing that Miss Kitty had left the room, sprang up and walked toward the kitchen door. Stoliker was on his feet in an instant, and made as though to follow him.

"Sit down," said the professor sharply, speaking for the first time. "He is not going to escape. Don't be afraid. He has done nothing, and has no fear of punishment. It is always the innocent that you stupid officials arrest. The woods all around you are full of real Fenians, but you take excellent care to keep out of their way, and give your attention to molesting perfectly inoffensive people."

"Good for you, professor!" cried Mrs. Bartlett emphatically. "That's the truth, if ever it was spoken. But are there Fenians in the woods?"

"Hundreds of them. They came on us in the tent about three o'clock this morning,—or at least an advance guard did,—and after talking of shooting us where we stood they marched us to the Fenian camp instead. Yates got a

242

pass, written by the Fenian general, so that we should not be troubled again. That is the precious document which this man thinks is deadly evidence. He never asked us a question, but clapped the handcuffs on our wrists, while the other fools held pistols to our heads."

"It isn't my place to ask questions," retorted Stoliker doggedly. "You can tell all this to the colonel or the sheriff; if they let you go, I'll say nothing against it."

Meanwhile, Yates had made his way into the kitchen, taking the precaution to shut the door after him. Kitty Bartlett looked quickly round as the door closed. Before she could speak the young man caught her by the plump shoulders—a thing which he certainly had no right to do.

"Miss Kitty Bartlett," he said, "you've been crying."

"I haven't; and if I had, it is nothing to you."

"Oh, I'm not so sure about that. Don't deny it. For whom were you crying? The professor?"

"No, nor for you either, although I suppose you have conceit enough to think so."

"Me conceited? Anything but that. Come, now, Kitty, for whom were you crying? I must know."

"Please let me go, Mr. Yates," said Kitty, with an effort at dignity.

"Dick is my name, Kit."

"Well, mine is not Kit."

"You're quite right. Now that you mention it, I will call you Kitty, which is much prettier than the abbreviation."

"I did not 'mention it.' Please let me go. Nobody has the right to call me anything but Miss Bartlett; that is, you haven't, anyhow."

"Well, Kitty, don't you think it is about time to give somebody the right? Why won't you look up at me, so that I can tell for sure whether I should have accused you of crying? Look up—Miss Bartlett."

"Please let me go, Mr. Yates. Mother will be here in a minute."

"Mother is a wise and thoughtful woman. We'll risk mother. Besides, I'm not in the least afraid of her, and I don't believe you are. I think she is at this moment giving poor Mr. Stoliker a piece of her mind; otherwise, I imagine, he would have followed me. I saw it in his eye."

"I hate that man," said Kitty inconsequently.

"I like him, because he brought me here, even if I was handcuffed. Kitty, why don't you look up at me? Are you afraid?"

"What should I be afraid of?" asked Kitty, giving him one swift glance from her pretty blue eyes. "Not of you, I hope."

"Well, Kitty, I sincerely hope not. Now, Miss Bartlett, do you know why I came out here?"

"For something more to eat, very likely," said the girl mischievously.

"Oh, I say, that to a man in captivity is both cruel and unkind. Besides, I had a first-rate breakfast, thank you. No such motive drew me into the kitchen. But I will tell you. You shall have it from my own lips. That was the reason!"

He suited the action to the word, and kissed her before she knew what was about to happen. At least, Yates, with all his experience, thought he had taken her unawares. Men often make mistakes in little matters of this kind. Kitty pushed him with apparent indignation from her, but she did not strike him across the face, as she had done before, when he merely attempted what he had now accomplished. Perhaps this was because she had been taken so completely by surprise.

"I shall call my mother," she threatened.

"Oh, no, you won't. Besides, she wouldn't come." Then this frivolous young man began to sing in a low voice the flippant refrain, "Here's to the girl that gets a kiss, and runs and tells her mother," ending with the wish that

244

she should live and die an old maid and never get another. Kitty should not have smiled, but she did; she should have rebuked his levity, but she didn't.

"It is about the great and disastrous consequences of living and dying an old maid that I want to speak to you. I have a plan for the prevention of such a catastrophe, and I would like to get your approval of it."

Yates had released the girl, partly because she had wrenched herself away from him, and partly because he heard a movement in the dining room, and expected the entrance of Stoliker or some of the others. Miss Kitty stood with her back to the table, her eyes fixed on a spring flower, which she had unconsciously taken from a vase standing on the window-ledge. She smoothed the petals this way and that, and seemed so interested in botanical investigation that Yates wondered whether she was paying attention to what he was saying or not. What his plan might have been can only be guessed; for the Fates ordained that they should be interrupted at this critical moment by the one person on earth who could make Yates' tongue falter.

The outer door to the kitchen burst open, and Margaret Howard stood on the threshold, her lovely face aflame with indignation, and her dark hair down over her shoulders, forming a picture of beauty that fairly took Yates' breath away. She did not notice him.

"O Kitty," she cried, "those wretches have stolen all our horses! Is your father here?"

"What wretches?" asked Kitty, ignoring the question, and startled by the sudden advent of her friend.

"The Fenians. They have taken all the horses that were in the fields, and your horses as well. So I ran over to tell you."

"Have they taken your own horse, too?"

"No. I always keep Gypsy in the stable. The thieves did not come near the house. Oh, Mr. Yates! I did not see you." And Margaret's hand, with the unconscious vanity of a woman, sought her disheveled hair, which Yates thought too becoming ever to be put in order again.

Margaret reddened as she realized, from Kitty's evident embarrassment, that she had impulsively broken in upon a conference of two.

"I must tell your father about it," she said hurriedly, and before Yates could open the door she had done so for herself. Again she was taken aback to see so many sitting round the table.

There was a moment's silence between the two in the kitchen, but the spell was broken.

"I—I don't suppose there will be any trouble about getting back the horses," said Yates hesitatingly. "If you lose them, the Government will have to pay."

"I presume so," answered Kitty coldly; then: "Excuse me, Mr. Yates; I mustn't stay here any longer." So saying, she followed Margaret into the other room.

Yates drew a long breath of relief. All his old difficulties of preference had arisen when the outer door burst open. He felt that he had had a narrow escape, and began to wonder if he had really committed himself. Then the fear swept over him that Margaret might have noticed her friend's evident confusion, and surmised its cause. He wondered whether this would help him or hurt him with Margaret, if he finally made up his mind to favor her with his serious attentions. Still, he reflected that, after all, they were both country girls, and would no doubt be only too eager to accept a chance to live in New York. Thus his mind gradually resumed its normal state of self-confidence; and he argued that, whatever Margaret's suspicions were, they could not but make him more precious in her eyes. He knew of instances where the very danger of losing a man had turned a woman's wavering mind entirely in the man's favor. When he had reached this point, the door from the dining room opened, and Stoliker appeared.

"We are waiting for you," said the constable.

"All right. I am ready."

As he entered the room he saw the two girls standing together talking earnestly.

"I wish I was a constable for twenty-four hours," cried Mrs. Bartlett. "I would be hunting horse thieves instead of handcuffing innocent men."

"Come along," said the impassive Stoliker, taking the handcuffs from his pocket.

"If you three men," continued Mrs. Bartlett, "cannot take those two to camp, or to jail, or anywhere else, without handcuffing them, I'll go along with you myself and protect you, and see that they don't escape. You ought to be ashamed of yourself, Sam Stoliker, if you have any manhood about you—which I doubt."

"I must do my duty."

The professor rose from his chair. "Mr. Stoliker," he said with determination, "my friend and myself will go with you quietly. We will make no attempt to escape, as we have done nothing to make us fear investigation. But I give you fair warning that if you attempt to put a handcuff on my wrist again I will smash you."

A cry of terror from one of the girls, at the prospect of a fight, caused the professor to realize where he was. He turned to them and said in a contrite voice:

"Oh! I forgot you were here. I sincerely beg your pardon."

Margaret, with blazing eyes, cried:

"Don't beg my pardon, but—smash him."

Then a consciousness of what she had said overcame her, and the excited girl hid her blushing face on her friend's shoulder, while Kitty lovingly stroked her dark, tangled hair.

Renmark took a step toward them, and stopped. Yates, with his usual quickness, came to the rescue, and his cheery voice relieved the tension of the situation.

"Come, come, Stoliker, don't be an idiot. I do not object in the least to the handcuffs; and, if you are dying to handcuff somebody, handcuff me. It hasn't struck your luminous mind that you have not the first tittle of evidence against my friend, and that, even if I were the greatest criminal in America, the fact of his being with me is no crime. The truth is, Stoliker, that I wouldn't be in your shoes for a good many dollars. You talk a great deal about doing your duty, but you have exceeded it in the case of the professor. I hope you have no property; for the professor can, if he likes, make you pay sweetly for putting the handcuffs on him without a warrant, or even without one jot of evidence. What is the penalty for false arrest, Hiram?" continued Yates, suddenly appealing to the old man. "I think it is a thousand dollars."

Hiram said gloomily that he didn't know. Stoliker was hit on a tender spot, for he owned a farm.

"Better apologize to the professor and let us get along. Good-by, all. Mrs. Bartlett, that breakfast was the very best I ever tasted."

The good woman smiled and shook hands with him.

"Good-by, Mr. Yates; and I hope you will soon come back to have another."

Stoliker slipped the handcuffs into his pocket again, and mounted his horse. The girls, from the veranda, watched the procession move up the dusty road. They were silent, and had even forgotten the exciting event of the stealing of the horses.

248

CHAPTER XVII.

When the two prisoners, with their three captors, came in sight of the Canadian volunteers, they beheld a scene which was much more military than the Fenian camp. They were promptly halted and questioned by a picket before coming to the main body; the sentry knew enough not to shoot until he had asked for the countersign. Passing the picket, they came in full view of the Canadian force, the men of which looked very spick and span in uniforms which seemed painfully new in the clear light of the fair June morning. The guns, topped by a bristle of bayonets which glittered as the rising sun shone on them, were stacked with neat precision here and there. The men were preparing their breakfast, and a temporary halt had been called for that purpose. The volunteers were scattered by the side of the road and in the fields. Renmark recognized the colors of the regiment from his own city, and noticed that there was with it a company that was strange to him. Although led to them a prisoner, he felt a glowing pride in the regiment and their trim appearance—a pride that was both national and civic. He instinctively held himself more erect as he approached.

"Renmark," said Yates, looking at him with a smile, "you are making a thoroughly British mistake."

"What do you mean? I haven't spoken."

"No, but I see it in your eye. You are underestimating the enemy. You think this pretty company is going to walk over that body of unkempt tramps we saw in the woods this morning."

"I do indeed, if the tramps wait to be walked over—which I very much doubt."

"That's just where you make a mistake. Most of these are raw boys, who know all that can be learned of war on a cricket field. They will be the worst whipped set of young fellows before night that this part of the country as ever seen. Wait till they see one of their comrades fall, with the blood gushing out of a wound in his breast. If they don't turn and run, then I'm a Dutchman. I've seen raw recruits before. They should have a company of older men here who have seen service to steady them. The fellows we saw this morning were sleeping like logs, in the damp woods, as we stepped over them. They are veterans. What will be but a mere skirmish to them will seem to these boys the most awful tragedy that ever happened. Why, many of them look as if they might be university lads."

"They are," said Renmark, with a pang of anguish.

"Well, I can't see what your stupid government means by sending them here alone. They should have at least one company of regulars with them."

"Probably the regulars are on the way."

"Perhaps; but they will have to put in an appearance mighty sudden, or the fight will be over. If these boys are not in a hurry with their meal, the Fenians will be upon them before they know it. If there is to be a fight, it will be before a very few hours—before one hour passes, you are going to see a miniature Bull Run."

Some of the volunteers crowded around the incomers, eagerly inquiring for news of the enemy. The Fenians had taken the precaution to cut all the telegraph wires leading out of Fort Erie, and hence those in command of the companies did not even know that the enemy had left that locality. They were now on their way to a point where they were to meet Colonel Peacocke's force of regulars—a point which they were destined never to reach. Stoliker sought an officer and delivered up his prisoners, together with the incriminating paper that Yates had handed to him. The officer's decision was short and sharp, as military decisions are generally supposed to be. He ordered the constable to take both the prisoners and put them in jail at Port Colborne. There was no time now for an inquiry into the case,—that could come afterward,—and so long as the men were safe in jail, everything would be all right. To this the constable mildly interposed two objections. In the first place, he said, he was with the volunteers not in his capacity as constable, but in the position of guide and man who knew the country. In the second place, there was no jail at Port Colborne.

"Where is the nearest jail?"

"The jail of the county is at Welland, the county town," replied the constable.

"Very well; take them there."

"But I am here as guide," repeated Stoliker.

The officer hesitated for a moment. "You haven't handcuffs with you, I presume?"

"Yes, I have," said Stoliker, producing the implements.

"Well, then, handcuff them together, and I will send one of the company over to Welland with them. How far is it across country?"

Stoliker told him.

The officer called one of the volunteers, and said to him:

"You are to make your way across country to Welland, and deliver these men up to the jailer there. They will be handcuffed together, but you take a revolver with you, and if they give you any trouble, shoot them."

The volunteer reddened, and drew himself up. "I am not a policeman," he said. "I am a soldier."

"Very well, then your first duty as a soldier is to obey orders. I order you to take these men to Welland."

The volunteers had crowded around as this discussion went on, and a murmur rose among them at the order of the officer. They evidently sympathized with their comrade's objection to the duties of a policeman. One of them made his way through the crowd, and cried:

"Hello! this is the professor. This is Mr. Renmark. He's no Fenian." Two or three more of the university students recognized Renmark, and, pushing up to him, greeted him warmly. He was evidently a favorite with his class. Among others young Howard pressed forward.

"It is nonsense," he cried, "talking about sending Professor Renmark to

251

jail! He is no more a Fenian than Governor-General Monck. We'll all go bail for the professor."

The officer wavered. "If you know him," he said, "that is a different matter. But this other man has a letter from the commander of the Fenians, recommending him to the consideration of all friends of the Fenian cause. I can't let him go free."

"Are you the chief in command here?" asked Renmark.

"No, I am not."

"Mr. Yates is a friend of mine who is here with me on his vacation. He is a New York journalist, and has nothing in common with the invaders. If you insist on sending him to Welland, I must demand that we be taken before the officer in command. In any case, he and I stand or fall together. I am exactly as guilty or innocent as he is."

"We can't bother the colonel about every triviality."

"A man's liberty is no triviality. What, in the name of common sense, are you fighting for but liberty?"

"Thanks, Renmark, thanks," said Yates; "but I don't care to see the colonel, and I shall welcome Welland jail. I am tired of all this bother. I came here for rest and quiet, and I am going to have them, if I have to go to jail for them. I'm coming reluctantly to the belief that jail's the most comfortable place in Canada, anyhow."

"But this is an outrage," cried the professor indignantly.

"Of course it is," replied Yates wearily; "but the woods are full of them. There's always outrages going on, especially in so-called free countries; therefore one more or less won't make much difference. Come, officer, who's going to take me to Welland? or shall I have to go by myself? I'm a Fenian from 'way back, and came here especially to overturn the throne and take it home with me. For Heaven's sake, know your own mind one way or other and let us end this conference."

The officer was wroth. He speedily gave the order to Stoliker to handcuf the prisoner to himself, and deliver him to the jailer at Welland.

"But I want assistance," objected Stoliker. "The prisoner is a bigger man than I am." The volunteers laughed as Stoliker mentioned this self-evident fact.

"If anyone likes to go with you, he can go. I shall give no orders."

No one volunteered to accompany the constable.

"Take this revolver with you," continued the officer, "and if he attempts to escape, shoot him. Besides, you know the way to Welland, so I can't send anybody in your place, even if I wanted to."

"Howard knows the way," persisted Stoliker. That young man spoke up with great indignation: "Yes, but Howard isn't constable, and Stoliker is. I'm not going."

Renmark went up to his friend.

"Who's acting foolishly now, Yates?" he said. "Why don't you insist on seeing the colonel? The chances are ten to one that you would be allowed off."

"Don't make any mistake. The colonel will very likely be some fussy individual who magnifies his own importance, and who will send a squad of volunteers to escort me, and I want to avoid that. These officers always stick by each other; they're bound to. I want to go alone with Stoliker. I have a score to settle with him."

"Now, don't do anything rash. You've done nothing so far; but if you assault an officer of the law, that will be a different matter."

"Satan reproving sin. Who prevented you from hitting Stoliker a short time since?"

"Well, I was wrong then. You are wrong now."

"See here, Renny," whispered Yates; "you get back to the tent, and see that everything's all right. I'll be with you in an hour or so. Don't look so frightened. I won't hurt Stoliker. But I want to see this fight, and I won't get there if the colonel sends an escort. I'm going to use Stoliker as a shield when the bullets begin flying."

The bugles sounded for the troops to fall in, and Stoliker very reluctantly attached one clasp of the handcuff around his own left wrist, while he snapped the other on the right wrist of Yates, who embarrassed him with kindly assistance. The two manacled men disappeared down the road, while the volunteers rapidly fell in to continue their morning's march.

Young Howard beckoned to the professor from his place in the ranks. "I say, professor, how did you happen to be down this way?"

"I have been camping out here for a week or more with Yates, who is an old schoolfellow of mine."

"What a shame to have him led off in that way! But he seemed to rather like the idea. Jolly fellow, I should say. How I wish I had known you were in this neighborhood. My folks live near here. They would only have been too glad to be of assistance to you."

"They have been of assistance to me, and exceedingly kind as well."

"What? You know them? All of them? Have you met Margaret?"

"Yes," said the professor slowly, but his glance fell as it encountered the eager eyes of the youth. It was evident that Margaret was the brother's favorite.

"Fall back, there!" cried the officer to Renmark.

"May I march along with them? or can you give me a gun, and let me take part?"

"No," said the officer with some hauteur; "this is no place for civilians." Again the professor smiled as he reflected that the whole company, as far as martial experience went, were merely civilians dressed in uniform; but he became grave again when he remembered Yates' ominous prediction regarding them.

"I say, Mr. Renmark," cried young Howard, as the company moved off, "if you see any of them, don't tell them I'm here—especially Margaret. It might make them uneasy. I'll get leave when this is over, and drop in on them."

The boy spoke with the hopeful confidence of youth, and had evidently no premonition of how his appointment would be kept. Renmark left the road, and struck across country in the direction of the tent.

Meanwhile, two men were tramping steadily along the dusty road toward Welland: the captor moody and silent, the prisoner talkative and entertaining—indeed, Yates' conversation often went beyond entertainment, and became, at times, instructive. He discussed the affairs of both countries, showed a way out of all political difficulties, gave reasons for the practical use of common sense in every emergency, passed opinions on the methods of agriculture adopted in various parts of the country, told stories of the war, gave instances of men in captivity murdering those who were in charge of them, deduced from these anecdotes the foolishness of resisting lawful authority lawfully exercised, and, in general, showed that he was a man who respected power and the exercise thereof. Suddenly branching to more practical matters, he exclaimed:

"Say, Stoliker, how many taverns are there between here and Welland?"

Stoliker had never counted them.

"Well, that's encouraging, anyhow. If there are so many that it requires an effort of the memory to enumerate them, we will likely have something to drink before long."

"I never drink while on duty," said Stoliker curtly.

"Oh, well, don't apologize for it. Every man has his failings. I'll be only too happy to give you some instructions. I have acquired the useful practice of being able to drink both on and off duty. Anything can be done, Stoliker, if you give your mind to it. I don't believe in the word 'can't,' either with or without the mark of elision."

Stoliker did not answer, and Yates yawned wearily.

"I wish you would hire a rig, constable. I'm tired of walking. I've been on my feet ever since three this morning."

"I have no authority to hire a buggy."

"But what do you do when a prisoner refuses to move?"

"I make him move," said Stoliker shortly.

"Ah, I see. That's a good plan, and saves bills at the livery stable."

They came to a tempting bank by the roadside, when Yates cried:

"Let's sit down and have a rest. I'm done out. The sun is hot, and the road dusty. You can let me have half an hour: the day's young, yet."

"I'll let you have fifteen minutes."

They sat down together. "I wish a team would come along," said Yates with a sigh.

"No chance of a team, with most of the horses in the neighborhood stolen, and the troops on the roads."

"That's so," assented Yates sleepily.

He was evidently tired out, for his chin dropped on his breast, and his eyes closed. His breathing came soft and regular, and his body leaned toward the constable, who sat bolt upright. Yates' left arm fell across the knees of Stoliker, and he leaned more and more heavily against him. The constable did not know whether he was shamming or not, but he took no risks. He kept his grasp firm on the butt of the revolver. Yet, he reflected, Yates could surely not meditate an attempt on his weapon, for he had, a few minutes before, told him a story about a prisoner who escaped in exactly that way. Stoliker was suspicious of the good intentions of the man he had in charge; he was altogether too polite and good-natured; and, besides, the constable dumbly felt that the prisoner was a much cleverer man than he.

"Here, sit up," he said gruffly. "I'm not paid to carry you, you know."

"What's that? What's that? What's that?" cried Yates rapidly, blinking hi eyes and straightening up. "Oh, it's only you, Stoliker. I thought it was my friend Renmark. Have I been asleep?"

"Either that or pretending—I don't know which, and I don't care."

"Oh! I must have been pretending," answered Yates drowsily; "I can't have dropped asleep. How long have we been here?"

"About five minutes."

"All right." And Yates' head began to droop again.

This time the constable felt no doubt about it. No man could imitate sleep so well. Several times Yates nearly fell forward, and each time saved himself, with the usual luck of a sleeper or a drunkard. Nevertheless, Stoliker never took his hand from his revolver. Suddenly, with a greater lurch than usual, Yates pitched head first down the bank, carrying the constable with him. The steel band of the handcuff nipped the wrist of Stoliker, who, with an oath and a cry of pain, instinctively grasped the links between with his right hand, to save his wrist. Like a cat, Yates was upon him, showing marvelous agility for a man who had just tumbled in a heap. The next instant he held aloft the revolver, crying triumphantly:

"How's that, umpire? Out, I expect."

The constable, with set teeth, still rubbed his wounded wrist, realizing the helplessness of a struggle.

"Now, Stoliker," said Yates, pointing the pistol at him, "what have you to say before I fire?"

"Nothing," answered the constable, "except that you will be hanged at Welland, instead of staying a few days in jail."

Yates laughed. "That's not bad, Stoliker; and I really believe there's some grit in you, if you are a man-catcher. Still, you were not in very much danger, as perhaps you knew. Now, if you should want this pistol again, just watch where it alights." And Yates, taking the weapon by the muzzle, tossed it as far as he could into the field.

Stoliker watched its flight intently, then, putting his hand into his pocket, he took out some small object and flung it as nearly as he could to the spot where the revolver fell.

"Is that how you mark the place?" asked Yates; "or is it some spell that will enable you to find the pistol?"

"Neither," answered the constable quietly. "It is the key of the handcuffs. The duplicate is at Welland."

Yates whistled a prolonged note, and looked with admiration at the little man. He saw the hopelessness of the situation. If he attempted to search for the key in the long grass, the chances were ten to one that Stoliker would stumble on the pistol before Yates found the key, in which case the reporter would be once more at the mercy of the law.

"Stoliker, you're evidently fonder of my company than I am of yours. That wasn't a bad strategic move on your part, but it may cause you some personal inconvenience before I get these handcuffs filed off. I'm not going to Welland this trip, as you may be disappointed to learn. I have gone with you as far as I intend to. You will now come with me."

"I shall not move," replied the constable firmly.

"Very well, stay there," said Yates, twisting his hand around so as to grasp the chain that joined the cuffs. Getting a firm grip, he walked up the road, down which they had tramped a few minutes before. Stoliker set his teeth and tried to hold his ground, but was forced to follow. Nothing was said by either until several hundred yards were thus traversed. Then Yates stopped.

"Having now demonstrated to you the fact that you must accompany me, I hope you will show yourself a sensible man, Stoliker, and come with me quietly. It will be less exhausting for both of us, and all the same in the end. You can do nothing until you get help. I am going to see the fight, which I feel sure will be a brief one, so I don't want to lose any more time in getting back. In order to avoid meeting people, and having me explain to them that you are my prisoner, I propose we go through the fields."

One difference between a fool and a wise man is that the wise man always accepts the inevitable. The constable was wise. The two crossed the rail fence into the fields, and walked along peaceably together—Stoliker silent, as usual, with the grim confidence of a man who is certain of ultimate success, who has the nation behind him, with all its machinery working in his favor; Yates talkative, argumentative, and instructive by turns, occasionally breaking forth into song when the unresponsiveness of the other rendered conversation difficult.

"Stoliker, how supremely lovely and quiet and restful are the silent, scented, spreading fields! How soothing to a spirit tired of the city's din is this solitude, broken only by the singing of the birds and the drowsy droning of the bee, erroneously termed 'bumble'! The green fields, the shady trees, the sweet freshness of the summer air, untainted by city smoke, and over all the eternal serenity of the blue unclouded sky—how can human spite and human passion exist in such a paradise? Does it all not make you feel as if you were an innocent child again, with motives pure and conscience white?"

If Stoliker felt like an innocent child, he did not look it. With clouded brow he eagerly scanned the empty fields, hoping for help. But, although the constable made no reply, there was an answer that electrified Yates, and put all thought of the beauty of the country out of his mind. The dull report of a musket, far in front of them, suddenly broke the silence, followed by several scattering shots, and then the roar of a volley. This was sharply answered by the ring of rifles to the right. With an oath, Yates broke into a run.

"They're at it!" he cried, "and all on account of your confounded obstinacy I shall miss the whole show. The Fenians have opened fire, and the Canadians have not been long in replying."

The din of the firing now became incessant. The veteran in Yates was aroused. He was like an old war horse who again feels the intoxicating smell of battle smoke. The lunacy of gunpower shone in his gleaming eye.

"Come on, you loitering idiot!" he cried to the constable, who had difficulty in keeping pace with him; "come on, or, by the gods! I'll break your wrist across a fence rail and tear this brutal iron from it."

The savage face of the prisoner was transformed with the passion of war, and, for the first time that day, Stoliker quailed before the insane glare of his eyes. But if he was afraid, he did not show his fear to Yates.

"Come on, you!" he shouted, springing ahead, and giving a twist to the handcuffs well known to those who have to deal with refractory criminals. "I am as eager to see the fight as you are."

The sharp pain brought Yates to his senses again. He laughed, and said: "That's the ticket, I'm with you. Perhaps you would not be in such a hurry if you knew that I am going into the thick the fight, and intend to use you as a shield from the bullets."

"That's all right," answered the little constable, panting. "Two sides are firing. I'll shield you on one side, and you'll have to shield me on the other."

Again Yates laughed, and they ran silently together. Avoiding the houses, they came out at the Ridge Road. The smoke rolled up above the trees, showing where the battle was going on some distance beyond. Yates made the constable cross the fence and the road, and take to the fields again, bringing him around behind Bartlett's house and barn. No one was visible near the house except Kitty Bartlett, who stood at the back watching, with pale and anxious face, the rolling smoke, now and then covering her ears with her hands as the sound of an extra loud volley assailed them. Stoliker lifted up his voice and shouted for help.

"If you do that again," cried Yates, clutching him by the throat, "I'll choke you!"

But he did not need to do it again. The girl heard the cry, turned with a frightened look, and was about to fly into the house when she recognized the two. Then she came toward them. Yates took his hand away from the constable's throat.

"Where is your father or your brother?" demanded the constable.

"I don't know."

"Where is your mother?"

"She is over with Mrs. Howard, who is ill."

260

"Are you all alone?"

"Yes."

"Then I command you, in the name of the Queen, to give no assistance to this prisoner, but to do as I tell you."

"And I command you, in the name of the President," cried Yates, "to keep your mouth shut, and not to address a lady like that. Kitty," he continued in a milder tone, "could you tell me where to get a file, so that I may cut these wrist ornaments? Don't you get it. You are to do nothing. Just indicate where the file is. The law mustn't have any hold on you, as it seems to have on me."

"Why don't you make him unlock them?" asked Kitty.

"Because the villain threw away the key in the fields."

"He couldn't have done that."

The constable caught his breath.

"But he did. I saw him."

"And I saw him unlock them at breakfast. The key was on the end of his watch chain. He hasn't thrown that away."

She made a move to take out his watch chain but Yates stopped her.

"Don't touch him. I'm playing a lone hand here." He jerked out the chain, and the real key dangled from it.

"Well, Stoliker," he said, "I don't know which to admire most—your cleverness and pluck, my stupidity, or Miss Bartlett's acuteness of observation. Can we get into the barn, Kitty?"

"Yes; but you mustn't hurt him."

"No fear. I think too much of him. Don't you come in. I'll be out in a moment, like the medium from a spiritualistic dark cabinet."

Entering the barn, Yates forced the constable up against the square oaken post which was part of the framework of the building, and which formed one side of the perpendicular ladder that led to the top of the hay mow.

"Now, Stoliker," he, said solemnly, "you realize, of course, that I don't want to hurt you yet you also realize that I must hurt you if you attempt any tricks. I can't take any risks, please remember that; and recollect that, by the time you are free again, I shall be in the State of New York. So don't compel me to smash your head against this post." He, with some trouble, unlocked the clasp on his own wrist; then, drawing Stoliker's right hand around the post, he snapped the same clasp on the constable's hitherto free wrist. The unfortunate man, with his cheek against the oak, was in the comical position of lovingly embracing the post.

"I'll get you a chair from the kitchen, so that you will be more comfortable—unless, like Samson, you can pull down the supports. Then I must bid you good-by."

Yates went out to the girl, who was waiting for him.

"I want to borrow a kitchen chair, Kitty," he said, "so that poor Stoliker will get a rest."

They walked toward the house. Yates noticed that the firing had ceased, except a desultory shot here and there across the country.

"I shall have to retreat over the border as quickly as I can," he continued. "This country is getting too hot for me."

"You are much safer here," said the girl, with downcast eyes. "A man has brought the news that the United States gunboats are sailing up and down the river, making prisoners of all who attempt to cross from this side."

"You don't say! Well, I might have known that. Then what am I to do with Stoliker? I can't keep him tied up here. Yet the moment he gets loose I'm done for."

"Perhaps mother could persuade him not to do anything more. Shall go for her?"

"I don't think it would be any use. Stoliker's a stubborn animal. He ha suffered too much at my hands to be in a forgiving mood. We'll bring him a chair anyhow, and see the effect of kindness on him."

When the chair was placed at Stoliker's disposal, he sat down upon it, still hugging the post with an enforced fervency that, in spite of the solemnity of the occasion, nearly made Kitty laugh, and lit up her eyes with the mischievousness that had always delighted Yates.

"How long am I to be kept here?" asked the constable.

"Oh, not long," answered Yates cheerily; "not a moment longer than is necessary. I'll telegraph when I'm safe in New York State; so you won't be here more than a day or two."

This assurance did not appear to bring much comfort to Stoliker.

"Look here," he said; "I guess I know as well as the next man when I'm beaten. I have been thinking all this over. I am under the sheriff's orders, and not under the orders of that officer. I don't believe you've done anything, anyhow, or you wouldn't have acted quite the way you did. If the sheriff had sent me, it would have been different. As it is, if you unlock those cuffs, I'll give you my word I'll do nothing more unless I'm ordered to. Like as not they've forgotten all about you by this time; and there's nothing on record, anyhow."

"Do you mean it? Will you act square?"

"Certainly I'll act square. I don't suppose you doubt that. I didn't ask any favors before, and I did what I could to hold you."

"Enough said," cried Yates. "I'll risk it."

Stoliker stretched his arms wearily above his head when he was released.

"I wonder," he said, now that Kitty was gone, "if there is anything to eat in the house?"

"Shake!" cried Yates, holding out his hand to him. "Another great and mutual sentiment unites us, Stoliker. Let us go and see."

CHAPTER XVIII.

The man who wanted to see the fight did not see it, and the man who did not want to see it saw it. Yates arrived on the field of conflict when all was over; Renmark found the battle raging around him before he realized that things had reached a crisis.

When Yates reached the tent, he found it empty and torn by bullets. The fortunes of war had smashed the jar, and the fragments were strewn before the entrance, probably by some disappointed man who had tried to sample the contents and had found nothing.

"Hang it all!" said Yates to himself, "I wonder what the five assistants that the Argus sent me have done with themselves? If they are with the Fenians, beating a retreat, or, worse, if they are captured by the Canadians, they won't be able to get an account of this scrimmage through to the paper. Now, this is evidently the biggest item of the year—it's international, by George! It may involve England and the United States in a war, if both sides are not extra mild and cautious. I can't run the chance of the paper being left in the lurch. Let me think a minute. Is it my tip to follow the Canadians or the Fenians? I wonder is which is running the faster? My men are evidently with the Fenians, if they were on the ground at all. If I go after the Irish Republic, I shall run the risk of duplicating things; but if I follow the Canadians, they may put me under arrest. Then we have more Fenian sympathizers among our readers than Canadians, so the account from the invasion side of the fence will be the more popular. Yet a Canadian version would be a good thing, if I were sure the rest of the boys got in their work, and the chances are that the other papers won't have any reporters among the Canucks. Heavens! What is a man to do? I'll toss up for it. Heads, the Fenians."

He spun the coin in the air, and caught it. "Heads it is! The Fenians are my victims. I'm camping on their trail, anyhow. Besides, it's safer than following the Canadians, even though Stoliker has got my pass."

Tired as he was, he stepped briskly through the forest. The scent of big item was in his nostrils, and it stimulated him like champagne. What was temporary loss of sleep compared to the joy of defeating the opposition press?

A blind man might have followed the trail of the retreating army. They had thrown away, as they passed through the woods, every article that impeded their progress. Once he came on a man lying with his face in the dead leaves. He turned him over.

"His troubles are past, poor devil," said Yates, as he pushed on.

"Halt! Throw up your hands!" came a cry from in front of him.

Yates saw no one, but he promptly threw up his hands, being an adaptable man.

"What's the trouble?" he shouted. "I'm retreating, too."

"Then retreat five steps farther. I'll count the steps. One."

Yates strode one step forward, and then saw that a man behind a tree was covering him with a gun. The next step revealed a second captor, with a huge upraised hammer, like a Hercules with his club. Both men had blackened faces, and resembled thoroughly disreputable fiends of the forest. Seated on the ground, in a semicircle, were half a dozen dejected prisoners. The man with the gun swore fearfully, but his comrade with the hammer was silent.

"Come," said the marksman, "you blank scoundrel, and take a seat with your fellow-scoundrels. If you attempt to run, blank blank you, I'll fill you full of buckshot!"

"Oh, I'm not going to run, Sandy," cried Yates, recognizing him. "Why should I? I've always enjoyed your company, and Macdonald's. How are you, Mac? Is this a little private raid of your own? For which side are you fighting? And I say, Sandy, what's the weight of that old-fashioned bar of iron you have in your hands? I'd like to decide a bet. Let me heft it, as you said in the shop."

"Oh, it's you, is it?" said Sandy in a disappointed tone, lowering his gun. "I thought we had raked in another of them. The old man and I want to make it an even dozen."

265

"Well, I don't think you'll capture any more. I saw nobody as I came through the woods. What are you going to do with this crowd?"

"Brain 'em," said Macdonald laconically, speaking for the first time. Then he added reluctantly: "If any of 'em tries to escape."

The prisoners were all evidently too tired and despondent to make any attempt at regaining their liberty. Sandy winked over Macdonald's shoulder at Yates, and by a slight side movement of his head he seemed to indicate that he would like to have some private conversation with the newspaper man.

"I'm not your prisoner, am I?" asked Yates.

"No," said Macdonald. "You may go if you like, but not in the direction the Fenians have gone."

"I guess I won't need to go any farther, if you will give me permission to interview your prisoners. I merely want to get some points about the fight."

"That's all right," said the blacksmith, "as long as you don't try to help them. If you do, I warn you there will be trouble."

Yates followed Sandy into the depths of the forest, out of hearing of the others, leaving Macdonald and his sledge-hammer on guard.

When at a safe distance, Sandy stopped and rested his arms on his gun, in a pathfinder attitude.

"Say," he began anxiously, "you haven't got some powder and shot on you by any chance?"

"Not an ounce. Haven't you any ammunition?"

"No, and haven't had all through the fight. You see, we left the shop in such a hurry we never thought about powder and ball. As soon as a man on horseback came by shouting that there was a fight on, the old man he grabbed his sledge, and I took this gun that had been left at the shop for repairs, and off we started. I'm not sure that it would shoot if I had ammunition, but I'd like to try. I've scared some of them Fee-neens nigh to death with it, but I was always afraid one of them would pull a real gun on me, and then I don't know just what I'd 'a' done."

Sandy sighed, and added, with the air of a man who saw his mistake, but was somewhat loath to acknowledge it: "Next battle there is you won't find me in it with a lame gun and no powder. I'd sooner have the old man's sledge. It don't miss fire." His eye brightened as he thought of Macdonald. "Say," he continued, with a jerk of his head back over his shoulder, "the boss is on the warpath in great style, aint he?"

"He is," said Yates, "but, for that matter, so are you. You can swear nearly as well as Macdonald himself. When did you take to it?"

"Oh, well, you see," said Sandy apologetically, "it don't come as natural to me as chewing, but, then, somebody's got to swear. The old man's converted, you know."

"Ah, hasn't he backslid yet?"

"No, he hasn't. I was afraid this scrimmage was going to do for him, but it didn't; and now I think that if somebody near by does a little cussing,—not that anyone can cuss like the boss,—he'll pull through. I think he'll stick this time. You'd ought to have seen him wading into them d—d Fee-neens, swinging his sledge, and singing 'Onward, Christian soldiers.' Then, with me to chip in a cuss word now and again when things got hot, he pulled through the day without ripping an oath. I tell you, it was a sight. He bowled 'em over like nine-pins. You ought to 'a' been there."

"Yes," said Yates regretfully. "I missed it, all on account of that accursed Stoliker. Well, there's no use crying over spilled milk, but I'll tell you one thing, Sandy: although I have no ammunition, I'll let you know what I have got. I have, in my pocket, one of the best plugs of tobacco that you ever put your teeth into."

Sandy's eyes glittered. "Bless you!" was all he could say, as he bit off a corner of the offered plug.

"You see, Sandy, there are compensations in this life, after all; I thought you were out."

"I haven't had a bite all day. That's the trouble with leaving in a hurry."

"Well, you may keep that plug, with my regards. Now, I want to get back and interview those fellows. There's no time to be lost."

When they reached the group, Macdonald said:

"Here's a man says he knows you, Mr. Yates. He claims he is a reporter, and that you will vouch for him."

Yates strode forward, and looked anxiously at the prisoners, hoping, yet fearing, to find one of his own men there. He was a selfish man, and wanted the glory of the day to be all his own. He soon recognized one of the prisoners as Jimmy Hawkins of the staff of a rival daily, the New York Blade. This was even worse than he had anticipated.

"Hello, Jimmy!" he said, "how did you get here?"

"I was raked in by that adjective fool with the unwashed face."

"Whose a—fool?" cried Macdonald in wrath, and grasping his hammer. He boggled slightly as he came to the "adjective," but got over it safely. It was evidently a close call, but Sandy sprang to the rescue, and cursed Hawkins until even the prisoners turned pale at the torrent of profanity. Macdonald looked with sad approbation at his pupil, not knowing that he was under the stimulus of newly acquired tobacco, wondering how he had attained such proficiency in malediction; for, like all true artists, he was quite unconscious of his own merit in that direction.

"Tell this hammer wielder that I'm no anvil. Tell him that I'm a newspaper man, and didn't come here to fight. He says that if you guarantee that I'm no Fenian he'll let me go."

Yates sat down on a fallen log, with a frown on his brow. He liked to do a favor to a fellow-creature when the act did not inconvenience himself, but he never forgot the fact that business was business.

"I can't conscientiously tell him that, Jimmy," said Yates soothingly. "How am I to know you are not a Fenian?"

"Bosh!" cried Hawkins angrily. "Conscientiously? A lot you think of conscience when there is an item to be had."

"We none of us live up to our better nature, Jimmy," continued Yates feelingly. "We can but do our best, which is not much. For reasons that you might fail to understand, I do not wish to run the risk of telling a lie. You appreciate my hesitation, don't you, Mr. Macdonald? You would not advise me to assert a thing I was not sure of, would you?"

"Certainly not," said the blacksmith earnestly.

"You want to keep me here because you are afraid of me," cried the indignant Blade man. "You know very well I'm not a Fenian."

"Excuse me, Jimmy, but I know nothing of the kind. I even suspect myself of Fenian leanings. How, then, can I be sure of you?"

"What's your game?" asked Hawkins more calmly, for he realized that he himself would not be slow to take advantage of a rival's dilemma.

"My game is to get a neat little account of this historical episode sent over the wires to the Argus. You see, Jimmy, this is my busy day. When the task is over, I will devote myself to your service, and will save you from being hanged, if I can; although I shall do so without prejudice, as the lawyers say, for I have always held that that will be the ultimate end of all the Blade staff.

"Look here, Yates; play fair. Don't run in any conscientious guff on a prisoner. You see, I have known you these many years."

"Yes, and little have you profited by a noble example. It is your knowledge of me that makes me wonder at your expecting me to let you out of your hole without due consideration."

"Are you willing to make a bargain?

"Always—when the balance of trade is on my side."

"Well, if you give me a fair start, I'll give you some exclusive information hat you can't get otherwise."

"What is it?"

269

"Oh, I wasn't born yesterday, Dick."

"That is interesting information, Jimmy, but I knew it before. Haven't you something more attractive to offer?"

"Yes, I have. I have the whole account of the expedition and the fight written out, all ready to send, if I could get my clutches on a telegraph wire. I'll hand it over to you, and allow you to read it, if you will get me out of this hole, as you call it. I'll give you permission to use the information in any way you choose, if you will extricate me, and all I ask is a fair start in the race for a telegraph office."

Yates pondered over the proposition for some moments.

"I'll tell you what I'll do, Jimmy," he finally said. "I'll buy that account from you, and give you more money than the Blade will. And when I get back to New York I'll place you on the staff of the Argus at a higher salary than the Blade gives you—taking your own word for the amount."

"What! And leave my paper in the lurch? Not likely."

"Your paper is going to be left in the lurch, anyhow."

"Perhaps. But it won't be sold by me. I'll burn my copy before I will let you have a glimpse of it. That don't need to interfere with your making me an offer of a better position when we get back to New York; but while my paper depends on me, I won't go back on it."

"Just as you please, Jimmy. Perhaps I would do the same myself. I always was weak where the interests of the Argus were concerned. You haven't any blank paper you could lend me, Jimmy?"

"I have, but I won't lend it."

Yates took out his pencil, and pulled down his cuff.

"Now, Mac," he said, "tell me all you saw of this fight."

The blacksmith talked, and Yates listened, putting now and then a mark on his cuff. Sandy spoke occasionally, but it was mostly to tell of sledge

270

hammer feats or to corroborate something the boss said. One after another Yates interviewed the prisoners, and gathered together all the materials for that excellent full-page account "by an eyewitness" that afterward appeared in the columns of the Argus. He had a wonderful memory, and simply jotted down figures with which he did not care to burden his mind. Hawkins laughed derisively now and then at the facts they were giving Yates, but the Argus man said nothing, merely setting down in shorthand some notes of the information Hawkins sneered at, which Yates considered was more than likely accurate and important. When he had got all he wanted, he rose.

"Shall I send you help, Mac?" he asked.

"No," said the smith; "I think I'll take these fellows to the shop, and hold them there till called for. You can't vouch for Hawkins, then, Mr. Yates?"

"Good Heavens, no! I look on him as the most dangerous of the lot. These half-educated criminals, who have no conscientious scruples, always seem to me a greater menace to society than their more ignorant co-conspirators. Well, good-by, Jimmy. I think you'll enjoy life down at Mac's shop. It's the best place I've struck since I've been in the district. Give my love to all the boys, when they come to gaze at you. I'll make careful inquiries into your opinions, and as soon as I am convinced that you can be set free with safety to the community I'll drop in on you and do all I can. Meanwhile, so long."

Yates' one desire now was to reach a telegraph office, and write his article as it was being clicked off on the machine. He had his fears about the speed of a country operator, but he dared not risk trying to get through to Buffalo in the then excited state of the country. He quickly made up his mind to go to the Bartlett place, borrow a horse, if the Fenians had not permanently made off with them all, and ride as rapidly as he could for the nearest telegraph office. He soon reached the edge of the woods, and made his way across the fields to the house. He found young Bartlett at the barn.

"Any news of the horses yet?" was the first question he asked.

"No," said young Bartlett gloomily; "guess they've rode away with them."

"Well, I must get a horse from somewhere to ride to the telegraph office.

271

Where is the likeliest place to find one?"

"I don't know where you can get one, unless you steal the telegraph boy's nag; it's in the stable now, having a feed."

"What telegraph boy?"

"Oh, didn't you see him? He went out to the tent to look for you, and I thought he had found you."

"No, I haven't been at the tent for ever so long. Perhaps he has some news for me. I'm going to the house to write, so send him in as soon as he gets back. Be sure you don't let him get away before I see him."

"I'll lock the stable," said young Bartlett, "and then he won't get the horse, at any rate."

Yates found Kitty in the kitchen, and he looked so flurried that the girl cried anxiously:

"Are they after you again, Mr. Yates?"

"No, Kitty; I'm after them. Say, I want all the blank paper you have in the house. Anything will do, so long as it will hold a lead-pencil mark."

"A copy book—such as the children use in school?"

"Just the thing."

In less than a minute the energetic girl had all the materials he required ready for him in the front room. Yates threw off his coat, and went to work as if he were in his own den in the Argus building.

"This is a —— of a vacation," he muttered to himself, as he drove his pencil at lightning speed over the surface of the paper. He took no note of the time until he had finished; then he roused himself and sprang to his feet.

"What in thunder has become of that telegraph boy?" he cried. "Well, it doesn't matter; I'll take the horse without his permission."

He gathered up his sheets, and rushed for the kitchen. He was somewhat

272

surprised to see the boy sitting there, gorging himself with the good things which that kitchen always afforded.

"Hello, youngster! how long have you been here?"

"I wouldn't let him go in to disturb you while you were writing," said Kitty, the boy's mouth being too full to permit of a reply.

"Ah, that was right. Now, sonny, gulp that down and come in here; I want to talk to you for a minute."

The boy followed him into the front room.

"Well, my son, I want to borrow your horse for the rest of the day."

"You can't have it," said the boy promptly.

"Can't have it? I must have it. Why, I'll take it. You don't imagine you can stop me, do you?"

The boy drew himself up, and folded his arms across his breast.

"What do you want with the horse, Mr. Yates?" he asked.

"I want to get to the nearest telegraph office. I'll pay you well for it."

"And what am I here for?"

"Why, to eat, of course. They'll feed you high while you wait."

"Canadian telegraph office?"

"Certainly."

"It's no good, Mr. Yates. Them Canadians couldn't telegraph all you've written in two weeks. I know 'em," said the boy with infinite scorn. "Besides, the Government has got hold of all the wires, and you can't get a private message through till it gets over its fright."

"By George!" cried Yates, taken aback, "I hadn't thought of that. Are you sure, boy?"

"Dead certain."

"Then what's to be done? I must get through to Buffalo."

"You can't. United States troops won't let you. They're stopping everybody—except me," he added, drawing himself up, as if he were the one individual who stood in with the United States Government.

"Can you get this dispatch through?"

"You bet! That's why I came back. I knew, as soon as I looked at you, that you would write two or three columns of telegraph; and your paper said 'Spare no expense,' you remember. So says I to myself: 'I'll help Mr. Yates to spare no expense. I'll get fifty dollars from that young man, seeing I'm the only person who can get across in time.'"

"You were mighty sure of it, weren't you?"

"You just bet I was. Now, the horse is fed and ready, I'm fed and ready, and we're losing valuable time waiting for that fifty dollars."

"Suppose you meet another newspaper man who wants to get his dispatch through to another paper, what will you do?"

"Charge him the same as I do you. If I meet two other newspaper men, that will be one hundred and fifty dollars; but if you want to make sure that I won't meet any more newspaper men, let us call it one hundred dollars, and I'll take the risk of the odd fifty for the ready cash; then if I meet a dozen newspaper men, I'll tell them I'm a telegraph boy on a vacation."

"Quite so. I think you will be able to take care of yourself in a cold and callous world. Now, look here, young man; I'll trust you if you'll trust me. I'm not a traveling mint, you know. Besides, I pay by results. If you don't get this dispatch through, you don't get anything. I'll give you an order for a hundred dollars, and as soon as I get to Buffalo I'll pay you the cash. I'll have to draw on the Argus when I get to Buffalo; if my article has appeared, you get your cash; if it hasn't, you're out. See?"

"Yes, I see. It won't do, Mr. Yates."

"Why won't it do?"

"Because I say it won't. This is a cash transaction. Money down, or you don't get the goods. I'll get it through all right, but if I just miss, I'm not going to lose the money."

"Very well, I'll take it to the Canadian telegraph office."

"All right, Mr. Yates. I'm disappointed in you. I thought you were some good. You aint got no sense, but I wish you luck. When I was at your tent, there was a man with a hammer taking a lot of men out of the woods. When one of them sees my uniform, he sings out he'd give me twenty-five dollars to take his stuff. I said I'd see him later, and I will. Good-by, Mr. Yates."

"Hold on, there! You're a young villain. You'll end in state's prison yet, but here's your money. Now, you ride like a house a-fire."

After watching the departing boy until he was out of sight Yates, with a feeling of relief, started back to the tent. He was worried about the interview the boy had had with Hawkins, and he wondered, now that it was too late, whether, after all, he had not Hawkins' manuscript in his pocket. He wished he had searched him. That trouble, however, did not prevent him from sleeping like the dead the moment he lay down in the tent.

CHAPTER XIX.

The result of the struggle was similar in effect to an American railway accident of the first class. One officer and five privates were killed on the Canadian side, one man was missing, and many were wounded. The number of the Fenians killed will probably never be known. Several were buried on the field of battle, others were taken back by O'Neill's brigade when they retreated.

Although the engagement ended as Yates had predicted, yet he was wrong in his estimate of the Canadians. Volunteers are invariably underrated by men of experience in military matters. The boys fought well, even when they saw their ensign fall dead before them. If the affair had been left entirely in their hands, the result might have been different—as was shown afterward, when the volunteers, unimpeded by regulars, quickly put down a much more formidable rising in the Northwest. But in the present case they were hampered by their dependence on the British troops, whose commander moved them with all the ponderous slowness of real war, and approached O'Neill as if he had been approaching Napoleon. He thus managed to get in a day after the fair on every occasion, being too late for the fight at Ridgeway, and too late to capture any considerable number of the flying Fenians at Fort Erie. The campaign, on the Canadian side, was magnificently planned and wretchedly carried out. The volunteers and regulars were to meet at a point close to where the fight took place, but the British commander delayed two hours in starting, which fact the Canadian colonel did not learn until too late. These blunders culminated in a ghastly mistake on the field. The Canadian colonel ordered his men to charge across an open field, and attack the Fenian force in the woods—a brilliant but foolish move. To the command the volunteers gallantly responded, but against stupidity the gods are powerless. In the field they were appalled to hear the order given to form square and receive cavalry. Even the schoolboys knew the Fenians could have no cavalry.

Having formed their square, the Canadians found themselves th helpless targets of the Fenians in the woods. If O'Neill's forces had shot with reasonable precision, they must have cut the volunteers to pieces. The latter were victorious, if they had only known it; but, in this hopeless square, panic seized them, and it was every man for himself; at the same time, the Fenians were also retreating as fast as they could. This farce is known as the battle of Ridgeway, and would have been comical had it not been that death hovered over it. The comedy, without the tragedy, was enacted a day or two before at a bloodless skirmish which took place near a hamlet called Waterloo, which affray is dignified in Canadian annals as the second battle of that name.

When the Canadian forces retreated, Renmark, who had watched the contest with all the helpless anxiety of a noncombatant, sharing the danger, but having no influence upon the result, followed them, making a wide detour to avoid the chance shots which were still flying. He expected to come up with the volunteers on the road, but was not successful. Through various miscalculations he did not succeed in finding them until toward evening. At first they told him that young Howard was with the company, and unhurt, but further inquiry soon disclosed the fact that he had not been seen since the fight. He was not among those who were killed or wounded, and it was nightfall before Renmark realized that opposite his name on the roll would be placed the ominous word "missing." Renmark remembered that the boy had said he would visit his home if he got leave; but no leave had been asked for. At last Renmark was convinced that young Howard was either badly wounded or dead. The possibility of his desertion the professor did not consider for a moment, although he admitted to himself that it was hard to tell what panic of fear might come over a boy who, for the first time in his life, found bullets flying about his ears.

With a heavy heart Renmark turned back and made his way to the fatal field. He found nothing on the Canadian side. Going over to the woods, he came across several bodies lying where they fell; but they were all those of strangers. Even in the darkness he would have had no difficulty in recognizing the volunteer uniform which he knew so well. He walked down to the Howard homestead, hoping, yet fearing, to hear the boy's voice—the voice of a deserter. Everything was silent about the house, although a light shone through an upper window, and also through one below. He paused at the gate, not knowing what to do. It was evident the boy was not here, yet how to find the father or brother, without alarming Margaret or her mother, puzzled him. As he stood there the door opened, and he recognized Mrs. Bartlett and Margaret standing in the light. He moved away from the gate, and heard the older woman say:

"Oh, she will be all right in the morning, now that she has fallen into a nice sleep. I wouldn't disturb her to-night, if I were you. It is nothing but nervousness and fright at that horrible firing. It's all over now, thank God. Good-night, Margaret."

The good woman came through the gate, and then ran, with all the speed of sixteen, toward her own home. Margaret stood in the doorway listening to the retreating footsteps. She was pale and anxious, but Renmark thought he had never seen anyone so lovely; and he was startled to find that he had a most un-professor-like longing to take her in his arms and comfort her. Instead of bringing her consolation, he feared it would be his fate to add to her anxiety; and it was not until he saw she was about to close the door that he found courage to speak.

"Margaret," he said.

The girl had never heard her name pronounced in that tone before, and the cadence of it went direct to her heart, frightening her with an unknown joy. She seemed unable to move or respond, and stood there, with wide eyes and suspended breath, gazing into the darkness. Renmark stepped into the light, and she saw his face was haggard with fatigue and anxiety.

"Margaret," he said again, "I want to speak with you a moment. Where is your brother?"

"He has gone with Mr. Bartlett to see if he can find the horses. There is something wrong," she continued, stepping down beside him. "I can see it in your face. What is it?"

"Is your father in the house?"

"Yes, but he is worried about mother. Tell me what it is. It is better to

278

tell me."

Renmark hesitated.

"Don't keep me in suspense like this," cried the girl in a low but intense voice. "You have said too much or too little. Has anything happened to Henry?"

"No. It is about Arthur I wanted to speak. You will not be alarmed?"

"I am alarmed. Tell, me quickly." And the girl in her excitement laid her hands imploringly on his.

"Arthur joined the volunteers in Toronto some time ago. Did you know that?"

"He never told me. I understand—I think so, but I hope not. He was in the battle today. Is he—has he been—hurt?"

"I don't know. I'm afraid so," said Renmark hurriedly, now that the truth had to come out; he realized, by the nervous tightening of the girl's unconscious grasp, how clumsily he was telling it. "He was with the volunteers this morning. He is not with them now. They don't know where he is. No one saw him hurt, but it is feared he was, and that he has been left behind. I have been all over the ground."

"Yes, yes?"

"But I could not find him. I came here hoping to find him."

"Take me to where the volunteers were," she sobbed. "I know what has happened. Come quickly."

"Will you not put something on your head?"

"No, no. Come at once." Then, pausing, she said: "Shall we need a lantern?"

"No; it is light enough when we get out from the shadow of the house."

Margaret ran along the road so swiftly that Renmark had some trouble in keeping pace with her. She turned at the side road, and sped up the gentle ascent to the spot where the volunteers had crossed it.

"Here is the place," said Renmark.

"He could not have been hit in the field," she cried breathlessly, "for then he might have reached the house at the corner without climbing a fence. If he was badly hurt, he would have been here. Did you search this field?"

"Every bit of it. He is not here."

"Then it must have happened after he crossed the road and the second fence. Did you see the battle?"

"Yes."

"Did the Fenians cross the field after the volunteers?"

"No; they did not leave the woods."

"Then, if he was struck, it could not have been far from the other side of the second fence. He would be the last to retreat; and that is why the others did not see him," said the girl, with confident pride in her brother's courage.

They crossed the first fence; the road, and the second fence, the girl walking ahead for a few paces. She stopped, and leaned for a moment against a tree. "It must have been about here," she said in a voice hardly audible. "Have you searched on this side?"

"Yes, for half a mile farther into the fields and woods."

"No, no, not there; but down along the fence. He knew every inch of this ground. If he were wounded here, he would at once try to reach our house. Search down along the fence. I—I cannot go."

Renmark walked along the fence, peering into the dark corners made by the zigzag of the rails; and he knew, without looking back, that Margaret, with feminine inconsistency, was following him. Suddenly she darted past him, and flung herself down in the long grass, wailing out a cry that cut Renmark like a knife.

280

The boy lay with his face in the grass, and his outstretched hand grasping the lower rail of the fence. He had dragged himself this far, and reached an insurmountable obstacle.

Renmark drew the weeping girl gently away, and rapidly ran his hand over the prostrate lad. He quickly opened his tunic, and a thrill of joy passed over him as he felt the faint beating of the heart.

"He is alive!" he cried. "He will get well, Margaret." A statement somewhat premature to make on so hasty an examination.

He rose, expecting a look of gratitude from the girl he loved. He was amazed to see her eyes almost luminous in the darkness, blazing with wrath.

"When did you know he was with the volunteers?"

"This morning—early," said the professor, taken aback.

"Why didn't you tell me?"

"He asked me not to do so."

"He is a mere boy. You are a man, and ought to have a man's sense. You had no right to mind what a boy said. It was my right to know, and your duty to tell me. Through your negligence and stupidity my brother has lain here all day—perhaps dying," she added with a break in her angry voice.

"If you had known—I didn't know anything was wrong until I saw the volunteers. I have not lost a moment since."

"I should have known he was missing, without going to the volunteers."

Renmark was so amazed at the unjust accusation, from a girl whom he had made the mistake of believing to be without a temper of her own, that he knew not what to say. He was, however, to have one more example of inconsistency.

"Why do you stand there doing nothing, now that I have found him?" he demanded.

It was on his tongue to say: "I stand here because you stand there unjustly quarreling with me," but he did not say it. Renmark was not a ready man, yet he did, for once, the right thing.

"Margaret," he said sternly, "throw down that fence."

This curt command, delivered in his most schoolmastery manner, was instantly obeyed. Such a task may seem a formidable one to set to a young woman, but it is a feat easily accomplished in some parts of America. A rail fence lends itself readily to demolition. Margaret tossed a rail to the right, one to the left, and to the right again, until an open gap took the place of that part of the fence. The professor examined the young soldier in the meantime, and found his leg had been broken by a musket ball. He raised him up tenderly in his arms, and was pleased to hear a groan escape his lips. He walked through the open gap and along the road toward the house, bearing the unconscious form of his pupil. Margaret silently kept close to his side, her fingers every now and then unconsciously caressing the damp, curly locks of her brother.

"We shall have to get a doctor?" Her assertion was half an inquiry.

"Certainly."

"We must not disturb anyone in the house. It is better that I should tell you what to do now, so that we need not talk when we reach there."

"We cannot help disturbing someone."

"I do not think it will be necessary. If you will stay with Arthur, I will go for the doctor, and no one need know."

"I will go for the doctor."

"You do not know the way. It is five or six miles. I will ride Gypsy, and will soon be back."

"But there are prowlers and stragglers all along the roads. It is not safe for you to go alone."

"It is perfectly safe. No horse that the stragglers have stolen can overtake Gypsy. Now, don't say anything more. It is best that I should go. I will run on ahead, and enter the house quietly. I will take the lamp to the room at the

282

side, where the window opens to the floor. Carry him around there. I will be waiting for you at the gate, and will show you the way."

With that the girl was off, and Renmark carried his burden alone. She was waiting for him at the gate, and silently led the way round the house, to where the door-window opened upon the bit of lawn under an apple tree. The light streamed out upon the grass. He placed the boy gently upon the dainty bed. It needed no second glance to tell Renmark whose room he was in. It was decorated with those pretty little knickknacks so dear to the heart of a girl in a snuggery she can call her own.

"It is not likely you will be disturbed here," she whispered, "until I come back. I will tap at the window when I come with the doctor."

"Don't you think it would be better and safer for me to go? I don't like the thought of your going alone."

"No, no. Please do just what I tell you. You do not know the way. I shall be very much quicker. If Arthur should—should—wake, he will know you, and will not be alarmed, as he might be if you were a stranger."

Margaret was gone before he could say anything more, and Renmark sat down, devoutly hoping no one would rap at the door of the room while he was there.

CHAPTER XX.

Margaret spoke caressingly to her horse, when she opened the stable door, and Gypsy replied with that affectionate, low guttural whinny which the Scotch graphically term "nickering." She patted the little animal; and if Gypsy was surprised at being saddled and bridled at that hour of the night, no protest was made, the horse merely rubbing its nose lovingly up and down Margaret's sleeve as she buckled the different straps. There was evidently a good understanding between the two.

"No, Gyp," she whispered, "I have nothing for you to-night—nothing but hard work and quick work. Now, you mustn't make a noise till we get past the house."

On her wrist she slipped the loop of a riding whip, which she always carried, but never used. Gyp had never felt the indignity of the lash, and was always willing to do what was required merely for a word.

Margaret opened the big gate before she saddled her horse, and there was therefore no delay in getting out upon the main road, although the passing of the house was an anxious moment. She feared that if her father heard the steps or the neighing of the horse he might come out to investigate. Halfway between her own home and Bartlett's house she sprang lightly into the saddle.

"Now, then, Gyp!"

No second word was required. Away they sped down the road toward the east, the mild June air coming sweet and cool and fresh from the distant lake, laden with the odors of the woods and the fields. The stillness was intense, broken only by the plaintive cry of the whippoorwill, America's one-phrased nightingale, or the still more weird and eerie note of a distant loon.

The houses along the road seemed deserted; no lights were shown anywhere. The wildest rumors were abroad concerning the slaughter of the day; and the population, scattered as it was, appeared to have retired into its shell. A spell of silence and darkness was over the land, and the rapid hoof beats of the horse sounded with startling distinctness on the harder portions of the road, emphasized by intervals of complete stillness, when the fetlocks sank in the sand and progress was more difficult for the plucky little animal. The only thrill of fear that Margaret felt on her night journey was when she entered the dark arch of an avenue of old forest trees that bordered the road, like a great, gloomy cathedral aisle, in the shadow of which anything might be hidden. Once the horse, with a jump of fear, started sideways and plunged ahead: Margaret caught her breath as she saw, or fancied she saw, several men stretched on the roadside, asleep or dead. Once in the open again she breathed more freely, and if it had not been for the jump of the horse, she would have accused her imagination of playing her a trick. Just as she had completely reassured herself a shadow moved from the fence to the middle of the road, and a sharp voice cried:

"Halt!"

The little horse, as if it knew the meaning of the word, planted its two front hoofs together, and slid along the ground for a moment, coming so quickly to a standstill that it was with some difficulty Margaret kept her seat. She saw in front of her a man holding a gun, evidently ready to fire if she attempted to disobey his command.

"Who are you, and where are you going?" he demanded.

"Oh, please let me pass!" pleaded Margaret with a tremor of fear in her voice. "I am going for a doctor—for my brother; he is badly wounded, and will perhaps die if I am delayed."

The man laughed.

"Oho!" he cried, coming closer; "a woman, is it? and a young one, too, or I'm a heathen. Now, miss or missus, you get down. I'll have to investigate this. The brother business won't work with an old soldier. It's your lover you're riding for at this time of the night, or I'm no judge of the sex. Just slip down, my lady, and see if you don't like me better than him; remember that all cats are black in the dark. Get down, I tell you."

"If you are a soldier, you will let me go. My brother is badly wounded.

I must get to the doctor."

"There's no 'must' with a bayonet in front of you. If he has been wounded, there's plenty of better men killed to-day. Come down, my dear."

Margaret gathered up the bridle rein, but, even in the darkness, the man saw her intention.

"You can't escape, my pretty. If you try it, you'll not be hurt, but I'll kill your horse. If you move, I'll put a bullet through him."

"Kill my horse?" breathed Margaret in horror, a fear coming over her that she had not felt at the thought of danger to herself.

"Yes, missy," said the man, approaching nearer, and laying his hand on Gypsy's bridle. "But there will be no need of that. Besides, it would make too much noise, and might bring us company, which would be inconvenient. So come down quietly, like the nice little girl you are."

"If you will let me go and tell the doctor, I will come back here and be your prisoner."

The man laughed again in low, tantalizing tones. This was a good joke.

"Oh, no, sweetheart. I wasn't born so recently as all that. A girl in the hand is worth a dozen a mile up the road. Now, come off that horse, or I'll take you off. This is war time, and I'm not going to waste any more pretty talk on you."

The man, who, she now saw, was hatless, leered up at her, and something in his sinister eyes made the girl quail. She had been so quiet that he apparently was not prepared for any sudden movement. Her right hand, hanging down at her side, had grasped the short riding whip, and, with a swiftness that gave him no chance to ward off the blow, she struck him one stinging, blinding cut across the eyes, and then brought down the lash on the flank of her horse drawing the animal round with her left over her enemy. With a wild snort of astonishment, the horse sprang forward, bringing man and gun down to the ground with a clatter that woke the echoes; then, with an indignant toss of the head, Gyp sped along the road like the wind. It was the first time he had ever felt the cut of a whip, and the blow was not forgiven. Margaret, fearing further obstruction on the road, turned her horse's head toward the rail fence, and went over it like a bird. In the field, where fast going in the dark had dangers, Margaret tried to slacken the pace, but the little horse would not have it so. He shook his head angrily whenever he thought of the indignity of that blow, while Margaret leaned over and tried to explain and beg pardon for her offense. The second fence was crossed with a clean-cut leap, and only once in the next field did the horse stumble, but quickly recovered and went on at the same breakneck gait. The next fence, gallantly vaulted over, brought them to the side road, half a mile up which stood the doctor's house. Margaret saw the futility of attempting a reconciliation until the goal was won. There, with difficulty, the horse was stopped, and the girl struck the panes of the upper window, through which a light shone, with her riding whip. The window was raised, and the situation speedily explained to the physician.

"I will be with you in a moment," he said.

Then Margaret slid from the saddle, and put her arms around the neck of the trembling horse. Gypsy would have nothing to do with her, and sniffed the air with offended dignity.

"It was a shame, Gyp," she cried, almost tearfully, stroking the glossy neck of her resentful friend; "it was, it was, and I know it; but what was I to do, Gyp? You were the only protector I had, and you did bowl him over beautifully; no other horse could have done it so well. It's wicked, but I do hope you hurt him, just because I had to strike you."

Gypsy was still wrathful, and indicated by a toss of the head that the wheedling of a woman did not make up for a blow. It was the insult more than the pain; and from her—there was the sting of it.

"I know—I know just how you feel, Gypsy dear; and I don't blame you for being angry. I might have spoken to you, of course, but there was no time to think, and it was really him I was striking. That's why it came down so hard. If I had said a word, he would have got out of the way, coward that he was, and then would have shot you—you, Gypsy! Think of it!"

If a man can be molded in any shape that pleases a clever woman, how can a horse expect to be exempt from her influence. Gypsy showed signs of melting, whinnying softly and forgivingly.

"And it will never happen again, Gypsy—never, never. As soon as we are safe home again I will burn that whip. You little pet, I knew you wouldn't——"

Gypsy's head rested on Margaret's shoulder, and we must draw a veil over the reconciliation. Some things are too sacred for a mere man to meddle with. The friends were friends once more, and on the altar of friendship the unoffending whip was doubtless offered as a burning sacrifice.

When the doctor came out, Margaret explained the danger of the road, and proposed that they should return by the longer and northern way—the Concession, as it was called.

They met no one on the silent road, and soon they saw the light in the window.

The doctor and the girl left their horses tied some distance from the house, and walked together to the window with the stealthy steps of a pair of housebreakers. Margaret listened breathlessly at the closed window, and thought she heard the low murmur of conversation. She tapped lightly on the pane, and the professor threw back the door-window.

"We were getting very anxious about you," he whispered.

"Hello, Peggy!" said the boy, with a wan smile, raising his head slightly from the pillow and dropping it back again.

Margaret stooped over and kissed him.

"My poor boy! what a fright you have given me!"

"Ah, Margery, think what a fright I got myself. I thought I was going to die within sight of the house."

The doctor gently pushed Margaret from the room. Renmark waited until the examination was over, and then went out to find her.

She sprang forward to meet him.

"It is all right," he said. "There is nothing to fear. He has been exhausted by loss of blood, but a few days' quiet will set that right. Then all you will have to contend against will be his impatience at being kept to his room, which may be necessary for some weeks."

"Oh, I am so glad! and—and I am so much obliged to you, Mr. Renmark!"

"I have done nothing—except make blunders," replied the professor with a bitterness that surprised and hurt her.

"How can you say that? You have done everything. We owe his life to you."

Renmark said nothing for a moment. Her unjust accusation in the earlier part of the night had deeply pained him, and he hoped for some hint of disclaimer from her. Belonging to the stupider sex, he did not realize that the words were spoken in a state of intense excitement and fear, that another woman would probably have expressed her condition of mind by fainting instead of talking, and that the whole episode had left absolutely no trace on the recollection of Margaret. At last Renmark spoke:

"I must be getting back to the tent, if it still exists. I think I had an appointment there with Yates some twelve hours ago, but up to this moment I had forgotten it. Good-night."

Margaret stood for a few moments alone, and wondered what she had done to offend him. He stumbled along the dark road, not heeding much the direction he took, but automatically going the nearest way to the tent. Fatigue and the want of sleep were heavy upon him, and his feet were as lead. Although dazed, he was conscious of a dull ache where his heart was supposed to be, and he vaguely hoped he had not made a fool of himself. He entered the tent, and was startled by the voice of Yates:

"Hello! hello! Is that you, Stoliker?"

"No; it is Renmark. Are you asleep?"

"I guess I have been. Hunger is the one sensation of the moment. Have you provided anything to eat within the last twenty-four hours?"

"There's a bag full of potatoes here, I believe. I haven't been near the tent since early morning."

"All right; only don't expect a recommendation from me as cook. I'm not yet hungry enough for raw potatoes. What time has it got to be?"

"I'm sure I don't know."

"Seems as if I had been asleep for weeks. I'm the latest edition of Rip Van Winkle, and expect to find my mustache gray in the morning. I was dreaming sweetly of Stoliker when you fell over the bunk."

"What have you done with him?"

"I'm not wide enough awake to remember. I think I killed him, but wouldn't be sure. So many of my good resolutions go wrong that very likely he is alive at this moment. Ask me in the morning. What have you been prowling after all night?"

There was no answer. Renmark was evidently asleep.

"I'll ask you in the morning," muttered Yates drowsily—after which there was silence in the tent.

CHAPTER XXI.

Yates had stubbornly refused to give up his search for rest and quiet in spite of the discomfort of living in a leaky and battered tent. He expressed regret that he had not originally camped in the middle of Broadway, as being a quieter and less exciting spot than the place he had chosen; but, having made the choice, he was going to see the last dog hung, he said. Renmark had become less and less of a comrade. He was silent, and almost as gloomy as Hiram Bartlett himself. When Yates tried to cheer him up by showing him how much worse another man's position might be, Renmark generally ended the talk by taking to the wood.

"Just reflect on my position," Yates would say. "Here I am dead in love with two lovely girls, both of whom are merely waiting for the word. To one of them I have nearly committed myself, which fact, to a man of my temperament, inclines me somewhat to the other. Here I am anxious to confide in you, and yet I feel that I risk a fight every time I talk about the complication. You have no sympathy for me, Renny, when I need sympathy; while I am bubbling over with sympathy for you, and you won't have it. Now, what would you do if you were in my fix? If you would take five minutes and show me clearly which of the two girls I really ought to marry, it would help me ever so much, for then I would be sure to settle on the other. It is the indecision that is slowly but surely sapping my vitality."

By this time, Renmark would have pulled his soft felt hat over his eyes, and, muttering words that would have echoed strangely in the silent halls of the university building, would plunge into the forest. Yates generally looked after his retreating figure without anger, but with mild wonder.

"Well, of all cantankerous cranks he is the worst," he would say with a sigh. "It is sad to see the temple of friendship tumble down about one's ears in this way." At their last talk of this kind Yates resolved not to discuss the problem again with the professor, unless a crisis came. The crisis came in the form of Stoliker, who dropped in on Yates as the latter lay in the hammock, smoking and enjoying a thrilling romance. The camp was strewn with these engrossing, paper-covered works, and Yates had read many of them, hoping to came across a case similar to his own, but up to the time of Stoliker's visit he had not succeeded.

"Hello, Stoliker! how's things? Got the cuffs in your pocket? Want to have another tour across country with me?"

"No. But I came to warn you. There will be a warrant out to-morrow or next day, and, if I were you, I would get over to the other side; though you need never say I told you. Of course, if they give the warrant to me, I shall have to arrest you; and although nothing may be done to you, still, the country is in a state of excitement, and you will at least be put to some inconvenience."

"Stoliker," cried Yates, springing out of the hammock, "you are a white man! You're a good fellow, Stoliker, and I'm ever so much obliged. If you ever come to New York, you call on me at the Argus office,—anybody will show you where it is,—and I'll give you the liveliest time you ever had in your life. It won't cost you a cent, either."

"That's all right," said the constable. "Now, if I were you, I would light out to-morrow at the latest."

"I will," said Yates.

Stoliker disappeared quietly among the trees, and Yates, after a moment's thought, began energetically to pack up his belongings. It was dark before he had finished, and Renmark returned.

"Stilly," cried the reporter cheerily, "there's a warrant out for my arrest. shall have to go to-morrow at the latest!"

"What! to jail?" cried his horrified friend, his conscience now troublin him, as the parting came, for his lack of kindness to an old comrade.

"Not if the court knows herself. But to Buffalo, which is pretty muc the same thing. Still, thank goodness, I don't need to stay there long. I'll b in New York before I'm many days older. I yearn to plunge into the aren once more. The still, calm peacefulness of this whole vacation has made me long for excitement again, and I'm glad the warrant has pushed me into the turmoil."

"Well, Richard, I'm sorry you have to go under such conditions. I'm afraid I have not been as companionable a comrade as you should have had."

"Oh, you're all right, Renny. The trouble with you is that you have drawn a little circle around Toronto University, and said to yourself: 'This is the world.' It isn't, you know. There is something outside of all that."

"Every man, doubtless, has his little circle. Yours is around the Argus office."

"Yes, but there are special wires from that little circle to all the rest of the world, and soon there will be an Atlantic cable."

"I do not hold that my circle is as large as yours; still, there is something outside of New York, even."

"You bet your life there is; and, now that you are in a more sympathetic frame of mind, it is that I want to talk with you about. Those two girls are outside my little circle, and I want to bring one of them within it. Now, Renmark, which of those girls would you choose if you were me?"

The professor drew in his breath sharply, and was silent for a moment. At last he said, speaking slowly:

"I am afraid, Mr. Yates, that you do not quite appreciate my point of view. As you may think I have acted in an unfriendly manner, I will try for the first and final time to explain it. I hold that any man who marries a good woman gets more than he deserves, no matter how worthy he may be. I have a profound respect for all women, and I think that your light chatter about choosing between two is an insult to both of them. I think either of them is infinitely too good for you—or for me either."

"Oh, you do, do you? Perhaps you think that you would make a much better husband than I. If that is the case, allow me to say you are entirely wrong. If your wife was sensitive, you would kill her with your gloomy fits. I wouldn't go off in the woods and sulk, anyhow."

"If you are referring to me, I will further inform you that I had either to go off in the woods or knock you down. I chose the less of two evils."

"Think you could do it, I suppose? Renny, you're conceited. You're not the first man who has made such a mistake, and found he was barking up the wrong tree when it was too late for anything but bandages and arnica."

"I have tried to show you how I feel regarding this matter. I might have known I should not succeed. We will end the discussion, if you please."

"Oh, no. The discussion is just beginning. Now, Renny, I'll tell you what you need. You need a good, sensible wife worse than any man I know. It is not yet too late to save you, but it soon will be. You will, before long, grow a crust on you like a snail, or a lobster, or any other cold-blooded animal that gets a shell on itself. Then nothing can be done for you. Now, let me save you, Renny, before it is too late. Here is my proposition: You choose one of those girls and marry her. I'll take the other. I'm not as unselfish as I may seem in this, for your choice will save me the worry of making up my own mind. According to your talk, either of the girls is too good for you, and for once I entirely agree with you. But let that pass. Now, which one is it to be?"

"Good God! man, do you think I am going to bargain with you about my future wife?"

"That's right, Renny. I like to hear you swear. It shows you are not yet the prig you would have folks believe. There's still hope for you, professor. Now, I'll go further with you. Although I cannot make up my mind just what to do myself, I can tell instantly which is the girl for you, and thus we solve both problems at one stroke. You need a wife who will take you in hand. You need one who will not put up with your tantrums, who will be cheerful, and who will make a man of you. Kitty Bartlett is the girl. She will tyrannize over you, just as her mother does over the old man. She will keep house to the queen's taste, and delight in getting you good things to eat. Why everything is as plain as a pikestaff. That shows the benefit of talking over a thing. You marry Kitty, and I'll marry Margaret. Come, let's shake hands ove it." Yates held up his right hand, ready to slap it down on the open palm of the professor, but there was no response. Yates' hand came down to his side again, but he had not yet lost the enthusiasm of his proposal. The more he thought of it the more fitting it seemed.

"Margaret is such a sensible, quiet, level-headed girl that, if I am as flippant as you say, she will be just the wife for me. There are depths in my character, Renmark, that you have not suspected."

"Oh, you're deep."

"I admit it. Well, a good, sober-minded woman would develop the best that is in me. Now, what do you say, Renny?"

"I say nothing. I am going into the woods again, dark as it is."

"Ah, well," said Yates with a sigh, "there's no doing anything with you or for you. I've tried my best; that is one consolation. Don't go away. I'll let fate decide. Here goes for a toss-up."

And Yates drew a silver half dollar from his pocket. "Heads for Margaret!" he cried. Renmark clinched his fist, took a step forward, then checked himself, remembering that this was his last night with the man who had at least once been his friend.

Yates merrily spun the coin in the air, caught it in one hand, and slapped the other over it.

"Now for the turning point in the lives of two innocent beings." He raised the covering hand, and peered at the coin in the gathering gloom. "Heads it is. Margaret Howard becomes Mrs. Richard Yates. Congratulate me, professor."

Renmark stood motionless as a statue, an object lesson in self-control. Yates set his hat more jauntily on his head, and slipped the epoch-making coin into his trousers pocket.

"Good-by, old man," he said. "I'll see you later, and tell you all the particulars."

Without waiting for the answer, for which he probably knew there would have been little use in delaying, Yates walked to the fence and sprang over it, with one hand on the top rail. Renmark stood still for some minutes, then, quietly gathering underbrush and sticks large and small, lighted a fire, and sat down on a log, with his head in his hands.

CHAPTER XXII.

Yates walked merrily down the road, whistling "Gayly the troubadour." Perhaps there is no moment in a man's life when he feels the joy of being alive more keenly than when he goes to propose to a girl of whose favorable answer he is reasonably sure—unless it be the moment he walks away an accepted lover. There is a magic about a June night, with its soft, velvety darkness and its sweet, mild air laden with the perfumes of wood and field. The enchantment of the hour threw its spell over the young man, and he resolved to live a better life, and be worthy of the girl he had chosen, or, rather, that fate had chosen for him. He paused a moment, leaning over the fence near the Howard homestead, for he had not yet settled in his own mind the details of the meeting. He would not go in, for in that case he knew he would have to talk, perhaps for hours, with everyone but the person he wished to meet. If he announced himself and asked to see Margaret alone, his doing so would embarrass her at the very beginning. Yates was naturally too much of a diplomat to begin awkwardly. As he stood there, wishing chance would bring her out of the house, there appeared a light in the door-window of the room where he knew the convalescent boy lay. Margaret's shadow formed a silhouette on the blind. Yates caught up a handful of sand, and flung it lightly against the pane. Its soft patter evidently attracted the attention of the girl, for, after a moment's pause, the window opened carefully, while Margaret stepped quickly out and closed it, quietly standing there.

"Margaret," whispered Yates hardly above his breath.

The girl advanced toward the fence.

"Is that you?" she whispered in return, with an accent on the last word that thrilled her listener. The accent told plainly as speech that the word represented the one man on earth to her.

"Yes," answered Yates, springing over the fence and approaching her.

"Oh!" cried Margaret, starting back, then checking herself, with a catch in her voice. "You—you startled me—Mr. Yates."

"Not Mr. Yates any more, Margaret, but Dick. Margaret, I wanted to see you alone. You know why I have come." He tried to grasp both her hands, but she put them resolutely behind her, seemingly wishing to retreat, yet standing her ground.

"Margaret, you must have seen long ago how it is with me. I love you, Margaret, loyally and truly. It seems as if I had loved you all my life. I certainly have since the first day I saw you."

"Oh, Mr. Yates, you must not talk to me like this."

"My darling, how else can I talk to you? It cannot be a surprise to you, Margaret. You must have known it long ago."

"I did not, indeed I did not—if you really mean it."

"Mean it? I never meant anything as I mean this. It is everything to me, and nothing else is anything. I have knocked about the world a good deal, I admit, but I never was in love before—never knew what love was until I met you. I tell you that——"

"Please, please, Mr. Yates, do not say anything more. If it is really true, I cannot tell you how sorry I am. I hope nothing I have said or done has made you believe that—that—Oh, I do not know what to say! I never thought you could be in earnest about anything."

"You surely cannot have so misjudged me, Margaret. Others have, but did not expect it of you. You are far and away better than I am. No one knows that so well as I. I do not pretend to be worthy of you, but I will be a devoted husband to you. Any man who gets the love of a good woman," continued Yates earnestly, plagiarizing Renmark, "gets more than he deserves; but surely such love as mine is not given merely to be scornfully trampled underfoot."

"I do not treat your—you scornfully. I am only sorry if what you say is true."

"Why do you say if it is true? Don't you know it is true?"

"Then I am very sorry—very, very sorry, and I hope it is through no fault of mine. But you will soon forget me. When you return to New York——"

"Margaret," said the young man bitterly, "I shall never forget you. Think what you are doing before it is too late. Think how much this means to me. If you finally refuse me, you will wreck my life. I am the sort of man that a woman can make or mar. Do not, I beg of you, ruin the life of the man who loves you."

"I am not a missionary," cried Margaret with sudden anger. "If your life is to be wrecked, it will be through your own foolishness, and not from any act of mine. I think it cowardly of you to say that I am to be held responsible. I have no wish to influence your future one way or another."

"Not for good, Margaret?" asked Yates with tender reproach.

"No. A man whose good or bad conduct depends on anyone but himself is not my ideal of a man."

"Tell me what your ideal is, so that I may try to attain it."

Margaret was silent.

"You think it will be useless for me to try?"

"As far as I am concerned, yes."

"Margaret, I want to ask you one more question. I have no right to, but I beg you to answer me. Are you in love with anyone else?"

"No!" cried Margaret hotly. "How dare you ask me such a question?"

"Oh, it is not a crime—that is, being in love with someone else is not. I'll tell you why I dare ask. I swear, by all the gods, that I shall win you—if not this year, then next; and if not next, then the year after. I was a coward to talk as I did; but I love you more now than I did even then. All I want to know is that you are not in love with another man.

"I think you are very cruel in persisting as you do, when you have had your answer. I say no. Never! never! never!—this year nor any other year. Is not that enough?"

"Not for me. A woman's 'no' may ultimately mean 'yes.'"

"That is true, Mr. Yates," replied Margaret, drawing herself up as one who makes a final plunge. "You remember the question you asked me just now?—whether I cared for anyone else? I said 'no.' That 'no' meant 'yes.'"

He was standing between her and the window, so she could not escape by the way she came. He saw she meditated flight, and made as though he would intercept her, but she was too quick for him. She ran around the house, and he heard a door open and shut.

He knew he was defeated. Dejectedly he turned to the fence, climbing slowly over where he had leaped so lightly a few minutes before, and walked down the road, cursing his fate. Although he admitted he was a coward for talking to her as he had done about his wrecked life, yet he knew now that every word he had spoken was true. What did the future hold out to him? Not even the incentive to live. He found himself walking toward the tent, but, not wishing to meet Renmark in his present frame of mind, he turned and came out on the Ridge Road. He was tired and broken, and resolved to stay in camp until they arrested him. Then perhaps she might have some pity on him. Who was the other man she loved? or had she merely said that to give finality to her refusal? In his present mood he pictured the worst, and imagined her the wife of some neighboring farmer—perhaps even of Stoliker. These country girls, he said to himself, never believed a man was worth looking at unless he owned a farm. He would save his money, and buy up the whole neighborhood; then she would realize what she had missed. He climbed up on the fence beside the road, and sat on the top rail, with his heels resting on a lower one, so that he might enjoy his misery without the fatigue of walking. His vivid imagination pictured himself as the owner in a few years' time of a large section of that part of the country, with mortgage on a good deal of the remainder, including the farm owned by Margaret's husband. He saw her now, a farmer's faded wife, coming to him and begging for further time in which to pay the seven per cent. due. He knew he would act magnanimously on such an occasion, and grandly give her husband all the

300

time he required. Perhaps then she would realize the mistake she had made. Or perhaps fame, rather than riches, would be his line. His name would ring throughout the land. He might become a great politician, and bankrupt Canada with a rigid tariff law. The unfairness of making the whole innocent people suffer for the inconsiderate act of one of them did not occur to him at the moment, for he was humiliated and hurt. There is no bitterness like that which assails the man who has been rejected by the girl he adores—while it lasts. His eye wandered toward the black mass of the Howard house. It was as dark as his thoughts. He turned his head slowly around, and, like a bright star of hope, there glimmered up the road a flickering light from the Bartletts' parlor window. Although time had stopped as far as he was concerned, he was convinced it could not be very late, or the Bartletts would have gone to bed. It is always difficult to realize that the greatest of catastrophes are generally over in a few minutes. It seemed an age since he walked so hopefully away from the tent. As he looked at the light the thought struck him that perhaps Kitty was alone in the parlor. She at least would not have treated him so badly as the other girl; and—and she was pretty, too, come to think of it. He always did like a blonde better than a brunette.

A fence rail is not a comfortable seat. It is used in some parts of the country in such a manner as to impress the sitter with the fact of its extreme discomfort, and as a gentle hint that his presence is not wanted in that immediate neighborhood. Yates recollected this, with a smile, as he slid off and stumbled into the ditch by the side of the road. His mind had been so preoccupied that he had forgotten about the ditch. As he walked along the road toward the star that guided him he remembered he had recklessly offered Miss Kitty to the callous professor. After all, no one knew about the episode of a short time before except himself and Margaret, and he felt convinced she was not a girl to boast of her conquests. Anyhow, it didn't matter. A man is surely master of himself.

As he neared the window he looked in. People are not particular about lowering the blinds in the country. He was rather disappointed to see Mrs. Bartlett sitting there knitting, like the industrious woman she was. Still it was consoling to note that none of the men-folks were present, and that Kitty,

301

with her fluffy hair half concealing her face, sat reading a book he had lent to her. He rapped at the door, and it was opened by Mrs. Bartlett, with some surprise.

"For the land's sake! is that you, Mr. Yates?"

"It is."

"Come right in. Why, what's the matter with you? You look as if you had lost your best friend. Ah, I see how it is,"—Yates started,—"you have run out of provisions, and are very likely as hungry as a bear."

"You've hit it first time, Mrs. Bartlett. I dropped around to see if I could borrow a loaf of bread. We don't bake till to-morrow."

Mrs. Bartlett laughed.

"Nice baking you would do if you tried it. I'll get you a loaf in a minute. Are you sure one is enough?"

"Quite enough, thank you."

The good woman bustled out to the other room for the loaf, and Yates made good use of her temporary absence.

"Kitty," he whispered, "I want to see you alone for a few minutes. I'll wait for you at the gate. Can you slip out?"

Kitty blushed very red and nodded.

"They have a warrant out for my arrest, and I'm off to-morrow before they can serve it. But I couldn't go without seeing you. You'll come, sure?"

Again Kitty nodded, after looking up at him in alarm when he spoke of the warrant. Before anything further could be said Mrs. Bartlett came in, and Kitty was absorbed in her book.

"Won't you have something to eat now before you go back?"

"Oh, no, thank you, Mrs. Bartlett. You see, the professor is waiting for me."

302

"Let him wait, if he didn't have sense enough to come."

"He didn't. I offered him the chance."

"It won't take us a moment to set the table. It is not the least trouble."

"Really, Mrs. Bartlett, you are very kind. I am not in the slightest degree hungry now. I am merely taking some thought of the morrow. No; I must be going, and thank you very much."

"Well," said Mrs. Bartlett, seeing him to the door, "if there's anything you want, come to me, and I will let you have it if it's in the house."

"You are too good to me," said the young man with genuine feeling, "and I don't deserve it; but I may remind you of your promise—to-morrow."

"See that you do," she answered. "Good-night."

Yates waited at the gate, placing the loaf on the post, where he forgot it, much to the astonishment of the donor in the morning. He did not have to wait long, for Kitty came around the house somewhat shrinkingly, as one who was doing the most wicked thing that had been done since the world began. Yates hastened to meet her, clasping one of her unresisting hands in his.

"I must be off to-morrow," he began.

"I am very sorry," answered Kitty in a whisper.

"Ah, Kitty, you are not half so sorry as I am. But I intend to come back, if you will let me. Kitty, you remember that talk we had in the kitchen, when we—when there was an interruption, and when I had to go away with our friend Stoliker?"

Kitty indicated that she remembered it.

"Well, of course you know what I wanted to say to you. Of course you now what I want to say to you now."

It seemed, however, that in this he was mistaken, for Kitty had not the slightest idea, and wanted to go into the house, for it was late, and her mother would miss her.

"Kitty, you darling little humbug, you know that I love you. You must know that I have loved you ever since the first day I saw you, when you laughed at me. Kitty, I want you to marry me and make something of me, if that is possible. I am a worthless fellow, not half good enough for a little pet like you; but, Kitty, if you will only say 'yes,' I will try, and try hard, to be a better man than I have ever been before."

Kitty did not say "yes" but she placed her disengaged hand, warm and soft, upon his, and Yates was not the man to have any hesitation about what to do next. To practical people it may seem an astonishing thing that, the object of the interview being happily accomplished, there should be any need of prolonging it; yet the two lingered there, and he told her much of his past life, and of how lonely and sordid it had been because he had no one to care for him—at which her pretty eyes filled with tears. She felt proud and happy to think she had won the first great love of a talented man's life, and hoped she would make him happy, and in a measure atone for the emptiness of the life that had gone before. She prayed that he might always be as fond of her as he was then, and resolved to be worthy of him if she could.

Strange to say, her wishes have been amply fulfilled, and few wives are as happy or as proud of their husbands as Kitty Yates. The one woman who might have put the drop of bitterness in her cup of life merely kissed her tenderly when Kitty told her of the great joy that had come to her, and said she was sure she would be happy; and thus for the second time Margaret told the thing that was not, but for once Margaret was wrong in her fears.

Yates walked to the tent a glorified man, leaving his loaf on the gatepost behind him. Few realize that it is quite as pleasant to be loved as to love. The verb "to love" has many conjugations. The earth he trod was like no other ground he had ever walked upon. The magic of the June night was never so enchanting before. He strode along with his head and his thoughts in the clouds, and the Providence that cares for the intoxicated looked after him, and saw that the accepted lover came to no harm. He leaped the fence without even putting his hand to it, and then was brought to earth again by the picture of a man sitting with his head in his hands beside a dying fire.

CHAPTER XXIII.

Yates stood for a moment regarding the dejected attitude of his friend.

"Hello, old man!" he cried, "you have the most 'hark-from-the-tombs' appearance I ever saw. What's the matter?"

Renmark looked up.

"Oh, it's you, is it?"

"Of course it's I. Been expecting anybody else?"

"No. I have been waiting for you, and thinking of a variety of things."

"You look it. Well, Renny, congratulate me, my boy. She's mine, and I'm hers—which are two ways of stating the same delightful fact. I'm up in a balloon, Renny. I'm engaged to the prettiest, sweetest, and most delightful girl there is from the Atlantic to the Pacific. What d'ye think of that? Say, Renmark, there's nothing on earth like it. You ought to reform and go in for being in love. It would make a man of you. Champagne isn't to be compared to it. Get up here and dance, and don't sit there like a bear nursing a sore paw. Do you comprehend that I am to be married to the darlingest girl that lives?"

"God help her!"

"That's what I say. Every day of her life, bless her! But I don't say it quite in that tone, Renmark. What's the matter with you? One would think you were in love with the girl yourself, if such a thing were possible."

"Why is it not possible?"

"If that is a conundrum, I can answer it the first time. Because you are a fossil. You are too good, Renny; therefore dull and uninteresting. Now, there is nothing a woman likes so much as to reclaim a man. It always annoys a woman to know that the man she is interested in has a past with which she has had nothing to do. If he is wicked and she can sort of make him over, like an old dress, she revels in the process. She flatters herself she makes a new man of him, and thinks she owns that new man by right of manufacture. We owe it to the sex, Renny, to give 'em a chance at reforming us. I have known men who hated tobacco take to smoking merely to give it up joyfully for the sake of the women they loved. Now, if a man is perfect to begin with, what is a dear, ministering angel of a woman to do with him? Manifestly nothing. The trouble with you, Renny, is that you are too evidently ruled by a good and well-trained conscience, and naturally all women you meet intuitively see this, and have no use for you. A little wickedness would be the making of you."

"You think, then, that if a man's impulse is to do what his conscience tells him is wrong, he should follow his impulse, and not his conscience?"

"You state the case with unnecessary seriousness. I believe that an occasional blow-out is good for a man. But if you ever have an impulse of that kind, I think you should give way to it for once, just to see how it feels. A man who is too good gets conceited about himself."

"I half believe you are right, Mr. Yates," said the professor, rising. "I will act on your advice, and, as you put it, see how it feels. My conscience tells me that I should congratulate you, and wish you a long and happy life with the girl you have—I won't say chosen, but tossed up for. The natural man in me, on the other hand, urges me to break every bone in your worthless body. Throw off your coat, Yates."

"Oh, I say, Renmark, you're crazy."

"Perhaps so. Be all the more on your guard, if you believe it. A lunatic is sometimes dangerous."

"Oh, go away. You're dreaming. You're talking in your sleep. What! Fight? Tonight? Nonsense!"

"Do you want me to strike you before you are ready?"

"No, Renny, no. My wants are always modest. I don't wish to fight at all, especially to-night. I'm a reformed man, I tell you. I have no desire to bid good-by to my best girl with a black eye to-morrow."

"Then stop talking, if you can, and defend yourself."

"It's impossible to fight here in the dark. Don't flatter yourself for a moment that I am afraid. You just spar with yourself and get limbered up, while I put some wood on the fire. This is too ridiculous."

Yates gathered some fuel, and managed to coax the dying embers into a blaze.

"There," he said, "that's better. Now, let me have a look at you. In the name of wonder, Renny, what do you want to fight me for to-night?"

"I refuse to give my reason."

"Then I refuse to fight. I'll run, and I can beat you in a foot race any day in the week. Why, you're worse than her father. He at least let me know why he fought me."

"Whose father?"

"Kitty's father, of course—my future father-in-law. And that's another ordeal ahead of me. I haven't spoken to the old man yet, and I need all my fighting grit for that."

"What are you talking about?"

"Isn't my language plain? It usually is."

"To whom are you engaged? As I understand your talk, it is to Miss Bartlett. Am I right?"

"Right as rain, Renny. This fire is dying down again. Say, can't we postpone our fracas until daylight? I don't want to gather any more wood. Besides, one of us is sure to be knocked into the fire, and thus ruin whatever is left of our clothes. What do you say?"

"Say? I say I am an idiot."

"Hello! reason is returning, Renny. I perfectly agree with you."

"Thank you. Then you did not propose to Mar—to Miss Howard?"

"Now, you touch upon a sore spot, Renmark, that I am trying to forget. You remember the unfortunate toss-up; in fact, I think you referred to it a moment ago, and you were justly indignant about it at the time. Well, I don't care to talk much about the sequel; but, as you know the beginning, you will have to know the end, because I want to wring a sacred promise from you. You are never to mention this episode of the toss-up, or of my confession, to any living soul. The telling of it might do harm, and it couldn't possibly do any good. Will you promise?"

"Certainly. But do not tell me unless you wish to."

"I don't exactly yearn to talk about it, but it is better you should understand how the land lies, so you won't make any mistake. Not on my account, you know, but I would not like it to come to Kitty's ears. Yes, I proposed to Margaret—first. She wouldn't look at me. Can you credit that?"

"Well, now that you mention it, I——"

"Exactly. I see you can credit it. Well, I couldn't at first; but Margaret knows her own mind, there's no question about that. Say! she's in love with some other fellow. I found out that much."

"You asked her, I presume."

"Well, it's my profession to find out things; and, naturally, if I do that for my paper, it is not likely I am going to be behindhand when it comes to myself. She denied it at first, but admitted it afterward, and then bolted."

"You must have used great tact and delicacy."

"See here, Renmark; I'm not going to stand any of your sneering. I told you this was a sore subject with me. I'm not telling you because I like to, but because I have to. Don't put me in fighting humor, Mr. Renmark. If I talk fight, I won't begin for no reason and then back out for no reason. I'll go on."

"I'll be discreet, and beg to take back all I said. What else?"

"Nothing else. Isn't that enough? It was more than enough for me—at the time. I tell you, Renmark, I spent a pretty bad half hour sitting on the

308

fence and thinking about it."

"So long as that?"

Yates rose from the fire indignantly.

"I take that back, too," cried the professor hastily. "I didn't mean it."

"It strikes me you've become awfully funny all of a sudden. Don't you think it's about time we took to our bunks? It's late."

Renmark agreed with him but did not turn in. He walked to the friendly fence, laid his arms along the top rail, and gazed at the friendly stars. He had not noticed before how lovely the night was, with its impressive stillness, as if the world had stopped, as a steamer stops in mid-ocean. After quieting his troubled spirit with the restful stars he climbed the fence and walked down the road, taking little heed of the direction. The still night was a soothing companion. He came at last to a sleeping village of wooden houses, and through the center of the town ran a single line of rails, an iron link connecting the unknown hamlet with all civilization. A red and a green light glimmered down the line, giving the only indication that a train ever came that way. As he went a mile or two farther the cool breath of the great lake made itself felt, and after crossing a field he suddenly came upon the water, finding all further progress in that direction barred. Huge sand dunes formed the shore, covered with sighing pines. At the foot of the dunes stretched a broad beach of firm sand, dimly visible in contrast with the darker water; and at long intervals fell the light ripple of the languid summer waves, running up the beach with a half-asleep whisper, that became softer and softer until it was merged in the silence beyond. Far out on the dark waters a point of light, like a floating star, showed where a steamer was slowly making her way; and so still was the night that he felt rather than heard her pulsating engines. It was the only sign of life visible from that enchanted bay—the bay of the silver beach.

Renmark threw himself down on the soft sand at the foot of a dune. The point of light gradually worked its way to the west, following, doubtless unconsciously, the star of empire, and disappeared around the headland, taking with it a certain vague sense of companionship. But the world is very small, and a man is never quite as much alone as he thinks he is. Renmark heard the low hoot of an owl among the trees, which cry he was astonished to hear answered from the water. He sat up and listened. Presently there grated on the sand the keel of a boat, and someone stepped ashore. From the woods there emerged the shadowy forms of three men. Nothing was said, but they got silently into the boat, which might have been Charon's craft for all he could see of it. The rattle of the rowlocks and the plash of oars followed, while a voice cautioned the rowers to make less noise. It was evident that some belated fugitives were eluding the authorities of both countries. Renmark thought, with a smile, that if Yates were in his place he would at least give them a fright. A sharp command to an imaginary company to load and fire would travel far on such a night, and would give the rowers a few moments of great discomfort. Renmark, however, did not shout, but treated the episode as part of the mystical dream, and lay down on the sand again. He noticed that the water in the east seemed to feel the approach of morning even before the sky. Gradually the day dawned, a slowly lightening gray at first, until the coming sun spattered a filmy cloud with gold and crimson. Renmark watched the glory of the sunrise, took one lingering look at the curved beauty of the bay shore, shook the sand from his clothing, and started back for the village and the camp beyond.

The village was astir when he reached it. He was surprised to see Stoliker on horseback in front of one of the taverns. Two assistants were with him, also seated on horses. The constable seemed disturbed by the sight of Renmark but he was there to do his duty.

"Hello!" he cried, "you're up early. I have a warrant for the arrest of you friend: I suppose you won't tell me where he is?"

"You can't expect me to give any information that will get a friend int trouble, can you? especially as he has done nothing."

"That's as may turn out before a jury," said one of the assistants gravely

"Yes," assented, Stoliker, winking quietly at the professor. "That is f judge and jury to determine—not you."

"Well," said Renmark, "I will not inform about anybody, unless I a compelled to do so, but I may save you some trouble by telling where I have been and what I have seen. I am on my way back from the lake. If you go down there, you will still see the mark of a boat's keel on the sand, and probably footprints. A boat came over from the other shore in the night, and a man got on board. I don't say who the man was, and I had nothing to do with the matter in any way except as a spectator. That is all the information I have to give."

Stoliker turned to his assistants, and nodded. "What did I tell you?" he asked. "We were right on his track."

"You said the railroad," grumbled the man who had spoken before.

"Well, we were within two miles of him. Let us go down to the lake and see the traces. Then we can return the warrant."

Renmark found Yates still asleep in the tent. He prepared breakfast without disturbing him. When the meal was ready, he roused the reporter and told him of his meeting with Stoliker, advising him to get back to New York without delay.

Yates yawned sleepily.

"Yes," he said, "I've been dreaming it all out. I'll get father-in-law to tote me out to Fort Erie to-night."

"Do you think it will be safe to put it off so long?"

"Safer than trying to get away during the day. After breakfast I'm going down to the Bartlett homestead. Must have a talk with the old folks, you know. I'll spend the rest of the day making up for that interview by talking with Kitty. Stoliker will never search for me there, and, now that he thinks I'm gone, he will likely make a visit to the tent. Stoliker is a good fellow, but his strong point is duty, you know; and if he's certain I'm gone, he'll give his country the worth of its money by searching. I won't be back for dinner, so you can put in your time reading my Dime Novels. I make no reflections on your cooking, Renny, now that the vacation is over; but I have my preferences, and they incline toward a final meal with the Bartletts. If I were you, I'd have a nap. You look tired out."

"I am," said the professor.

Renmark intended to lie down for a few moments until Yates was clear of the camp, after which he determined to pay a visit; but Nature, when she got him locked up in sleep, took her revenge. He did not hear Stoliker and his satellites search the premises, just as Yates had predicted they would; and when he finally awoke, he found to his astonishment that it was nearly dark. But he was all the better for his sleep, and he attended to his personal appearance with more than ordinary care.

Old Hiram Bartlett accepted the situation with the patient and grim stolidity of a man who takes a blow dealt him by a Providence known by him to be inscrutable. What he had done to deserve it was beyond his comprehension. He silently hitched up his horses, and, for the first time in his life, drove into Fort Erie without any reasonable excuse for going there. He tied his team at the usual corner, after which he sat at one of the taverns and drank strong waters that had no apparent effect on him. He even went so far as to smoke two native cigars; and a man who can do that can do anything. To bring up a daughter who would deliberately accept a man from "the States," and to have a wife who would aid and abet such an action, giving comfort and support to the enemy, seemed to him traitorous to all the traditions of 1812, or any other date in the history of the two countries. At times wild ideas of getting blind full, and going home to break every breakable thing in the house, rose in his mind; but prudence whispered that he had to live all the rest of his life with his wife, and he realized that this scheme of vengeance had its drawbacks. Finally, he untied his patient team, after paying his bill, and drove silently home, not having returned, even by a nod, any of the salutations tendered to him that day. He was somewhat relieved to find no questions were asked, and that his wife recognized the fact that he was passing through a crisis. Nevertheless, there was a steely glitter in her eye under which he uneasily quailed, for it told him a line had been reached which it would not be well for him to cross. She forgave, but it must not go any further.

When Yates kissed Kitty good-night at the gate, he asked her, with som trepidation, whether she had told anyone of their engagement.

"No one but Margaret," said Kitty.

"And what did she say?" asked Yates, as if, after all, her opinion was of no importance.

"She said she was sure I should be happy, and she knew you would make a good husband."

"She's rather a nice girl, is Margaret," remarked Yates, with the air of a man willing to concede good qualities to a girl other than his own, but indicating, after all, that there was but one on earth for him.

"She is a lovely girl," said Kitty enthusiastically. "I wonder, Dick, when you knew her, why you ever fell in love with me."

"The idea! I haven't a word to say against Margaret; but, compared with my girl——"

And he finished his sentence with a practical illustration of his frame of mind.

As he walked alone down the road he reflected that Margaret had acted very handsomely, and he resolved to drop in and wish her good-by. But as he approached the house his courage began to fail him, and he thought it better to sit on the fence, near the place where he had sat the night before, and think it over. It took a good deal of thinking. But as he sat there it was destined that Yates should receive some information which would simplify matters. Two persons came slowly out of the gate in the gathering darkness. They strolled together up the road past him, absorbed in themselves. When directly opposite the reporter, Renmark put his arm around Margaret's waist, and Yates nearly fell off the fence. He held his breath until they were safely out of hearing, then slid down and crawled along in the shadow until he came to the side road, up which he walked, thoughtfully pausing every few moments to remark: "Well, I'll be——" But speech seemed to have failed him; he could get no further.

He stopped at the fence and leaned against it, gazing for the last time at the tent, glimmering white, like a misshapen ghost, among the somber trees. He had no energy left to climb over.

"Well, I'm a chimpanzee," he muttered to himself at last. "The highest bidder can have me, with no upset price. Dick Yates, I wouldn't have believed it of you. You a newspaper man? You a reporter from 'way back? You up to snuff? Yates, I'm ashamed to be seen in your company! Go back to New York, and let the youngest reporter in from a country newspaper scoop the daylight out of you. To think that this thing has been going on right under your well-developed nose, and you never saw it—worse, never had the faintest suspicion of it; that it was thrust at you twenty times a day—nearly got your stupid head smashed on account of it; yet you bleated away like the innocent little lamb that you are, and never even suspected! Dick, you're a three-sheet-poster fool in colored ink. And to think that both of them know all about the first proposal! Both of them! Well, thank Heaven, Toronto is a long way from New York."

THE END.

About Author

Robert Barr (16 September 1849 – 21 October 1912) was a Scottish-Canadian short story writer and novelist.

Early years in Canada

Robert Barr was born in Barony, Lanark, Scotland to Robert Barr and Jane Watson. In 1854, he emigrated with his parents to Upper Canada at the age of four years old. His family settled on a farm near the village of Muirkirk. Barr assisted his father with his job as a carpenter, and developed a sound work ethic. Robert Barr then worked as a steel smelter for a number of years before he was educated at Toronto Normal School in 1873 to train as a teacher.

After graduating Toronto Normal School, Barr became a teacher, and eventually headmaster/principal of the Central School of Windsor, Ontario in 1874. While Barr worked as head master of the Central School of Windsor, Ontario, he began to contribute short stories—often based on personal experiences, and recorded his work. On August 1876, when he was 27, Robert Barr married Ontario-born Eva Bennett, who was 21. According to the 1891 England Census, the couple appears to have had three children, Laura, William, and Andrew.

In 1876, Barr quit his teaching position to become a staff member of publication, and later on became the news editor for the Detroit Free Press. Barr wrote for this newspaper under the pseudonym, "Luke Sharp." The idea for this pseudonym was inspired during his morning commute to work when Barr saw a sign that read "Luke Sharp, Undertaker." In 1881, Barr left Canada to return to England in order to start a new weekly version of "The Detroit Free Press Magazine."

London years

In 1881 Barr decided to "vamoose the ranch", as he called the process of immigration in search of literary fame outside of Canada, and relocated to London to continue to write/establish the weekly English edition of the Detroit Free Press. During the 1890s, he broadened his literary works, and started writing novels from the popular crime genre. In 1892 he founded the magazine The Idler, choosing Jerome K. Jerome as his collaborator (wanting, as Jerome said, "a popular name"). He retired from its co-editorship in 1895.

In London of the 1890s Barr became a more prolific author—publishing a book a year—and was familiar with many of the best-selling authors of his day, including :Arnold Bennett, Horatio Gilbert Parker, Joseph Conrad, Bret Harte, Rudyard Kipling, H. Rider Haggard, H. G. Wells, and George Robert Gissing. Barr was well-spoken, well-cultured due to travel, and considered a "socializer."

Because most of Barr's literary output was of the crime genre, his works were highly in vogue. As Sherlock Holmes stories were becoming well-known, Barr wrote and published in the Idler the first Holmes parody, "The Adventures of "Sherlaw Kombs" (1892), a spoof that was continued a decade later in another Barr story, "The Adventure of the Second Swag" (1904). Despite those jibes at the growing Holmes phenomenon, Barr remained on very good terms with its creator Arthur Conan Doyle. In Memories and Adventures, a serial memoir published 1923–24, Doyle described him as "a volcanic Anglo—or rather Scot-American, with a violent manner, a wealth of strong adjectives, and one of the kindest natures underneath it all".

In 1904, Robert Barr completed an unfinished novel for Methuen & Co. by the recently deceased American author Stephen Crane entitled The O'Ruddy, a romance.Despite his reservations at taking on the project, Barr reluctantly finished the last eight chapters due to his longstanding friendship with Crane and his common-law wife, Cora, the war correspondent and bordello owner.

Death

The 1911 census places Robert Barr, "a writer of fiction," at Hillhead Woldingham, Surrey, a small village southeast of London, living with his wife, Eva, their son William, and two female servants. At this home, the author died from heart disease on 21 October 1912.

Writing Style

Barr's volumes of short stories were often written with an ironic twist in the story with a witty, appealing narrator telling the story. Barr's other works also include numerous fiction and non-fiction contributions to periodicals. A few of his mystery stories and stories of the supernatural were put in anthologies, and a few novels have been republished. His writings have also attracted scholarly attention. His narrative personae also featured moral and editorial interpolations within their tales. Barr's achievements were recognized by an honorary degree from the University of Michigan in 1900.

His protagonists were journalists, princes, detectives, deserving commercial and social climbers, financiers, the new woman of bright wit and aggressive accomplishment, and lords. Often, his characters were stereotypical and romanticized.

Barr wrote fiction in an episode-like format. He developed this style when working as an editor for the newspaper Detroit Press. Barr developed his skill with the anecdote and vignette; often only the central character serves to link the nearly self-contained chapters of the novels. (Source: Wikipedia)

NOTABLE WORKS

In a Steamer Chair and Other Stories (Thirteen short stories by one of the most famous writers in his day -1892)

"The Face And The Mask" (1894) consists of twenty-four delightful short stories.

In the Midst of Alarms (1894, 1900, 1912), a story of the attempted Fenian invasion of Canada in 1866.

From Whose Bourne (1896) Novel in which the main character, William Brenton, searches for truth to set his wife free.

One Day's Courtship (1896)

Revenge! (Collection of 20 short stories, Alfred Hitchcock-like style, thriller with a surprise ending)

The Strong Arm

A Woman Intervenes (1896), a story of love, finance, and American journalism.

Tekla: A Romance of Love and War (1898)

Jennie Baxter, Journalist (1899)

The Unchanging East (1900)

The Victors (1901)

A Prince of Good Fellows (1902)

Over The Border: A Romance (1903)

The O'Ruddy, A Romance, with Stephen Crane (1903)

A Chicago Princess (1904)

The Speculations of John Steele (1905)

The Tempestuous Petticoat (1905–12)

A Rock in the Baltic (1906)

The Triumphs of Eugène Valmont (1906)

The Measure of the Rule (1907)

Stranleigh's Millions (1909)

The Sword Maker (Medieval action/adventure novel, genre: Historical Fiction-1910)

The Palace of Logs (1912)

"The Ambassadors Pigeons" (1899)

"And the Rigor of the Game" (1892)

"Converted" (1896)

"Count Conrad's Courtship" (1896)

"The Count's Apology" (1896)

"A Deal on Change " (1896)

"The Exposure of Lord Stanford" (1896)

"Gentlemen: The King!"

"The Hour-Glass" (1899)

"An invitation" (1892)

" A Ladies Man"

"The Long Ladder" (1899)

"Mrs. Tremain" (1892)

" Transformation" (1896)

"The Understudy" (1896)

" The Vengeance of the Dead" (1896)

"The Bromley Gibbert's Story" (1896)

" Out of Thun" (1896)

"The Shadow of Greenback" (1896)

"Flight of the Red Dog" (fiction)

"Lord Stranleigh Abroad" (1913)

"One Day's Courtship and the Herald's of Fame" (1896)

"Cardillac"

"Dr. Barr's Tales"

"The Triumphs of Eugene Valmont"

CPSIA information can be obtained
at www.ICGtesting.com
Printed in the USA
LVHW040044010820
662074LV00010B/202